KU-757-264

M. E. MORRIS

The Icemen

GRAFTON BOOKS

A Division of the Collins Publishing Group

LONDON GLASGOW
TORONTO SYDNEY AUCKLAND

Grafton Books
A Division of the Collins Publishing Group
8 Grafton Street, London W1X 3LA

A Grafton UK Paperback Original 1990

Copyright © 1988 by M. E. Morris

ISBN 0-586-20798-8

Printed and bound in Great Britain by
Collins, Glasgow

Set in Times

All rights reserved. No part of this publication may
be reproduced, stored in a retrieval system, or
transmitted, in any form, or by any means, electronic,
mechanical, photocopying, recording or otherwise,
without the prior permission of the publishers.

This book is sold subject to the condition that it
shall not, by way of trade or otherwise, be lent,
re-sold, hired out or otherwise circulated
without the publisher's prior consent in any
form of binding or cover other than that in
which it is published and without a similar
condition including this condition being imposed
on the subsequent purchaser.

The characters in this story are entirely fictional and do not
represent any individual or collective person. Any such resem-
blance is purely coincidental and unintentional.

For all the Icemen
past, present, and future,
who have gone down to the White Continent
and will remain there – forever.

. . . I have therefore resolved to remain in Berlin and there to choose death of my own will at the very moment when, as I believe, the seat of the Fuehrer and Chancellor can no longer be defended. I die with a joyful heart in the awareness of the immeasurable deeds and achievements of our soldiers at the front, and the contribution, unique in history, of our youth, which bears my name.

It goes without saying that I thank them all from the bottom of my heart and that it is also my desire that in spite of everything they should not give up the struggle, but continue fighting wherever they may be, faithful to the great Clausewitz, against the enemies of the Fatherland. From the sacrifices of our soldiers and from my own comradeship with them, there will come in one way or another into German history the seed of a brilliant renaissance of the National Socialist Movement and thus the realization of a true national community . . .

Given at Berlin, 29 April 1945, 4 A.M.

/s/ ADOLF HITLER*

* Excerpt from Hitler's final Political Testament, dated and signed as indicated, and witnessed by Dr Joseph Goebbels, Martin Bormann, William Burgdorf, and Hans Krebs.

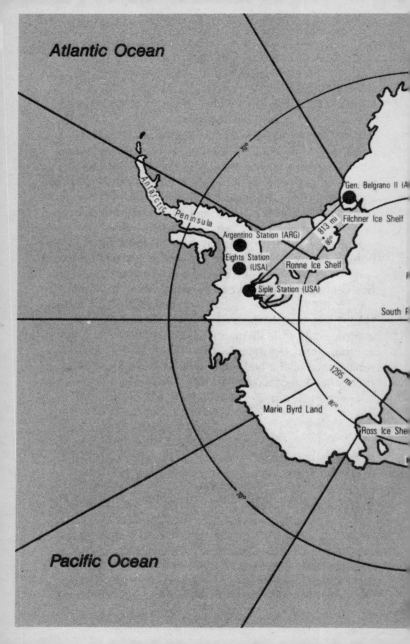

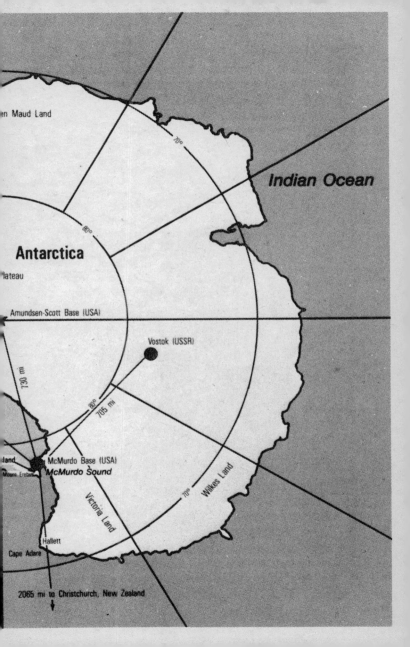

Prologue

East Falkland Island
June 25, 1982

Sergeant Major William Dawson of Her Majesty's Royal Marines cursed and let up on the accelerator of the Land Rover. He should not have let that dink in Transport talk him out of a snowcat – hindsight was so bloody infallible. No need to concern himself with that, now, however. Other problems were rapidly developing. The cold dawn mist that had soaked him even before he had crawled into the vehicle back at Port San Carlos had turned first into frigid rain, then sleet, and was now about half sleet and half wet snow. It was driving against his windscreen from dead ahead and already forming a slush in the area not swept by his wipers. The wind must be close to twenty knots. Great. With the outside air obviously below freezing, the chill factor had to be somewhere in the minus temperatures.

Holding the door open against the wind, Dawson stuck his head out and checked the wheels. Flamin' shit! They were sunk in the peat up to their hubs. What a piss-poor country for a war, especially a war that, in his view, nobody really wanted and had been fought over a pair of islands that were of little use to anyone. He looked around at the terrain, what he could see of it. Treeless, it looked as if some giant hand had scoured it with a huge steel brush, exposing the underlying clay subsoil in great open patches. Rocks littered the entire area, some large enough

11

to require detouring whether you were in a vehicle or on foot. Broad fields of peat, like the one that he was in now, were everywhere. The two ruts that served as a road – make that trail – from Port San Carlos to Port Stanley were little more than irregular ditches, so deep in spots that vehicles sometimes rode along on their undersides, progressing only by timely bursts of acceleration. As long as they were going fast enough, they would make it, scraping along the center ridge until the ruts shallowed and the wheels could gain traction once again.

That wasn't Dawson's problem at the moment. Just the opposite. Instead of high and dry on a clay ridge, his Land Rover was axle deep in the moist peat.

He closed the door and jerked the gear lever into reverse. Carefully, he released the clutch, just enough to feel the Land Rover tighten in response to the initial engagement of the gears. The vehicle moved backwards perhaps an inch before the wheels began to spin. He shifted into low. Again, he released the clutch. The Rover rocked back and forth, gained an overall movement of something less than six inches, and settled still deeper into the churned peat.

Snorting in disgust, Dawson shut off the ignition. He would have to dig himself out. Now his hindsight really began to twist his insides. Before setting out from Port San Carlos, why hadn't he grabbed a lance corporal to handle such menial tasks? *William, m'lad, you're not thinkin' too clearly this mornin'.* Shaking his head, he turned the ignition back on and hit the starter. No need to freeze yet. He should leave the heater on while he dug; that way he'd have a warm compartment to climb back into.

It took only a moment to pull the trenching tool from its storage brackets on the side of the vehicle. Might as well try the rears first.

12

Ridiculous. As fast as he scooped up the soggy peat, a new blob would slide into its place. He tried again. Same result. At this rate, he could succeed in completely burying his vehicle. For a moment, he was even tempted to do just that. It would serve the stupid Rover right!

In just the few minutes that he had been outside, he was chilled to the bone. Hastily, he slung the shovel into the rear of the vehicle and climbed back behind the wheel. The inside was like an oven. At least the heater worked. He would just have to wait it out. Trying to hike out in this weather would be suicidal.

Thankfully, fighting was over and there would be no danger of being discovered by an Argentine patrol, even if one would have been able to move around in this stuff. He figured his position was probably just about halfway between Port San Carlos and Port Stanley. That meant hills – although someone had the gall to list those on East Falkland as mountains on local maps – to the south, his right. To his left should be lowlands, and probably Teal Inlet.

He checked his watch. A convoy of POWs would be leaving Port San Carlos at noon. That would be another three hours and he was a good two along the road. Five hours before they would reach him, provided that they used snowcats. Or, maybe the weather would cause a delay. No need to try the radio again. Reception had been weak and garbled several kilometers back. Still, maybe he could send blind. Someone might hear him. With no great expectations, he triggered the hand mike. He couldn't even get a side tone. The ice must be shorting out his antenna.

No real sweat. He was warm and had almost a full tank of petrol for the motor, and thus the heater. There were rations behind the rear seat, smokes in his pocket. Too bad he hadn't brought one of the Port San Carlos lasses

13

with him. There were only a few among the twenty or thirty residents who were still there, but any one of the less-than-impressive lot would have done for the moment.

What a way to wind up a quick combat tour. The occupation troops who came in on the QE2 could have this bloody place. As far as the fight itself, it had gone well. The Argentines had put on a pretty good show at first – the bloody bastards had cost his battalion eighty-three good marines – but, they had been ill-trained to counter elite British forces. Hell, they had even left the high ground unoccupied. He winced, thinking of the navy's problems, however. The Argentine pilots had been shit-hot good, with balls of steel. Thank the Almighty they hadn't concentrated on the ground forces. Of course, the Harriers had helped in that respect. The short-legged little duffers had taken on the Mirages and American-built A-4s and generally waxed their asses over land. The vertical-take-off-and-landing Harriers were revered as guardian angels by the sergeant major and his marines.

It looked like the wind was letting up. Good. That would improve the visibility. Dawson pulled up the collar of his combat jacket and scooted down in the seat. By twisting just the right way, he could stretch his legs over to the far side and gain some small degree of comfort. With the wind whistling around the Land Rover considerably less noisy than before, and the warmth of the car heater, he had to let his eyelids drop.

A transient beam of sunlight wakened him. The snow-fall was much lighter and there were breaks in the low overcast, through which he could catch glimpses of blue sky. Blue sky! That was only the second time he'd seen the heavens since landing on this terrible place, 7,000 miles from home.

Sitting upright, he scanned the surrounding horizon with his binoculars. Visibility was good, although the cloud base could not be more than several hundred meters. The 'mountains' rose to his right, their rounded tops just below the base of the overcast. Off to his left stretched the flatland, a moorlike area of peat bogs and clay. At the far reaches were splashes of grasslands, a welcome sight even if they were brown spotted and ragged. One, in particular, aroused his interest. Probably four or five kilometers away, it surrounded a building! A white clapboard, two-story structure. Arranged before it were what looked like foundations for other buildings, and there were several stacks of lumber off to one side. He could see no movement and actually expected none. The marines' main thrust after landing at Port San Carlos had carried them right through this area on their way to Port Stanley. Considering the weather at that time, and the lack of Argentine resistance inland, they might have even bypassed the building. It sat low in a hollow, and with the rise and fall of the road, it could have been undetected. There weren't even any sheep in the grassed area. He had yet to see grass without sheep on East Falkland Island. It *must* be deserted.

His marine's instinct told him that it was worth investigating. There might be the danger of an ambush, but he doubted that. The cease-fire was already in effect and he knew for a fact that the Argentine forces had laid down their arms with some relief. They had tired of the cold and wet and isolation of the open terrain and had eagerly sought the paved streets and civilized POW compounds in Port Stanley. He recalled that on his last trip over, there had been so many prisoners, the force commanders were calling for a ship lift to take them off the island. The white building was most probably quite empty and a reconnaissance of it would help pass the time until help came along. Besides, it was in keeping with his duty. A combat marine had no business sitting on his sore cheeks,

15

stuffing down rations and waiting to be rescued like some army fairy.

Grabbing his weapon, he dropped out of the Land Rover and started plodding north. The first several hundred yards were sloshy going, each step sinking him almost a foot into the soft peat. But eventually, it shallowed and began to break up and the clay was much more solid. Within forty-five minutes, he reached the grassland surrounding the white building. A metal flagpole stood before it, lanyards still rigged and slapping the metal under the force of the wind, which was now quite variable in its direction. There were, indeed, foundations already dug for three other buildings, and foundation pillars and several floor joists were complete on one.

He started to yell a hello, but if there were anyone inside they surely would have seen him approaching over the open country.

Cautiously, he walked around the building. There was a back door at ground level and a small balcony jutting from the lone second-story opening – a door as well. Returning to the front of the building, he flipped off the safety of his weapon and used the tip of the barrel to push open the door. It led into a hallway, at the far end of which was a flight of stairs; along each side of the hall was a series of doors. He opened the first to his right. It appeared to be an abandoned office. Inside were a bare table and a broken wooden chair.

Each of the other rooms was either empty or cluttered with bits of debris. In the last space before the stairs, he found a metal trash can with some charred papers in the bottom. He fished out one of the larger remnants, a scrap roughly one by three inches. On it was what appeared to be a letterhead, although the fragment was scarred brown from the heat of the fire set to destroy it. Not a very competent job, thought Dawson. Someone had been in

16

too much of a hurry. He held the paper up to the light from the window and tried to make out the printing. Yes, some of the characters could be identified, but they were in an unfamiliar font and didn't make sense. Then, with an uncomfortable feeling of surprise and confusion, he realized why. The words were written in German script.

Curious, he searched through the remainder of the papers. Several more pieces displayed portions of German words, the printing arrangement suggesting letterheads. He placed the scraps in his wallet and turned to the stairway.

The brief respite in the weather had ended and the cloud bases were again lowering. The snow and wind were back also and the light inside the building was rapidly fading. There was no door at the top of the stairs, just a wide opening that led into a large room that occupied the entire second story. It was crammed with tumbled and scattered folding chairs and bits of colored paper and cloth. At the far end of the room was a raised platform framed by a railing that enclosed a waist-high podium. But Sergeant Major Dawson saw not the chairs nor debris, nor even took note of the platform or the podium. In astonishment, he riveted his eyes on the blood-red banner which hung from ceiling to floor. It was easily five feet wide and had in its middle a white disk, which, even in the dim light allowed in the room by the storm, provided a vivid background for the enclosed black swastika. The emblem of the Third Reich of Hitler's Germany was hanging before his very eyes. Dawson took several steps forward, unable to take his eyes off the banner. Why here, forty-three years after the last Nazi died in Berlin?

A metallic click, instantly recognized by the combat marine, ended the hypnotic spell of the flag and Dawson whirled around raising his weapon to its firing position.

He never saw the figure that squeezed the trigger of the Luger and put a hollow-pointed bullet into his head.

The shot reverberated throughout the cavernous room, creating a thousand echoes and filling the chamber with a sharp, if only momentary, clap of lethal thunder. The figure who fired it lowered his gun hand, then crossed his body with it and slipped the still-smoking automatic into the inside pocket of his heavy parka.

The assassin let the trace of a smile modify his look of hate. He felt good inside. It had been forty-three years since he had shot his last British soldier.

Stepping across the sergeant major's body, the old Nazi removed the banner, folded it carefully, stuffed it inside his parka next to the Luger, and walked back down the stairs. Outside, there was the muffled clanking sound of an approaching tracked vehicle.

His pickup had finally arrived. Checking carefully that it was indeed the case, he hurried outside and met the heavily armored personnel carrier on the run. It slowed for only a moment as two tattered and battle-weary Argentine officers pulled him into the vehicle. Crouching down on one of the bench seats in the rear, he steadied himself with both hands as the personnel carrier careened across the moors. They still had to evade British patrols and make their way to a secluded cove where they could wait for nightfall. Provided the submarine had escaped the British fleet, he would return to Argentina. The Falklands campaign had failed and the clandestine reestablishment of the Third Reich would have to wait for another day. But that day would come.

1

The Present Time

The temperature rose to minus seventy-three degrees Fahrenheit. The ground blizzard that had laced the camp with driving snow for the past four days slowed to an amiable breeze, and the whiteness that had obscured even the jet-black oil drums marking the location of the drifted-over skiway settled onto the surface of the plateau of snow and ice. The pristine beauty of the mile-and-a-half-high plateau was marred only by a black geodetic dome that rose just to the side of the landing area; it seemed to come from the depths of the snow, but, actually, it was slowly being buried by the annual winter snow accumulation. Beneath its massive protective form were entire buildings filled with scientific instruments and men and women who had worked in relative comfort through the long antarctic winter. A few yards away, from the top of the glistening steel flagpole standing in solitary splendor at the exact bottom of the globe called Earth, the red, white, and blue flag of the United States of America fluttered quietly, casting a flickering shadow across the face of a weathered plywood sign. It stood firmly staked into the solid sastrugi, silently proclaiming:

WELCOME
SOUTH POLE INTERNATIONAL AIRPORT
AMUNDSEN-SCOTT STATION
ELEVATION: 9,301 FEET

Spring was coming to Antarctica.

At the precise moment that the antarctic sun climbed over the polar horizon, three seemingly unrelated events were taking place.

The first was the death of Myron Lubel, a mousey little man by personality and stature, but a valued upper-echelon member of the Mossad, the Israeli secret service. He died propped up against a high red-brick wall facing a dark alley in a suburb of Punta Arenas, Chile. The wall provided privacy for the place of business of one Maria Theresa, a madam of international acclaim. At the moment, her busy young ladies and their male clientele inside the ornate and very posh bordello had not the slightest thought that outside, in the early morning chill, lay a dead Jew with a half-inch-diameter stainless steel rod driven in one ear and out the other.

The second event was occurring in the private office of the director of the Central Intelligence Agency at that organization's headquarters in Langley, Virginia. The director and a senior agent, Raphael Minochetti, were reviewing a classified report prepared by the latter. They sat side by side at a polished mahogany writing table once owned by Benedict Arnold. Amid the paper debris and empty coffee cups of an all-night session, Minochetti was checking the report format under the personal supervision of the director.

'Action only to the Commander, Naval Support Forces, Antarctica?' queried Minochetti.

'His eyes only,' replied the director. 'And cross out those info addees.'

'How about the White House? This could be top drawer.'

'I'll brief the chief of staff. If he wants to present it to the president, that's fine. But, I think we need a bit more firm evidence.'

'Incredible, isn't it?'

'Shit, nothing surprises me these days. But, I don't want to make the decision to tell the president. He's up to his ass in domestic problems all this week. The international scene is quiet. I can't throw this at him, not yet. Let's get good solid confirmation.'

'How do you want to transmit this? COMNAVSUPFORANT doesn't have any crypto gear at Christchurch. Through the embassy at Wellington?'

'No. Time's not a factor yet and I'd rather no one sees this except COMNAVSUPFORANT, not even comm personnel. Use a courier.'

'Right.' Minochetti nodded and left the director's office.

The director poured himself a final cup of coffee from the chrome decanter on the side table and settled into his winged leather office chair. He was getting too old for these all-night sessions. Perhaps, it was time to hang it up. Sell the damn DC townhouse and hunker down on his secluded sixty-five acres of Connecticut backland. Grow apples or something.

Calmed somewhat by the coffee and the realization that the night's long session was over, he picked up the small stack of intelligence reports and read them for the umpteenth time. Reports on Nazis in Argentina were nothing new. He'd been seeing such reports cross his various desks for thirty years. Once the biggies had been tracked down and extradited by the Israelis, the pitiful few remaining in South America presented no threat to the world they had tried so desperately to conquer. Another ten years and they'd all be gone. Even that old bastard Hess was dead now, gone with most of the rest of the big Nazis. But several of the papers before him were disturb-

21

ing. One was a report, yet to be verified, that the Argentine government finally had a bellyful of the old Germans and was making plans to isolate the remaining few in one of their experimental colonies in Antarctica. The director had a good friend in the Antarctic Research Programs Office of the National Science Foundation and he had spent many pleasant hours listening to his friend extol the virtues and promises of the lone untainted continent on earth. What a shock his friend had coming. Nazis in Antarctica.

That sure as hell ought to bring property values down, thought the director. But there was no humor in the contents of a related message.

Ten months back, an American geological party, after taking soil and rock samples in the foothills that ran across part of what was generally referred to as Argentine Antarctica, had routinely shipped the samples back to several universities for detailed analysis. The findings were spectacular, to say the least: there could very well be the world's richest deposits of several critical metals, perhaps even uranium ore, right where the Argentines were placing their newest colonization camp, the one they planned to use to house their Nazi community.

So what?

The director knew so what. Antarctica was the one place on the planet where old and new Nazis could live undisturbed. It was an open continent, and no nation had any jurisdiction over it. Somewhere down the line, it was just possible that those very same Nazis, or to be more exact, their descendents, would have the means not only to reenter the world community but to destroy it as well. Farfetched? Not any more farfetched than a Bavarian paperhanger becoming the most powerful dictator of all time.

* * *

22

The third event taking place at the precise moment that the antarctic sun climbed over the polar horizon would appear to the casual eye, if such sinister things could be viewed by a *casual* eye, as quite unrelated to the other two. That was not exactly the case, however.

In a compound in the village of Tell Mardikh – an eruption of the mud and dirt that makes up the northeastern portion of the Great Syrian Desert – three men squatted on a large square of Damascus carpet and talked in low tones. The roof of the room was domed, not unlike the inside of a beehive, and the room itself was only one of a countless number of similar rooms that made up the 200-year-old ocher clay compound. Adjoining the village was the site of ancient Ebla, now an archaeological dig that had already stimulated startling revisions of man's understanding of the early civilizations of the area. Two hundred and fifty kilometers to the south lay Damascus, fifty kilometers to the northwest were the beaches where on a clear day one could almost see across the blue Mediterranean to the island of Cyprus.

The oldest of the three men, Ahmad Diah, breathed more in low gasps than in a normal rhythm, and frequently shook his head as if to provide an unsteady landing site for the small winged insects that buzzed in and out of the room. In the way of a man who had endured such irritation for more than sixty years, his head shaking was the only acknowledgement of the insects. To his right squatted Mulhammad al-Kalaji, his right arm an eight-inch stump that bulged from his shoulder and made that side of his tunic stick out as if he were always trying to point to something. He was easily twenty years the junior of Diah. Across from them both, his arms loosely resting in the deep fold of his outer garment as it covered his denim-clothed legs, the third occupant of the room, Ibrahim al-Abbadi, spoke in low tones. The youngest of the three had a quiet, steady voice that was in marked contrast to the fire in his dark eyes. The fingers of his right hand continually fondled a small metal pair of TWA passenger wings, the type that flight attendants pinned on small children. They were a constant reminder of his role in the April 1986 assault on TWA Flight 840. He should have achieved his destiny on that day, high in the sky between New York and Athens. But, he had not been high enough. The Boeing 727 was only at 15,000 feet when Ibrahim pressed the button on the small transmitter credit card in his wallet. Instead of blowing the airliner out of the sky, the explosive device he had placed below the window seat in row 10 merely blasted a jagged hole in the fuselage. Nevertheless, four American passengers were blown through the hole and fell to their deaths, four few infidels and servants of Israel.

A member of the Ezzedine Kassam Unit of the Arab Revolutionary Cells, Ibrahim had at least extracted some vengeance for the American devils' bold confrontation with his fellow soldiers of God in the skies over the Gulf of Sidra. Next time, he would depart this world in an act that would ensure his resurrection as a most favored descendent of his namesake.

'God must be pleased,' said the old man, Ahmad Diah. 'This unexpected emergence of a new ally gives us renewed life in our purpose.'

'It is so,' added Mulhammad al-Kalaji.

'We have the money?' asked Ibrahim.

'Yes. Twenty million American dollars as a binder. Our brothers assure us that they will provide additional monies as we require,' answered Ahmad. 'When do you leave?'

'Tonight, from Damascus. I will meet with the technical people to receive a briefing on the weapon and to hear the time frame for its deliverance to us.'

'You must be firm on the exchange. We must think of

24

those who provide our funds. Their resources are not unlimited.'

'For the elimination of Israel, any price is right,' countered Ibrahim.

'True in the wisdom of God. But our brothers who dig deep into their pockets have also a grasp of earthly needs, more so than you and I. Their questions will be polite at first, but sharp if the cost seems too high. I have their confidence only up to a point.' Ahmad's wheeze escalated into a tight cough and with considerable effort he forced enough phlegm up into his mouth to spit. 'God must let me live to see this. It is his will.'

2

Eight thousand nautical miles beyond the hand-lettered, tongue-in-cheek airport sign that stood rigid in the south polar snow, and due north along the 118th west meridian, the rays of the sun bled across the horizon of the San Gabriel Mountains and began to illuminate the coastal city of Oxnard, California. It was the last of summer, although the environmental gods of that region paid little heed to the seasons, and a warm September night was ending.

Commander Marc Bradford opened his eyes, blinked the sleep out, and stared lazily at the ceiling. From the window over the head of his bed, a small wedge of sparkling sunlight probed the drawn drapes and stabbed across the room. Marc focused on the widening shaft of light, and for a moment watched the dancing bits of dust mill about in hopeless confusion. He lay there for several minutes, enjoying that luxurious period between waking and rising. Eventually, he made a reluctant effort to start his day. As he swung his legs gently over the side of the bed, he glanced beside him at the still-sleeping form of his wife. She lay facing the opposite wall, her legs tucked up tightly in the fetal position. Auburn hair, touched almost imperceptibly by premature gray, tumbled over her shoulders, a stimulating fall that ended on the sheet at upper back level. He touched it and let his hand slide down to feel the warmth of her flawless skin, deeply curving spine, and twin mounds of flesh where her thighs disappeared under the covers. She stirred slightly, reaching back with one arm, even in her sleep, to rest her hand lightly on his. Cautiously, he slid his hand away, hesitating to move further until her breathing returned to its deep slumber state. He smiled. Sometime in the early morning, she must have risen and slipped on her gown. Twenty years of married intimacy with the same man had failed to overcome her almost virginal shyness about sleeping nude. He reached over to the nightstand, found the lighter, and lit a cigarette. Wincing at the bitter taste, he immediately snuffed it out. What a useless habit. From the kitchen came the soft whir of the refrigerator motor.

A glance at his watch revealed that it was almost seven, a full hour past his usual wake-up time. Sex did that. Standing, he fumbled around the room until he located his robe on the floor at the foot of the bed, then softly shuffled into the kitchen.

The sun completed its climb over the horizon while he prepared the coffee. Squinting out the window over the sink, he switched off the kitchen light.

A veteran of almost twenty-three years in the navy, he had married Dorothy on the day he received his gold wings at Pensacola. A product of the Navy ROTC program at Stanford, he had held his own with his contemporaries from the Academy. He was a good aviator and a promising career officer. Together, he and Dorothy had withstood the rigors and demands of navy life. Now, they were beginning to reap the rewards of all his junior tours and they felt very comfortable within the unique professional and social life of the service.

He had progressed through a series of responsible flying, shipboard, and desk jobs until he had been selected for command and given one of the navy's special mission squadrons. As of this mid-September morning, he had commanded the elite unit for less than three months after serving the previous two years as its operations and then executive officer. In a few hours, he would be leading the

27

unit south for its annual five-month deployment to Antarctica.

On the spur of the moment, he selected a carton of eggs from the refrigerator, cracked them into a cereal bowl, stirred them with a fork, and poured them onto a hot griddle. He dropped two pieces of bread into the toaster before uncovering the butter and pouring himself a cup of coffee. It was strong and black, good navy brew. Sipping it slowly, he let his thoughts drift back to the events of the previous evening.

It had been a good party, a typical final-night bash, but he had been glad to see that his officers were tempering their drinking. Even his two marine pilots stayed sober. The modern-day MADD programs and law-enforcement emphasis on keeping the drinkers off the road were having their effect on the traditional navy bashes. The spirit was still there, however, and the Officers' Club had provided a well-staffed bar, a generous buffet, and a combo who were equally skilled in the music of the eighties and the more frantic rock of the nostalgic sixties.

Marc and Dorothy had remained until almost midnight. After paying their compliments to the party chairman and the club manager, they walked arm in arm to the parking lot, retrieved their station wagon, and drove home under a cloudless sky. They rode in weary silence for a while; then Dorothy sighed contently as she slid closer to Marc and observed, 'It was a nice party.'

'It was okay,' agreed Marc. 'The last one for a while.'

They rode the rest of the way home in silence, enjoying the nearness of each other, savoring their final hours together.

After a short time, their driveway appeared and Marc swung the car easily into its familiar path, stopping just short of the closed garage door.

They kissed lightly as he shut off the ignition. Climbing out of the car, he glanced upward at the starlit sky. 'We'll leave it out tonight,' he announced with mock solemnity.

The house was quiet. Their son, fourteen-year-old Jim, lay sprawled on the sofa in front of a flickering television, which was wheezing with snow noise. Dorothy shut off the set and laid her hand softly on the boy's forehead. At first startled, he sat stiffly upright, then smiled sheepishly before ambling off to bed.

Marc selected a bottle of Early Times from an ornately carved teakwood bar, poured a generous two fingers of the golden bourbon, and walked into the kitchen. Dorothy was rinsing out an empty milk glass. For a moment, he was unnoticed and stood in the shadows, filled with a warm feeling of love for the woman busy over the sink. As she wiped up the crumbs from their son's late-night snack, Marc offered his glass. 'Nightcap?'

'Nope. Some gentlemen take advantage of young ladies who let liquor cross their lips.'

'This is whiskey, not liquor.'

'Same thing.'

'Ah! And just as suitable for me purpose, m'dear.'

'All right, Long John Silver, now out of my way. It's past my bedtime.'

'Aye, that it is, m'luvley. I'll be crawlin' between the sheets right beside ya.'

'Silly.'

He stirred in a splash of tap water with his forefinger while Dorothy gathered her night things and retired to the bathroom. Her nightly ritual was still a source of bewilderment to her husband. What on earth could she do in there for so long a time? The bourbon glass had been licked dry by the time she joined him. It was good to lie there, feeling the warmth of each other's presence, enjoying the faint body odors that mingled together and heightened even more the acute awareness each had for the other. For a while, neither spoke nor moved.

'It's going to be hard – leaving tomorrow,' Marc whispered.

'It's always hard, Marc. Jim will miss you so.'

'Jim?'

'Me, too. You know that.'

They kissed.

Marc rolled toward his wife. 'We've been married a long time. Seems like it would get easier – leaving, I mean.'

'Well, it doesn't.'

'No,' agreed Marc. He pulled her close to him and laid his free hand across her stomach. 'Hey! You're getting a little pot? Nothing else, I trust.'

She giggled and patted his waist. 'You should talk.'

A hint of flab had appeared on the big-boned aviator the past year. Still, he carried his 190 pounds well on his six-foot-one frame. He laughed and leaned over to his wife, who returned his kisses with ill-concealed anticipation.

'I surely do love you,' he murmured.

Dorothy felt his hands start to tug at her gown, and she arched her back as he slid the filmy garment up and over her head. 'Put it where I can find it . . .' she began. Marc dropped the gown on the floor beside the bed and silenced further comments with his lips. They slid easily into each other's embrace, he pulling her beneath him and nuzzling her breasts.

She was as anxious as he, and their bodies closed, each eagerly seeking the other in their familiar pattern of lovemaking. It would be the last time for many months, and that realization raised Marc's endurance to the level of his wife's passion. Finally, exhausted and relaxed in each other's arms, they slipped into a deep sleep.

* * *

Marc was jolted from his thoughts by the smell of the eggs he was frying. They were dark brown and an overcast of gray smoke was enveloping the griddle. Grabbing a handy fork, he scraped the scarred remains into the garbage disposal and spun it into action. In his haste, he lost his grip on the piece of flatware and it disappeared into the drain, where it was fiercely attacked by the metal shredder arms. The resultant clatter rang within the hollow unit with a shrill that rivaled the sound of a thousand banshees.

'Son of a b – .' Marc swallowed the last word as Jim walked sleepy-eyed into the kitchen.

'Cookin' again, Dad?'

Marc flipped off the disposal and it ground to a gurgling halt. 'I was fixing scrambled eggs.'

The boy already had produced a box of cereal. 'No thanks, Dad. Too much carbon is bad for me.' His son was fanning away the smoke over the stove as he opened the refrigerator.

Dorothy padded in, drawing on her robe. Marc met her curious frown with a sheepish grin as he looked up from his chore of fishing out the mangled fork.

'If it's all the same to you, chef, I'll just have coffee.' Dorothy held out her cup.

'Something dropped into the disposal.' Marc continued probing for the elusive fork.

'Uh huh. I wonder who.'

'Well, I can't be a great lover and a good cook, too.'

Dorothy brushed a kiss across his cheek. 'One out of two isn't bad,' she said quietly.

'I can always learn how to cook.'

'Coffee, please.'

'I take it, then, madam agrees with the adjective "great"?'

'Full to the rim, please.'

'How about "capable"?' Marc pleaded.

'You went to sleep first.'

'I did not.'

'Okay, I concede. Capable.' Her statement was as enthusiastic as the moist kiss she planted on his cheek.

'Mushy, mushy,' commented their son.

'Eat your breakfast,' instructed Marc as he slid his wife's mouth around to his.

Jim ignored him and poured a second heaping bowl of cereal.

'Now,' said Dorothy, pulling away, 'may I pul-leese have my damn coffee?'

Marc acquiesced and filled her cup.

The short drive to the squadron spaces on Point Mugu Naval Air Station was nervously quiet. Marc attempted to ease the situation with small talk.

'You'll be the man of the house, again, Jim. I expect you to take care of your mother.'

'Sure, Dad.'

'I don't know what I'd do without him,' commented Dorothy.

Marc was relieved to see the squadron parking area ahead and he swung into the space marked: Commanding Officer, Antarctic Development Squadron SIX.

Two youthful sailors appeared, saluted smartly, and began lifting out his bags.

'Morning, Skipper,' greeted the taller of the two.

Marc returned the salutes. 'Good morning, Wood . . . Spencer. You two all ready to go?'

'Yes, sir,' Wood replied, then he added, 'Morning, Mrs Bradford. I see the whole crew's turned out for the big day.' Winking at Jim, he turned back to Marc. 'We'll put your gear on board, sir.'

'Thanks.'

Marc led his wife and son through the side door of the silver hangar and they climbed the steel stairway to the second-level balcony. It ran down the entire side of the huge enclosure and overlooked the indoor working area. Marc's office was midway down the railed overhang. His executive officer was waiting inside.

'Anything earthshaking?' asked Marc.

'No, we're all set, Captain. Our departure message needs your release.' The exec held out the message board.

Marc scribbled his initials on the bottom of the message draft, leafed through the remaining papers, and handed back the clipboard.

'Have a good cruise, Don,' offered Dorothy.

'You bet, Dorothy,' returned the exec. 'With Marc, here, at the helm, it will be. 'Bye, Jim.'

'Goodbye, Commander Donovan,' returned the boy.

The exec shut the door behind him.

Marc opened his gear locker and pulled out the bright blue flying suit. Two wide golden stripes dropped down the right side from the shoulder seam to the waist. He donned the garment over his uniform, put on the bright yellow ball cap with the black CO on its crown, and handed his bridge cap and briefcase to a waiting yeoman. The sailor scurried off. Marc turned to his wife and son.

There was a slight moistness in Dorothy's eyes, but no redness. It was a look Marc had seen too many times before. 'Last time for a while,' he stated flatly.

Dorothy nodded. 'We'll be fine.'

'Well, lover, let's get on with it.'

They kissed warmly and he gave his son a long hug.

'Penguin feathers, this time, Dad?'

'For sure.' Marc always promised to bring some back for his son, but always forgot. He didn't dare this last time.

They walked back down the balcony and stairs and passed through the open hangar doors. The five Lockheed

LC-130R Hercules aircraft were positioned in a nose-to-tail column, with a spacing between them of about twenty feet. A white nylon restraining line had been rigged some fifty feet from the aircraft, and white-uniformed sentries were patrolling back and forth, occasionally intercepting running children whose spontaneous bursts of energy threatened to carry them under the rope and interfere with loading operations.

A sizable crowd of dependents was saying goodbye to their men; some embraced, others talked and held hands, still others passed squirming toddlers back and forth as daddies gave their goodbye kisses.

The stately Hercules were waiting, their flat landing-gear skis retracted but still only a few inches above the concrete ramp surface, making the sausage-shaped fuselages appear to be squatting on great webbed feet.

Seeing his crew all aboard and the line crewmen in position under the noses of the Hercules, Marc realized that it was time. He pulled Dorothy to him one last time.

'Goodbye, my love. Take care of things.'

'We will. You be careful.'

Jim returned his father's hug with appropriate embarrassment.

One last meeting of the eyes and Marc turned and walked briskly to the lead Hercules. As he reached the steps formed by the lowered crew entrance hatch, his macho reserve weakened and he slipped a pair of dark sunglasses over his eyes and tried unsuccessfully to swallow the lump in his throat. Climbing up onto the spacious flight deck, he nodded to his crew and strapped himself into the command pilot's seat.

To his right sat his regularly assigned copilot, Lt Sheila Kohn. An aircraft commander in her own right, the young woman was the lone aviator among eight females assigned to the squadron. 'Frosty' Kohn, as she was known throughout a large segment of the naval aviation community, was already establishing herself as a 'comer' with her professionalism, her expertise both as an aviator and a naval officer, and her no-nonsense demeanor, which Marc had early on diagnosed as a cover-up for her desire to be thought of as a naval officer first and a woman second. With that body, strapped so confidently in the seat opposite his, the woman would be forever fighting *that* battle. Seven years out of the Academy, this was her second year in VXE-6. She held an unrestricted instrument rating and was carrier qualified, having spent her last tour delivering F-14s and Hornets to squadrons embarked at sea. Marc had no doubt she would be early selected for lieutenant commander. He had to admire her steadfast determination to be not just the best female in the navy, but the best, period.

Five feet six, the raven-haired aviatrix fit into a flight suit like it was painted on. Reluctantly recognizing that, she never allowed her weight to vary more than half a pound, and exercised like a professional jock. She had been a marathon runner since her Academy days, could swim like a dolphin, and with her mastery of the giant Hercules, it was no exaggeration to say that she could fly like a bird. Still, with all of her qualifications, her ability in one area was unknown. Every man in the squadron wondered how she would be in bed.

Marc's flight engineer and navigator were also in position, and on the lower of the two seat bunks that stretched athwartships across the rear of the flight deck sat one of the crew's relief pilots and the squadron flight surgeon, Lieutenant Holley. As the next senior crew member, the young doctor-aviator, affectionately dubbed 'the Quack' by his fellow officers, was intently loading a professional-looking reflex camera.

'We're ready to start, Captain,' reported Kohn.

35

'Number three, clear!' came the crisp intercom voice of the outside observer.

'Roger, turning number three.' As he spoke, Marc triggered the interplane circuit and immediately pushed the start button for the starboard inside engine. All five Hercules simultaneously roared into life.

The outside observer coiled his long interphone cord and jumped up into the aircraft, pulling the entrance door shut behind him. The chocks had already been removed from in front of the ski-draped tandem main wheels and on Marc's signal the Hercules column moved out.

The wives and children continued to wave, straining to catch a final glimpse of their men, until the last aircraft taxied beyond their view.

Slowly, the scattered groups dispersed. The sailor-sentries began taking down the guard lines, and a blue-dungaree-clad working party commenced policing up the area.

Almost half a world away, it was six o'clock in the early evening and the director of Israel's secret service was deep in thought as he stood by the window in his office, which overlooked the darkening blue waters of a nervous corner of the Mediterranean Sea. He was contemplating the sinister significance of the decoded intelligence dispatch he held in front of him. It had just been hand-delivered, and after his first reading he had immediately called the one person he knew would have the strongest interest in the startling report.

The information had been procured at the cost of the life of one of his most valuable agents. Fortunately, the man had been a widower, and the director would not have the sad task of informing a next of kin. In fact, Myron Lubel had no family at all.

36

There was a quiet knock on the director's door. That would be Berel.

'Come in,' invited the director. He crossed over to the door and held out his hand as his visitor entered.

'What is it?' immediately asked Berel. In his late sixties, with a monk's fringe of gray hair wrapped around a shiny scalp, Berel Kosciusco joined hands with his old friend and eagerly accepted the director's offer to sit. Long of waist, with short, fat legs that barely reached the floor, Kosciusco was almost the same height sitting as standing, which was a plump five feet five. He wore his customary open-necked white shirt, over which was a wrinkled wash-and-wear seersucker sport coat. He had an endless supply of them, it seemed, all bought in the early years after the war when he had first migrated to the United States after the horror of Auschwitz. Like the tattoo on his wrist, the coats were his tie to an era that he had never left. His trousers were a concession to modern times, being a cotton-polyester mix, and having baggy pockets, which were kept constantly crammed with little notes he always seemed to be writing to himself. An Israeli for the past thirty-eight years, of noble Polish lineage, his only purpose in life was pursuing and bringing to justice those who had raped the dignities and extinguished the lives of six million of his kind. His wife was a scratched and dented four-drawer file cabinet crammed with histories of his forays around the world and his encounters with the human rodents who had survived for so many years after his liberation. His children were also files, but even more precious ones, filled with media accounts of the successful prosecution of those he had found in the back corners and sewers of the world. Like his friend, Myron Lubel, of whose death he was about to learn, he had no other family besides his life's work.

'Berel,' began the director as gently as he could, 'Myron

is dead.' How else could he have said it? No other way would have been any less considerate, for Kosciusco was a man who lived in a world of cold facts, and superfluous words were as much a waste of time as superfluous actions.

The rotund figure seated on the sofa merely nodded his head.

'But, my friend, before he died he had visited one of our contacts in Chile and gave her this message. He died with victory in his heart, Berel. Read this.'

Kosciusco took the paper, fished rimless glasses from his shirt pocket, and read the short report. Handing the paper back to the director, he used his handkerchief to wipe both his glasses and his eyes. 'Erich Scnell,' he said, with another nod of his head. 'I am very close, now, to the end of my journey.'

The director understood fully. Scnell was one of the last, perhaps the very last. All the others who might still be alive had been minor figures in that most terrible of times. Scnell, however, was one of those who had worked with the infamous Mengele, the creature who had stained the title Doktor for all time. Scnell, also, had used little children and women, as well as men, in his 'genetic' research. An animal who carved and cut live persons in his quest for pain tolerance perimeters to better the interrogation techniques of the SS, he had been one of Mengele's favored assistants. Now, according to the report, Scnell had been found. With a group of other non-South American Argentines, he was a member of that country's scientific staff at their base, General Belgrano, on the Antarctic Peninsula. The perfect hiding place. The Israelis had never considered Antarctica as a haven for such persons. But, in the light of Lubel's finding, why not? For years, Argentina had been establishing small colonies of families on the peninsula. Argentine children had been conceived and born there, the very first Antarctica natives. National mail was regularly posted, and the Argentine Parliament met once a year on that bleak finger of rock to pass and confirm national laws, all activities they could use to support their claim of sovereignty over a strategic wedge of the Antarctic continent once the Antarctic Treaty expired. Until then, as had all other treaty nations, they had agreed to hold any territorial claims in abeyance. Meanwhile, they were taking all possible steps to be able to justify their claim when the day came. And Doktor Erich Scnell was hidden from the outside world as part of that effort. Hidden, that is, until Kosciusco's fellow unrelenting ferret, Myron Lubel, had learned of Scnell's whereabouts. To die for such an act was a noble death.

'He will still be difficult to get to, Berel.'

'Yes, but there is a way. There is always a way.'

'Argentina will never cooperate.'

'We do not need Argentina's cooperation.'

'The Americans?'

Kosciusco's face was aglow with his thought of final triumph. 'Of course. Who else has access to all of Antarctica, if not the Americans? They will take me to Scnell.'

3

As they led the elephantine column of Hercules toward the duty runway, Marc and his crew performed the routine checks of the aircraft's systems and engines. By the time they reached the number one spot for takeoff, Kohn had requested and received their instrument flight clearance to Honolulu.

'Okay, Sheila, takeoff check.'

Kohn began reading aloud the long list of items to be sighted, set, or aligned prior to their taking of the runway. With each challenge, Marc would sight the individual lever, knob, or instrument and give the proper response. The two experienced pilots took nothing for granted and their procedure was professional and brief.

'Point Mugu Tower, Navy four-nine-one-two-nine, ready to go,' reported Kohn.

'Roger, one-two-nine, I have your release. Maintain runway heading to flight level one-two-zero . . . cleared for left turn passing one-two-zero . . . climb on course to flight level two-seven-zero . . . squawk code one-one-zero-zero, monitor GUARD . . . read back. Over.'

Kohn read back the clearance verbatim and the voice of the tower controller returned, 'Roger, one-two-nine, the firing range is inactive, contact San Francisco Overseas Radio when established on course . . . cleared for takeoff . . . have a good cruise, Icemen.'

'Roger, tower, see you next spring.' As she spoke, Kohn gave Marc a thumbs-up. Marc released the brakes and guided the loaded Hercules onto the west runway. They would be taking off to seaward. The Point Mugu

Naval Air Station sat just to the south of coastal Oxnard, the airfield itself just a few hundred yards inland from the lapping surf. The control tower of the naval air station, home of the Pacific Missile Test Center, was obligated to ensure that traffic pattern aircraft did not stray into the missile test range and 129s assigned climbout to 12,000 feet would take the C-130 through the eastern edge. With the range inactive, however, there should be no peril. Still, Frosty Kohn liked to double-check such things.

'We're rolling, tower,' she reported, then added, 'Understand range is inactive.'

'That is affirmative, one-two-nine,' confirmed the tower operator, his tone indicative of a slight irritation that his previous information was being questioned.

She gave Marc one of her rare grins. 'I guess I triggered his male ego. But it's our asses that are in this thing. I'd hate to lose mine through some tower error.'

Atta girl, Frosty, I'm with you, Marc said to himself as he advanced the power levels smoothly to their forward stop. The churning propellers launched the Hercules with such a pronounced motion that the crew could feel the satisfying pressure of the rapid acceleration against their seat backs. Marc shifted his primary scan to the airspeed indicator and as the needle approached fifty-five knots he switched his left-hand grip from the nosewheel steering wheel to the flight-control yoke. At sixty knots he gave a firm pull and the nose of the aircraft rose confidently to its takeoff attitude. He could not see back to his left, but he knew that Dorothy and Jim were somewhere back there, watching the takeoff and sharing that heavy, lonely feeling that gave this particular departure a special flavor. But his attention stayed with the aircraft.

He had entered the airman's world, and the responsibility of guiding eighty tons of man and machine into the morning air was his only concern. On the right, toward the rear of the flight deck, sat his navigator, marine M. Sgt David Wineman, busily arranging his route charts and making initial adjustments to his inertial flight navigation gear. He would be primarily a monitor on the overwater route to New Zealand. Sophisticated electronic navigation equipment now took over the mundane chores that only two decades back his predecessors in the earlier F models of the Hercules had performed with sextants, LORAN, and dead reckoning. All four of the squadron's F models had been lost on the Ice, but Wineman and his fellow crew members had escaped unscratched when the last F model had blown off its number two engine with an errant JATO bottle during an open field takeoff. Wineman had philosophized at the accident hearing, 'At least, now we'll get more modern aircraft.' And true to his somewhat callous prediction, the LC-130R was a quantum jump over the early Hercules flown by VXE-6, with more power and thus improved speed, range, and payload capacity. At the moment, Wineman had his boxer's build hunched over the navigation table, enjoying the feel of the powerful takeoff acceleration, arranging his various charts and papers before him in order of importance, and making preliminary entries into his navigation log.

Across the rear bulkhead were two crew bunks – relatively luxurious four-inch slabs of rubber encased in gray plastic. On the top bunk lay several brown leather flight jackets, two small pillows with clean white covers, and several assorted magazines. On the bottom bunk, which also served as a seat for extra flight-deck personnel, sat the crew's junior pilot, Lt (jg) 'Zin' Zinwicki, and the flight surgeon. Both were securely strapped in and looking rather bored with the whole affair. The Quack held an empty paper cup on his lap, obviously waiting for the point in their departure procedure where he could lean forward and extract a portion of thick black navy coffee from a stainless steel container in the galley on the left rear side of the flight deck.

The newly commissioned flight surgeon had reported to the squadron fresh out of indoctrination training, having volunteered for the antarctic program. He had reported aboard as a well-qualified physician but a rather naïve naval officer. His strict New England upbringing and his years of formal schooling and training had ill-prepared him for his first assignment with the irreverent professionals of VXE-6. Marc still had to smile whenever he recalled the doctor's introduction to the assembly at Holley's first 'all officers' meeting in the hangar ready room. The exec had asked him to stand and be recognized as he introduced, '. . . our new flight surgeon, Doctor Harold P. Holley!' The room had immediately erupted into a loud chorus of fake duck calls, 'Quack . . . quack . . . quack! . . .' as everyone, including Marc, cupped their hands over their mouths and gave the squadron's traditional greeting to a stunned medical officer. Holley was almost in a state of shock for the remainder of the meeting. It took him only a few weeks to realize, however, that the irreverent nickname was really a mark of respect. The men knew, and Holley was soon to learn, that the task of the flight surgeon on the Ice would be one of the most demanding and dangerous tours a military doctor could undertake. Holley was now very proud of his christening, and his little black bag, strapped somewhere back in the cargo compartment, carried the inscription 'Squadron Quack,' stenciled in large, bold print just below his name.

'One hundred and five knots,' intoned Kohn, indicating the reaching of refusal speed. Beyond that point, should an engine fail or a propeller malfunction, the takeoff could be continued on the three remaining power plants and the great aircraft's reserve energy would ensure a safe climbout and return to the field. At 116 knots, Marc sensed the aircraft's will to fly and allowed it to rise without adjusting the graceful takeoff attitude. At fifty feet, he called for the retraction of the landing gear, lowered the nose slightly to expedite the airspeed buildup, and at 135 knots signaled Kohn to bring up the flaps. She was already on their departure frequency and reporting their takeoff time and flight status. In answer to the departure controller's instructions, she set a new code on the IFF transponder.

'Roger, one-two-nine,' came the detached voice of departure control, 'radar contact . . . out.' The absence of any further instructions implied that Navy 129 could continue with its climbout as instructed in the clearance.

Back in the cavernous cargo compartment, accompanied by the piercing noise of the overhead ventilation fan and a heaping mound of cargo boxes and luggage, the eight squadron passengers assigned to the lead Hercules began moving about in search of more comfortable positions. Several left their webbed troop seats and sought sleeping nooks atop the strapped cargo. Blankets and flight jackets were rolled and wadded into crude pillows. One experience air traveler had already settled down for the eight-hour flight to Honolulu, curled on the cold deck in a sleeping bag cocoon, arms folded comfortably across his chest and the foot of the bag draped through a loose cargo strap. Someone had passed around a box of doughnuts. Three sailors sat on the incline of the tailgate ramp and began a spirited card game. A fourth had declined and was rigging a litter to the topmost tier of fittings. Vaulting into it, he thumbed through a well-used copy of *Playboy*, quickly becoming oblivious to his surroundings.

A truly classical cargo carrier, the C-130 was definitely not a passenger's airplane. Nevertheless, the sky sailors who regularly rode the rear adjusted quickly to the situation with characteristic enlisted ingenuity and sometimes sheer cunning. The American sailor was infamous for his ability to sleep in any conceivable position, and these sky sailors could always manage to jury-rig a spot where they could ride in relative comfort. In any one group, someone was constantly on the prowl, searching for unread magazines or climbing over the stacked cargo aft to one of the two white-enameled urinals hung on the fuselage sides beyond the paratrooper exit doors. As a concession to their female pilot, a privacy curtain was rigged around the chemical stool, and each man knew to make sure the woman was engaged in flight-deck duties before relieving themselves at the urinals.

After a few hours in the air, the scattered paper cups and magazines and overflowing ashtrays would give the cargo bay a real lived-in atmosphere. After all, in the present case, eight people meant sixteen armpits, and if the cargo compartment were allowed to get too warm there was no mistaking the presence of healthy male odors – the sort of thick fragrance that wasn't exactly offensive, but mighty good to get away from at the first landing break. Several on board at the moment were veterans of Frosty's first transpacific flight and recalled her pointed hint upon leaving Honolulu when she strategically placed several spray cans of deodorant in the cargo compartments. Not wishing to repeat that experience of living in a Garden Rose environment, they had brought along their own cans of Brut and Stud, and with devilish anticipation, lay in wait for her first foray aft.

Marc leveled at 27,000 feet and engaged the autopilot. The air was crystal clear above the heavy layer of smog that perennially blanketed the water off the coast of southern California. Except for a few budding cumuli far off to the southwest, visibility was unrestricted and the Hercules rode the still air like a canoe on calm water.

'Watch it for a minute, Sheila. I'm going aft. Want some coffee?'

'Black, please,' replied Kohn, loosening her shoulder straps for a more comfortable ride.

Marc released his lap belt and slid back the seat. With the increased leg room, even a man of his size could easily step back onto the flight deck.

The relaxed flight engineer, one leg dangling over the arm of his slightly elevated seat behind and between the two pilots, was nonchalantly recording the level-off engine readings in his log.

'How's it look, Tom?' inquired Marc.

'Okay, Skipper,' the tow-headed technician replied. First Class Petty Officer Thomas P. Dare was typical of the flight crewmen. In his early thirties, this was his third year with VXE-6. An aviation electrician's mate by rating, he had nevertheless become a qualified flight engineer.

Marc made his way down the short ladder from the flight deck and picked his way aft over the sprawled bodies. While he stood by the portside urinal, he steadied his stance with a one-handed grip on the ramp restraining bar and gave the cargo compartment a cursory inspection. Funny how he could go on a local flight of maybe three or four hours and never have to leave his seat, but take off on a transpacific jaunt and his bladder required attention within the first hour. Having contributed his bit of moisture to the smog far below, he took his time returning to the flight deck.

He spent a few minutes talking to his loadmaster, like Wineman a marine sergeant and one of the six enlisted marines assigned to the squadron. Along with the two USMC pilots, the eight-man contingent were all veteran airmen, specifically picked by the corps for the elite antarctic duty. After hearing the sergeant's latest philosophy on world affairs and sex, Marc chatted briefly with

46

the *Playboy*-engrossed crewman and added his praise to the sailor's somewhat obscene comment about the center-fold's mammary glands. The twenty-year-old aviation mechanic would be part of the two crews evaluating a DeHaviland Ranger during the coming months on the Ice. He had his work cut out for him. The Canadian-built DHC-7R would be a civilian plane, leased by the navy for the trials. One of Marc's more experienced pilots, Lt Comdr 'Bud' Tilley, was back at the plant picking up the special cold-weather version of the aircraft and would be bringing it down across the Pacific a few weeks after the squadron reached McMurdo. DeHaviland was installing special long-range internal fuel tanks for the long Pacific legs. Skis and passenger seats would come down by priority air in the air force C-141 lift and be reinstalled once the Ranger was safely on the Ice. Marc was not too enthused about the program, particularly the flight down across the Pacific, but the squadron had deployed the ancient C-47s along the same route during the early years and they had all made it. He also recalled that they invariably experienced long delays waiting for favorable winds at Alameda and later Christchurch. The Ranger was not that much better an aircraft when it came to cruising range, but with more powerful and reliable engines, not to mention state-of-the-art avionics and nav gear, the odds were considerably better for an event-free crossing. In the old Dakotas, Marc recalled reading in squadron reports, even the heaters had been inadequate.

Prolonged conversation was all but impossible amid the roar of the engines and the high-pitched scream of the ventilation fans, which filled the packed cargo cavern with an unrelenting E-string vibration. Even small talk was usually reserved for the flight deck, where the padded fuselage and distance from engines and cargo compart-ment air blowers provided a relatively quiet zone. As he picked his way forward, a strong whiff of Brut crossed his nostrils.

Returning to the flight deck, he drew two coffees for himself and Kohn. Stepping forward, he noted that the Quack had commandeered the command pilot's seat and was leaning toward the side, camera glued to his face and his fingers busily aligning, focusing, and snapping pictures as if he owned all of the film in the world. For the life of him, Marc could not fathom the need to take more than one or two shots, considering that they were almost five miles high over open ocean. Leaning back to reload, the doctor sensed Marc's presence behind him.

'Want your seat, Skipper?' he asked.

Marc reached across in front of Dare and handed Kohn her coffee. 'Wouldn't dream of it, Doctor. Log some seat time. Lieutenant Kohn, don't let him touch anything.'

'Hey,' began the Quack defensively, 'I am a qualified pilot, too, you know.'

'Not in this bird,' retorted Kohn.

The Quack switched his argument to his seatmate. 'Women should be maintained in a state of successive pregnancies and without footwear, not mingling up here with us professional warriors.'

Kohn warmed to the exchange. 'God help the woman who ever has a baby with you in attendance.'

'An event those of you who have chosen the life of an Amazon will never experience.'

'Amazon? You, the squadron Quack, have the nerve to call me an Amazon? I wouldn't let you remove my tonsils.'

'I don't do tonsils.'

Kohn shook her head in surrender and went back to monitoring the flight instruments. The light-hearted conversation was typical of the banter that she and the Quack

48

often engaged in, much to the amusement of their squadron mates. No one else had the nerve to parry with Frosty; she could be ruthless. Actually, the new doctor was one of her most ardent fans and felt much safer with her at the controls than some of the squadron hot rods, and she felt comfortable around him, as he was the one officer she could confide in. Their words might not show it, but they had a good professional relationship and the beginnings of a personal one, at least as much of a beginning as Frosty allowed herself with any man.

The Quack went back to his picture taking. Kohn could give and take with the best of them, and while Holley hated to admit it, she was by far the superior naval officer. Maybe, with time and experience, he would feel as at home in the US Navy as she. Meanwhile, he would content himself with the thought that he was the only man in the squadron for whom she would remove her clothes.

Marc sat down on the lower bunk with his coffee. Zinwicki was stretched out in the upper. The other four aircraft should be behind 129 at about twenty-minute intervals. The sixth Hercules was already in Christchurch, having made an early flight to the Ice to deliver the first load of scientific personnel. Actually, 129 had sat in Christchurch as a search and rescue aircraft during that preseasonal turnaround and had returned to Mugu only three days back, so Marc's crew was getting the short end of the stick on predeployment free time. He would have to see if he could spring an extra day in Christchurch for them, provided their schedule permitted. If not, that was the roll of the dice.

His mind kept returning to Tilley and the Ranger. There would be two critical stretches on the route between the States and McMurdo Station. The first would be between the West Coast and Honolulu. Even with the extra internal fuel tanks, Tilley would have to wait for a projected zero in-flight wind component, not a frequent condition this time of year, when the prevailing winds were westerlies. He didn't relish the thought of what would be an overgross takeoff, the new DeHaviland propelled into the air by four JATO bottles, their racks alone an unproven modification to the civilian passenger carrier. At least, enroute on that first long leg, they would be over warm, well-traveled water. An unfavorable wind change, once they passed their point of no return, could conceivably result in Tilley and his two-man crew swimming the last few miles to Oahu.

The real pucker would come later, after the Ranger's ball-busting marathon down through Pago Pago in American Samoa on its South Pacific route to New Zealand. There, Tilley would stop for any needed maintenance, then head for Invercargill on the southeastern coast of South Island, once more to wait for favorable winds for the final perilous leg to Antarctica.

Another by-guess-and-by-God, four-bottle blast into the cold southern latitudes air. That final flight to the Ice, so routine to the Hercules, would be across 2,400 miles of the most inhospitable seas on earth. The loss of an engine, a major malfunction of the aircraft's navigational equipment, or a sudden change in the always-unpredictable antarctic weather could place the DHC-7 in deepest peril. The antarctic Pacific was no place to ditch. No warm-water wait in a bright yellow raft under sunny Pacific skies; quite the opposite – an icy plunge into frigid, thrashing waters. Even if by some miracle the crew managed to nurse a crippled craft to the continent, floundering along in an unpredictable antarctic storm, the end could very well come in a grinding crash against a snow-shrouded 12,000-foot-high block of ice. Either way, their fate would be the same.

The pilots and crewmen of the Hercules certainly didn't

envy Tilley and his crew, they just admired them and respected their raw courage and airmen's ability to coax a short-range passenger airplane over several very long-range, overwater flights. The fact that such a feat would be typical of VXE-6's thirty-three-year performance record was of little comfort to the commanding officer, whose responsibility it was to ensure that the flight was made safely. Marc breathed a silent prayer for that singular operation as he finished his coffee and opened his briefcase. He was soon absorbed in the pile of paperwork that had escaped his attention in the hectic days prior to deployment.

One-two-nine droned on across the water, gaining time against the sun as the miles passed.

Frosty Kohn watched the buildup of a large cumulus off to their left. A few hours from now, the arid sands of Baja California would have a welcome drink of water. But the ocean below was calm, almost glassy. That should change before too long. The weather briefing back at Mugu had included the remark that a large bubble of unstable air lay right on course midway to Honolulu. At 27,000 feet, they should be well above any visible condensation, but the unrest of such an air mass would undoubtedly cause them to remain strapped in while they crossed the area. Actually, even a little clear air turbulence would be welcome. The scenery was certainly monotonous; something would have to keep them awake. Kohn much preferred flight conditions that challenged her a bit more.

4

The Aeritalia G222 STOL transport of the Comando de Aviacion del Ejercito – Argentina's Army Aviation Command – carried a lone passenger as it droned westward with its tail toward the late morning sun, its twin turboprop engines humming happily in their relaxed cruise settings. Ahead, the clear air visibility belied the actual distance to the southernmost range of the Andes. A view from the cockpit would seem to place the jagged, snow-covered peaks within a veritable stone's throw, yet the radar picture on the small scope that sat between the pilots' controls confirmed that the closest ice escarpment was still more than 120 kilometers away. Five thousand meters below lay the southernmost portion of the windswept Patagonian desert. To the south, only 300 kilometers away, was the Strait of Magellan, and to the south-southeast at a considerably larger distance – 800 kilometers – were the Islas Malvinas.

The 2,300-mile-long southeastern portion of South America that was Argentina was a flipflop image, in topography and climate, of the North American stretch of land that ran northward from Mexico's Yucatan to Canada's Hudson Bay.

Argentina's northeastern jungle was almost indistinguishable from the southeastern rain forests of Yucatan, the Pampas easily reminiscent of the American prairie. The great Paraná River, Argentina's Mississippi, was even occasionally referred to as 'old man river'; and finally, the Andes, the southern hemisphere's counterpart of the Rocky Mountains, but a mile and a half higher at its tallest peaks. Argentina was cold in the south and warm in the north, seeming to confirm that nature had whimsically played a creative game of opposites. It was spring here, and in keeping with that season of renewal, it was a time of political renewal in that most European of South American countries.

With a population that was 95 percent Spanish, Italian, and other European stock, Argentina was only six years out of a fascist political system that had extended from the time of Juan Perón in 1946 to the overthrow of the Galtieri junta in 1983, the direct result of the country's ill-fated 1982 incursion into the Malvinas.

Argentina had not ventured onto foreign soil since its Paraguay adventure, 112 years before its invasion of the antarctic islands. During the interim, its military forces had fired on no people except its own. And with the results of that 1982 error in judgement toppling the last fascist regime, the new government was determined to accomplish dramatic changes in the economy, system of government, and world image of Argentina. The mission of the lone passenger in the army transport was a part of that overall reshaping of Argentina.

Ahead, at the base of the Andes, lay Lake Argentino, its westernmost tongue fed by the massive Moreno Glacier, which calved gigantic chunks of ice into its waters. The Moreno provided a relief for the tremendous pressures of the 400-kilometer-long continental ice cap sitting atop the southern tip of the Andes. Sixty-four kilometers wide, the ice cap, every moment during the day, stretched and pushed a dozen significant glaciers toward the sea to the west and the lowland to the east.

An impressive hacienda on the southwestern edge of Lake Argentino was the eventual destination of the man in the Aeritalia G222, but first he must transfer to ground transportation, for there was no suitable landing area within walking distance of the homestead. To that end, the pilot now began a high-speed descent toward a bare strip of land carved from the scrub; it was several kilometers short of his destination and actually closer to the village of Califate, which sat on the southeastern tip of the lake. Indicative of the seclusion provided by the isolated hacienda was the fact that few villagers of Califate even knew of its existence, and certainly none had been there.

As if it were on an attack, the G222 roared across the primitive landing strip, then pulled sharply up and to the left to configure itself for the landing. The pilot used his full measure of landing flaps, automatically changing the configuration of the leading edge of the wing to produce a lifting surface of maximum efficiency. Nose high, the aircraft approached the strip, its speed just above its stalling point and its lowered wheels skimming the tops of the scrub grass. At the instant the aircraft crossed the edge of the strip, the pilot cut his power, allowed the transport to drop sharply onto the dirt surface, and created his own miniature dust storm by placing his propellers into their full reverse position. The Aeritalia stopped within 100 meters, exactly opposite a four-wheel-drive Blazer. The smooth-running turboprop engines wound down to a stop.

'Good morning, Senor Mignone,' greeted the man standing beside the car as the Aeritalia's passenger approached.

'Herr Eisner,' responded the passenger, extending his hand.

Both men were about the same age, in their late sixties, but there was a marked difference in their appearance. The German was tall and lean, almost gaunt. At five feet ten, the Argentine was several inches shorter and his stocky frame was accented by a small paunch, which caused the front of his parka to hang forward, away from his legs. The German's hair was close-cropped and dyed black; the Argentine's was missing and a thickly knitted cap protected his bald pate from the cold. Quickly, both of them climbed into the Blazer and the German gunned it away from the strip.

'I trust your flight was pleasant.'

'Comfortable enough, but not exactly first class.'

'I'm sure, but then the transport was designed to carry combat troops, not high-level government officials. You come bearing gifts?' Eisner indicated with his head the box that one of the aircraft crewmen had placed in the rear of the Blazer.

'Some fresh fruit and a few bottles of wine to replenish your cellar.'

'Ah, how thoughtful. We can look forward to enjoying a treat during dinner this evening. You will stay, of course.'

'The plane will be waiting for me.'

'I will send someone to take the crew into Califate. It is a very small village, but several families there will welcome and entertain them. The army men will find the hospitality a rare diversion from their normal duties.'

'In that case, I shall look forward to joining you.'

'Good.'

They were now heading west, paralleling the southern edge of Lake Argentino. The dirt road was still very hard from the long winter's cold, and the Blazer dipped and swayed as the German kept the speed just below the point where the bumps and ditches would throw them out of control. Patches of dirty snow dotted the surrounding terrain, becoming more widespread as they began a gradual climb toward the towering Andes. Within minutes they were a hundred meters above the level of the sparkling blue lake, threading along a narrow ridge that fell away sharply toward the water on Mignone's side.

The view was awesome. Jagged peaks reached toward the brilliant blue sky, with white cap clouds hovering just above several. Below each peak was the gray haze of falling snow. Moreno Glacier was now clearly in view at the far edge of the lake, a gigantic flow of crevassed ice and snow imperceptibly descending from the high mountain valleys.

The Blazer topped a ridge, and as they reached the crest Mignone caught his first view of the hacienda. The white stucco structure was a perfect square and single-storied. The square was hollow, the home completely enclosing an interior garden. Large rectangular windows were evenly spaced around the exterior wall, and around the garden was a covered walkway that shielded the inside wall windows. To the rear was an annex, similarly constructed, rectangular in shape. The entire complex was roofed with thick clay tile, Spanish in design, ocher in color. Apparently, lake water was piped to the surrounding grounds, for there was a generous spread of healthy grass extending several hundred meters on all sides. Several outbuildings, one appearing to be a stable, sat on the back edge of the grounds. There was no shrubbery, and only a few scrawny trees, hardy specimens that annually fought the extreme cold and harsh winds of winter. The house sat at lake level, with the water perhaps a kilometer away. The Blazer continued on, now gradually making its way down from the ridge.

'It has been a while since I've had the pleasure of enjoying your hospitality,' commented Mignone.

'I sense your visit this time concerns serious matters.'

'It does that.'

'Well,' said the German with a shrug, 'let us warm ourselves first with some *yerba mate*.'

56

'I am ready for that.' The hot herbal tea would be most welcome in southern Argentina's chilly September spring. A glance at his watch revealed it was almost noon. The sun was about as high as it would be, which at these latitudes was not very high at all, and the low angle of its rays were not providing as much warmth as its brilliance might suggest.

The German stopped the Blazer beneath the shelter of the covered entranceway. A young man took Mignone's parka and cap as they entered. The tea was already waiting for them in the comfortable library, and the great stone fireplace that sat between two tiers of windows was filling the room with delicious warmth from an expansive bed of cherry-red coals. The windows, six in all and each three by eight feet in size, opened the room to the west, affording the occupants a splendid view of the lake and the Moreno in the distance. Eisner led Mignone over to the group of high-backed leather chairs in front of the fireplace. They were arranged around a circular coffee table, on which sat the tea.

'Well, old friend, tell me. What is this all about?'

Alberto Mignone was, indeed, an old friend of Kurt Eisner. They had played together as children when Eisner's father had been a minor official in the German Embassy in Buenos Aires during the years before World War II. In 1941, Eisner had returned to his homeland with his parents; Mignone, perhaps impressed by the opulence and ceremonial activities of the embassy, had impatiently finished his schooling and entered his own country's foreign service. They had seen each other only once during the war, when Mignone had been a member of a foreign service mission to Berlin, where the neutralist Argentines had discussed a program of mutual benefit between their country and Nazi Germany. The popularity of Hitler, the stunning successes of the early stages of the war, and the sight of thousands of Germans, ecstatically shouting their devotion to their fuehrer, had convinced the young Mignone that the National Socialist Movement was indeed the wave of the future. Mignone had taken special pride when his ancestral Italy had fought side by side with the charismatic Hitler. Then, when the war ended disastrously for the Axis, Mignone, by then an official of some importance, had been instrumental in the settling of the hordes of Germans, most of them National Socialists, who had made their way to Argentina. Once more, he had been reunited with his friend Eisner.

Mignone was a survivor, having served the fascist regimes of Perón through Galtieri, and even finding a post suitable to his long experience within the new government of Presidente Alfonsin. Having been deeply involved in the German situation, he had during the past forty-three years been the prime liaison between the Argentine government and the exiles. His mission today was another instance of his diplomatic ability in conveying Argentina's concern for its old friends. But, this time, the message was radically different.

Eisner had sensed that the moment Mignone had stepped down from his transport aircraft. The two had been in association for such a long time that each could read the other even before words were spoken.

The German had prospered in Nazi Germany, becoming one of the elite before the dream of Hitler collapsed. A fanatical officer in the fuehrer's personal bodyguard, he was one of that group's youngest colonels and a favorite of Hitler's personal staff. To Col. Kurt Eisner, the Third Reich had not died in Berlin; it had only been forced into exile and was still a viable force that one day, in fulfillment of his fuehrer's prophecy, would rise and again encompass the world. Perhaps not in his lifetime, however. Therefore, he had only one duty: to keep the dream alive. Most of his fellow Nazis were gone, either having died of natural causes or having been imprisoned or executed after being exposed by the devil Jews, who now had more control of the world than before the Reich's heroic effort to exterminate them. But a hard core of National Socialists was still alive, old men but determined leaders, and their followers were still legion. This very place, this most secret, isolated, remote facility in southwestern Argentina, was their headquarters, the seat of the true German government in exile.

Mignone finished his tea and accepted a refill from Eisner.

'Times have changed, my dear friend.'

'Times are always changing,' replied the German.

'We have a new government, Herr Eisner, and there are new demands on our economy and our associations with other countries. There are new opportunities. Be patient with me while I explain.'

'I have patience for everything except the delay of the return of the new order.'

Mignone nodded. 'Yes, yes, of course. But to fully understand the purpose of my visit, you must first understand the position of Argentina in the world today. It is not the same, now. The people have tired of the dominance of the military. The shame and disappointment of our disastrous campaign in the Malvinas gave rise to a new force in this country, a force of the people. The trial of Galtieri and his associates, General Dozo and Admiral Anaya, who so ineptly fought the British, brought cries for reform and a new beginning. We are a rich country in resources. Our beef is the world's finest, our sheep and wool industry extensive and efficient, our oil resources respectable. Along with New Zealand and several minor countries, we are one of the few truly agricultural economies in the world. But, we are broke, on the verge of bankruptcy. Why? Because of the misuse of our wealth. Even I must admit that, and I have had a small hand in creating that predicament. Let me give you a recent example. In the six years between 1978 and 1983, we borrowed more than thirty-seven billion dollars from foreign banks. Twenty billion – *billion* – was used to build up our military; *plata dulce* – sweet money – siphoned off the top to buy guns and line the pockets of Galtieri and his cronies. And what did we get for it? An army that could not fight, a navy that *would not fight!* And an air force of prima donnas, although I must give them their due. They, alone, fought brilliantly against the British.'

'You need not remind me of the Malvinas disgrace. We had more than a passing interest in that decision.'

'Yes. I am aware of our promises to you. The Malvinas would have been ideal for the settlement and growth of the German government in exile. After all, that was one of our prime purposes in the campaign, a purpose that some of your people almost compromised by that premature activation of a headquarters complex. Can you imagine the position we would have found ourselves in should that have been discovered?'

We were closer to compromise than you think! thought Eisner. I can still see the Royal Marine's face when I put a bullet in him. 'We had no idea that the great military state of Argentina could be defeated by a small expeditionary force based 7,000 miles away. *Gott!* As I say, I am impatient for the return of the Third Reich.'

'Herr Eisner, our progress now depends upon our relationship with other countries. We can no longer afford a detachment from the advantages of world association. We must have trade. Last year, the Soviet Union purchased eleven million tons of grain. We are the world's second largest exporters of that commodity. We are beginning to taste our first full economic meal in decades.'

'And we of the National Socialist Movement are happy for our friends who have sheltered us so long.'

'Escuchemé! – listen to me – the Soviets can become a major trade partner, but they have already laid down a condition.'

'A condition?'

'Yes. They know that there are still remnants of the Third Reich in this country . . .'

'Remnants! You suddenly refer to those of us who have maintained a complete government in exile, with a chancellery, and ministers of departments, and a planning force, as *remnants!*'

Mignon immediately regretted his choice of words. 'Hear me out. We have not forgotten our friends. It is just that we must make adjustments.'

'The Soviets know nothing of this place, or our activities.'

'Perhaps not. But they know the history of our association.'

'It is the Jews! You are caving in to the demands of international Jewry!'

'My old friend, do you actually think the Jews have any influence over the Soviet Union? Come now, think of the humor in such a thought. With respect to the Jews, the Soviets carry on the work of the Reich.'

'I was referring to the Jews in Argentina.'

'A handful. Of no consequence and of even lesser influence.'

'Ohhh, do not fool yourself. Who do you think controls the international banking community? Do you think that thirty-seven billion dollars was loaned to you for some intrinsic assets? The interest on that money is of little value compared to *control*. That is the aim of the Jews. Financial control of the world.'

'You must let me continue.'

Eisner threw up his hands in disgust.

'We have made provisions. For several years, as you are aware, Doctor Scnell has been serving our interests in Antarctica, performing as the medical officer at one of our colonies.'

Eisner nodded. He was well aware of Doctor Scnell's presence in Belgrano. And he was also aware of the doctor's real work, work which still served the Third Reich.

Mignone continued, 'We are colonizing Antarctica, Herr Eisner. Families are living there, children are being conceived and born in Argentine territory – the very first antarctic natives are of Argentine heritage. We are developing ways of living on that desolate continent. We post mail with the cachets of our country, and once a year representatives of our government travel to those colonies and sit in official session. We pass laws and confirm statutes, all on the rocky soil of Antarctica. We are exercising sovereignty over our claims.'

Eisner wasn't sure just what that had to do with him and the others, but he knew his friend Mignone well enough to know that whatever the Argentine was leading up to would affect the entire German colony in Argentina. Too many signs had been reported to him by his people in Buenos Aires. For the moment, he would be patient and hear out his friend. He responded to Mignone's assertion. 'You are exercising sovereignty over claims that you have given up by acquiescence to the Antarctic Treaty. You see, I am aware of such things. Do not forget that before our great struggle, we had an interest in that terrible place. German expeditions had tested the waters off the coast and German pilots had photomapped more than 400,000 square miles of territory.'

'Claims that we have agreed to hold in abeyance, not given up.'

'There is a difference? The United States and the Soviet Union are the biggest exploiters of Antarctica. Do you think they will recognize your claims?'

'When the time comes, yes. But this is not the time to argue the point. Because of our advances in Antarctica, our pioneering efforts have been quite successful. We – and I am speaking for the Presidente – are prepared to offer your people a part in that future.'

Eisner's heart began to jump. The hint of what he now knew was coming had appeared in Mignone's opening words. Still, he must suppress his building excitement at a turn of events that would play right into his hands. 'The other countries will not stand for such a thing,' he argued with a forced show of sincerity.

'They have no choice. Antarctica is an open continent. Anyone may go there, anyone may settle there.'

'And anyone may starve and freeze there.' He must appear negative to the proposal.

'No, we are living there, now. There are ways. We are prepared to establish a new colony and give it our full support. At some later time, you may declare your independence from Argentina and openly occupy whatever part of the continent you choose within our dependency. You will be infringing on no other's rights and there can be no international objection, again because of the status of Antarctica under the treaty. You will not be a treaty signatory, so you are not bound by it.'

'You are quite sincere about this, aren't you.'

'The government of Argentina is quite sincere.'

'I think it is an impossibility,' Eisner continued, playing out the scene.

'No, to the contrary, it is the *only* possibility.'

'We will not do it. We cannot do it.' Silently he marveled, we will be ecstatic, foolish friend, it will give us exactly the platform we need.

Mignone droned on, 'My friend, and I use that term because you are my friend, I believe in your cause, although I must confess I do not have your confidence that it will survive. I and a number of my associates who are also sympathetic to your struggle have argued long and hard for this. We have laid our careers on the line for a last chance for you and your people. Believe me, if you do not take this offer, the Presidente will outlaw your organization and charge you with sedition. He has no choice. While the extent of your existence in this country is not even suspected by the common citizen, that same citizen lives with rumors that surviving members of the National Socialist Party still live in Argentina. We can no longer live with even the rumor.'

'We are more than a rumor, Senor Mignone, much more. I am the senior member of a thirty-man Reichchancellery and all of my ministers are survivors of personal relationships with Adolf Hitler, himself. We lead a community of more than 12,000 Germans, pure Germans who are second-generation offspring of the thousands of countrymen who migrated to this country, from the valiant crewmen of the *Graf Spee* in 1939 to the refugees of 1945 and after. Our people are present in all facets of your society. They are oilmen, ranchers, Buenos Aires businessmen and women, teachers, military people, and even government workers. Underneath, however, they have unshakable confidence in the 1,000-year existence of the Third Reich. We have educated them, ourselves. They are our children, and they are our successors. Do you want them to take to the streets in protest at this betrayal? We are small in number, perhaps, but so were the Montoñeros of the early seventies, and I assure you that the rabble of the People's Revolutionary Army had not the devotion or organization of the National Socialist Movement. We can throw your country into turmoil

64

overnight.' Eisner was now enjoying the game. Put up resistance, and gain even more favorable terms for the relocation.

'That may be, but in doing so, you guarantee the complete annihilation of your party. The people will not tolerate fascism in their own government any longer, so why should they tolerate a foreign fascist government in exile? The walls of Buenos Aires are covered with graffiti. *'No mas fanaticos! Nunca mas!'* they are saying. You must agree to our plan. It is the only way to accomplish both of our aims. Our realignment with the world community can proceed, and your status can be preserved. There may come a ripe time when your opportunity will return. It will never, if your last blood flows in the streets of Argentina. And, believe me, that would be the will of the people.'

Eisner let his erect posture weaken and he sank back into his chair. It was time to indicate surrender. And time to show Mignone the real perseverance of German intent. 'You have no idea as to what we truly are, and how we have preserved ourselves. But I know you are carrying the message of your government, so we must respond. But first, I am going to present you to someone. You will be the first outsider to realize the true depth of our commitment. There has never been a cause such as ours. Not the Communist, not even the Catholic Church. The Third Reich will survive a thousand years, and I am about to show you why. Please, have some more tea, although it has perhaps lost its comfort within the context of our most serious discussion.' Eisner rose. 'I must make sure arrangements are ready.' Excusing himself with a stiff bow, he left the room.

Mignone refilled his cup, surprised to see that the tea was still hot. He really did not care for more, but it was a ritual that men of the world used when they needed to think. He alone had proposed the relocation plan for the Germans. They must be removed from the country, even he realized that, despite his strong sympathy with their cause. To most of the world, the Nazis were history; to the latest generation, ancient history. But he knew that Eisner and his followers were still a group to be reckoned with, and Eisner's remarks during their discussion had revealed that they were even more viable than he had imagined. What was puzzling to him was the lack of any real resistance to the move. He had expected Eisner to flare up at his first mention of any relocation. Instead, the German had only voiced a token resistance.

Perhaps, Eisner understood that the Argentine colonies in Antarctica were proving to be livable places, within certain limits, of course. As for the Argentine outlook, the Germans could exist there and continue with their dreams until the natural course of human life overtook them. And the daily struggle to cope with such an environment would allow them little extra energy to continue with their plans, whatever they were. There was another argument for their relocation. They would be doing Argentina a service, demonstrating the requirements for the support of older people on the continent. Until now, only young, physically fit citizens had been settled on the bleak Antarctic Peninsula, which jutted out to within 600 miles of the tip of South America. It was a good solution to a very sticky problem. And time for it.

Eisner had been gone for almost forty-five minutes and Mignone was both startled and surprised to see him return. He had changed clothes and now wore the colorful but sinister black uniform of the SS Leibstandarte Adolf Hitler, Hitler's personal bodyguard troops.

'It is arranged,' he announced. 'Please, follow me.'

They walked through an outside door and along the covered walkway that bordered the enclosed garden until they reached the rear wing. There, they reentered the main house and proceeded halfway down the rear hall, where an entry into the annex awaited them. When they passed through that door, Mignone found himself in another world. This time, there was a shorter hall, but one with combat banners of various World War II German military units lining each side, the colorful cloths hanging loosely around individual staffs and each illuminated with the soft glow of a baby blue spotlight. At the far end was still another door. On it was a large cast bronze plaque of the eagle-swastika emblem of the Third Reich.

They passed into what appeared to be an outer administrative office. There were file cabinets and two desks, a larger one for an overseer and a smaller one for secretarial work. The lone occupant of the office, wearing an immaculately tailored uniform of a Wehrmacht sergeant, was standing stiffly at attention beside the smaller desk. But it was the space behind the larger desk that caught Mignone's eyes. A life-size portrait of Adolf Hitler dominated not only the wall, but the entire room. Face on, the leader of Nazi Germany wore a casual uniform of tan tunic, brown riding breeches, and black boots. His arms were crossed, his right hand resting loosely on the Nazi armband that enclosed his upper left arm. His legs were spread and at one side lay an alert wolfhound. Behind him stretched valley scenery reminiscent of the area around his East Prussian hideaway, *Wolfsschanze* – Wolf's Lair. It was an heroic pose, painted in the Teutonic fashion so popular with the Nazi leader.

Finally, there was another door, of rich wood but unadorned with either symbol or legend. Eisner rapped his gloved knuckles lightly and opened the door. He stepped aside as Mignone followed him through the entrance.

The Argentine official was as unprepared for what he saw as for anything he had viewed in his sixty-eight years. The room was a reincarnation of the official spaces of the Third Reich. A series of Nazi banners covered all walls, the blood reds, white disks, and enclosed swastikas completely overpowering the eye. The carpet was pure white, as was the ceiling. But the most impressive feature of the furnishings was a magnificently carved desk. Some sensitive and emotional carpenter had obviously loved and treated the woods as he did his women. Easily eight feet long, it was half again as wide. Dark mahogany, the polished and impressive desk was bare on top except for a leather desk pad, a black pen in its marble holder, and a small pewter statue of a winged eagle. But even the walls and banners and desk paled before the image of the unbelievable creature that stood in the center of the room.

The man was a human skeleton, not more than five-and-a-half feet tall, although his humped back prevented any accurate estimate of his height in his youth. The wrinkled yellow skin hung over his bones as a dust cover would drape over a piece of protected furniture, loosely and in folds. He had once been much bigger, probably even fat. There was no hair on his head, but gray sprouts of it remained over his eyes and in his nostrils and a ragged patch covered the center of his upper lip. He stood without assistance, close to a large wingbacked leather chair, which must have been placed purposely in the center of the room. Two plain straight chairs sat opposite it.

But it was the eyes that held Mignone's attention. Those piercing orbs were sparkling with hate.

The man must be close to 100 years old. He was certainly the oldest human Mignone had ever seen, flesh and blood barely in human form, wearing the exact same uniform that clothed the figure in the portrait.

For an instant, Mignone allowed an impossible thought to flash through his mind. Could it be Adolf Hitler? Reason quickly returned. Eisner raised his right arm in a stiff, outstretched salute.

'Mein Fuehrer!' His greeting was accented by a sharp clicking of his heels.

The creature raised his arm with some effort, then draped his upturned palm backward over his right shoulder. 'Come in, Eisner. So, this is our friend, Senor Mignone, of whom you have spoken so often.'

Mignone took the outstretched hand. The flesh was warm.

'Please, sit down.'

Mignone took one of the two straight chairs, Eisner the other. The gaunt figure remained standing.

'I am Martin Bormann.' The voice was clear and strong.

Mignone let his jaw drop as he sat back into his chair.

'I see you are having difficulty with this.'

'I thought you were dead.'

'Of course. So does everyone. But I did not die in Berlin in 1945. I did plead with my fuehrer to allow that, but he was insistent that the Third Reich must be preserved. As you can see, it is.'

Mignone studied the living death mask that was the man's face. Martin Ludwig Bormann, Hitler's first deputy, condemned to death in absentia during the 1946 Nuremberg Trials. If Mignone's memory was correct, Bormann would be in his late eighties, maybe ninety. It was possible.

'My trusted deputy, Herr Eisner, tells me there is a plan for us. I am not too interested in the details, but I must ask, this is approved by your president?' Before the tongue-tied Mignone could reply, Bormann held up his hand and answered himself. 'Of course, it must be. You would not have such authority, yourself. Well, I must say, I do not like it.'

Mignone was surprised to hear his own voice steady. His body certainly was anything but! 'It is imperative that your people comply.'

'Ha! My people! Only *my people!* I am free to stay?'

'Of course I meant you also . . . Fuehrer,' Mignone answered, inadvertently using Eisner's term of addressing Bormann.

Bormann lowered his head and gazed sternly into Mignone's eyes. His puckered lip raised the sparse mustache even closer against his nostrils and the remnants of his eyebrows dropped closer to his eyes.

'We will discuss it. Thank you, Senor Mignone.'

That was it? Summarily dismissed?

'Thank you, Mein Fuehrer!' responded Eisner.

Mignone felt himself being assisted from the chair. His senses returned, but not his composure. 'Yes . . . thank you, . . .' he muttered, and followed Eisner from the room.

Over and over, Mignone reviewed the brief meeting as he and Eisner returned to the library. The walk back from Bormann's office seemed ten times longer than the walk to it. As they once again sat beside the circular coffee table, Eisner poured each of them a beaker of cherry schnapps. Very inappropriate, thought Mignone, but he needed something.

'You look disturbed, old friend,' commented Eisner, a trace of self-satisfaction in his voice.

'I really didn't see what I just saw, did I?'

Eisner chuckled. 'Of course you did. And, I might add, you are the first person outside of our community to be aware of our fuehrer's existence.'

Mignone sipped his schnapps. He was a loyal, lifetime

supporter of the German exiles, a sympathizer with their lost cause. But his estimate of their viability had always been that they were a dying breed who had missed a singular chance for glory. The existence of Martin Bormann did not change that in his mind, but it did add a new, sinister depth to their organization. Under no circumstances must Argentina allow Bormann's existence to become public knowledge. It would be a political self-crucifixion. And Eisner's purpose was clear. Argentina would have to support the Nazi community in Antarctica, above and beyond the support they planned for their own purposes. Eisner had a trump card, an insurance policy, a backup system, to ensure that support.

Mignone drained the last of his schnapps. Eisner poured him another. 'For a moment, I thought it was Hitler,' muttered Mignone.

'It almost was.'

Mignone stopped in midsip.

'Yes, yes, if our plans had gone right, you would have met the son of our great fuehrer on this day.'

'I don't understand,' ventured Mignone.

'A postscript to the most ambitious adventure in world history. As it was, the Allies did not give us quite enough time.' Eisner nodded smugly. 'But we did have limited success. For several weeks, we had the son of Adolf Hitler. We can credit Scnell with that great achievement. Artificial insemination, my friend. We were well on our way to perfecting such techniques. At first, we even tried preserving sperm by the use of chemicals – incidentally, we must with considerable reluctance give credit to some of the Jews who so graciously donated themselves for the development of the technique. We had no use to promulgate their kind, of course, and there were some difficulties. The chemical solution did preserve the sperm, but considerable gene damage resulted. Some of those Jew babies looked exactly how Jews should look. Ha! It would not have done for such monsters to have been created inside the bodies of German women. We were developing the technique of freezing when the war ended.'

'You mentioned a son of Hitler.'

'During the last days, immediately after Hitler married Eva Braun, we persuaded him to contribute a sperm specimen.'

Once more, Mignone reached for the cherry schnapps. It tasted terrible, but that was incidental to its effect.

'We impregnated a healthy woman of pure Germanic stock. We got a fetus, but it spontaneously aborted in the third month. We were *that* close, Mignone! But we still have Bormann, our new fuehrer and successor to the founder of the Third Reich! He is the cement that holds together the building blocks of the future.'

Mignone hesitated to ask, but it was a logical question. 'And after Bormann?'

'We have someone groomed. Bormann's son, actually. He carries the blood of the Third Reich. Now, I must ask you. You must continue to be our champion with your government. We must have continued support in our new home, for as long as it takes. If we do not, then the world must know that Argentina harbored Bormann for decades after the war. That would have the strongest political ramifications.'

'I will talk immediately to my government.'

'No one else must know of our fuehrer yet.'

'I will keep that confidence, you can be sure.'

'Then, we are in complete agreement. I have a room prepared for you. Rest, and we will dine and talk of old times.'

Alberto Mignone stared out of the small oval window in the Aeritalia G222 as the aircraft pulled away from its parking place. The dinner had been very pleasant, he sharing the table not only with Eisner but several of the older group who made up the ministers of Bormann's cabinet. Bormann himself had joined them for after-dinner coffee and some German documentary films of early World War II victories.

Now, Eisner stood on the tarmac, waving a final time. Mignone had a new appreciation for his German friend and his purpose. Imagine. Bormann alive – and kept hidden for so many years. As they waited at the takeoff end of the strip, another aircraft passed in front of them and settled onto the grass. The civilian twin turboprop was taxiing over to the parking area as Mignone's airplane started its takeoff run. Strangely enough, Eisner was still standing where he had last shook Mignone's hand, as if he were waiting for the new arrival.

Eisner tugged at his parka, ensuring that it fit smoothly across his upper body, and checked the angle of his Tyrolean hat. The T-tailed Beechcraft stopped directly in front of him. Thirty minutes later, its passenger and he were sitting at a conference table in the Lake Argentino villa along with a Wehrmacht sergeant-secretary. Across from him sat his new visitor, Ibrahim al-Abbadi.

'You have come a long way, Mr Abbadi,' said Eisner in English, unsure as to how to address someone with an 'al-' in front of his name. The Arab took no notice.

'I take it you are the one with whom we are to deal.'

'Yes. I have personally been responsible for the contact of our subordinates.'

'Then, the first order of business is the status of the weapon,' continued al-Abbadi.

'Progressing nicely. We have just received an unexpected boost to our project. You noticed the departing Argentina Air Force plane as you landed, no doubt?'

73

'Yes.'

'That was a representative of the Argentine government. They are moving us to a field station they have established in Antarctica.'

The Arab's eyes tightened. 'What does that do to our arrangement?'

'It enhances it, my friend, it enhances it greatly. We will have absolute security.'

'But the equipment and materials for the weapon?'

'Already in our laboratory here, of course. This is where we have been developing it.'

'Then, I will assume this move will not delay our transaction.'

'The only delay will be your ability to provide the proper signatures on the agreement.'

'May I see it?'

The sergeant extracted a document from his file folder. Eisner divided the papers into two groups and handed one to al-Abbadi.

'This is a mutual support agreement, a treaty actually, between us, the Third Reich of the New Germany, and the United Arab Republic. I assume you can speak for them?'

'You assume too much. I am Syrian, that is all. But I will take this agreement and see that it gets into the proper hands.'

'It must have the support of the United Arab Republic.'

'God will it.'

'Shall we cover the provisions?'

'We pay you money and you provide us with the weapon.'

Eisner grunted. 'It is slightly more than that. For a sum of money to develop the weapon, we give you the weapon, yes. But part and parcel of this treaty is a political arrangement between the UAR and the Third Reich.'

'I have no need to go into that, nor have I that kind of authority. The papers will receive the proper assessment at a level beyond me.'

'No, you do need to understand, for the weapon is not yours until we have the required signatures and verification of the treaty.'

'Then, tell me. I am a simple man.'

'In exchange for our services, the UAR will recognize us as a legitimate government in exile and offer us protection and support. That protection will include defense of our government in the United Nations and a military response should any nation act against us.'

Ibrahim al-Abbadi pushed back his chair. 'We Arabs have no forces capable of fighting in this part of the world. That, I know.'

'You do not need any. Your present tactics will suffice to keep the Western nations away from us. They will merely have to be intensified.'

'Go on.'

'Once the Israelites are gone, you will have absolute control over the Middle East. We will expect funds and political support to reunite with our fellow Germans.'

'As I said, I am a simple soldier of God, but I know enough to realize the Soviet Union would not allow that.'

'They will, for a united Germany will be their political ally, just as it was in 1940, and relieve them of an embarrassing occupation. Are you not aware of the Israeli saying, "The enemy of my enemy is my friend"? What a twist, yes? We have the technical ability they lack, the sophisticated scientific brains to provide them with the technical leadership they need to wage economic and political war against the West. In any case, that problem is ours. Our immediate need from the UAR is recognition and support as indicated in the treaty.'

'You are asking a lot.'

'For the elimination of the Jews?'

Ibrahim nodded, apparently satisfied in his own mind. The world of broader international politics was largely beyond him. He was a practitioner of cause and effect.

'We are bedfellows, you and I, my friend,' continued Eisner, 'very good for each other, and our home is full of other friends who sleep with us, all with a common enemy, the Jews, who will rule the world if we do not act. Already, they have taken your lands and have economic and political control over your most capable enemy, the United States. Most of the world has recognized this fact. Africa will side with us in the face of America's support of apartheid. South America has always resented her big bully neighbor to the north. Central America is inconsequential, but they have an equal vote in world affairs. The other Third World countries have all declared themselves opposed to worldwide US capitalistic goals, which include the draining of the earth's resources and enforced poverty. The world revolution will not be socialistic in the Marxist sense, but purification and progress by the elimination of Western decadence.'

Al-Abbadi was not sure he understood all of the words so emphatically spoken by the German, but they sounded as if the speaker knew what he was talking about. Al-Abbadi could not care less about the coming world revolution. First must come the elimination of Israel and the reinstatement of Arab dominance over his part of the world.

'Do you have the binder money?' asked Eisner.

'Twenty million dollars, US,' responded al-Abbadi, 'deposited as you instructed. When do we get the weapon?'

76

'February. At that time, the balance of the payment, five hundred million dollars, will be due from the UAR as part of the agreement.'

'It will be done.'

'Well, then,' announced Eisner, standing. 'Will you join me in a celebration of our agreement?'

'I will make my thanks to God. That is celebration enough. Have you a driver to return me to the airfield?'

'Of course. Come.'

Eisner watched the Blazer pull away. He had his doubts about such a person having any legitimate contact with the United Arab Republic. But the agreement would get some response. In the meantime, the Third Reich had an additional twenty million dollars and that would be ample reward for providing the terrorist with a weapon that would destroy the Israelites. The rest of world Jewry could wait until the Third Reich resumed its sacred task.

5

Marc and his crew were preparing for their arrival at Honolulu about the time Ibrahim al-Abbadi was growing drowsy aboard his departing air transport from Lake Argentino. The Arab was relaxed yet anticipatory in the knowledge that in just four short months he and his fellow members of the Ezzedine Kassam Unit of the Arab Revolutionary Cells would have a weapon worthy of their efforts against Israel.

The passengers back in the cargo compartment of 129 were tidying up their particular space and engaging each other in lively conversation. They were only 100 miles out from Oahu; about another twenty-five minutes and they could start a four-day rest and relaxation period prior to continuing on to the Ice. The crew was also looking forward to the once-a-year stay in the islands. Their operations order specified that the layover was for 'necessary maintenance and upkeep of squadron aircraft,' but all were aware that if there were no major discrepancies with 129, the four days were essentially theirs to do with as they would. And the aircraft had been thoroughly checked and the systems completely readied back at Mugu, so there was little chance that much work would be required at Honolulu. In typical navy fashion, they planned to make the best of whatever time they had. It was one of those fringe benefits that helped compensate them for the five months of around-the-clock work that lay ahead. Work hard, play hard was a slogan that the crew of VXE-6 understood fully.

On the flight deck, Marc was still on the lower bunk,

sipping coffee and trying to coax his senses back into an alert state following a three-hour nap. He had slept soundly after completing the last of the paperwork that had overflowed from the last days into his briefcase. Like all multi-engine aviators on aircraft that had provisions for such crew rest, he could sleep like a baby amid the muffled roar of the engines, the soft sound of the pressurization system, and the comforting presence of flight-deck chatter as the crew went about their functions. Noise was no problem; it was a change in the noise level, even a subtle one, that would wake a sleeping aviator. Just as a parent, no matter how fatigued and in need of sleep, can sense the slight irregularity in an infant's breath in the still of the night, the men who flew the long hours on patrol or transport could sense the slightest change in the mix of noises that were the life sound of an aircraft. Marc had slept undisturbed.

The eight-hour flight itself was not particularly tiring, but boredom was as bad an influence as fatigue, thus the practice of catching naps on such flights was routine. He suspected his pilots had switched around and refreshed themselves in similar fashion, for Frosty Kohn was in the command seat and Zinwicki in the copilot's position. As Marc stood and stretched, he noticed the Quack logging a few Zs in the upper bunk.

'How we doin', Sarge?' he asked, bending over Wineman.

'Right on schedule, Skipper,' replied the marine. 'We're ninety-six miles out.'

'That forecaster back at Mugu was right on, then?'

'Not really. We've been up and down like a damn yo-yo to find a decent flight level.'

'How about the other airplanes?'

'Right behind us, strung out about twenty minutes apart.'

That's the way it's supposed to work, thought Marc as he moved to stand behind Zinwicki. Even if he had not checked their position, he knew that they were approaching Hawaii. The sky had that special hue that would continue all the way south to New Zealand, a beautifully clear, invigorating blue. His thoughts returned briefly to Dorothy and Jim, but they were in his other world now. He would think of them often during the next months and miss them and become more anxious every day to return to them. But the real world from this point on would be the objects and people around him, just as his only physical concern at the moment was the steadily cruising Hercules and those members of his crew quietly performing their tasks on the flight deck.

This would be his last year with VXE-6. It would be on to War College or perhaps a joint staff. He would no longer be separated from his family, but he would miss the comradeship and professional association within his unique squadron. Realistically, he also had to admit that this was probably his last operational flying duty. In the US Navy, seniority meant increased administrative and staff duty; he'd be flying a desk for the next few years. Then, it would be ship's company. Even aviators were naval officers first and fly-boys second, so he would get his chance to master the sea as he had the sky. He already had a short tour aboard the USS *Lexington* behind him, his training command duty, the bane of every aviator. At least he had not spent it in the rear seat of a T-34 or TA-4, holding on for dear life while some embryo naval aviator up front mastered the fundamentals of flight – the navy way. The Lex was an old carrier, but she *was* a carrier and he had logged valuable duty as her flight-deck officer. So the next time he stepped aboard ship, it would be as department head or perhaps exec.

'Want a seat, Captain?' asked Zinwicki.

'Might as well, I've goofed off most of this flight.'

'Privileges of command,' kidded his young copilot.

As he strapped in, Frosty reported, 'About 15 minutes out, you can see the islands up ahead.'

True enough, the dull purple, mountainous outline of Oahu crouched low on the horizon directly in front of them. Off to their left rose the twin volcanos of the big island, Mauna Loa breathing lightly into the air with her white sulphur breath. Pele was quiet today.

Kohn would fly the approach and landing. And Dare, from his flight engineer's throne, would begin his record keeping of pilot proficiency – for the most natural of a sailor's ulterior motives. There would be three landings between now and New Zealand. Kohn would shoot the one at Honolulu, Zinwicki the one at Pago Pago, and Marc the final at Harewood International Airport, Christchurch. With more than 3,000 hours in the C-130s, Dare considered himself an expert on judging the landing performance of his pilots and would assign each of them a numerical grade of one to ten. Low man – or woman, should Kohn find herself in that unenviable position – would buy the arrival booze for the crew once they reached Kiwiland. It was a traditional game with the captain's crew and it served a useful purpose, for each pilot had to take his turn. No allowances were made for nighttime, gusty winds, or any circumstances that might turn a routine landing into one of considerable challenge. When it became your turn, you hacked it, and Dare would jot down his score, licking his lips in anticipation of that New Zealand whiskey. There was no way he and the crew could lose!

Marc figured he could take the young Zinwicki. After all, the junior pilot was only a year out of C-130 school and had just qualified as First Pilot. But Frosty was another matter. She was a greaser when it came to setting down a lumbering Hercules. Marc had ridden through a number of minimum-visibility, stormy-night, and shifting-wind approaches with her and she treated them all the same. The airplane was just an extension of her body, and she took good care of her body. He had yet to see her skip, bounce, or drop in a bit hard. No C-130 would dare to cross Frosty Kohn.

They passed down the east side of Oahu, descending from their cruise altitude, and as they swung wide around Diamond Head they were passed from Approach Control over to Honolulu Tower. Traffic must be light. Marc set his watch to Honolulu time: 1532.

Frosty placed the Hercules on downwind and they ran through the prelanding check.

One-two-nine rode the traffic pattern altitude as if on rails, the sure hands of Frosty Kohn in complete control. From seaward, they made their right-hand turn onto base leg and then onto final. The civil field lay adjacent to the old deactivated runways of Hickam Field. Technology had long ago overtaken the key Pacific military airdrome and military aircraft now shared the long, updated runways with the more numerous commercial carriers. After landing, it would be an inconvenient ten- to fifteen-minute taxi to the vast parking apron of the air base; otherwise the dual-purpose landing area served both civil and military aircraft quite well.

As anticipated, Frosty touched her wheels down with the barest whisper of contact. Out of the corner of his eye, Marc could see Dare penciling in her score. It had to be a ten – the flight engineer wrote two numbers. Damn. Just once, he'd like to see the woman blow one. Well, Zinwicki had to be his salvation.

A fat, blue air force crew bus was waiting to take them to the billeting office, the energetic young airman assigned as driver jumping down from his seat and helping load their baggage. Marc noted that the lad was particularly solicitous of Lieutenant Kohn's gear. In a matter of minutes, the enlisted crew and passengers had been dropped off at their barracks and the officers were standing in the transient officers' quarters being greeted by a portly Polynesian staff sergeant.

'Aloha, gentlemen and lady, I have your room assignments ready.' He handed out five-by-seven registration cards and started stacking keys, small bars of soap, and fluffy white towels on the counter.

'May I have another towel, please?' requested Frosty.

'I'm sorry, Captain, we can issue only one daily.'

'It's Lieutenant, Sergeant,' corrected Frosty, obviously irritated that the sergeant didn't recognize the difference between her 'railroad track' insignia and that worn by an air force type. Then her look softened, 'I'm sure no one would mind. I really need a two-towel shower. It's been a long flight.'

The sergeant's mental image of her in the shower completely overrode any regard for petty regulations. Smiling, he placed another towel in front of her.

'I'll have one, also,' stated Zinwicki, jumping on the bandwagon. Trapped, the sergeant pulled a second towel from under the counter for the jaygee, pleading with his large brown eyes as he looked questioningly at Marc.

'One will do me fine, Sergeant.'

'Thank you, sir. Sir, would you be Commander Bradford?'

'Yes.'

'I have a message for you, sir.'

Marc took the offered envelope and tore off one end. There was a single, neatly typed page inside.

Commander Bradford:
Could you please give me a call, Naval Base extension 299, if

83

you arrive before 1600, otherwise my home number (Ext. 330). I have a classified piece of correspondence for RADM Brady.

/s/ Jack Rushwood
Captain, US Navy
Deputy COS Operations
CINCPACFLT

What could this be all about? Marc had an uneasy feeling that his four days of relaxation in Honolulu might be jeopardized. Maybe not. A check of his watch revealed it was already 1638. He'd clean up and give the captain a call at his home. He couldn't help wondering what information for Brady would be classified, providing it referred to antarctic operations. They simply conducted no classified tasks. Of course, it could be something else. Strange how the request bothered him. There was no need for that; it was probably just some routine report, maybe personnel figures that some overzealous yeoman had overclassified. He tried to shrug off any concern about it, but deep inside he had a sort of pilot's instinct that all was not as it should be.

Picking up his assigned key, soap and single towel, he followed the others down the hall to his room.

There was no answer to his call to Rushwood. Deciding to try later, he showered and enjoyed a brisk toweling. Afterwards, he sat on the edge of his bed, debating whether he should try to find someone to go into town with or just take it easy and stay on the base, perhaps take a predinner swim. The late afternoon shower had completely revitalized him, the pulsating blasts of cold water and the therapeutic action of a hard scrubbing having driven out any remaining vestiges of flight fatigue. He slipped on his trunks and located one of his flowered aloha shirts. Joe Tourist: that was the image the mirror reflected back. Why not?

As he closed the door to his room, Zinwicki and the Quack approached.

'Gonna hit the beach, Skipper?' queried the Quack.

'No, I think I'll lie around the pool for a while and grab a bite here on base.'

'We're picking up a rental,' declared Zinwicki, obviously continuing the offer. 'The Quack wants to see some sights. We'd sure like to have you go with us.'

'No, maybe tomorrow. I don't get much quiet time,' replied Marc, remembering his obligation to call Rush-wood. 'Have a good time.'

'We'll check with you in the morning.'

'Thanks.'

The two adventurers hurriedly resumed their walk down the passageway.

A few swimmers were paddling around in the Officers' Club pool, which overlooked the channel into Pearl Harbor. Marc stopped by the poolside bar and ordered a Bloody Mary. Settling down on one of the plastic webbed chaise lounges, he sipped his drink and idly watched the inflow of afternoon water traffic. Fat fishing craft, their gunwales almost down to the water's surface from the weight of the day's catch; sleek naval destroyers returning from exercises off Oahu; pleasure craft riding high and full of happy couples; a nuclear attack submarine, possibly returning from an extended cruise in the western Pacific, its black paint in sober contrast to the white of the small craft around it – all were typical of the daily traffic into and out of Pearl. The gentle wakes of the slow-moving craft rippled across the serene blue surface and softly lapped against the sandy shore in a hushed litany of respect to those who would forever wear these waters as a holy shroud. It was hallowed water, made so by the Japanese on a Sunday morning almost a half century back, but the memory in the islands was as strong as if the deed had been committed yesterday. The swift silver

Zeros had swooped down from the Pali pass and christened the harbor waters with steel, hurled from the skies in surprise and deceit. Their baptism of fire had driven scores of deadly metal fish through the sides and into the bowels of sleeping ships, and the waters had been sanctified for all time by the blood and viscera of their victims. A great number of the dead still rested in the waters, most of them in a rusting hulk that was the tabernacle in the shrine.

Marc lay there for more than an hour, periodically interrupting his reverie with a quick plunge into the cool pool and a brief but strenuous swim. At six, he decided to try Captain Rushwood again.

'Hello?'

'Hello, this is Commander Bradford. May I speak with Captain Rushwood, please?'

There was a short wait while the child who had answered the phone summoned her father.

'Good evening, Commander!' came a cheery voice, the words slightly garbled as if the speaker were chewing on something. 'I've been waiting on your call. I hated to interrupt your stay in the islands, but I did want to make sure this material went with you. Apparently, it arrived on the West Coast after you had left, so they slapped it on a C-141 that was coming across. Say, we're just having an informal happy hour here before a late dinner. Would you like to join us? Just the family.'

'No, thank you, Captain. I have some obligations,' lied Marc.

'Yes, yes, I understand, but you would be most welcome. Listen, this envelope for Admiral Brady carries a secret classification, for Brady's eyes only. Originated at CIA headquarters. I thought you folks ran a clean operation down there.'

'We don't deal, ordinarily, in classified matters. The treaty, you know.'

'Not allowed any?'

'Well, not in the spirit of the thing, anyhow. It's a different operation from what we're used to in the navy.'

'So I understand. Well, anyhow, I'll keep the envelope in my safe until you leave. Just be sure you let me know if your departure time changes. I'll have it brought planeside, say, thirty minutes before takeoff?'

'That would be fine, sir.'

'You got it. Have a pleasant stay, and if I can be of any service, give me a ring.'

'Thanks, Captain.'

Well, that was simple enough, thought Marc. Now, time for one more dip before dinner. As he walked out of the phone area back to poolside, his eye was caught by a new arrival. The young woman certainly had not been there when he had left to call Rushwood. That body would never have gone unnoticed. Stretched face down on an issue white towel, black string bikini strained to its limits by the bounty of firm curves, raven hair framing the sidecast face . . . raven hair? Frosty! It was his copilot! He had never seen her unclothed; and the bikini certainly couldn't qualify as any type of body cover. Embarrassed, he could see that she had spotted him, gaping like a schoolboy at a nudist camp. Too late, now. He returned her smile and walked over to where she lay.

'Sheila. Not much sun left.'

'Enough to feel good, Captain. How's the water?'

'Just right. I didn't see you before; I've been here an hour or so.'

'I just walked over. You looked like you were deep in thought over there.'

'Oh. That note I got when we checked in. We have a piece of classified to take to the admiral.'

'That's a new twist.'

'Yes.' *Stop staring, Marc Bradford, you're a happily married man with a child. That's just another naval aviator on that towel.* For a fleeting moment, he tried to picture that body belonging someday to a new chief of naval operations. Fortunately, Frosty was too navy to think that her commanding officer could have any thoughts about her beyond her role in the squadron. She lay there, quite matter-of-factly, enjoying the smell of the sea air. Every male poolside was having an anxiety attack each time she adjusted her position.

Marc was enjoying the envy of the men, but reason had returned. Frosty did indeed belong to him, but only as a very competent and professional officer. 'Well, I'm going to go dress. You have any dinner plans? Maybe we can rustle up some of the other crews and have chow at the club?' Immediately upon extending the invitation, he felt awkward. It was innocent enough, but like a male counterpart of Caesar's wife, he should avoid even the appearance of impropriety. To hell with it. She was one of his officers and this was the new navy. He would extend to her the same courtesy he would to any of his officers.

Frosty solved his dilemma by her answer. 'Thank you, but I have some friends here in the islands. I'm committed to a quiet home-cooked meal over in Kailua.'

'Great. Have a good evening. I'll see you tomorrow.'

'Yes, sir. I'll check on the airplane first thing. We didn't have any discrepancies and the crew was supposed to finish fueling tonight.'

Yes, *sir*, she had replied. That put things back in the proper perspective. Good. Marc usually vacillated between pro and con concerning the increasingly coed navy. But, on this postcard-perfect Hawaiian afternoon, walking away but still casually keeping his eyes back toward Frosty and her black string bikini, he was definitely pro.

6

The early morning sky was tourist blue as Marc lifted 129 from Honolulu International Airport and swung the gracefully climbing Hercules around to the south. His turn away from the south shore of Oahu would place them on course for their first refueling stop, Pago Pago in American Samoa, on their journey across the South Pacific to New Zealand. Frosty Kohn was riding the copilot seat and Lieutenant Zinwicki was relaxed on the bottom flight-deck bunk, listening to the Quack expound on the virtues of the new telephoto lens he had picked up at the Pearl Harbor Naval Base Exchange.

As promised, the classified envelope for Rear Admiral Brady had arrived at planeside a few minutes before their taxi time, in the hands of Captain Rushwood, no less.

'Good morning, Commander, looks like you're all set to go,' the chubby four-striper had said, climbing up the short ladder onto the flight deck.

'Yes, sir, but this is a hard place to leave, especially at five-thirty in the morning. We didn't expect such a high-priced courier,' responded Marc.

'Well, I've been feeling guilty about not having you over for at least a drink while you were here. At least I can wish you a safe flight and a good cruise.'

'Thank you, sir. We appreciate it.' Marc took the envelope and signed the top copy of the classified material transfer receipt. He handed it and Rushwood's pen back to the captain, placed the remaining receipt copies in the upper pocket of his flight suit, and tossed the envelope back to Zinwicki. He watched Zin place it in his briefcase;

if there was one thing Marc was meticulous about, it was the handling of classified matter. He would, in turn, get a signed receipt when he delivered it to the admiral, and like all prudent officers would keep his copy until his death or the end of the world, whichever came first. A broken chain of receipts on a misplaced piece of classified had ended more than one budding career.

'Incidentally, I thought the commander of the naval support force was a captain's billet,' commented Rushwood.

'Since the late sixties, it has been – until this year. It was originally a two-star job, starting with Dufek, so it's not a precedent.'

'Any reason for the change?'

'None that I know of. I just carry the mail,' replied Marc with a grin. He didn't really want to discuss antarctic politics. Perhaps the interest of the UN and Third World in antarctic affairs was a factor, or the coming expiration of the Antarctic Treaty. Whatever the case, his takeoff time was only twenty minutes away. Rushwood sensed Marc's slight impatience.

'Say hello to all the penguins,' joked the genial captain, offering his hand. 'If we can be of any service, let us know, and give me a call when you come back through. There are still a couple out-of-the-way places around here you might enjoy. You, too, Lieutenant,' he added, giving Frosty a friendly wave. She nodded and raised her right hand in an abbreviated salute.

'Will do, see you in the spring,' Marc called as Rushwood disappeared down the flight-deck ladder.

'God . . . it's just beautiful,' observed Frosty as they leveled at 26,000 feet. They were well on top of the remaining night clouds and the morning buildups had yet to bud forth their first blossoms of climbing cumulus. The few white patches that were present, tired remnants of the last evening's island thunderstorms, drifted lazily across the awakening ocean, looking all the while like a loose parade of puffy cotton clowns.

Marc double-checked 129's heading against the penciled numbers on the small slip of paper provided by Wineman just prior to takeoff and engaged the autopilot. 'Beautiful it is, Sheila. I never fail to get the chills whenever we do this.' They were engulfed in blue space, with the darker rippling surface of the Pacific below them, the thin dark blue line of morning horizon all around them, and the lighter, continually changing blue in the heavens above.

Frosty smiled in agreement. 'We better enjoy it while we can. After today, the whole world changes.' They would refuel in Pago Pago before continuing on for the final six and a half hours to Christchurch. Considering their Honolulu takeoff time and the crossing of several time zones, their arrival at Harewood International Airport should be about ten in the evening. They would have crossed the equator and the International Date Line and lost a day. Gazing out her side window, Frosty mused, 'You know, we think we're hot stuff, cruising down across these waters, across thousands of miles of open ocean, but the Polynesians were sailing their log canoes all over the Pacific before Columbus discovered America or the Vikings ever thought about forays to the west.'

'I didn't realize you were such a historian,' observed Marc. 'It does make you feel a bit humble, doesn't it? Here we are, cruising five miles high over the waves and weather, guided by little black boxes and sophisticated techniques, while they were doing just as well with a string-and-stick sextant and a couple pandanus leaves full of breadfruit. We're pretty damn presumptuous to imagine ourselves in the same league as those folks.'

Frosty slid her seat back a notch and toggled her

headrest to a less steep angle in order to raise her feet and place them on the footrests that hung below the instrument panel. 'Well, this sure beats riding an outrigger, but I'm not sure it's progress.'

The time to Pago Pago passed slowly. Zinwicki shot the approach and landing, monitored by Marc, who had taken Frosty's seat. The young jaygee came in a bit fast and skipped slightly on touchdown, but Marc noticed Dare still gave him a respectable nine and a half. He began to suspect a conspiracy. He would have given Zinwicki an eight, certainly no more. Now, he would have to come up with a perfect ten at Christchurch or buy the arrival booze, and the forecaster back at Pago Pago had predicted showers and gusty winds at their ETA, not to mention a very black night from the low overcast. Oh, well, he could hack it. After all, the skipper was supposed to be better than any of his pilots.

By the time they had climbed out from the lush green Samoa Islands, the late afternoon thunderstorms were at their worst, dumping sheets of rain on the ocean below and firing great streaks of silver lightning through the skies. Marc threaded 129 skillfully through the spaces between the buildups, and by the time they had regained their cruising altitude the characteristic turbulence associated with such storms had begun to diminish. Wineman passed up their revised Christchurch ETA: 2244, local time. They were only fifteen minutes behind schedule.

The islands fell far behind them and as the sun began to ease below the horizon they were well out over the last remaining stretch of open water between them and New Zealand, penetrating the deep southern latitudes. The temperatures would be cooling, now.

Christchurch, midway down the east coast of South Island and surrounded on three sides by the fertile Canterbury plains, was just entering the first days of austral spring. It would be a cool night when they arrived and the evening showers would be hovering over the coastal city. This was the lambing and planting season and the jagged peaks of the Southern Alps would be shrugging off the winter snows. The South Island fjords would be shimmering in the spring air as they were again fed by the glacial melt. The holiday season would be approaching.

Marc and Sheila sat in respectful silence as they watched the incomparable South Pacific sunset. The ocean faded into nothingness, and they adjusted the flight-deck lights to a low amber glow to preserve their night vision.

One-two-nine slipped effortlessly through the darkening night, slowed only slightly by the mild headwind that spun off a low-pressure cell stagnated over the east coast of Australia. In a few hours they would have completed the long marathon flight from California to New Zealand, the island nation that the ancient travelers from the Society Islands named Aotearoa, the land of the long white cloud; the home of the flightless kiwi and Tiki, the Maori god of fertility. New Zealand's two main islands sat at the southwestern corner of the great Polynesian triangle of Pacific waters that had Hawaii at the apex and Easter Island as its easternmost point.

Marc was anxious to get to Christchurch. This would be his third and final year on the Ice and he had yet to see any of the magnificent land of the Maori, except from the air. However, this season there was a series of planning conferences in Christchurch and there was a possibility he might have some time to explore at least the area around Christchurch. The senior USARPs – scientists who used the acronym of the United States Antarctic Research Programs as their nickname – would be presenting their airlift requirements to the staff planners. VXE-6 had only to provide a representative for coordination planning and

Marc had already tapped the exec for that mundane chore. If things went well and no problems arose, he intended to get away for a few days and enjoy the countryside. Perhaps a drive down the east coast through Ashburton and Timaru, or southwest over to Mount Cook.

Abruptly, his thoughts of a rare holiday opportunity were interrupted by the recollection of the brown manila envelope that was secure inside his briefcase. If that damn thing interfered with his last chance to see a bit of Kiwiland South! . . . The more he thought about it, the more he had some misgivings about this being a routine season.

It was time for their fourth hourly position report. Wineman was tuned in to Whangarei Radio and the bearing confirmed that they were approaching the 100-mile distance from landfall on North Island. Frosty keyed her mike button.

'Hello . . . Auckland Control . . . this is navy one-two-niner. Over.'

A distinctly Kiwi voice replied, properly British in overall inflection but tainted with that special New Zealand casualness that gently clips the edges of the King's English and makes the language more informal. 'Well, hello, Yanks! That's a right pleasant voice to hear this time o' night. Welcome back to another Deep Freeze year. If you chaps have any reasonable idea of where you might be, I have some altimeter settings and meteorological data for you . . . over.'

The good-natured ribbing of American aerial navigational expertise was like an open door with a large welcome sign over it. Frosty rose to the occasion. 'Roger, Auckland, we're *exactly* one hundred miles out at flight level two-eight-zero, estimating Tauranga at one-eight past the hour. If you can stop shearing sheep long enough

94

to make a guess at the weather, we'd appreciate a Christchurch forecast . . . that's a coastal city down on your South Island.'

'Nasty, nasty, wun-two-niner,' replied the controller against a background noise of guffaws. 'Altimeter, two-niner-niner-zero, winds aloft at your flight level are two-five-zero at two-two knots . . . Christchurch is currently experiencing light rain showers under a broken overcast, ceiling ragged at six hundred feet. By your arrival I suspect a slightly higher cloud cover with winds gusting from the north at fifteen to twenty-five knots. I have an amended clearance for you.'

'Go ahead.'

'Wun-two-niner cleared from present position direct to Harewood Airport . . . descend to and maintain flight level wun-aight-zero . . . contact Christchurch Approach Control when fifty miles out . . . copy?'

Frosty read back the clearance verbatim.

'That is correct, wun-two-niner. Your only traffic will be National Airways Flight Twelve enroute Wellington to Auckland at twelve thousand . . . I have already alerted them that there is an American aircraft entering our area.'

Frosty couldn't ignore the subtle dig. 'Thank you, Auckland, you can go back to your telly now.'

The Kiwi surrendered. 'Thank *you*, wun-two-niner . . . have a pleasant flight, and welcome back.'

The rain showers were waiting at Christchurch just as forecast. When 129 reported fifty miles out, the approach controller gave an enroute descent pattern with instructions to report twenty miles north of Harewood.

Clear of all terrain at 12,000 feet, Frosty reported in. 'One-two-niner, twenty miles north, twelve thousand.'

'Cleared for ILS approach, runway three-six, no reported traffic, contact Harewood Tower over outer marker inbound.'

Typical. They had the whole airport to themselves. The Kiwis curled their toes and settled down when the sun set.

The bright lights of Christchurch filled the night as 129 passed 3,000 feet outbound, descending through broken clouds, and the Harewood strobes reached out like an electronic welcome mat as the Hercules rolled out of its procedure turn and passed over the outer marker.

'Outer marker, inbound . . . field in sight,' reported Frosty.

'Cleared to land, wun-two-niner . . . we have you . . . winds light and variable.'

Light and variable? thought Marc. He was working the yoke and adjusting his power continually as he guided 129 down the glide slope, watching his airspeed jump with turbulent-air palsy.

'Half flaps.'

Frosty leaned forward and flipped down the flap lever. Marc felt the welcome drag and attitude change as the slabs dropped from the bottom of the wing. Half flaps should be plenty with the gusting winds.

'Wipers.' The rain had intensified, and in response to his request, Frosty reached down on her side console and placed the wiper knob to low. Seeing that the setting was inadequate, she immediately placed the knob to high.

'Damn!' As soon as Marc would raise one wing, the other would drop. 'Get the winds again, Sheila.'

'Harewood Tower, verify your winds. We're all over the sky out here.'

'Roger, wun-two-niner, we do show an increase in velocity . . . now indicating two-five knots with gusts to three-five . . . holding steady from the north . . . there is a heavy rain shower in your position . . . cleared to land at your discretion . . . we don't expect any further increase. Over.'

'Roger.' Frosty switched to intercom. 'Did you hear

that genius? We're on an underwater roller coaster and he reports a rain shower in our position. Love that Kiwi trait of understatement.'

Marc kept an additional ten knots above the recommended approach speed, and thanked his own judgement as the wind abruptly ceased just as he flared. The Hercules dropped onto the runway like a clubbed elephant. They had arrived, and he had just bought the arrival booze.

Slowly, they taxied through the rain to the special section of the air terminal set aside for Deep Freeze operations. Pulling into the lighted parking area, Marc could see a sizable crowd of US personnel and New Zealand well-wishers waiting to greet them, including a bevy of local beauties whose faces and dress were quite familiar to the men of VXE-6. The Chi Chi girls were in from the surrounding countryside to spread their hospitality among the Deep Freeze troops. Some of the relationships would grow into full-fledged romances; the squadron regularly took several new brides back to the States at the end of a season.

The local TV station had a lone cameraman standing behind the ground crewman, holding his rain-soaked camera on one shoulder. Marc pressed the brakes and 129 eased to a halt. It was 2241. They were three minutes early.

Happy bedlam surrounded the aircraft as the passengers and crew disembarked and spotted old friends and shipmates who had preceded them on commercial airlift. The cargo ramp was lowered and everyone retrieved his bags before hurrying through the rain into the shelter of the customs room.

'Well, Sheila, let's go meet the press.'

'My hair will be a mess!' exclaimed Frosty, forgetting for just a rare moment that she was a naval officer first

97

and a woman second. She quickly recovered. 'After you, Captain.'

An overweight and overage lieutenant commander was waved through the terminal gate into the customs room as Marc and his crew were stacking their luggage. It was the officer in charge of the squadron's Christchurch detachment, Bob Christian.

'Welcome back, Captain.' Christian extended one hand and reached out for one of Marc's bags. 'You've already cleared through customs. My car's right outside.'

Marc thanked the senior customs official for the courtesy as they passed through the gate into the terminal proper. It was just a few steps to the double glass doors of the exit and they tossed the bags into the rear of Christian's station wagon. Marc held his briefcase on his lap as they drove away from the arc-shaped terminal building.

'We've got you billeted at The White Heron,' said Christian.

'Good. I stayed there last year. I've got some classified material for the admiral, Bob. Do you still have a safe?'

'Classified? Gosh, I have the small office safe. What's the classification?'

'Secret, Special Intelligence. CIA originated.'

'Whoo! What are we doing with something like that? My safe and building security probably don't meet the necessary criteria. We better stow it in the staff's safe for the night. On the other hand, I'm not sure the staff's safe is authorized for SI.'

Marc thought for a moment. 'Listen, I'm pretty bushed and won't be leaving my room. I'll just sleep on the damned thing. It'll be secure enough.' He grinned at Christian. 'Just forget I mentioned it.'

'Mentioned what?' Christian asked innocently. They were still chuckling as they eased to a stop in front of the motel. 'Incidentally, the admiral has invited you to breakfast in his office at eight in the morning,' said Christian as he led Marc to his room at the end of a hall.

'Room 118, away from the noise,' he announced as he unlocked the door and handed Marc the key.

'Put Zinwicki at the other end,' joked Marc, mentally cringing at the thought of his junior pilot entertaining the Chi Chi girls at all hours. The lad did have a reputation.

'Frosty will be just across the hall . . . 117.'

Marc did not appreciate the implication of Christian's pursed lips comment. 'Good, I like to have her nearby. And just to set the record straight, I don't really appreciate innuendo. I would hope all of my officers appreciate the position of Lieutenant Kohn in this squadron.'

'I would appreciate Lieutenant Kohn in any position,' continued Christian, undaunted by the mild reproach.

Marc remembered why he disliked the man. He was a holdover from the old days when a female navy person was considered to be just a 'sailor you could screw face to face.' Two years back, as operations officer, he had reluctantly concurred with the approval of Christian's appointment as O-in-C of the Christchurch detachment, but had retained certain reservations because of the man's rough manner. A disgruntled divorcé, the medically grounded aviator would stay at his present rank until mandatory retirement. Thank God that was only a year away. But he was a decent manager and administrator and a hard worker when he stayed off the sauce. Before his assignment, they had sat down to a no-holds-barred, man-to-man talk during which Marc made sure Christian understood his obligations, and the promise that if he failed to meet them, he wouldn't be allowed to stay in the navy until mandatory retirement. That would mean a cut in retirement pay, and the passed-over officer had generally performed well. The remark about Frosty indicated, however, that he still had his same old attitude toward anything and anyone who was not 'old navy.' He was one of the rare old salts who just could not adjust.

'Bob, you've got a year to go. Don't screw it up either by showing the Kiwis your bad side or rubbing me the wrong way.'

'Hell, Skipper, I don't mean anything against Frosty – or you. Women just don't belong in my career field.'

'Your *career field?* If you were half the officer Sheila Kohn is, you'd be retiring as a four-striper and not as a passed-over light commander.' Marc knew his words were a bit harsh, but it took that kind of talk to get through to Christian.

As for Christian, he could see that he had pushed his CO too far. After a long winter of being his own man with none of the brass looking over his shoulder, he would have to readjust his attitude until the summer tourists left. Twelve more months and they could have the whole bag of bolts. 'I'll get back down to the terminal and see that everyone gets settled.'

'That's a good idea, Bob. You do that.'

'Goodnight, Skipper.'

Marc unpacked his hanging bag and hung the contents in the closet. There was beer and milk in the small refrigerator and he opted for the beer while undressing. The shower refreshed him but failed to remove the irritation of Christian's crude attitude. Drying, he pulled on a pair of pajama bottoms and flopped onto the bed. It was short but firm, and gave good support to his back, which ached from the long flight down across the Pacific.

Remembering the classification of the contents of his briefcase, he got up to ensure that the door was locked.

He would finish unpacking in the morning, and he and the brown manila envelope would have breakfast with the admiral.

7

Chief scientist Anatolii Vladimirovich Kakushkin wearily
pushed back the four woolen blankets that had warmed
him during the past ten hours of vodka-assisted sleep. His
round-faced table clock, a constant reminder of his schedule, had buzzed itself to death without waking him, the
slim black hands stopping at 8:18. How much later it was
at this moment was a mystery to him and of no great
concern. He had only one major task for the day and that
would be in the early afternoon. Nevertheless, he had
slept through breakfast, a not uncommon fault of his to
which the rumbling in his stomach took loud exception.
However, if it wasn't too late, the cook would provide
him with something. Shivering from the chill in his
sleeping compartment, he fumbled with his clothes until
he located his pocket watch. Only 8:45 A.M., still time to
sip some tea and cajole the cook into providing some
solid sustenance. He quickly dressed and padded down
the narrow hall to the washroom. Afterwards, he sat in
the deserted dining area and drank the tea, letting it also
warm his hands through the glass as it brought back some
of the warmth the blankets had provided. The cook, a
soft touch when you paid him the right compliment, had
also supplied him with some black bread and jam. He had
offered tinned meat and borscht left from the night
before, but Kakushkin was becoming increasingly aware
of the tightness of his trouser waistband.

It was still early dawn outside and the spring temperature hovered in the mid minus forties. But he might get a
few things done as soon as the sun climbed a little higher.

His one vital task would take priority, of course. For the moment, however, he could sit and savor the tea and thick bread. The spacious room, with its great round dining table and high-backed oak chairs, enjoyed the additional heat of the constantly active kitchen. With the massive buffet dominating one wall, and the faded wallpaper that once had vividly portrayed a colorful montage of pastoral scenes, the dining room was a comfortable place to rest and allow his bones to soften from the night stiffness. They seemed even more tired this morning than when he had laid them on the cotton pile mattress the evening before. Fifty-nine winters, the last two in this awful place, had taken their toll on what had once been a pretty fit body. At least he still had all of his hair and most of his teeth, although several were capped with that stainless steel the camp dentist had been so proud of. He would get the unsightly repairs replaced as soon as he returned to Moscow.

The antarctic winter had been a frigid hell and there was absolutely no consolation in knowing that he had endured it in the most remote of all antarctic camps, which also just happened to be the coldest spot on earth. It would be a while before the record minus 129 degrees of a few years back was surpassed, although this past winter had seen some days within ten degrees of that reading.

Vostok Station sat more than 3,400 meters above sea level – if one could imagine a continent squashed under a three-kilometer-thick layer of ice and snow. The boxy, wooden living quarters were roof deep in the accumulated winter drift, with only the flat tops and a smattering of antennae betraying the presence of any camp at all. The structures were well sealed, but the bitter cold habitually forced its way through tiny cracks around the double-doored entranceways and the less-than-perfect joining of walls and roofs. Kakushkin's room was normally warm, but today outside air seemed to be leaking in. He made a mental note to voice a complaint to the station leader.

Fortunately, his duties had been light over the winter and now, with the approach of the summer relief party, he would have only to clean up a few loose ends and he could return home. This entire assignment had struck him as a needless waste of talent, anyhow. He had spent a lifetime infiltrating the scientific community as a senior KGB agent, his loyalties almost equally divided now between his appreciation of the Soviet scientific achievements and the need for a special force to provide the government with worldwide intelligence. Certainly, there had been little in Antarctica to report, and the station political leader could tend to the routine duties of party education. All in all, Kakushkin felt like a second thumb on a hand that had not been very busy the past twenty-four months. With the exception of a short visit to the American base at McMurdo last January, there had been little opportunity for his covert specialty.

While he was sipping the last of his tea, the station avionics specialist joined him.

'Good morning, Seva, have you things ready for my contact today?'

'Yes, Comrade, I gave the radio a checkout last evening. It is working well. I regret the main station unit is still inoperative.'

So did Kakushkin. The primary camp long-range radio had suffered a crippling malfunction several weeks back. They had several backup radios available and could talk to almost anyone they wanted, but the main radio gave them direct access to Moscow via satellite. His requirement today was to talk to his superiors back at the headquarters of the Committee for State Security.

He could still do that by utilizing one of the special

103

aircraft radios. Seva's function had been to dig out the multi-engined Ilyushin Il-18 transport, which had been forced to winter over, staked down in the hard snow and completely buried by the succession of winter blizzards. The number four engine required replacement parts before the aircraft could be flown, but the other three engines would provide more than ample electrical power for the sophisticated radio equipment that was standard on the big turbo-prop.

'My schedule requires a 1400 contact. Will you be available?'

'Yes, comrade,' replied Seva.

'Then I shall see you after lunch.' Kakushkin rose and returned to his room. To his pleasure, the heat was back at its normal level and the room was quite comfortable. He opened the small compartment over his desk, pulled out a stack of reports, and began completing his winter-over papers.

After lunch, he returned once more to his room and began to dress for the outside. He slipped on a second pair of long cotton underwear, followed by thick leather trousers, carefully tucking in the long tails of the two woolen shirts before placing the wide canvas suspenders over his shoulders. He tapped his outside shirt pocket to make certain his tobacco pouch was nested inside. Regretfully, the good stuff that the Americans had traded him last summer was long gone, but he still had an ample supply of the Russian leaf. Not quite as smooth tasting as the more refined American tobacco, but familiar to his tongue and reminiscent of his home in western Russia.

He thrust his arms into the sleeves of the wolf-fur parka and stretched up to retrieve his black leather cap from the top shelf of his locker. He set it full on his head, leaving the earflaps tied on top. He would lower them over his bare ears just before going outside. Finally, he probed his deep parka pockets and extracted two pairs of gloves, pulling the woolen ones on first, then the leather outer shells.

A soft knock on his door signaled the arrival of Seva. Together, they stepped into the storm lock and cautiously opened the outer door. The cold didn't feel bad. Pleased, he stepped out into the trench dug to the surface. Then, it hit him. The supercooled air of the polar plateau sliced into him like a chilled knife and the moisture around his lips and eyes immediately began to scratch as tiny ice crystals fought to overcome his natural body heat. He tried to sniff back the irritating drippings that the intense cold drew from his steaming nostrils, but the twin syrupy streams froze solid just as they reached the top of his upper lip.

Seva plowed on ahead of him, bareheaded. The Siberian native seemed to consider the sunny day a treat. The sky was sparkling clear, an intense blue with the complete absence of any pollutants to dull its sheen, and there was only the whisper of a wind. The lifeline that ran from the various hut clusters forming the camp had been relocated on top of the snow. Thank goodness that job had fallen to one of the maintenance men. Regardless of status, the routine tasks of the camp had been evenly divided among all; happily, Kakushkin had only an occasional outside job of filling the snow melter. To rig those lines must have taken hours.

The cold was bringing a flood of moisture from his eyes, which reflex action almost closed in response to the brilliance of the white surface. He closed them completely until he could slip on his dark sunglasses. That was much better, but he should have brought his snow goggles; they would have provided even better protection. There was no chill factor, just the perennial cold of the frozen continent, which was quite sufficient to prompt him to

105

swing his arms and move his fingers inside the two layers of gloves. His blood flowed well. He would meet his schedule.

It was almost a full kilometer to the outdoor aircraft stowage area. The small aerial armada assigned to the camp was all but completely buried. Only the main rotors of the three Mikhail helicopters protruded above the winter accumulation. As for the ancient Antonov biplane, anchored just beyond the helos, only the tip of the tail and the top wing were visible. Beyond that, Kakushkin could see the Il-18. Seva had put many hours into clearing the snow away from the airframe and engines, undoubtedly using the power shovel for most of the dig, but surely resorting to a hand shovel when close the fragile aluminum. There was no way he could have placed an access stairway next to the aircraft. Instead, a front loader was in position, its diesel clacking loudly and a staccato of white puffs streaming from its exhaust.

'Hop in the scoop, comrade, and I will lift you to the entry door,' directed Seva.

Kakushkin swung himself over the lip of the deep scoop and Seva lifted him to the level required.

'The entrance door is frozen shut!' he yelled over his shoulder. Seva climbed up beside him.

'Damn! I just freed it less than an hour ago. Here, let's pound the edges and give it a pull together.'

The strategy worked. Stepping inside, Kakuskin recoiled at the even more chilling bite of the deep freeze environment within the fuselage. The Il-18 had cold-soaked during its eight months of inactivity.

'No wonder the pilots are always saying that if they go down, it is worse to stay inside than erect shelters in the snow,' exclaimed Kakushkin.

'Yes, indeed. The aluminum sops up the cold like bread

106

does soup, and the sun angle is too low to provide any degree of rapid reheating.'

At least most of the fuselage had been tightly sealed. Very little drifted snow had forced its way through the weatherstripping around the doors, probably none once the ice had sealed them. Only one small pile of white powder betrayed a tiny leak, below one of the emergency exist windows. Seva made a mental note to check it later, as it could mean a defect in the pressurization capability of the cabin. It wasn't unusual, for the Ilyushin had been banged onto the ice repeatedly over its years of antarctic service, often overloaded, and almost always flown with that Russian disregard for severe surface conditions. They expected their aircraft, like themselves, to be hearty and capable of much cold-weather punishment.

Seva climbed into the cockpit and began throwing switches. 'I'll see if we can get it started. I put fresh batteries in this morning.' Even as he spoke, the auxiliary power unit far to the rear of the passenger cabin whined into life and almost immediately settled into a healthy roar. 'Now, we have all the power we need.'

'If only the engines start that easily,' commented Kakushkin.

'They will, comrade. Once that little bastard in the tail lights off, we should have no great difficulty. I have the engine preheats on. We have only to be patient for a few minutes.'

Kakushkin settled himself in the radio position and rubbed his gloved hands across his leather trousers to force a more positive blood flow. The radio gear appeared to be normal. He was familiar with the unit they would be using for their communications with Moscow, having sat with the aircraft radioman on numerous flights. As he refamiliarized himself with the equipment, he felt the first gentle vibrations of one of the main engine turbines.

Within just a few minutes the three healthy engines were up to speed and Kakushkin could feel the first welcome flow of heated air. While the cabin warmed, he turned on the radio gear and checked the transmitter antenna load. Not wishing to share his contact with Seva, he placed the earphones on his head after carefully rubbing the rubber cups to removed the stiffness as well as the cold. Carefully he dialed in the appropriate frequency and gave his mike a tentative key. The noise crackling in the headset indicated all was ready.

Pulling a small notebook from his parka pocket, he referred to one of the middle pages. 'Hello, High Path . . . hello, High Path . . . this is Dog Star. Do you read? Over.'

The immediate response came back in a hollow-sounding voice, typical of long-range transmissions. 'Dog Star, loud and clear. Do you read?'

'Loud and clear.'

'Let us go to scramble mode three.'

'Switching to scramble mode three.' Kakushkin reached back and extracted a small black box from its stowage rack on the bulkhead separating the crew compartment from the passenger cabin. Loosening a panel on the front of the transceiver, he slid the coding component into position, locking it in place with two thumbscrews. 'This is Dog Star, scramble mode three.' As he spoke, tiny electronic chips changed the pitch and frequencies of his words into a series of random sounding beeps that traveled line of sight over the 22,000-mile distance to the geosynchronous orbiting communication satellite. There, the signals were amplified and beamed to their Moscow destination, where a similar black box converted the beeps back into Kakushkin's words.

'Dog Star, I have an assignment for you.'

'Go ahead.'

'Toliya, this is Vladlen Malyshkin. I have with me comrade Rozen from the office of German War Reparations. We have received information that a former Nazi doctor by the name of Erich Scnell is present at an Argentine antarctic site, probably their General Belgrano I camp over on the peninsular. Are you familiar with it?'

'Yes, I know of it but have never been there. Who is this Scnell?'

'A war criminal, a murderer of our countrymen. We thought he was dead. We want to make sure. However, that is not the most important part of our intelligence. You are most probably aware that we have routinely monitored exiled-Nazi activity since 1945. Most of them are gone now, of course, but there has been one cell in Argentina that has seemed to have remained active. If Scnell is alive, he most probably comes from that group. Are you still receiving me clearly?'

'Yes, go ahead.'

'Our contact in the Argentine village of Califate, which is on Lake Argentino, where the German community has a villa, has given us a series of disturbing reports. The main thrust is that it appears the community is going to be relocated to an Argentine station in Antarctica. I assume this is all news to you.'

'Of course. I have been here for the past year. We get no intelligence. This has been a worthless assignment for me.'

'We understand that, Comrade Kakushkin, but it has been necessary. However, in the light of this development, we have a worthwhile assignment for you.'

'I am due for relief.'

'We have arranged with the Americans for you to serve as our exchange scientist for the summer season. You can anticipate an American airlift in early November.'

Kakushkin's heart tumbled into the pit of his stomach.

109

This would be the third Christmas season away from his wife, daughter, son-in-law, and granddaughter. The little girl had been only six years old when he had left Sverdlovsk. She would be a strapping ten-year-old before he saw her next and perhaps would not know him. He would not question his orders, however, for in just a few years he could think of semiretirement as a middle-grade bureaucrat in the KGB section at some remote embassy. This would not be the time to resist an assignment.

'Very well, comrade. Am I to try and bring him back? Who will accept jurisdiction?'

'That is a very sticky aspect to this assignment. We are not really concerned about trying to extract him from Belgrano. We have many more important things to do than hunt out old Nazis. The Jews are doing that for us. But we are concerned about the purpose of Argentina's continued support of the community, which seems to be thriving, even to the extent of providing them with a new home.'

'The Nazis should be harmless. They are old and dying out and certainly they can present no threat isolated in this white hell.'

'We are not so sure. The Germans have always been extremely unhappy about a divided country, and the emergence of West Germany as a European financial center, with a solid technical and economic base, has caused some unrest and less than tactful dissent in the German Democratic Republic. All we need now is an emergence of the old traditionalism and patriotic fervor for Germany as a nation of destiny and we may have serious troubles on hand. There has always been an undercurrent of that characteristic militarism that causes Germany to erupt every few decades. And the establishing of a Nazi community in Antarctica presents a whole new set of international problems. I'm sure you understand that.'

110

'Yes.' Kakushkin could see the possible ramifications, but he couldn't see himself being extended another six months or year. 'I don't see what I can do about that situation.'

'The Americans are hosting an international inspection team this season, in accordance with the Antarctic Treaty provisions. We have made arrangements for you to be included in that team. Go to the Belgrano Station. See if Scnell is there. Try and pick up any information about the Germans. How you accomplish your task is up to you. We have no objections to Scnell being eliminated, but we do not wish to have a violation of the treaty before us. Do you fully understand that?'

'Of course.'

'Then you must proceed with a great deal of caution. Under no circumstances must you act overtly in any way that will suggest we are engaged in this task.'

'I understand, but I must also add that I believe I should be relieved at the end of the summer season. Let someone else have a chance at this choice duty.' Kakushkin was sure that the sarcasm in his voice would get his point across without unnecessarily needling his superiors. He was correct.

'Of course, comrade. We understand the imposition in this assignment, but there is some urgency.'

'I understand. But how will I recognize this Scnell?'

'We are dispatching a packet to you. It will be delivered at McMurdo. There are pictures, although outdated. But we have some detailed data that will enable you to positively identify him.'

'Good.'

'We have routine traffic for your station. Unscramble.'

Kakushkin removed the scramble device and switched to the intercommunications circuit within the aircraft.

'Comrade Shvedin, the remainder of this contact concerns routine matters. I am turning the frequency over to you.'

'I am switching,' Seva replied.

Kakushkin removed his headset and reached for his parka. His assignment was a disappointment. He had already psyched himself up for a return to Sverdlovsk. Now, it would be another five months. The saving grace was that five months at the American station at McMurdo would be like a holiday after the winter at Vostok. And maybe as a bonus he would eliminate Scnell. After all, he would extract some pleasure at the sight of any ex-Nazi's expression as he exchanged the last brief breath of his miserable life for the eternity of hell.

8

Marc was sleeping soundly when the alarm went off, his night's rest deep and relaxed. The concern of the long deployment flight was over and the trials of the coming season on the Ice had yet to begin. There was a quality about New Zealand, a sort of romantic aura that seemed to hang over the islands. Perhaps it was the violent yet romantic history of the Maori who had first discovered and inhabited the isolated land long before the white man had come. Perhaps it was the realization that here sat a California-sized Garden of Eden of fertile soil and ideal climate for the growth of man and plant, yet home to a mere three million people. Whatever it was he had learned or felt about the islands, whenever he entered the realm of the kiwi and the Tiki his whole being seemed to enter a physical and mental high, and deep sleep, like that from which he had just awakened, was one of the familiar manifestations of that unique feeling.

It felt even better to take a hot shower and shave. His aviation-green uniform had survived the six-day journey in excellent shape. Despite cramped stowage in his suit-bag, it still displayed the sharp creases of the stateside press job. It felt warm in the chilly morning air as he walked outside the motel and was met by a staff car and driver.

'Good morning, Commander,' greeted the driver.

'That it is,' Marc responded, sliding into the front seat beside the sailor.

The drive to Deep Freeze headquarters took only a few

minutes, and promptly at 0755, Marc entered Brady's outer office and was met by the flag officer's aide.

'Well, hello, Commander Bradford, how was the flight down?'

'Great. I suppose the admiral's expecting me.'

The tall surface lieutenant nodded. 'Go on in, sir.'

Marc gave a single, courteous rap and opened the newly varnished door labeled COMMANDER, US NAVAL SUPPORT FORCE, ANTARCTICA. A bulldog figure, wrapped handsomely in service dress blues, strode across the room to meet him, right arm outstretched and a welcoming grin across a craggy face that had seen more than its share of salt air.

'Well, how was the flight?' asked Brady.

'Fine, sir. We sort of hated to leave Honolulu, though.'

'I can imagine.' Brady was the picture-book two star complete with a list when he walked and the rasp of a wooden mast when he spoke. He had a square jaw and an unruly shock of predominantly gray hair, not the distinguished silver gray of the mature executive but the healthy gray of the outdoorsman, streaked with stubborn remnants of its original rust. Only the faintest hint of a massive neck joined it to a stocky, big-boned body that appeared to be as wide as it was tall. No fat, just muscle and sinew. The old seadog could walk through a brick wall without breaking stride. He motioned Marc over to a side table that was covered with a white linen cloth and set for breakfast. Orange juice and coffee were already poured. A tall clear glass vase in the exact middle of the square table held a lone red flower unfamiliar to Marc. It looked something like an orchid, with long, pointed petals. Brady noticed Marc's curiosity and explained, 'Kaka Beak – after the bush parrot. Looks like his big beak. Damn near extinct in the wild. Pretty little thing, isn't it?'

114

'Very unusual, and like you say, very pretty.'

They sat down and pulled their napkins from the stainless steel rings while a white-jacketed Filipino messman brought in a plate of doughnuts, hot and fresh from the fryer.

'How would you like your eggs, Commander?' asked the messman.

'Over medium, please.'

'Milk or juice, sir?'

'Orange juice . . . no, make that milk,' decided Marc, remembering the rich product of the New Zealand dairy cattle.

The messman hurried out.

'I have a piece of classified for you, Admiral. CINCPACFLT relayed it to me at Honolulu.'

'Oh? Who's the originator?'

'CIA.'

'Spooks? That's unusual. What's the classification?' As he questioned Marc, Brady lifted the plate of doughnuts and offered them. Marc lifted the top one onto his bread plate.

'Thank you. Secret, Special Intelligence.'

'I'll be damned. I hope it doesn't make a big bow wave. This operation normally has pretty smooth sailing.'

'Would you like to see it now, sir?'

'No. Let's enjoy breakfast.' The admiral seemed only mildly interested, despite his previous comment. Plunging a doughnut into his coffee, he asked, 'How's Mrs Bradford? And Jim?'

'They're fine, Admiral, and looking forward to the end of this season.'

'You're a lucky man, Marc. Jim's a fine lad . . . we always wanted children . . . just didn't happen. God knows, we tried hard enough.' Brady chuckled and selected another doughnut.

115

'Is Mrs Brady here with you?'

'Oh, hell, yes . . . I can't set foot out of Washington without her. We've been the toast of the Kiwi social set since we arrived. These New Zealanders are the best damn people on earth. They take you in and make you feel like family. I love 'em. May come down here when I hang it up. They can outdrink a marine, outlie a sailor, and outpray the Pope. Nobody on earth like a Kiwi. I don't think the word "stranger" is even in their vocabulary. And the older generation still have vivid memories of those dark days early in World War II when the Japs were on their doorstep and starting to blast the door off the hinges. Then we saved their ass at the battle of the Coral Sea and since then a Yank can do no wrong. Don't misunderstand me; we fought that battle to save our own skin, too, and the Kiwis were right there splashing their blood all over the Pacific alongside our boys. They don't have to bow their heads to any man. Were right there in 'Nam, too. Didn't see too many of our so-called allies baring their asses over that one. 'Course, that dip-shit decision to ban our ships from their ports has put a temporary crimp in things. But once the government goes through another cycle, that'll change. Damn liberals.'

While Brady finished his second doughnut, Marc studied the veteran officer's face. As rugged as it was, it was the most straight-forward countenance one could imagine. And that was Brady. Sincere, highly professional, the admiral might be a bit rough around the edges, but the dark blue ribbon of a Navy Cross and two Purple Hearts topped a six-row display of combat and service ribbons that were the perfect complement to the gold wings pinned over them. He had earned his stars by consistent, superb performance. However, diamonds in the rough didn't fit in too well with the upper echelon of the

Washington scene, especially those overage in grade, so he had been shunted off to his antarctic command.

The messman returned with their eggs. They were prepared exactly to order and served with two thick grilled lamb chops. Mint jelly, a slice of honeydew melon, and a sprig of parsley completed the attractive plate. The Filipino also placed a rack of crisp toast beside the vase holding the Kaka Beak.

The admiral sighed with satisfaction and looked up at the white-jacketed sailor. 'Ramon, if you weren't so damned ugly, I'd leave Mrs Brady and marry you.' The messman smiled self-consciously, revealing a mouthful of silver-capped teeth. Brady turned back to Marc. 'Best damn cook in the fleet. Swiped him from the CNO's mess. Those dumb bastards had him fixing TV dinners, for Christ's sake!'

'I'll bring more coffee, sir,' interjected the embarrassed Ramon as he turned and retrieved a long-handled pewter pot from a service cart.

The breakfast was delicious, the milk ice cold, the butter spread generously on the crusty toast. Even the lamb, not normally Marc's choice for the first meal of the day, had a vigorous, sweet flavor that complemented the eggs and gave the breakfast the hearty satisfaction characteristic of Kiwi dining.

Marc marveled at the admiral's ability to stow away several of the doughnuts, the plate of eggs and lamb, most of the toast, and several cups of coffee without any apparent concern over the bountiful calories. He suspected that within the admiral's rugged physique, no self-respecting calorie would dare turn itself into fat.

As they finished, Brady slid back his chair and poured himself another cup of coffee. 'Okay, let's take a look at that correspondence.'

Marc took the envelope from his briefcase and handed the envelope to Brady.

'I'll have my aide give you a receipt,' offered Brady, relieving Marc of the awkward question. He ripped open the flap and took out the two-page document. Fishing his reading glasses from his coat pocket, he sipped his coffee and studied the contents, pursing his lips from time to time and nodding his head as if in agreement with the provisions of the letter. He reread it before placing it on the table.

'What's your clearance?'

'Top Secret, sir.'

'Special Intelligence?'

'No, sir, no SI.'

'Well, you have one now.' The decision was pure Brady. Get the job done and take care of the paperwork later. 'It seems we may have a bit of international intrigue on the Ice.'

'Intrigue?' Marc was suddenly more excited about the material.

'We may have a Nazi war criminal hiding out at General Belgrano.'

'I thought they had all been found. Wasn't Mengele the last of the biggies?'

'There are a few of the bastards left. I doubt they'll all be uncovered – haven't given it much thought. We all have the same end, eventually, and have to go stand before the Man. This is a Doctor Erich Scnell. Israeli intelligence has placed him as the medical officer over at Belgrano or possibly one of the new colonization stations. We can expect a visit from an Israeli agent sometime before December.'

'That'll be a first.'

'Sure as hell will. According to this letter, we are asked

to include him on our scheduled treaty inspection visit to the Argentine stations.'

'That sounds a bit awkward – and obvious. What does he hope to accomplish?'

'Just confirmation, I suppose. This could turn into a rather sensitive situation. There's more. There have been indications – unconfirmed rumors more than anything else – that there is still a cell of devoted Nazis in Argentina. They could be embarrassing to the Alfonsin government. Apparently, the people at Langley feel that the Argentines are going to try to shunt them all to the Ice.'

'Fantastic. Nazis in Antarctica.'

'Well, they were here in '39, but the old bastards can't stand that environment today. They'll kick off fast.'

'Maybe that's what the Argentines have in mind.'

'Probably. But you never know in the political arena just what the hell is going on. I've never read what it was during the war that made Argentina such a close friend of Nazi Germany or why they have felt some obligations over the years.'

'Fellow fascists, I would guess.'

'I've always thought it was more than that, as if Hitler had something on them, or had made some wild promises about cutting them in on the spoils when he took over the world. But that still doesn't explain why they tolerated the survivors for so long, right up to now, it appears.'

Brady studied the letter a third time.

'Admiral, it appears to me that by aiding the Israelis in this, we may be setting up a potentially embarrassing situation of our own if we're not careful.'

'Well, we've time to think about the matter. The Belgrano inspection isn't scheduled until November. I think we better keep this under our hats in the meantime. There may be more to it than we know since they

119

classified it SI – I don't see that the content itself warrants that sensitive a classification. I think we can anticipate some amplifying information after we get on the Ice. If we don't receive it by November, I'll contact some people.'

'And until then?'

'Business as usual.'

'I planned a few days out of Christchurch, Admiral. Have you any objections?'

'No, of course not. As a matter of fact, I was going to suggest you get back in the bush and see some of this country. I know it's your last chance, unless you want to come back on my staff?' Brady's impish grin betrayed the humor with which he made the offer.

'I'll take a pass, Admiral. No offense.'

'Ha! I figured that'd rattle your chain. Okay, leave a contact point with my aide. I'm sure that your XO can handle the planning meeting . . .' The intercom buzzer interrupted Brady's comment.

'The chief of staff on one, Admiral,' crackled the box.

'Well, be on your way, Marc. We'll be going to work soon enough.'

Marc returned the bulldog handclasp and left Brady's office. Outside, the aide handed him a pink telephone memo slip.

'A Father O'Gorley,' amplified the aide.

'Thanks.' Great timing. He was going to call the priest at first chance, anyhow. If anyone could give him some suggestions for a holiday, it would be Patrick Joseph O'Gorley. It would be good to see the old Irishman again.

But first, he had a very necessary chore. It was roughly three-quarters of a mile to the flight line. There, a small, single-story clapboard building housed the Christchurch offices of VXE-6's detachment. Bob Christian was walking out the door as Marc arrived.

'Have a good sleep?' inquired Marc's O-in-C.

'Like a baby.'

'How's the admiral this morning?'

'Charging, as always.'

'The classified contain anything interesting?'

'No,' replied Marc. No reason to cut in Christian on the information. 'Staff business, I guess.'

Together they strolled back to the ramp in front of the squadron hangar.

'Listen, Skipper, I'm sorry I took the wrong tack last night. I should have known better,' apologized Christian.

'That you should have. No offense taken, but you have to remember that female aviators still are a rarity and it's easy to place the wrong emphasis on them. I, for one, would welcome more in the squadron. With all the skirted scientists running around now, it's no big deal that the Ice is coed. It's a different world, Bob. We have to adjust.' He deliberately used the first person plural to indicate that he held some sympathy for Christian's feelings.

One-two-nine was nosed into the open hangar bay and several of the crew and a group of the squadron maintenance personnel were swarming over it, pulling off inspection panels and making minor adjustments on the various systems. Dare walked over, grinning and rubbing together the thumb and forefinger of his right hand.

'I believe it is payoff time,' commented Marc's plane captain. 'Would you like to see the recorded grades Skipper?' he continued, reaching into his shirt pocket for his little black book.

'Only as a formality, Dare. I already know the results. However, I would expect a bit more objective grading in the future. Zinwicki's landing at Pago Pago wasn't that hot – or, should I say, *was* hot. Hell, he floated halfway down the runway.'

121

'True. But then, you put an awful strain on my tires with that ker-plunk here, sir.'

'The wind played out.'

'As did your airspeed, my captain.'

Marc glanced at the scores: Frosty, a ten at Honolulu; Zinwicki with that undeserved nine and a half at Pago Pago; and his nine at Harewood.

'How's the airplane?' asked Marc, handing back the book with two twenties tucked between the pages. Dare lifted them out and touched them to his lips.

'Thank you, sir. The bird's fine. A couple minor gripes. We'll have her out of the hangar in another hour or so. Any flight requirements while we're here?'

'No. If you need a test hop, get hold of Lieutenant Kohn. She'll be available, along with Mr Zinwicki. I'll be tied up for a few days – with a pair of skis and a goatskin of Kiwi wine, I hope.'

'Hey! You're finally going to Mount Cook. Great. I wish I were going with you, but then us enlisted . . .' Dare's voice trailed off in mock martyrdom.

'In every society, there has to be a privileged class,' Marc needled. Dare retaliated by giving the two twenties another kiss.

'Ah, yes,' gloated the sailor, 'the better to pay off obligations.'

'You guys don't have to drink all that up tonight, you know. And don't forget what I said about more objective grading in the future.'

'I just call 'em as I see 'em.'

'Then see 'em more objectively,' insisted Marc.

Dare turned back toward 129. 'Have a good time, sir.'

Marc watched him climb a work stand and flaunt the two bills to the rest of the crew. Two twenties wouldn't bankrupt him and the goodwill such a relationship generated within his crew was priceless. The few bottles of whiskey the money would buy would be more than repaid by the long hours his men would be working on the Ice, and they were mature; the booze would be spread over several after-work sea story sessions.

He entered Christian's office and dialed O'Gorley's number.

'Saint Benedict's rectory . . .' He recognized the precise, cultured voice. It was O'Gorley's elderly housekeeper.

'Yes, this is Commander Bradford . . . is Father O'Gorley in?'

'Why, welcome back, Commander. Yes, just a moment while I fetch the old crab.' Marc smiled at her candid reply and heard her voice in the background, 'Father! Ye're wanted on the telephone! It's Commander Bradford.'

The phone clacked noisily as she laid it down. Within a few moments, it was picked up. 'Marc! How in the divil are ya?'

'Fine, Father. I got your call. How've you been?'

'Like a Stradivarius! A wee bit old, but still finely tuned and worth a fortune! Ya didn't keep yer promise and drop me a line. I hope ya treat yer family in the States better!'

'I'm sorry about that. Things just seemed to pile up and before I knew it, I was back on my way down here. How about lunch?'

'Foin! I'll pick ya up about eleven. I've a few chores to do. Mrs Divin is givin' me the dickens 'bout me room . . . says it looks like the leavin's of a charity sale – so, now, is eleven all right fer ya?'

'I'll see you then . . . I hope we can spend some time together, maybe even get back in the bush.'

'That we can . . . see ya at eleven.'

Marc replaced the phone in its cradle and reached for the morning message board, more out of habit than interest. As he leafed through the messages, he thought of his friendship with the old priest. Father O'Gorley was a frequent visitor to the Ice, usually as a guest of the New Zealanders. Something of a legend, his stocky, white-bearded figure was a common sight on the trail as well as in the major camps as he made himself available to the men for personal services. More than a few had received his tongue lashings about infrequent letters home or his severe counsel when one of the Chi Chi girls turned up with a Yank-induced pregnancy. Others, both Kiwis and Americans, had been comforted by his special brand of solace when bad news arrived. There were assigned chaplains on the Ice, both Catholic and Protestant, but the ecumenical and international O'Gorley was always a welcome addition to their ranks.

Pushing seventy, he was the mental and physical equal of men half his age, regularly skiing the Southern Alps of South Island, and usually making it to the States every couple of years to tackle the slopes of Colorado. He had a passion for observing the penguins and was considered something of an unofficial authority. Consistently, he roamed the rookeries, being careful not to disturb the nesting birds but on the lookout for fallen feathers, which he would gather and distribute to the children back at Christchurch. His shock of white hair, always uncovered unless the weather was extreme, and his special black parka made him blend into the rookeries as just another penguin, although a super-sized one.

Marc strolled leisurely back toward the headquarters complex. Almost in spite of himself, he was beginning to enjoy his first off-duty time in months, and plans for the next few days began to materialize in his thoughts as he observed the morning activities around the airport. Automobile traffic was light, as was the aircraft traffic. He could see the big golden tail of a Continental DC-10 sticking up beyond the low terminal roof. Probably a contract flight, bringing down the ground pounders of the staff and scientific community. A lone low-winged Piper putt-putted overhead as it made its way around a deserted traffic pattern, dipping its wings in a graceful turn as the pilot banked to approach the runway. Two yellow taxis sat silently in front of the terminal, their casually uniformed drivers leaning against the front fender of the lead cab as they chatted and watched for fares.

Marc retrieved his rental car and by eleven had changed into slacks and a sport coat. He browsed through the *Christchurch Star* while waiting in front of The White Heron for Father O'Gorley.

A worn 1979 Toyota Corolla, in desperate need of new piston rings and a wash job, stopped abruptly in front of him.

'Ah, there ya are!' exclaimed the priest as he hurried from the car and reached out his arms. Marc returned the warm embrace as they patted each other on the back. 'Ya've put on a pound 'r two, eh?' commented O'Gorley without waiting for an answer. 'Let's be off! I'm treatin' ya to the foinest lunch in South Island. . . .'n they keep their beer extra cold fer Yanks.' As an afterthought, he shook his head sadly and added in an undertone, 'What a terrible thing t'do to a good draught . . .'

They climbed into the Corolla and O'Gorley pulled away from the curb without bothering to look back or signal. Fortunately there was little traffic; still, Marc spent a few anxious minutes readjusting to the left-hand traffic flow. O'Gorley continued, 'Tell me, how's the family?'

'All well. Dorothy said to be sure and tell you hello and we're anxious for you to visit us next time you come to the States.'

'She sounds like a luvley woman . . . must be to sit back there so patiently every winter while ya come down

125

to play in the snow. Why didn't ya bring her along this time? The admiral does.'

Marc laughed at the obvious. 'I'm not the admiral! Besides, you know how little time I usually have in Christchurch.'

The priest braked to a sudden stop in the middle of the street, again without the hint of a check rearward – it would seem he had blind faith in Saint Christopher. 'Ah! Gabbin' so much, I missed me turn.' He muscled the Toyota around in a tire-screeching U-turn and back-tracked toward the center of the city. In a few minutes they were crossing over one of many arched bridges that spanned the willow-lined banks of the gentle Avon River and making their way through the bustling downtown traffic. The traffic policemen touched the tips of their caps as they recognized the old priest. For anyone else who drove like that, they'd undoubtedly set up a roadblock! The car sped on through Cathedral Square in the heart of the business district. The majestic, Gothic, Anglican Christchurch Cathedral sat at the focal point of the square, dominating it with its ornate 215-foot spire. O'Gorley skillfully threaded the charging Corolla through the noon automobile and bus traffic like a Notre Dame tailback breaking loose into the secondary and continued on east toward the coast. Christchurch blended into its seaside suburb of New Brighton, and after a confusing series of left and right turns through the patchwork of two-lane streets, they broke out of the residential clutter onto a coastal road. Ahead, reaching out over the water on tall, thin wooden stilts that seemed much too flimsy to hold the overhanging box structure, perched a rustic restaurant. As they drew closer, Marc could read the hand-lettered sign: Jerry's Seaside Pub and Take Away.

The parking lot was full, but O'Gorley pulled in behind a black Ford Cortina. 'Jerry's car,' he explained, obviously reasoning that the owner would not be leaving over the profitable noon hour.

Inside, they were greeted like visiting cardinals. The big Englishman, wearing a food- and liquid-stained white apron, ushered them to a window table overlooking the water. The reserved sign was discreetly moved to a dark inside table. As O'Gorley claimed, the beer was ice cold, and the lunch the best Marc had ever enjoyed in New Zealand.

Half a world away, if one traveled due east along the imaginary line that delineated the forty-four-degree south latitude slice of planet Earth, Martin Bormann, chancellor of the Third Reich of the New German State-in-Exile, stood behind his desk and stared angrily at his deputy, Kurt Eisner. Bormann's lowered head, glowering eyes, and tightly closed mouth were all hauntingly familiar to Eisner. Bormann always assumed the same countenance when he felt events were preceding his decision or concurrence. 'I am not sure we should allow those halfbreed superiors of Mignone to dictate the course of the Third Reich,' he began. 'We were promised sanctuary here, *in perpetuity*, by Juan Perón! The fuehrer himself put his signature to the paper. You are aware of that, Eisner; you carried the agreement between them.'

'That is true, but we must recognize the unprecedented change in political conditions. And this move is not bad for us. We can grow more rapidly, perhaps even more openly when we have a piece of ground to call our own. Imagine it, Mein Fuehrer, the seed of a New Germany! Our own territory!'

'Our own shitty block of snow and ice! We will be completely dependent upon the whims of the Argentines.'

'No more than we are now. And we have a new project going that has already raised twenty million dollars.'

'Yes, yes, the deal with the Arabs. But I shall not let Argentina forget what we have done for them. We gave the best of our military knowledge to Argentina. We showed them the way to absolute power. They wear the helmet and pride of our own Wehrmacht German forces and parade with the same proud step of progress that we used to march across Europe. And need I remind you, Herr Eisner, that we have paid our own way. It was German gold that established and provided the initial support for Perón. It was German gold that enabled Argentina to build a place for itself in South America unique to this continent, a European country among Indians and illiterate mixed bloods! There is an Aryan heritage in Argentina. They *owe* us, Eisner!'

And, thought Eisner, they collapsed under the pressure of a small British expeditionary force, which in my day we would have annihilated with two squadrons of Goering's worst. 'They are repaying that debt. We have been cared for, for forty-three years, my God! We have been allowed to flourish – in our own way. But it is over and we must adjust to that. We must make this move, and I repeat, it is an excellent development and we have the means to exploit what they feel is a ploy to be rid of us.'

Bormann continued to express displeasure. 'I am not sure I have your confidence.'

'Mein Fuehrer,' counseled Eisner, his voice a gentle vibration of steel resolve, 'As our infallible leader, you must see the eventual wisdom of this move. It is the hand of destiny picking us up once again from in front of our enemies and giving us another beginning.'

The look of Martin Bormann softened. He had performed the scene well. It was sometimes necessary to remind Eisner of his subordinate position. 'My ministers, have they been told?'

'They have been briefed on the proposal. They await your decision.'

'I will not talk to them until you have relayed me their thoughts on this.'

'They are in agreement with the move.'

'Then I will give them my decision. Call a meeting for tonight at midnight. I will have my statement prepared by then.'

And, as always, old man, you will follow my lead. Eisner saluted with an upraised arm and backed out of the room.

9

Lieutenant Kohn taxied 129 to its loading spot in front of the Deep Freeze terminal and cut the engines. She and Dare secured the myriad of levers and switches before she left the flight deck and ambled into the passenger waiting room. Lieutenant Zinwicki was waiting for her.

'Our flight plan's filed, ma'am,' reported the junior pilot, handing Kohn their copy of the weather briefing. 'Looks like about eight and a half hours.'

Kohn scanned the sheet. 'Headwinds aren't too bad, but that terminal forecast looks a bit shaky. We're going to be heavier than usual with cargo and passengers; that cuts down on our fuel load. We'll have to watch it closely.'

'With your permission, ma'am, I have a friend in the terminal who's seeing me off.'

'Sure, Zin. I think we're all set. Just be sure you're back before we load the passengers.'

'Will do.' Zinwicki hurried into the main terminal lobby, not even noticing Marc entering through the other side of the double doors. Like Kohn, Marc had exchanged his normal uniform and civilian clothes for antarctic gear, including his green Byrd cloth parka, a rare holdover from the early days of squadron operations. Over his right breast was sewn the squadron patch, an embroidered shield-shaped insignia that featured the words 'Puckered Penguins' in a scroll across the bottom and an obviously mistreated, oversexed, hungover Adélie penguin staring blankly ahead through bloodshot eyes. Lipstick smudged the hapless bird's otherwise spotlessly white chest, a smoldering cigarette dangled from its beak, and a sailor's white hat was perched askew on its head.

Kohn checked her watch. 2140. Marc was a few minutes early. 'Good evening, Captain. We're all set and should be loading the passengers in about five minutes.'

'How's the weather?'

'McMurdo's forecasting a middle stratus layer, light winds.'

'I understand we've got some headwinds enroute.' Marc allowed Kohn to take his briefcase, keeping his seabag beside him.

'May have thirty knots on the nose until sixty degrees south . . . should lessen after that.'

'That'll be the day,' remarked Marc. They both grinned. Antarctica was eight and a half hours away; a lot could happen in eight hours, especially when one considered that they would be approaching a continent half again as large as the United States with only a dozen or so reliable weather-reporting stations. There were more than that between San Diego and San Francisco.

'The aide said the admiral will be here about 2215,' advised Kohn. 'How was your holiday? Get out of the city?'

'That I did, and it was great. Spent a quiet four days up at Lake Tekapo. A friend of Father O'Gorley's let me use his cabin. Father even joined me for a couple of days of fishing. Didn't catch a thing. The rest of the time I just loafed and walked through the Kiwi bush like a tourist. It was a great feeling, to be away like that, all by myself.'

'How is the old leprechaun?'

'Hale and hearty as ever. He expects to come down to the Ice and spend some time, probably in December. Where's Zinwicki?'

'In the terminal, saying goodbye to a friend.'

'Oh? Opposite sex?'

131

'To him and you,' replied Kohn, a humorous twinkle in her eyes. 'He says he's met his true love.'

'Zinwicki? Our for-life bachelor? In just five days? Not a Chi Chi girl?'

'An Air New Zealand flight attendant. He has all the symptoms.' Together, Kohn and Marc walked nearer the glass partition and peered into the lobby. 'There they are,' said Kohn.

Zinwicki was energetically embracing a petite blond who exactly fit her bright blue flight uniform. They certainly looked serious. After a long minute, they separated and exchanged a final word before Zinwicki started back toward the Deep Freeze area. Immediately seeing Marc and Kohn eyeballing his approach, he wiped his lips and joined them.

'True love?' suggested Marc.

'May be, Skipper . . . she's really nice. I'm serious.'

The young aviator's words did sound sincere, despite his embarrassed grin. The blond was standing where he had left her, waving and blowing kisses.

Kohn nodded toward the terminal entrance. 'I think that's the admiral's car. I'll see you at planeside.' She departed for the floodlit Hercules.

'I'll go lend a hand with the passengers,' added Zinwicki.

'Thanks, Zin. We'll be right out, I imagine.' Marc strode out into the lobby. Brady was just entering, followed by a small entourage of staff members. His wife was on his arm.

'Good evening, Admiral . . . Mrs Brady.' Marc took the woman's extended hand. A good ten years younger than her husband, with a face and figure that erased an additional five or so years, the petite Mrs Brady wore her tailored two-piece wool suit with the air of a lady who had established herself within the circle of her husband's

132

profession and was loving every minute of it. Vivacious, with a sparkling personality that featured a quick wit, a delicious sense of humor, and a social presence that was the perfect complement to her husband's responsibilities, Mrs Brady had not a pretentious bone in her body. Washington's loss was certainly Christchurch's gain.

'Listen, Marc,' she instructed, 'you make it a point to get back here before the season's over so Thomas and I can have you to lunch and we can talk.'

Marc had to stifle a laugh. *No one* called the admiral 'Thomas' – except his auburn-haired spouse. Even now, she received a scowl as Brady hurried her on.

'I'll surely try, Mrs Brady, thank you,' responded Marc.

'And take care of yourselves on the Ice . . .' Her words were interrupted by a reporter team from the *Star* who asked if they could interview the admiral. Marc excused himself and headed for 129.

Kohn and Dare were strapping in and Wineman was discussing the navigational requirements with his relief navigator. Marc slung his parka onto the top flight-deck bunk and took the command pilot's seat. Dare turned down the flight-deck lights to allow their eyes to adjust to the low-intensity instrument lighting.

'Nice night,' commented Marc.

'Yes, I could use a few more here. What a beautiful city,' remarked Kohn, tightening her shoulder straps and adjusting her headset. Marc could see her profile outlined by the outside lights. The slight tilt of her nose, full lips, and sweep of hair that was pressed down on top by the gray plastic headset gave her a quiet beauty that was both feminine and professional. As they sat in silence, waiting for the appearance of the admiral, there was an invisible rapport between them. For the next eight hours they would be as one, sharing the responsibilities and aviator's pleasures of controlling the flight of the loaded Hercules across the most inhospitable seas on earth. The relationship was one of the intangible rewards that made both Marc and Kohn proud of their demanding profession and confident about their ability to meet every challenge they would encounter in the coming months. No words to that effect were ever exchanged between them, but they both understood the closeness of their relationship as the pilot crew of 129. There was no male-female aspect to that relationship, just the affection and admiration of two professionals in the unique world of military aviation. Marc was particularly pleased that Kohn would be Zinwicki's mentor during the cruise. The youthful aviator had much to learn, and he could learn it from no better pilot than the one who now was sitting to Marc's right.

Kohn was also utilizing the lull in activity to recall some of her most private thoughts. She was on an aviator's high, waiting patiently for the moment when she would meld with the rest of the crew in taking the Hercules and its cargo of materiel and passengers to the hostile continent of Antarctica. This was not a routine flight; the precarious journey from Christchurch to the unpredictable environment of the White Continent was never routine, despite the impressive capability of the aircraft. This night, because of their cargo weight requirement, the teardrop fuel tanks that hung below the wing would be practically empty. Certainly there was sufficient fuel for the flight as well as a reasonable change in enroute and/or terminal weather conditions. Yet, they would be operating the C-130 on the edge of its capability envelope. There would be no margin for a bad decision or a mismanagement of the aircraft's flight abilities. Flying the big cargo carrier was not the same as the exhilarating job of taking a jet fighter out to sea, but there were compensations. She and Marc would have nineteen souls in their care. That made a big mental difference. When she had tasted the real thrill of naval aviation, ferrying the sleek FA-18 Hornets out to the carriers at sea, she had only her own well-being to preserve. If there were an emergency, she could act with a single purpose – to save the aircraft, if possible; if not, to save herself. Tonight, although the chances of such an occurrence were not as great, they were there and the consequences could be even more disastrous. There was that element of danger, challenge, responsibility that filled Sheila Kohn with an excitement of pending achievement. She was a privileged individual and an even more privileged female individual, and that realization was not lost on her. This was *the* life!

'Here comes the admiral,' announced Marc, his words bringing Kohn back to the present, 'let's turn number three.'

By the time Brady had joined them on the darkened flight deck, all four engines were whining into life. They pulled away from the terminal as Marc noted the time: 2238. Brady was leaning over his shoulder, waving a vigorous farewell to his staff and wife. As they disappeared from view, the bulldog figure removed his parka and slung it on the upper bunk, plopped down on the lower seat bunk, and strapped in.

Marc guided the sluggish Hercules slowly along the blue-lighted taxiway. Not only did he have their computed gross weight figure in his mind, the feel of the aircraft in its non-natural element of being earthbound was telling him that they were at their maximum allowable takeoff weight. As usual at this hour, the airport was quiet. They had the whole airfield to themselves. He braked smoothly to a stop in the warm-up spot for runway 20.

'Ready to go, Harewood,' report Kohn.

'Roger, one-two-niner, you are cleared for takeoff . . . winds light and variable . . . say hello to all the chaps on the Ice and have a good flight.'

They moved onto the runway and lined up on the white center line.

'Going to grid,' reported Wineman. He switched off the magnetic compass input to the aircraft's compass system. The lines of magnetic variation in the polar area would fluctuate so rapidly that the magnetic signals would be useless. Instead, they would fly the artificial system used in polar aerial navigation, which set up a pattern of north-south, east-west reference lines across Antarctica. In effect, the south pole would then sit on the grid equator. Their inertial navigation system would keep track of their actual latitude and longitude, but they would maintain a grid chart for cross-reference as a navigational check. All courses and directions would be given in grid headings.

As Wineman set the master compass, the slaved repeaters on the pilot's and copilot's instrument panels locked in on the master setting. Runway 20, representing a magnetic heading of 200 degrees, now became runway 35 in the grid system, with a grid heading of 357 degrees. To the noninitiated, the system seemed hopelessly confusing. For example, although the crew would be flying almost due south to reach Antarctica, they would be flying a grid heading of almost due north! At the particular longitude of Christchurch, the magnetic and grid headings were 157 degrees apart. The pilots and navigators quickly adjusted to the grid system, consequently the artificial navigational system became second nature to the Icemen.

The actual navigation between Christchurch and McMurdo would be relatively simple, the crew relying on their inertial navigation system to take them along their desired track, but there were precious few checkmarks along the way, only several tiny islands along the 2,000-mile route. Radar confirmation of their position would be sparse until they could pick up the rugged coast of the continent. In the event they were forced to rely on their backup systems, Wineman would carry a chart plot and shoot a few star shots enroute.

'I have grid three-five-seven set in,' announced Wineman. Kohn and Marc checked their instruments and confirmed the reading.

'Okay, let's do it.' Marc advanced the power levers to their takeoff setting and felt the warm touch of Kohn's gloved hand as she backed him up.

One-two-nine accelerated and roared toward the dark at the far end of the runway. Marc used Kohn's computed speeds for rotation and lift-off and 129 powered its way into the cool night air in less than half the length of the runway. Wings bowed upward by the combination of lift and weight, the Hercules swung around to the south – grid north – for the east coast city of Dunedin, 200 miles ahead. The aircraft would be under the control of the New Zealand air traffic control system until over the coastal city.

An hour later, 129 was over open ocean and South Island was falling rapidly behind. Marc left his seat and joined Brady for a cup of coffee. The admiral offered him a shortbread cookie from a brown paper bag.

'Very tasty,' remarked Marc. 'Mrs Brady bake them?'

'God, no,' replied the admiral, 'if she had, you'd break your teeth.' Marc doubted it.

'Anything new on our German situation?'

'No', answered Brady, muching on one of the cookies. 'I suspect I'll get a visitor soon, probably on my first trip back to Christchurch. I called a friend of mine in the Pentagon on the embassy's secure phone in Wellington.'

They sat in silence, sipping the hot coffee and feeling very secure on the warm, darkened flight deck, the steady muffled roar of the four turboprop engines providing a background symphony of smooth power. The reliable sound occasionally resonated with a low rumble as the four propellers temporarily eased out of synchronization and the automatic controls eased them back into an exact match of RPMs. The outside air had already dropped to minus thirty-five degrees Fahrenheit at their 26,000-foot flight altitude. The coffee filled a psychological need as well as a physical one.

Marc leaned over Wineman's shoulder and examined their progress logs. Fuel consumption and distance traveled were right on the prediction. They would have a point of no return, a location along their track where the winds and remaining fuel were such that they would be committed to a landing on the Antarctic continent. Until then, should they encounter any difficulty, they could reverse their course and return to Christchurch, and until then there was always the uncertainty of a successful trip to the Ice.

The Hercules droned on south, the outside air dropping slowly but consistently. The second navigator relieved Wineman.

Marc returned to his seat and he and Kohn took turns catching catnaps as the aircraft flew rock steady under the positive control of the autopilot. One set of closed eyes in the cockpit presented no hazard; in all of this portion of the southern skies, 129 was the only aircraft aloft, 129 and the following four Hercules strung out at thirty-minute intervals.

It was now 0245 on October 1, the traditional date for the first seasonal flight to Antarctica. They had been airborne for four hours and were almost halfway through their journey. Four and a half nautical miles below them, a lone New Zealand navy frigate pitched and rolled on the tossing sea. The ship was steaming in a large rectangular path, or at least trying to! In these waters, the worst in the world, the valiant Kiwi station ship would remain for a month at a time, providing navigational and communications assistance and search and rescue facilities as needed. It was time for 129 to check in.

The ship had been bobbing on and off the radar for the past thirty minutes and the intermittent blip was almost lost in the heavy sea return. The radar range marker indicated eighteen miles, and the blip sat just to the right of dead ahead.

Kohn triggered her mike, '*Arcturus, Arcturus* . . . Navy one-two-niner, over.'

The reply crackled back immediately, 'Bloody cripes, that's a luvley, comfortin' voice! It must be the renowned Frosty Kohn, aviatrix extraordinaire.'

'Your reputation has preceded you, Sheila,' offered Marc.

Kohn shook her head, embarrassed but flattered by the recognition. 'Good morning, *Arcturus,* you have the advantage. With whom am I speaking?'

'This is Barry, Sheila. This valiant ship, which is slowly being battered into small bits by a most ferocious sea, is all mine – for a year, that is. What a comfort it is to hear your sweet tones out here on the edge of the earth.'

'Commander Barry Gordon,' explained Kohn over the intercom. 'He was my escort to several Kiwi functions last season while we were redeploying. I didn't realize he was up for command.' Switching back to the ship's UHF frequency, she continued with her report. 'We hold you dead ahead at twelve miles, *Arcturus.*'

'More or less,' replied the ship's voice. 'We've been painting you for the last hundred miles. Looks like you're right on course. I have some upper air winds for you, over.'

Kohn copied the winds; Wineman acknowledged them over the intercom. 'Roger, copy,' Kohn continued. 'How are you riding down there, Barry?'

139

'Up and down, m'dear, up and down! How about you folks?'

'Smooth as silk.'

'You fly-boys – and -girls – ought to go to sea with the real navy, sometime; get your sea legs!'

'I've got my sea legs . . . it's the sea stomach I lack.'

'I know what you mean . . . most of my crew stopped eating three days ago. Think of all the provisions money we're saving for the bureaucratic chaps back in Wellington.'

'Well, we appreciate you being down there, *Arcturus*.'

'Anything for you Yanks . . . oops! . . . stand by a second, my helmsman just surrendered his stomach contents to the fickle god of the southern seas.'

Kohn switched back to intercom. 'That is rough duty.'

Marc nodded agreement. 'Let me talk to them a moment.'

'Hello, *Arcturus*, this is the VXE-6 commanding officer. Please tell your crew that they are pretty important to us. This sky gets awfully big about now, and it's mighty comforting to know you guys are down there in case we have to go for an early-morning swim. Believe me, we appreciate it.'

'Thanks, Captain . . . you're piped over the ship's system and I'm sure the crew appreciates your compliment. If you don't need anything else, I think I'll go tie myself to the mast! Frosty, you owe me a dinner and a night out for this!'

'You got it, Barry. I'll buy. Hang in there. See you next trip.'

'Roger. *Arcturus*, out.' The transmission was obviously hurried.

'The helmsman's probably barfing all over the binnacle again,' came Brady's voice over the intercom.

'I didn't know you were on the phones, Admiral,' said Marc.

'Poor bastards down there. I'll have to make sure I write them up for a commendation once the season's over. That commanding officer is surely right. That's the real navy taking a pounding. Imagine a frigate in those seas. Lieutenant Kohn, your young man sounds like quite a leader.'

'He's not my young man, Admiral, but he is a friend and is fun to be with.'

'Oh.'

Marc noticed Dare was paying particular attention to his overhead gauges. 'Anything unusual?' he asked.

'Number four's using a bit of oil, Skipper,' reported Dare between bites on a lunchmeat sandwich, 'reading six gallons.'

The Allison turbos ran tight and needed only an eleven-gallon tank; however, five gallons usage in four hours was excessive.

'Tap it,' suggested Kohn.

Dare rapped the gauge sharply with his knuckles. The needle jerked up to six and a half. He took another hungry bite of his sandwich and continued studying the gauge while he chewed. 'I'll watch it.'

Marc acknowledged with a nod. Six and a half was still a skosh low at this point. The increasing cold could be brittling up some seals or squeezing open a line fitting. No problem, yet.

An hour and a half later, they were approaching their point of no return. It was decision time.

'McMurdo, one-two-niner, approaching PNR . . . what's your weather?' radioed Kohn.

'Present McMurdo weather is ceiling and visibility unlimited with surface winds from two-six-zero at ten knots, over.' McMurdo's figures were in grid, also.

'Sounds inviting, Mac . . . we'll see you in a couple of hours,' responded Kohn. No reason to be concerned with that report.

'We're ready for you!' added the McMurdo voice. After all, the speaker, along with a hundred or so other lonely souls, had not seen anyone else since the preceding February except for the few hours the Winter-Fly aircraft had visited them. They were obviously anticipating the end of their long winter duty. Their only consolation was that their comrades at the South Pole Station would have another month's wait before the temperatures warmed enough to permit aircraft operations at the precise bottom of the earth.

The next hour passed uneventfully. Marc estimated that he'd passed a gallon of coffee through his system since leaving Harewood, probably an exaggeration but certainly an impression. Otherwise, he was almost bored with the smoothness of the flight.

Almost.

'Holy shit!' The profanity shot through the intercom system like a shot as the navigator sat bolt upright in his seat. His words even carried to those on the flight deck who were not wearing earphones. 'We're getting seventy-five-knot headwinds!'

Marc was about to question the report but Frosty was already up on the circuit. 'Seventy-five-knots? We've been steady at twenty for the past two hours. What's happened?'

'I dunno,' answered the perplexed navigator, 'but they're picking up even more.'

'How's our howgozit?' interjected Marc. The navigator was already plotting his position on the distance versus fuel chart, which provided them with a constant check on the safe progress of their flight. A red diagonal line ran from the bottom left upward to the top right and his latest plot sat exactly on the red line.

'We're on the red,' reported the navigator.

'And committed to McMurdo,' added Kohn. They were well past their point of no return.

During the next twenty minutes the wind velocity increased to 125 knots. Somewhere out there, invisible in the emerging light of the antarctic dawn, was a very tight low-pressure cell, probably off to their left, spinning violent winds directly onto their nose. That would mean a radical change in the McMurdo weather.

As if on cue, McMurdo came up on the air, 'One-two-niner, we have a special weather observation for you . . . over.'

Kohn looked at Marc. 'Here it comes,' she muttered before switching to the McMurdo frequency. 'Go ahead, Mac . . . but, be gentle.'

'We're getting a ground blizzard rolling in over Minna Bluff. Right now, winds at Williams Field are forty knots in blowing snow. What's your estimated time of arrival?'

'ETA is zero-seven-one-eight at the moment, but that will change. We're hitting winds in excess of a hundred knots, right on the proboscis,' replied Kohn.

Minna Bluff lay twenty-three miles south of McMurdo, across the Ross Sea on the near edge of the continent. It was a 'seaman's eye' weather indicator, as it was located directly in the path of approaching storms. What you saw at Minna Bluff you'd be seeing at McMurdo a half hour later or so.

'Welcome to Antarctica,' sourly commented Dare. 'Now that they've coaxed their mail and fresh veggies past the PNR, we get the *real* weather.'

'Take an even strain, Tom, this is just typical. Mother Ice is letting us know nothing's changed . . . the Ice is still

the Ice.' Marc didn't want to show it, but he felt snook-
ered, also.

'Too damned typical,' agreed Kohn. 'Just once, I'd like
to fly in and see where we're landing.'

'We're getting one hundred and fifty knots, Skipper,'
reported the navigator.

It was time to fight back.

'Let's cut numbers one and four,' ordered Marc. 'We'll
loiter an hour or so. As fast as those winds have come up,
that cell is moving rapidly. Let's see if it doesn't let up.'
His stomach muscles tightened under his lap belt. He
loosened the strap, knowing that it wouldn't help.

Kohn feathered their two outboard engines and secured
the engines. 'Cargo, we're shutting down the outboards
for a while,' she reported to the loadmaster, who was
manning the phones back in the cargo compartment. 'You
might want to brief the passengers in case they ask about
it.'

The procedure was routine, but Sheila knew some of
their riders might be startled to look out and see half of
their engines stopped.

Their indicated airspeed slowed to 145 knots as Marc
adjusted the power levers. Considering the outside air
temperature and their flight altitude, their true airspeed
was only 209 knots. With the headwind, they were creeping across the sky at a ground speed of only fifty-nine
nautical miles per hour!

It was time for another howgozit plot. This time they
were below the red line. If the winds continued, they
would not make McMurdo on their remaining fuel.
Sergeant Wineman had returned to the flight deck and
both navigators were busily checking their instrument
readouts, trying to come up with a recommendation to
place the aircraft in a more favorable position or altitude.
The activity caused Admiral Brady to climb down from

the upper bunk and slip on the spare headset that hung over the navigator's station. He leaned over Marc's shoulder. 'Problems?'

'Winds, Admiral. We're trying to wait them out.' Marc motioned toward the stilled outboard propellers.

'How far out are we?' queried Brady.

'A little more than four hundred miles to go, which at our present sixty-knot ground speed will take seven hours.'

'Jesus Christ! Excuse me . . .' Brady, suddenly fully awake, quickly regained his composure. Smiling, he offered, 'Maybe I should go back and throw over some of our passengers.'

Marc joined his chuckle. 'You might get some opposition back there.'

'What are your plans?'

'Well, we'll wait it out for a while. If worst comes to worst, we may be able to go into Hallett.' The abandoned joint US–New Zealand station sat on the near edge of the continent, roughly 350 miles closer than McMurdo. Marc knew that unless the winds slackened, even Hallett was out of reach. That could mean a landing on sea ice. Dawn was breaking fast and the sky was clear ahead, but a landing on the rough frozen sea surface would be almost as hazardous as an outright ditching as far out as they would be from the solid portion of the shelf.

'Nav, would we gain anything by altering course over toward Wilkes Land, perhaps one of the coastal stations?' asked Kohn.

'I doubt it, Lieutenant,' replied Wineman. 'It would still be just about as far, and we'd have a terrific crab to compensate for this wind.'

'I think we're committed to dead ahead,' added Marc. 'At least we'll maintain a maximum closure speed toward the continent.'

'Should I alert the passengers, sir?' The loadmaster, isolated back in the darkened cargo compartment, was feeling the first pangs of nervousness.

'No, not yet,' answered Marc. 'We'll ride with this for another hour and then make some decisions if necessary. I think we'll pick up some ground speed before long.'

Before long turned out to be only twenty minutes. Wineman reported that the winds were dropping in velocity and swinging slightly off to port. They were down to eighty-five knots.

Marc gave McMurdo a call, then wished he hadn't. The entire area was engulfed in blowing snow with visibilities in the one-half- to one-mile range. His disappointment was immediately softened by Wineman's next winds report.

'Seventy knots,' reported the marine, 'and they're shifting nicely. Right now, I'm reading three-zero-zero grid.'

'Okay, let's crank up the outboards,' decided Marc.

By 0530 the winds were back to a twenty-knot headwind component and 129 was back on four engines, clocking a 280-knot ground speed. The green trace on the radar scope was outlining their first landfall, Cape Adare. They were on track and had lost only an hour.

The ice-covered Ross Sea was beneath them and the morning sun was bouncing off the snow-mantled mountains of Victoria Land. White peaks glided by their starboard side as they continued south toward McMurdo. Hallett passed, dormant beneath the fast-drifting, broken layer of low scud clouds.

By 0700, the aircraft was 100 miles out from McMurdo and those on the flight deck could see the tip of Mount Erebus poking through the thick white blanket of the ground blizzard. The wind-whipped snow was being deflected upward as it roared across from Minna Bluff

146

and struck the rising hills of Ross Island. A steady wisp of steam rose from the volcanic crater, and as it reached the rim it was sheared away by the force of the horizontal storm winds.

McMurdo came up on the radio and confirmed their worst suspicions. The blizzard had struck with full fury and the airstrip was submerged in blinding snow that was being driven violently against every object it encountered by seventy-knot winds.

'There must be several tight cells coming down from the plateau. I figured we had it made once those flight-level winds died down,' observed Marc. But their situation was still tight. 'What's our endurance?' he asked, to no one in particular.

Dare checked his fuel quantity and flow gauges. 'We can hang on for another ninety minutes.'

Marc made some fast mental calculations. At their present airspeed, it was only another twenty minutes to the airfield; but, why rush? They would be better off conserving fuel again, and arriving later would give the winds a chance to die down – or pick up. 'Okay, Sheila, let's cut the outboards again.'

The Hercules wallowed along nose high, steady at its 160-knot true airspeed, sipping its precious fuel rather than taking the long gulps it enjoyed at regular cruise speeds. They used up the better part of an hour before reporting over Williams Field and began a leisurely race-track pattern over the approach aid radio beacon. Williams had the TACAN system of electronic aerial navigation, which would give them constant bearings and distances to the airstrip, and a precision radar approach system staffed by one of the best GCA (ground-controlled approach) controllers in the navy. An outmoded system, or considered such by commercial aviators, who relied primarily on ILS, an automatic instrument landing

147

system, GCA was still second nature to navy pilots who flew the antarctic weather. ILS equipment required a stable ground installation, and the sea ice of Williams Field was forever shifting. So the confident voice of a GCA controller would be talking down 129.

By 0830 they were looking at their last thirty minutes of fuel, having bested Dare's endurance estimate by a good half hour. Williams Tower was reporting surface winds from 320 degrees at fifty-five knots and visibility zero in blowing snow. They would have a crosswind component of forty knots. Too much.

'Well, we can put it down on the ice shelf at outer Williams,' suggested Kohn. 'We would at least be into the wind.' She started thumbing through her need pad charts for the emergency area approach plate.

'It'll put us ten miles out from Williams and the crash equipment. The briefers said the area hasn't been looked at in a month. The sastrugi could be as much as six inches high and hard as steel. Let's just hold up on it until we see if we can get into Williams. We'll stick with the skiway for two passes. If we can't get in, we'll consider the shelf.' Marc glanced at the admiral, who was still wearing his headset. Brady nodded his concurrence.

Marc nosed the Hercules over and pegged the airspeed at 250 knots. The fuel-saving jet penetration would place them in position for radar pickup by the GCA controller. 'We'll start the outboards turning inbound,' instructed Marc. That would give them the full power of all four engines if they had to go around. Smoothly, he laid the Hercules over into its reversal turn.

Kohn reported in, 'Willie Radar, we're in procedure turn, passing eight thousand feet.'

'Roger, one-two-niner . . . radar contact seventeen miles east . . . report steady inbound on heading two-five-five degrees . . . descend to and maintain one thousand feet. Over.'

The calm, reassuring voice of the chief air controlman conducting the approach filled the headsets. The winter-over unit had its pick of controllers and the chief was the best of the best. An experienced antarctic veteran, he had spent the long, lonely eight months at McMurdo for just this one moment, and Marc's stomach muscles unwound a bit at the fatherly sound of the chief's baritone. If anyone could bring them in, that deep, articulate voice could. The chief knew it and Marc and his crew knew it. No ego involved on either end of the radio link, just professionalism that at the moment held the fate of nineteen lives within its grasp.

'One thousand feet,' report Kohn. She and Dare started the outboard engines.

'Roger, turn farther right, heading two-six-zero . . . you're eleven miles from touchdown.'

The winds had pushed them over their desired track a few degrees. The steady voice continued, 'Ten miles from touchdown . . . perform your landing cockpit check.' The formal over and out commands were not necessary, the chief and Marc instinctively knowing when a transmission ended. They had played the scene a hundred times before. Marc, Kohn, and Dare had already performed most of the landing check; now they executed the remaining actions with the exception of the flaps and landing gear.

'Nine miles from touchdown . . . turn farther right, heading two-six-five.'

'Two-six-five,' parroted Kohn, her mind acting in concert with Marc's as they both mentally visualized the skiway and wind relationship. The skiway heading was 250 degrees; at their heading of 265, they were holding a 15-degree drift correction.

'Slightly left of centerline . . . correcting nicely . . . eight miles from touchdown . . . two-six-five your assigned heading.'

149

Marc and Kohn realized that if 15 degrees were correcting them toward their desired track, the winds must have decreased or swung around more on their nose. Marc wanted to know. 'What's your wind, radar?' he asked.

'Two-niner-zero at fifty knots . . . turn left, heading two-six-three . . . seven miles from touchdown.'

Good! The wind *had* shifted! Their crosswind component was down to thirty knots. They could handle that. Now, if they could just see. The Hercules settled into the top of the ground blizzard, an airborne submersible diving through the depths of the driven snow. Outside the windows there was absolute white; they were flying inside a ping-pong ball, bouncing and tilting from the force of the gusts around them.

'Five miles from touchdown . . . approaching glide path . . . you're a skosh high . . . check your altitude.'

Marc had let the Hercules edge up a few feet. A minor adjustment on the control column glued it back down at 1,000 feet.

'That's better . . . you're right on . . . approaching glide path . . . begin your normal rate of descent.'

Marc eased the nose over as Kohn lowered the landing gear and placed the ski lever in the down position. 'Gear down, skis down,' she reported. One-two-nine began its blind, gradual descent toward the hard plate of ice over McMurdo Sound.

'You're on glide path . . . good transition . . . on centerline . . . four miles from touchdown . . . do not acknowledge any further transmissions . . .' From this point on, the chief would do all the talking; the crew of 129 would fly the airplane. 'Turn farther left two-six-two degrees.'

One degree. Marc eased in just a touch of rudder and let his gyro heading indicator nail the 262 mark. The chief called for one degree, and one degree is what he got. This was the ultimate in precision control and response.

'Three miles from touchdown . . . check gear and skis down and locked . . . cleared for landing . . . on center-line . . . on glide path . . . two-six-two your heading . . . tracking nicely . . . excellent rate of descent . . .'

They were locked on the glide slope and it felt good. Kohn was leaning forward, her pert nose almost to the windshield, as she strained to see through the ocean of snow. The wipers were useless. Marc would keep his eyes on the instruments; Kohn would sing out the instant she saw the runway. The only markers leading up to the scraped snow were black-painted fifty-five-gallon oil drums. No fancy stateside strobe lights flashing in the white void, no buzzing or cockpit indications from inner marker signals – just the waiting oil drums.

'Two miles from touchdown . . . on centerline . . . on glide path . . .'

So far, so good.

'Half flaps,' requested Marc and with his peripheral vision he could see Kohn position the flap lever and felt the increased drag. He adjusted the power levers to keep his rate of descent constant. The lowered trailing edge slabs set up a familiar vibration.

'One mile from touchdown . . . on centerline . . . on glide path . . .' The wind was holding steady. Frosty should sight something soon. 'One-half mile . . . on glide path . . . one-quarter mile at GCA minimums . . .'

Not in Antarctica, thought Marc, continuing his approach.

Kohn shook her head. 'Nothing, Skipper . . .'

'Going around!' Marc shoved the power levers full forward, paying particular attention to his rate of descent indicator to ensure it stopped and started indicating an increase in altitude. Simultaneously, Kohn retracted the

151

gear and skis, eased the flaps up slowly, and sat back in her seat. Same as always! Doodle!

'See anything?' asked the chief. He would be relighting his cigar about now.

'Not a thing. Let's try it again. Fifteen minutes of fuel on board.' Marc made the report matter-of-factly, then added to his crew over the intercom, 'Okay, gents – and lady – we're putting this hummer on the deck.' His decision drew a nod of approval from Kohn and Dare. 'As soon as we touch down, Sheila, you and Tom watch for those drums. I'm going to stay on the gauges and I'll go into full reverse as soon as we touch. Okay?'

'Gotcha, Skipper,' replied Dare, taking an extra hitch in his shoulder harness. The air on the flight deck was thick with concentration and suspense and hung like fog. You could feel it. The three bodies controlling the airplane and the one below, in the darkened radar shack, were one, their movements and emotions joined in an intimate act of complete mutual trust and teamwork. They were going to set down the Hercules at better than seventy knots on an unseen snow surface between menacing thick plywood skiway markers that were barely a wingspan apart and spaced every 1,000 feet along each side of a 13,000-foot bobsled run.

It took only five minutes for the chief to work them around in an abbreviated pattern to the final approach. Two minutes later, they were three and a half miles from touchdown, on glide path, on centerline.

Marc was on an airman's high, locked in mortal combat with all the nasty gods of the air as they swirled around him, hurling their great bursts of wind, blinding snow, and unpredictable turbulence – all combining to hide the surface he sought. They were clamoring for their just due from this mere mortal who dared challenge their supremacy of the antarctic environment. The battle was joined

152

and the juices flowed thickly within the four principals of the life-or-death drama. Marc and his crew, along with the chief in the dark hut, were committed to meld their individual skills in a gamble that had been thrust upon them by a casual quirk of the unpredictable south polar weather. The lives of the nineteen souls inside the aluminum tube were the stakes; yet, if years of training and experience could balance the scales, the odds were at least even.

'One mile from touchdown . . .'

Marc slowed the Hercules to eighty knots.

'Full flaps.'

Once more, Kohn pushed down the flap lever.

The wide Teflon-coated skis hung below the aircraft like the grasping claws of some giant bird, ready to plow into the unseen snow surface and drag the hurling beast to a perilous halt.

'One-quarter mile . . . GCA minimums . . .' The chief continued calling centerline and glide slope and would do so until the Hercules touched down or disappeared in a gigantic ball of orange flame.

Kohn's words were to herself, but they carried over her microphone so that all on the flight deck could hear, 'No joy! Gentlemen, prepare to earn your flight pay!'

Marc raised the nose very cautiously and set his airspeed at seventy-five knots. The rate of descent showed fifty feet per minute. Then, a final adjustment to seventy knots.

Twenty-five feet per minute.

The radar altimeter read fifty feet – and thirty-five feet of that was snow penetration.

The chief continued his monotone, 'Over touchdown . . .'

Marc felt the rapid ticking of the rear edge of the main skis as they began to nip the snow surface. He pulled the

153

power levers rapidly back into their reverse thrust position. The charging C-130 settled onto the snow, the four Allisons roaring their defiance at the storm. The reversed propellers screamed in unison and the Hercules groaned to a stop in less than four fuselage lengths!

Marc quickly placed the power levers in their ground-idle position as the snow tornado generated by their unorthodox touchdown swirled about them. The admiral joined Marc and Kohn in searching out the windows.

'I can't see a goddamned thing,' reported Brady. 'Hell, I can't even see the snow surface.'

'If I didn't know better, I'd say we were still up in the air, sitting on a hard cloud,' added Kohn.

'Welcome to Antarctica,' muttered the loadmaster, his voice low but no longer edgy.

By way of contrast, the GCA chief was exuberant. 'I have you on deck!'

Marc sat quietly, horse-whipped, his legs with no feeling from the knees down. The deployment was off to a lousy – but safe – start. The planning conference back at Christchurch had added too many flight hours to an already overtaxed schedule. The arrival weather was crappy. The brown manila envelope and the news about the Nazis gave a whole new aspect to the season. *Balls*. He must shake the feeling. Depressing his mike button, he called, 'Damned good job, Chief. You can date my daughter any time!'

'You have a son,' rejoined Frosty, openly laughing with relief.

'Then, he can date my son!'

Behind him, the flight-deck tension had disappeared, just as a thick fog in a heavy wind, the moment they slid to a halt. Dare caught Marc's eyes and they exchanged grins of satisfaction. Everyone had done his and her job as well as they could have been done. That's what this

154

flying game was all about. Brady even had his arms around Dare's shoulders and the young sailor wore a sheepish expression as Brady kept repeating in his ear, 'Nice . . . damned nice . . .' He wasn't used to the enthusiastic hugs of flag officers.

'I've got a follow-me vehicle on the way,' reported the chief. 'I'm giving him vectors . . . you're smack in the middle of the skiway, about a hundred yards down from the touchdown point.'

'A hundred yards,' repeated Marc on the intercom. 'A tad close. We could have stretched it a bit.' Switching back to the GCA frequency, he continued, 'We aren't going anywhere.' There was no way he would taxi without some guidance. Old 318, the first LC-130F assigned to the squadron, had been lost in similar circumstances. The crew had taxied during a whiteout, inadvertently climbed over a snow ridge and dug one wing into the surface. The wing fuel tank ruptured and old 318 burned up on the spot. Marc called the chief again, 'We don't see any markers. Where are the closest ones?'

'You're sitting right between a pair. You do good work, Commander.'

Marc nodded in silent appreciation of the compliment, knowing full well that the landing had been a joint effort. He also knew that the chief had shown once more that when he placed his hairy hands on the console of his radar set, he played a symphony of electronic detection that could track a jay-walking penguin, should one be foolish enough to waddle across the chief's touchdown point.

Suddenly, dead ahead, a bouncing gray tractor slid to a just-in-time stop under 129's nose, its rubber-soled steel tracks undulating in frantic recoil at the sudden brake application. Two fur-engulfed sailors stood in the open vehicle and waved, their goggled eyes only partially visible. With an exaggerated show of enthusiasm, they

155

unfurled and held aloft a crudely lettered banner which proclaimed in bold black print: WELCOME TO THE ICE, FISH! The last word was the time-honored label for new arrivals to the continent.

For thirty minutes, Marc edged the Hercules ahead through the storm, following the creeping ex-army Weasel. Finally, he received a stop signal.

A ghostly horde, dark and silent, slowly materialized out of the whiteness that still engulfed 129, staring at the propellers as they coasted to a stop. They were the men of the winter, wrapped in layers of bulky cold-weather clothing, faces covered with masks and scarves. All wore goggles to ward off the stinging wind, and beyond the dark lenses unseen eyes were locked on the airplane as if it were an apparition rather than a reality. No one waved or stepped forward. Within the rigid, wrapped bodies were the subdued personalities of the winter-over crew, victims of the world's worst isolation. Months back, the outside world had simply ceased to exist. They were on another planet, where the sun went from a low circle around the horizon to a few weeks of dipping and reappearing to finally disappearing completely for several months.

It would take them a few minutes before they realized that the silver, whalelike aluminum form squatting before them was actually a forerunner of their relief, with all sorts of forgotten pleasures. Tonight, they would dine on fresh green lettuce and real eggs. They would munch brightly colored fruit only days away from the trees while they read and reread letters from a distant land called home and shared pictures of sons and daughters whom they had yet to see.

Brady zipped his parka and stepped down from the plane, greeting the men with a smile and waves of his mittened hands. He followed the officer in charge of the winter-over party through the snow drifts, anxiously seeking the warmth and security of a nearby Jamesway hut.

The crew and passengers followed, the first timers cringing in disbelief at the fury and cold of the storm. They weren't at all sure of where they were to go and even less sure of just where they were! In any event, it was a terrible place. But, led by the shadowy snow figures who triumphantly shouted, 'This way, fish!' over the wind noise, they soon disappeared into a round frame and canvas-covered hut. There they were welcomed with hot coffee and soup and they could rub some of the cold from their bones.

Marc gathered his seabag and briefcase and led his small flight-deck crew into the hut to join the others. The cook had prepared peanut butter and Span hors d'oeuvres.

'The weather's got the helos grounded,' the O-in-C was telling the admiral.

'What about surface transportation?' asked Brady, nibbling on a peanut butter and Spam cracker.

'We've got snowcats warmed and ready, but I would advise waiting and letting the visibility pick up some. Coming down, we lost the trail flags several times,' replied the brown-bearded commander. Marc noticed a nest of cracker crumbs in the man's facial hair.

McMurdo Station, on the tip of Hut Point Peninsula, a volcanic dust finger of Ross Island that jutted south into McMurdo Sound, was still seven miles away across sea ice.

By the time the second cups of soup were being poured and the cook was wrestling with a new tin of peanut butter, the wail of the wind had softened to a steady whine, an octave lower in pitch. The storm was weakening.

'I think we should do it,' proclaimed Brady. Marc and

his pilots followed the bulldog figure outside where two wide-tracked snowcats were waiting, their bright red paint subdued in the shadow of the storm and their hearty diesels mixing steady streams of black exhaust with the blowing snow.

The rolling, pitching ride across the sea ice toward Ross Island took better than an hour. Five times, the creeping two-tractor convoy had to stop and wait for a lull in the fierce winds before the drivers could see the next trail marker. Marc's watch was reading noon by the time they were climbing over the snow-whipped black volcanic ash floor of the pass across Hut Point Peninsula, between the New Zealander's Scott Base and the weather-hidden heights of Observation Hill. Doggedly, they continued on into the confines of McMurdo Station, where Antarctica's largest base boasted more than thirty buildings, including several scientific laboratories, a tank farm, a supply yard, and a complete operational center, all connected by above-ground insulated fuel- and waterlines. The boxy structures of the complex broke up the raging winds, and periodic glimpses of the streets and other features could be caught as the snowcats stopped in front of Brady's quarters. The simple rectangular hut sat on the edge of the camp, facing across McMurdo Sound toward the continent, twenty-three miles beyond the hut's card-table-sized picture window.

Brady tumbled out, followed by Ramon, who assisted the admiral with his gear. The two quickly disappeared through the double-doored storm entrance.

Within minutes, Marc and his pilots were disembarking by their quarters in the personnel building, barely managing to grab their bags off the rear rack of the snowcat before it rumbled off.

The blizzard was less intense 'downtown'; at the far end of the station the ice pier could be seen, and beyond that the original hut used by the English explorer, Sir Robert Scott. The small frame building, its bare board sides weathered but still remarkably intact, was set aside as an international shrine of sorts, and the steel-springed cots and tinned rations still waited inside for the return of the ill-fated expedition that had set out for the South Pole seventy-eight years earlier.

Marc dropped his gear on the bed in his cubicle and walked down the narrow passageway to the small lounge. It was deserted. A hot pot of coffee was on the single electric burner. Next to it sat a portable broiler-oven, its glass front stained a dark brown from the splattering of countless steaks prepared over the winter. Scattered magazines lay about on the scratched and dented tables nested against the ends of a sagging sofa, its gray plastic covering cracked and brittle. A tarnished brass floor lamp sat between the sofa and a matching chair. The room was just as Marc had left it seven months back. He sat, sipping a mug of the coffee, which must have been brewed several days prior to their arrival, and listened to the wind. Dorothy and Jim, the technology and industry of the United States, the vast blue waters of the Polynesian Pacific, the gentle rolling plains around Christchurch all were no longer a part of his world. Now, his existence, along with that of his 73 officers and 475 men and women, would be confined to 5,500,000 square miles of sunken continent, depressed by 7,000,000 cubic miles of centuries-old ice and snow.

Sheila Kohn entered the lounge and sat in the chair by the lamp, the movement of her body jarring the loose light bulb and breaking the electrical connection. Marc reached over and tightened it and the light returned.

'Coffee?' he offered.

'No, thanks. It looks thick.'

'Probably last season's.'

'Wouldn't doubt it.'

Outside, the dying blizzard was slinging its last gusts through the station, rattling the wooden buildings and depositing a new layer of ancient snow, which it had swept from the high polar plateau and carried across the continent to McMurdo. The faint whir of a laboring oil heater, secluded in a small space off the lounge, rose and fell as the wind whipping across its vent pipe caused intermittent bursts of back pressure.

Marc raised his cup. 'To a safe season.'

Frosty raised an imaginary cup. 'I'll drink to that.'

They both exchanged silly grins. Their love-hate relationship with Antarctica had returned.

The Icemen were back on the Ice.

10

The bus ride from Damascus would try the patience of the dead, thought Ibrahim al-Abbadi. The gray passenger box that was attached to the worn frame of the vehicle vibrated and emitted noises that were the mechanical equivalent of the voices of souls who were forever doomed to the depths of darkness. Conversely, al-Abbadi's fellow passengers, including the goats and chickens, had been whipped into a silent stupor within the first hour out of the capital city. By the time they had passed through Homs, halfway to Ibrahim's destination and the crossing point of the great oil line that fed the black gold from the northern fields to the seaside loading reservoirs, Ibrahim was beginning to think he should have taken one of the more modern conveyances. The sleek, air-ride diesels passed his shaky transport at regular intervals, their slipstreams causing the ancient bus carrying Ibrahim to rock and almost veer off the road. But on this miserable vehicle, he would pass unnoticed, where in air-conditioned comfort, his Palestinian heritage might be detected among the Druzes and Kurds who could more properly call Syria their homeland. Not that a Palestinian was out of place in the country; indeed, there were many training in the secret camps to the east, which were quite isolated but close enough to the waters of the Euphrates to afford some measure of cleanliness and comfort between training sessions. But there were also those who took Western dollars for information, and the report of a lone Palestinian of Ibrahim's age and intense demeanor could be the tiny irregular and almost unidentifiable piece that completed someone's political jigsaw puzzle. There were also the hated ones, those of Arab blood who sold their souls to the American CIA. Such men were worse than infidels. They were few in number, but it would take only one to identify Ibrahim and complete a puzzle.

He tried to sleep but it was impossible if for no other reason than his seatmate, a woman of enormous proportions who hid all of her physical being beneath her clothing except for her breath, which each jolt of the bus brought forth as a combined exhalation and cough. Anything that smelled that bad must be able to be seen, but all Ibrahim could detect was the brown dust that blew in all of the windows.

When he finally swung his battered frame down onto the ground at Tell Mardikh, it was time for prayers, and he knelt and placed his head toward Mecca. By the time he finished talking to his God, the bus was long gone and the air was clear and enticing with the smell of cooking. The village compound was a feast of aromas as he made his way among the corridors and rooms to his two companions. He would eat, but first he must report on his visit to the Germans in Argentina.

'Welcome on your return, Ibrahim,' greeted the old man Ahmad Diah.

'God is good,' returned Ibrahim.

'Sit and tell us,' invited Mulhammad al-Kalaji, swinging his arm stump in an exaggerated gesture of hospitality.

'The Germans want a treaty with the United Arab Republic,' announced Ibrahim.

'What kind of treaty?' asked Diah.

'A protective treaty. The Argentines are sending the Germans to Antarctica but are giving them a station that will eventually be a sovereign state.'

'Do they understand the lack of real solidarity in what passes for the UAR?' asked Diah. 'Right now, there is much dissent and lack of commonality in how the organization pursues its goals. That is why people like you and me exist. We have taken the holy struggle into our own hands. The Germans should be seeking a treaty with us.'

'We are even more divided than the UAR,' commented al-Kalaji.

'And more credible,' added Diah with a smile.

'Nevertheless, that is their wish.'

'And the weapon?'

'It will be ready in February,' answered Ibrahim.

'We cannot go to Antarctica to pick it up,' stated al-Kalaji. 'We know nothing of such a land.'

'We will not have to do that. The Germans will make arrangements,' answered Ibrahim. 'Delivery of the weapon is no problem; securing a signature on a piece of paper is our problem.'

'We start with those who are providing the funds,' said Diah. 'They are important people and will know who must agree to the conditions of the treaty. We will let them decide about this. Meanwhile we can make preparations for the employment of the weapon. We must ensure that our own people are spared. That will be a great task and one which we must go about very carefully, for not a single Jew must suspect that they are going to die in February.'

'What if the UAR refuses to sign?' insisted al-Kalaji.

'We will have a signed treaty when it is time,' announced Diah, throwing his head back and shaking it in joy. 'The Germans in their isolation know little about the impotence of the UAR, and the signatures and seals on the piece of paper will be worthless regardless who signs it. Therefore, who puts the pen to the paper is immaterial as long as he can write the correct names. We will have the balance of the money, that is the important thing. That will ensure the Germans give us the weapon. The piece of paper they can put in their files someplace and it will wither into nothingness before their day returns. God has preserved them for us, nothing more.'

11

October was a short month. Immediately upon their arrival at McMurdo, two Hercules began a series of turnaround flights between Christchurch and the Ice, bringing in the remainder of the squadron personnel, the first scientists, and priority air cargo. Meanwhile, the four C-130s remaining on the Ice began the long sequence of logistic support flights to the inland stations, which were the main requirements for the season. The first flights carried relief 'fish,' and by the last week of the month all of the tired winter-over personnel had been flown back to Christchurch. The squadron personality on the Ice had taken on the enthusiasm of a new crew.

Wop-wopping Bell UH-1N helicopters, heavily laden with anxious biologists and their camping equipment, visited the nearby penguin rookeries. An efficient shuttle service between McMurdo, squatting in the volcanic ash of Ross Island, and the hard ice of Williams Field was established by the reliable Hueys.

By the end of the month, the early-season field parties had been put in place and the first flight to South Pole Station was scheduled for Halloween night. Night in the current sense was a two-hour-long dusk, as the spring sun merely dipped below the horizon as one would momentarily dunk an orange-frosted doughnut into a heavily creamed cup of coffee.

The month also saw the first arrival of the news media crowd, who immediately began to move about the camp, often entering busy areas uninvited – and more than not, unwelcomed – in their never-ending quest for the true story of Antarctica. Each evening, they glued themselves to the makeshift Officers' Club bar to absorb 'atmosphere' and record the colorful talk of the personnel, who really only wanted an hour away from their duties and their constant working companions. One of the great contrasts of Antarctica, the most isolated continent on earth, was the lack of privacy, and the few moments stolen by a quiet drink at the bar were not easily sacrificed to the probing questions of the persistent newsmen and -women. Frosty Kohn particularly took offense at their lack of tact and discretion.

October 30 had been a very long day and Kohn was scheduled for the next evening's South Pole flight. Thirty days on the Ice and her flight log book had 178 newly recorded flight hours, the crew 53 more, for Marc had found time to relieve her on ten of the flights. Poor Zinwicki, the lone copilot, was getting that deployment stare of blank eyes and robot movement as he flew practically all of 129's demanding schedule. He was right at 200 hours and the Quack had grounded him for fatigue. One of the other Hercules crew members, who had less time for the month, would provide Frosty with her copilot for the premier South Pole flight.

Kohn sat on a stool at the far end of the bar, sipping a rum and Coke.

'Good evening, Lieutenant.'

Frosty glanced aside at the speaker, apparently a self-styled God's gift to womanhood, as the man pulled his adjacent stool close enough to touch thighs.

'Norm Collier, *Brooksdale Gazette-News*. Buy you another?'

Where the hell is Brooksdale? thought Frosty as she moved her leg away from his. 'Good evening, Mr Collier. No, thank you. One is my limit.'

'Call me Norm, and you?'

'I'm *Lieutenant* Kohn. Sheila Kohn.'

'A pleasure, Sheila.'

Frosty would have preferred to stay with 'Lieutenant,' but there was also that public relations aspect to her position in the squadron.

'What is your job, Sheila? Administration? I bet there's quite a bit of paperwork involved in an operation of this type.' The man was not getting off to a good start.

Frostly wondered why the gold wings above her woolen shirt pocket hadn't clued the clod as to her specialty. Of course, the pair of beady eyes that crawled over her face and body as if they were trying to peer through her khaki fatigues would pass right over a gilded piece of metal. His oversight added little credibility to his efforts to strike up a conversation.

'I'm a C-130 aircraft commander,' she replied, the tone of her voice equal to the temperature of the ice outside.

The man had whipped out his notebook. 'I beg your pardon?'

'I'm a naval aviator, Mister Collier. I fly the C-130s.'

'A pilot? How 'bout that!'

No, clod, I'm an aviator. Air force jocks are pilots. Outwardly, Frosty ignored the comment.

The newsman smelled a story. A female pilot in the US Navy. The good people of Brooksdale were going to get a scoop.

'How long have you been a pilot, Sheila?'

'Since graduation.' *Let him toy with that for a while.*

Collier scribbled something in his notebook. 'I find that fascinating. I thought women were prevented from going into combat.'

Frosty partially turned toward the reporter. 'Mister Collier, women have been an integral part of the United States Navy since before you experienced what I suspect was some weird type of puberty. We are active in all

167

branches of the navy, indeed, of all the services. As for combat, this is hardly that, although if you ever get your skinny little ass off that bar stool and take a flight with us, you may be fortunate enough to ride through an antarctic blizzard or a whiteout or an open-field landing, which on the hazardous duty ladder is only one rung below combat.'

'Hey, Lieutenant, no offense meant.' The man was finally getting the message. 'Could I? Fly with you on one of your flights?'

'See the staff public affairs officer. If he wants to schedule you, and there's room, you can go to Pole with me tomorrow.'

'I'll do that. Tell me, don't you run into problems being a woman pilot?'

'What kind of problems?'

'Oh, you know, the crew members, flying with a woman and all that?'

This guy's only one generation removed from a cave, mused Sheila. 'My crew has every confidence in me, and I in them. What sex we are is immaterial, Mister Collier. I have received the same training and operational assignments as any naval aviator.'

'Yeh, but the men fly off aircraft carriers. Wouldn't you like to be a man and do that?'

Frosty was having trouble recognizing that here was a person who was a member of the news media and yet had such a narrow concept of the military in modern times. As for her wanting to be a man, it would be nice to be a male long enough to ask him to step outside for a moment. She was even tempted as a female. 'I have fifty-seven carrier landings, in three different combatant aircraft including FA-18 Hornets. You really need to educate yourself, Mister Collier, on the role women play in the modern military. Where is Brooksdale? On the dark side of the moon?'

'North Dakota,' replied Collier, scribbling again in his notebook.

'Same thing,' observed Frosty, taking another sip of her rum and Coke.

'Well, I know about women in the military. But, listen, off the record, you must get hit on a lot, being down here with all these men in such isolated duty. I can count the women on this continent on my two hands and maybe a couple toes. But hey, after all, human nature is human nature. That would make one hell of a human interest side to my story – you know, how does a female naval officer maintain her femininity and still do her job surrounded by sailors? Now, if there is one thing I know, it's sailors. I did a four-year hitch, back in the late seventies. Trying to find myself, you know? It was good for me. I've never regretted it.'

'What was your rating?'

'Journalist. I was a lead writer on the station paper at North Island.'

Figures, thought Frosty.

'Look, we could collaborate on a great story here. I think I could even get it on the wires for national exposure. How about we work together on this one? I'll see you get a byline.'

'Mister Collier, I have neither the time nor the inclination to work with you on any story. I have considerable responsibilities, which occupy me full time. Also, I think it would be improper for me to engage in such an activity as an active duty naval officer. And that is what I am, a naval officer who takes considerable pride in giving the taxpayers, who provide my salary and instruments of my work, my undivided attention.'

'That's a great quote, Sheila. I like that. Hey, call me Norm, huh? Time for us to relax. Workday's over, right?' The man closed his notebook and slipped it back into his shirt pocket. 'Playtime. A couple drinks together, between professionals. A little chitchat, get to know each other. You like good scotch? I mean, good stuff, *eighteen years* old. Brought a bottle with me. We can slip down to my room and enjoy. My roommate's at the flick. Know what I'm saying? You need to unwind, Sheila. I concede you're a good naval officer and a crack pilot. But you're a woman, too. I can be good for you.'

Frosty could not believe she was actually hearing those words. Norm Collier was a throwback to the dark ages of B-movies and Hollywood reporters. In civilian clothes he probably wore a crushed fedora with a press card sticking from the hatband. A guest of the National Science Foundation and the US Navy, he had, in less than fifteen minutes, shown himself to be a complete ass with Frosty. She would like to respect his status as a working visitor to the Ice, but the man did need a course in couth.

Frosty let the trace of a smile part her lips and spoke almost in a whisper. 'Why not skip the chitchat, Norm? Let's go sample that scotch.'

Norm Collier, associate editor and investigative reporter of the *Brooksdale Gazette-News*, circulation 37,218, practically fell off his bar stool. He was about to score with a delicious female navy type whose cool exterior undoubtedly hid an insatiable capacity for sexual activity. Maybe she was even a nympho. By God, he had known it all along!

The walk to his room was a short one. Once inside, Collier hastily searched through his carryall until he found the bottle of scotch. Turning around, he started to lift it in a symbolic toast to his conquest. Instead, he caught a stinging open palm that snapped his head around so sharply that a loud crack sounded from the slipping together of two neck discs. Off balance, he fell backward onto his bunk.

170

'That's for openers, Mister Collier. I have never been so insulted in all my life. I don't know what kind of weight you carry around in Brooksdale, but down here you are a guest of your government and taking up valuable space that could be used by a legitimate reporter. You are a textbook chauvinist and I suspect that when I report your behavior to my skipper, you'll be off the Ice by tomorrow night.'

'Hey, listen, honey . . .' Collier winced, as even speaking aggravated the pain in his neck.

'No, you don't call me honey. Not you, with an anus where your mouth ought to be. You lie there and listen. First thing in the morning, you're going to get an interview with a member of the admiral's staff. My skipper will see to that. Then I suspect you will find yourself with a number one priority on the next flight to Christchurch. You stay away from me, and don't you dare print a word about this or I'm coming to little old Brooksdale and will raise such a stink with your publisher that you'll not be able to get a job writing advertising copy.'

'You can't . . . talk that way to me.'

'Bullshit, I can't. You've overstepped your bounds, Mister, and I'm personally flushing your press credentials down the drain. You're right about one thing. I am a woman, so my reaction can't be that of a man; otherwise, you'd be leaving with your teeth packed away in a little plastic bag. But, and you listen to this, I am a member of the United States Navy and a professional. I will regret that I lost my temper and struck you, but by Almighty God, it felt good.'

Collier was on his feet. Humiliation was not a new experience for him, but the past few minutes of Frosty's tongue lashing called for some response. Still, he was enough of a newsman to know that his position would certainly be in serious jeopardy if he satisfied his urge to strike that lovely face.

'I apologize, Lieutenant. You've blown this all out of proportion. But, I do apologize.' *I need this story.*.

'You're off the Ice, Collier.' Frosty stalked out the door.

October was a wasted month for Admiral Brady. He would have much preferred to participate in more of the actual work of establishing logistic support for the scientific community. But, outside of going along on the first flights to the isolated inland stations and congratulating the men for a successful winter-over season, most of his activities had to be devoted to welcoming and hosting the various visitors who showed up, courtesy of the National Science Foundation's and the navy's public relations program. With typical bulldog charm, he escorted the congressional VIPs who chose to visit during the first hectic month of operations. As the senior US representative on the continent, he made an early point of a visit to the New Zealanders over at Scott Base, hardly more than a stone's throw from McMurdo. He hosted the Kiwis at dinner in his hut and accepted their invitation to ride their sled dogs around the sea ice off their camp.

Dealing with the press was a sensitive chore. The wrong word or phrase could result in a damaging misquote, and part of the lifeblood of Deep Freeze operations was the favorable reports of the members of the news media. That made the taxpayers happy, and happy taxpayers meant happy congressmen, and happy congressmen meant funds for continued operations. He couldn't help but wonder why the one representative of that North Dakota paper – what was it, the *Brooksdale Gazette* or something like that? – had left the Ice so abruptly. He guessed the man just didn't like the cold.

Finally, the first month was about over; the stream of visitors would slow and he could get some work done. There was the new station to be established over on the base of the Antarctic Peninsula. There was a tremendous requirement for bulk jet fuel and fuel oil at South Pole Station. The November and December field party support requirements would be record setting in themselves. He would have to ensure that a Vostok flight was made in mid-November to pick up the new Soviet exchange scientist, Doctor Anatolii Vladimirovich Kakushkin. Brady always looked forward to working with the Soviets. They were so uninhibited on the Ice, and great drinking partners.

There would be several foreign camp inspections, all sanctioned by the Antarctic Treaty: Vostok; Mirnyy; the Japanese Showa Station; the Aussies' Davis coastal camp; and the Argentines over at Belgrano and, perhaps, at their new advanced concept station on the Joerg Plateau not far from the old US Eights Station. For Argentino Station, the Argentines had borrowed a page from the Americans and were utilizing a dome similar to the one at South Pole, only smaller. Inside were to be berthing structures and laboratories, as well as a compact nuclear reactor to provide heat, electricity, and snow-melting capability. In keeping with their pioneering efforts, the Argentine camp would be a permanent settlement, with families who would live there year-round. It would be the farthest inland they had ventured with their colonization program and the conditions would be even more harsh than out on the Antarctic Peninsula. Brady was quite anxious to inspect Argentino Station.

Marc spent the month tending to command details. He monitored the flight operations and ensured that his itchy-pants winter-over sailors were given the highest priority

173

in returning to Christchurch. The Chi Chi girls would be in for a couple of hard weeks. Fortunately, he had been able to spell Frosty on some of the logistic flights, but not as many as he would have liked. The squadron was performing well, and October goals were being met. Except for the week's loss of 131, which had to be flown to Christchurch with a fractured nose gear strut, the aircraft were holding up well.

No disciplinary problems. There had been that unpleasant business with the North Dakota reporter, having to throw him off the Ice after his ill-mannered approach to Frosty. The incident had made the rounds of all the camps and every VXE-6 man and woman felt additional pride in their female aviator. Most would have given a week's pay to see Frosty uncork that right to the pressworm's cheek.

Frosty's first seasonal flight to South Pole Station had gone off without a hitch, despite the early date and minus sixty-three degrees surface temperature at the high plateau station. Frosty had suffered a mild embarrassment when she stopped at the end of her landing run and her skis froze to the ice. But, in typical professional fashion, she had unstuck them without a great deal of effort and continued her taxi to the refueling bladder without incident.

It was early November when Marc caught a helo shuttle down to Williams Field to see Brady off for Christchurch. The admiral would be working back at his New Zealand headquarters for the next two weeks and on his return he would be bringing with him the multinational inspection party, which included one Berel Kosciusco, the Israeli Nazi hunter. He would be under cover, ostensibly a member of the American team.

Marc caught the admiral just before he climbed aboard the waiting Hercules.

'Have a good trip, Admiral. Say hello to Mrs Brady for me.'

Brady paused at the crew entrance hatch. 'Keep it rolling, Marc! We're off to a good start. Watch those damned reporters . . . they're all looking for the big story, so don't prang any airplanes!' He laughed at the thought of how that type of thing could be reported out of context to the danger of antarctic flying. 'I'll be back by the middle of the month – with Kosciusco. Be glad when he can do his poking around and get off the Ice.' Brady disappeared through the open hatchway in the manner of a grizzly crawling into its hibernating hole. The Hercules taxied off and Marc remained standing at the spot until the aircraft lifted from the smooth skiway and dipped its wings in a turn north toward New Zealand.

He decided to play hooky from his paperwork-stacked desk back on Ross Island and ambled over to the airstrip dispensary. There was a fresh coat of white paint on the outside of the plywood structure, and over the large red cross was a new identity for the Williams Field medical facility: The Quack Shack. He entered the storm lock and stood in the Quack's tiny outer office. Holley's voice called out from the other side of a privacy curtain, 'Be right with you!' Almost immediately, the grinning face of the Quack peered around the curtain. He was up to his elbows in white plaster.

'Anything serious?' queried Marc, accepting Holley's unspoken invitation to join him and the patient.

One of the squadron loadmasters was sitting on the edge of the examination table while Holley and one of his corpsmen were putting the finishing touches on a forearm cast.

Marc examined the arm. 'What happened, Delaney?'

'Busted my friggin' forearm, Cap'n.'

'Tried to stop a falling crate,' explained the Quack.

'Dumb,' muttered the sailor, then his face brightened. 'Ought to be worth a couple days recuperatin' leave in Christchurch, eh, Doc?'

'Light duty for twenty-four hours – it's just a hairline crack.' The Quack gave a few last smoothing strokes to the fast-setting plaster. 'Would hate to pull you off flight status,' he continued hesitantly.

The loadmaster apparently reconsidered the situation. 'It's just a hairline crack, Cap'n,' he repeated, 'no problem.'

Marc grinned. A little thing like a broken arm couldn't keep a good loadmaster down, especially when flight pay was involved. He would just work his striker harder.

Holley cleaned the plaster off his arms and left his corpsman to finish up. 'Going flying, Skipper?' he asked.

'No, just saw the admiral off to Christchurch. How's everything in the tend and mend business?'

'Good. No serious injuries, yet. A few raw noses from the cold, one or two busted ones from after-hours playtime. Had to give one of the USARPs a shot of penicillin for a possible penguin-induced infection.'

'You're kidding?'

'No. He was over at Cape Crozier, letting it all hang out while he took a leak, and one of the Emperors zapped him right on the end of his penis. Cut an inch gash.'

'I don't believe it!' exclaimed Marc, laughing uncontrollably.

'That's not all of it. Seems he's marrying a Kiwi next week in Chi Chi and things are still going to be sore.'

'Oh, God, the fun we have on the Ice. Incidentally, some of the flight crews are getting a bit high on flight time. Keep a weather eye on them.'

'I've been getting out with them as much as I can. I

don't like to be away from here too much – never can tell when we might get another penguin attack.'

Marc grinned at the Quack. 'The exec's crew is pushing it hard. You better go along with them next trip.'

'Will do. Coffee?' The Quack lifted a chrome pot off the single electric burner and poured the hot water over a small pile of instant coffee in the bottom of his mug. He poured another for Marc.

The hot liquid practically cooked the flesh off Marc's lips. 'My God! That's hot!' he exclaimed.

'That's because you didn't filter it first,' replied the Quack, sipping his own through a three-week growth of scraggly black mustache. He was certainly adapting to Antarctica, hair and all.

'It comes off tonight. Just don't have enough whiskers for a good one.'

'I'll second that. It looks like the rear end of a horse with mange!' Marc put down his drained coffee cup and waved goodbye to the Quack as he left. He still had time to walk around and observe the strip activity.

It was good to chat with his men and hear their news from home. Most volunteered some succinct opinions as to how the operation was going. Morale was high. The flight crews were either in the air, working on their aircraft, or grabbing a few hours of much-needed sleep. C-130 one-three-two had a leaky nose gear hydraulic seal and Marc kibitzed a while until the plane captain tactfully suggested he might get chilled standing outside in the cold air. He took the hint and left the sailor to his work. Passing the cargo yard, he returned the cheerful waves of several of the cargo handlers and stopped to watch one of the tractor drivers maneuvering a heavy D-8 Caterpillar around the crowded yard. The driver was hatless, his face glowing ruddy red around his dark sunglasses. Clenched teeth gripped an obscene-looking panatela and from time

177

to time the driver reached into his parka jacket to bring up a can of beer to his lips. Between shifting and working the lift control levers he would throw back his head and down great gulps of the brew.

It was a routine scene for Antarctica, where navy men exchanged waves instead of salutes and drank beer while handling valuable cargo. But the waves *were* salutes, and the beer drinking, while technically an infraction, was not a pressed issue unless the privilege was abused. A cold beer was a small concession for a sixteen-hour day in the frigid cargo yard. The system was irregular, but it worked. In a way life here was a lot like combat, combat with the elements.

A Huey was whining into life on the ice parking apron and Marc hailed it just as the wop-wopping of the rotors signified that the pilot was about ready to go. Five minutes later, Marc was back on Ross Island, in his small squadron office at McMurdo, immersed in the end-of-the-month reports.

Back in Honolulu, after waiting two weeks at Alameda for favorable winds and another two at Hickam for a generator replacement, Lt Comdr Bud Tilley and his crew were lifting their DeHaviland DHC-7 into the warm Hawaiian air and pointing its nose southwest toward Pago Pago. Tilley and his three-man crew were broke, exhausted, impatient, and in dire need of a quiet few days in Christchurch. If the four turboprops kept humming as smoothly as they were on their climbout from Pearl, they would have that quiet time in just one more day. The transpac fuel tanks were proving to be an excellent modification. No leaks, trouble-free operation, and up to the task of ensuring that the Ranger would make its way across the rest of the South Pacific with an ample reserve of fuel. The pucker was over – until they flew that last leg from Christchurch to the Ice.

12

Once more, Alberto Mignone sat across from his long-time associate, Kurt Eisner. This was his third and final visit to the hacienda by Lake Argentino. On his second, he had conveyed the intentions of his government to go ahead with the relocation of the Germans and had received some requests for certain concessions from Eisner, who had presented them as conditions that Bormann required before agreeing to a quiet move.

'We have looked over the list of families that you wish to make up the complement of Argentino Station. We approve of all of them, and have added several others that we would rather see leave Argentina with you. Of course, there will be a contingent of our own people to assist in running the station until your people are well versed in its operation.'

Eisner studied the additions to the list. 'We approve.'

Mignone sighed inwardly with relief. The completed list now contained all of the old Nazis; the second-generation fanatics who made up Bormann's ministry; the strongest sympathizers plucked from their everyday participation in Argentine life; and the additions he had indicated, several officers of the armed services who had advanced to such seniority as to be dangerous should Eisner have fought the relocation. In all, there were 123 people, including 23 families with a total of 31 children, 19 unmarried Germans, and 27 Argentine nationals who would initially supervise the running of the station, most of the blue collar force being assigned to the nuclear power plant.

'We wish to start the movement in five days.'

Eisner did not like the short notice, but during the last meeting with Bormann and the ministers all had decided not to obstruct whatever specific plans the Argentines had for the move. 'Very well. We will be ready.'

'Your people here will be flown directly to Argentino Station. Our housekeeping people are already there, of course, and the station is in readiness. The others will be collected and assembled at an army base south of here and will follow on a regular schedule. By the end of the month, the new home of the New Germany government-in-exile will be established. Does that not please you?'

'The fuehrer is convinced that there is some advantage to the move. We can refine our theoretical doctrine and prepare for the day when our cause can reemerge, which may not be that far in the future.'

Mignone did not reply so Eisner continued. 'Old friend, the world as you know it is doomed. The Communists and the Americans are on a headlong course toward mutual destruction – either the physical destruction of their two lands or the political destruction of their ways of life. It is inevitable, perhaps not in my lifetime, but in my childrens', who I remind you are a continuation of the Third Reich. In the first case, the Northern Hemisphere will be desolated and civilization will disappear as we know it under the nuclear winter. Much of the Southern Hemisphere will be destroyed also, of course; but there may very well be a small pocket of survivability, perhaps here, and Australia, New Zealand, and Antarctica. With our sense of purpose and organization, we shall be in a position to grab the leadership of the world from the survivors. In the second case, the political upheaval caused by the emerging Third World will be prefaced by a complete destruction of Israel. The Jews will be gone and the Middle East will be back in the hands of its rightful owners. The power and wealth of an all-encompassing United Arab Republic will prepare the world for a final division. That will be our new time. Our countrymen over at Filchner Station will be the first to benefit from the new order as we provide leadership to the scientists there. It is only a jump back across the water to here, where our power will be recognized by the European stock of Argentina. Such is our destiny, and we go now to Antarctica not in any euphoria of idealism, but in the reality of what I have just said. The doctrine of Marxism-Leninism – world export of revolution and the rise of the working class – is in direct conflict with capitalism and can accomplish only one thing: catastrophic encounter within the Western world. What irony, that our two most powerful enemies, the United States and the Soviet Union, will make possible the return of the Third Reich.'

Herr Eisner, my old friend, thought Mignone, your isolation even here has driven you over the brink of reality into the chasm of madness. The extreme isolation of Antarctica will end your dream and that of the creature you serve. It is over. All that remains is for the terrible continent to bring back enough of that reality that you see as I do. We have come up with the perfect solution for our dilemma and what you will come to see as an acceptable one for yours.

'Do you not see it, Mignone?'

'What you say is possible. But I cannot see into the future. That is why we take this course in the present.'

'And that is why we accept this course.'

'Then, our business is finished. I will call from Buenos Aires and give you the time you must have your people at the strip outside Califate.'

'We will be there.'

* * *

181

Mignone watched the village of Califate fade into the haze as his transport climbed east, away from Lake Argentino and the hacienda of the Third Reich. There was a great lightness to his shoulders, as if he had just relieved himself of a heavy load, and indeed he had. The touchy political question of what to do with the Germans was solved, and they seemed quite resigned to their fate. Perhaps, because their idea of their fate was different than that which lay in his mind. It might be that Eisner really believed in his theory that the world was about to self-destruct, but more than likely, the old Nazi was grasping at the proverbial straw, refusing to give up his dream of forty-three years. Perhaps they knew something he didn't.

Mignone adjusted his seat back and closed his eyes.

13

Anatolii Kakushkin sat in the quiet seclusion of his room and opened the packet that had arrived from Moscow by way of the Soviet Embassy in Wellington and the Deep Freeze mailbag from Christchurch. He pulled out a one-page briefing sheet, which gave him a summary of the intelligence reports indicating there might be a possible move of the Nazi colony at Lake Argentino to the Argentino Station in Antarctica.

There was also a handwritten note of just a few sentences:

Comrade Kakushkin:
  It may be that you have an opportunity to give the attached medication to Doctor Scnell. That way your trip to Belgrano I may give you some personal satisfaction.

There was no signature, but stapled to the note were a five-by-seven photograph of a man in a white clinical coat coming through a door that seemed to be located in some sort of medical facility, and a small plastic packet that contained a tiny gray pill. The man was in his late sixties, perhaps older, lean, slightly stooped, and wearing wire-framed glasses. He had bags under his eyes and his shiny head was devoid of any hair, as was his face except for a trace of light eyebrows. It would be an extremely easy face to recognize.

On the back of the photograph was an explanation:

  The photograph was taken last year at Belgrano Station and acquired by us in Chile. The man is the medical officer at the station.

Kakushkin touched a match to the typed briefing paper and studied the pill attached to the handwritten note. He had used it before. And for the approaching target of opportunity, there would be no trace of any unnatural irregularity within the body of the man, who was from this moment a corpse.

14

Colonel Kurt Eisner slumped in the canvas sling of the troop seat aboard the bouncing LC-47 of the 1 Escuadron Antarctico – Number One Antarctic Squadron of the Argentine Air Force – seriously second-guessing his agreement with the Argentine's recommendation for the relocation of the New Germany community to Antarctica. He was miserably cold, more than slightly nauseous, and extremely uncomfortable as he unsuccessfully tried to conform his body to the contour of the cloth sling. Almost immediately after departing Rio Gallegos, the airplane had encountered multiple cloud layers and turbulence. Now, midway up the Antarctic Peninsula and straining to maintain the 13,000-foot altitude that kept them well above the jagged terrain below, the ancient Douglas transport was breathing heavily as it forced its way through moist snow and gusty winds. The interior of the passenger cabin was piled high with cartons, boxes, and crates of all descriptions, lashed to the metal deck with nylon cargo straps that creaked and snapped under the changing gravitational forces of the bumpy ride. Eisner's face was hot and moist with nervous sweat while his mouth was dry and seemingly filled with cotton balls, but there was no way he was going to risk unfastening his seat belt for a trip forward to the metal canister of water strapped to the bulkhead behind the pilots' compartment. If he did leave his seat, it would be to deposit his stomach contents somewhere other than in his lap, which was an ever-increasing possibility. The other passengers – the last six from the hacienda at Lake Argentino – seemed to be in similar distress, except for Martin Bormann, who despite his advanced age was resting comfortably in the only litter rigged in the packed fuselage. Tended by two yellow-haired nurses, he was almost lost under the pile of heavy covers and had only to turn his head slightly to sip through a large straw the hot vegetable soup kept at his side. He was also positioned such that by turning the other way he could lean slightly forward and watch the aircraft's passage through the storm outside the small square window. He seemed to like that, and at the moment was apparently engrossed in the dark, turbulent clouds, occasionally nodding and pointing at the brief appearances of the rock, snow, and ice below. The man must have a cast-iron stomach, thought Eisner, and be totally ignorant of the danger the storm was presenting to the aircraft's southern passage. They were probably half-way to Argentino Station, Eisner reasoned. Perhaps the air would turn smoother farther inland. As the second ranking officer of the governing core of the Third Reich, he was not pleased at the prospect of arriving at Argentino and stepping off the plane amid the welcoming salutes of his comrades only to vomit at their feet.

The LC-47 – the L designator standing for a special cold-weather configuration – had seen many such flights, having been a prime carrier of Argentine antarctic personnel since the early sixties, when it had been stripped and prepared for such work. The inside of the fuselage was covered with a thick blanket material, snapped securely to the aluminum formers and stuffed into every nook and cranny of the circular cabin. Strangely enough, the after bulkhead, which had provided some insulation from the unheated tail compartment, had been largely removed, probably to accommodate the jet engine. This unique modification was employed by the Argentine Air Force to give the outdated LC-47 a better takeoff ability when operating from the rough snows of Antarctica. The jet engine sat silent now, its hungry fire no asset when airborne since its voracious appetite consumed fuel at an incredible rate, fuel that was not available for the heavy cargo run to Argentino.

Eisner could see forward also, and the fact that the four crewmen – two pilots, one navigator, and a plane captain – had been engaged in serious discussion for the past forty minutes worried him. They should be relaxed and nonchalant in the way of airmen who were confident in their control of the aircraft and mastery of the situation. Animated discussion, frequent head shaking, and worried glances out the windshield were not the marks of such men. The cockpit windshield was coated with frost, and one of the pilots would periodically reach out with a gloved hand and wipe a viewing area. For what purpose, Eisner was not quite sure. Speeding along into the heavy snow, the aircraft was flying blind and at 13,000 feet was still several thousand feet below Antarctica's highest mountain peaks; however, Eisner did seem to recall that such elevations were several hundred miles farther inland. Small comfort. One placed flying into a mountain secondary to the present situation, which seemed to indicate that the plane crew was quite concerned about merely keeping the Douglas Skytrain in the air!

An anxious hour passed. The snow was still heavy, the clouds still thick, but the ride was smoother and Eisner gathered the courage to release his lap belt and make his way forward along the narrow aisle between the unoccupied troop seats and the jumbled cargo. The drink of water settled him further and the attitude of the crew bolstered his shaky morale. The two pilots were sitting silently in their seats, sucking up hot coffee from steaming mugs. The navigator was bent over his tiny table, clucking to himself in apparent satisfaction, and the mechanic even smiled as Eisner squeezed forward behind the pilots.

'How are we doing?' asked the German.

'Much better than a few minutes back, sir,' responded the copilot.

'It looked as if you were having quite a discussion,' ventured Eisner.

The pilot chuckled. A big man, made even bigger by his bulky flying garments and with the ruddy face and gray speckled hair of a seasoned navigator, he spoke reassuringly, 'We were concerned about the weather. The forecast was that it would begin to improve over the peninsula. Obviously, it had not at that point. There was a possibility we might have to return to Rio Gallegos. But you can see now. It is better.'

Not to Eisner. He could see nothing outside except white.

'Notice how the turbulence has diminished? That is a good sign. We are riding smoother now and we have burned sufficient fuel to be considerably lighter. If the need arises, we can climb higher.'

'I can hardly breathe at this altitude,' complained Eisner.

'Ha! I understand. Do not worry. We should be able to descend before long. I have just talked to Argentino and they say the weather is breaking. They can see patches of blue sky to the southeast.'

'How much longer?' asked Eisner.

'I would say about ninety minutes and we should start our letdown.'

'Good.'

'How is our fuehrer riding?' asked the big man.

'Very comfortably, it appears. He seemed to have a fascination for the storm. Most of us were fighting our stomachs while he sipped soup and talked with his attendants.'

'He is a great man and has been through much worse than this.'

'That is true,' remarked Eisner. 'Well, thank you. This is a historic flight.' Eisner felt much better. The confident demeanor of the two pilots calmed him. Walking toward his seat, he stopped and stood next to Bormann. 'The weather is improving. We should be there in another hour and a half, Mein Fuehrer.'

'This is not a very glorious way to arrive at our new home, is it, Eisner?'

Eisner shrugged. 'This aircraft is especially equipped for such flights.'

'It is the same aircraft that carried Allied paratroopers and dumped them onto German soil forty-five years ago.'

'Our return will be more suitable to our station. I am confident of that.'

'That is the plan.' Bormann stuck out his jaw and the fire of his eyes intensified. 'Every single indignity visited upon the protectors of the Third Reich will be avenged one hundred fold.'

Ja, Mein Fuehrer – that is the plan, Eisner agreed silently.

'Tell me, Eisner, how do you feel our women and children will adapt here? You have no wife, of course.'

'They are all Germans. They will survive as before, confident in the future. The Argentines have lived on the continent for well over a decade. Can Germans do less than that?'

'Well said. But we do have some young unattached men, several more than unattached women. I am concerned about that.'

'They are all breeders. They will be satisfied.'

'We can tolerate no jealousy. I will not stand for that!

The wives must not be approached. The sanctity of the German family must be maintained. I hold you responsible for that, Eisner. You are old and may have forgotten the urgency of young men's juices. There can be problems.'

'I am not *that* old. I will see that the men are kept busy. That slows down the flow of the "juices," as you so aptly put it. And our breeding program provides for each man to satisfy his needs.'

'I want you to keep several women aside. Do not allow them to become pregnant. They will be a safety valve.'

Why this sudden interest in such matters? wondered Eisner as he assured the old man, 'I have already planned for that.'

'Good. And I, as their fuehrer, must ensure that those women are in turn rewarded later with children. Do you understand that, Eisner? They will be disappointed that they are not allowed to bear children right away for the Reich. You must reassure them of their role in our plan.'

The deep snow of the Joerg Plateau appeared through the break in the clouds. Several holes had been passed during the last twenty minutes and the radio navigational gauge showed that Argentino Station was dead ahead at a distance of eighty nautical miles.

'We will try the next one,' said the pilot. 'Turn on the Fasten Seat Belt and No Smoking signs.'

The copilot reached overhead and pushed up a small silver toggle switch.

'We are there!' announced Eisner, directing the other passengers' attention to the illumination of the sign on the forward bulkhead. The sign was a formality. No one was smoking and all had kept their seat belts securely fastened after the long bout with the bouncy air.

A few minutes later, they heard the diminished roar of the engines as the pilot retarded the throttles.

'This looks wide enough,' announced the pilot to his companion in the right seat. The break in the clouds was several kilometers wide. He dropped his left wing and began a tight spiral toward the snow below.

Eisner turned and peered through the canvas mesh of his seat back and out his window. They were dropping fast, in a very steep bank. What was it his air force friends used to say about a sucker hole, an inviting break in the cloud cover that, once entered, closed back up and left the pilot confused until he lost control or smashed into the mountains? This seemed to be such a situation. The montage of snow below and clouds around was spinning rapidly and at times he was not sure which substance he was viewing, the precipitated water in the sky or the solid water on the surface.

Abruptly, the pilot reversed the direction of the turn and pulled off even more power. The Skytrain dropped like a shotgunned duck, passing for a moment through a curtain of clouds and then breaking again into the clear. The bank was almost vertical and Eisner could not only see the surface and the clouds but the blue of the sky above. Surely the fool up forward was not going to try acrobatics to remain within the sucker hole!

The wings leveled and the aircraft screamed down the steep invisible slope of its desperate descent. Then they were underneath. The nose pulled up to level flight and the reassuring surge of power told Eisner that they were now back on their course to Argentino Station. Perhaps this was everyday stuff to the men in the cockpit; to Eisner, it was only a bad decision away from sheer madness. He judged their distance above the surface to be only a thousand meters or so, with the base of the clouds only a few score meters above the cruising Skytrain. The multilayered clouds were diffusing the sun's rays, which made any definitive examination of the plateau very difficult. Only the presence of the coastal mountains to their left prevented a complete whiteout situation. Thankfully, the dark rocky outcroppings gave some reference points, for the human eye was easily confused by the common color of the snow and the clouds. Several severely crevassed glaciers flowed from between the various peaks onto the plateau floor, spreading out in fan-shaped tongues of crumbled ice, the enormous force of their weight creating pressure ridges far out on the plateau itself. Argentino Station was not in the most desirable spot on the Antarctic continent. But the mountains could contain valuable minerals for future exploitation, and just beyond them was the great slab of the Filchner Ice Shelf, which could be an alternate avenue of supply should the treacherous weather over the Antarctic Peninsula preclude air support.

Suddenly a great blue dome flashed by beneath the LC-47, its surface swept clean of the falling snow by winds from the same storm. Eisner had only time for a quick look before the structure passed from his view, but there had been time enough to spot a smooth snow airstrip and the dark blotches of several small outbuildings. The Skytrain resumed its descent and leaned into a graceful turn back toward the dome. Eisner could see the main landing gear skis lower slowly below the wide wing and felt the vibration as they disrupted the airflow. As soon as they clunked into place, the wing flaps dropped to their lowered position and the aircraft steadied into its final descent. The snow was racing under the skis when the pilot reduced his power to idle and raised the nose. The Skytrain hung for a moment only inches above the snow, then the skis settled onto the surface, rocking back and forth as they followed the uneven contours of the skiway. Despite their undulating action, the landing was smooth and the tail of the twin-engined Douglas dropped as the plane slowed. They had arrived.

A twelve-man honor guard, unarmed but in the warm alpine uniforms of Wehrmacht mountain troops and wearing on their left arms colorful red, white, and black swastika armbands, were at rigid attention, and beyond them was a small group of station personnel. Eisner recognized the Argentine station adviser and his chief scientific assistant, Bormann's five ministers, and the fuehrer's wife.

He and the other passengers stood aside as Bormann stepped down the flimsy aluminum ladder from the open cargo hatch, steadied by the solicitous hands of two of his special guards.

'Sieg!'
'Heil!'
'Sieg!'
'Heil!'
'Sieg!'
'Heil!'

Bormann raised his right arm and allowed his hand to flop backward, palm up. As he lowered it, the honor guard and others dropped their stiff salutes in unison. The station adviser bowed slightly and led him toward the entrance of the dome.

Eisner followed, along with the other four passengers. The impressive metal dome was a good seventy meters in diameter, its rounded top supporting the flapping sky-blue and white flag of Argentina. Eisner judged the dome to be twenty meters in height. Entering the personnel storm lock, he found his estimate to be correct with respect to the outside snow surface, but well short of the overall dimension of the dome. It sat over a deep, round depression. The inside height to the top of the dome was at least forty meters and he immediately noticed a rise in temperature, probably to a level near ten degrees Centigrade. The inside temperature of the buildings was undoubtedly at a normal living level. The dome was supported by a complex interweaving of arched steel beams joined to a massive reinforcing plate at their apogee. Off to the left was a larger inside door, obviously a passage for the vehicles attached to the station. An array of snowcats, front loaders, scrapers, tractors, and snowmobiles was parked near the wide door. The entire interior under the dome was softly lighted with a series of fluorescent-rod clusters, giving a twilight effect. A single UH-34 Sikorsky helicopter sat nearest the vehicle door, its bulbous nose and vertical tail plane painted international orange. The old reciprocating-engine workhorse was apparently the station's primary search and rescue vehicle.

Bormann and his party were led into the building that sat farthest from the entrance. The advance party had done its work well. The colorful military banners that had lined the hacienda annex hall back at Lake Argentino were positioned around the walls of a central hall, a meeting room thirteen meters square. At the far end, the group passed through a single door into an anteroom and beyond it into Bormann's office. The two spaces were duplicates of those back in Argentina. There was one difference, however. On the right wall of Bormann's office was another door and he was directed to it.

'Our living quarters,' explained his wife as an aide opened the door.

Bormann turned. 'I will take a few moments to refresh myself.'

'Certainly, Mein Fuehrer,' responded Eisner. 'I will see that the others are settled.'

'You will be showing me the entire complex soon?' inquired Bormann of the station adviser.

'At your convenience, of course.'

'In twenty minutes.' Without waiting for confirmation, Bormann disappeared into his quarters and his wife closed the door behind them.

The complex under the dome was a complete minicity. Living and berthing quarters were arranged around a dining and recreation area, all within the largest structure under the dome. Families were provided suites; single personnel had individual two-room compartments, except for the military detachment, consisting of the honor guard and a security force, who were berthed in a single barracks divided into two sections. The second section housed individual cubicles and a central lounge for the unmarried females.

A complete medical and dental facility occupied one of the smaller huts and a geological laboratory filled another. Behind the medical facility was the special laboratory. An education and library hut sat beside the main personnel structure. Finally, there was a cluster of huts to house the station support facilities and a larger, more sophisticated one within which hummed the nuclear energy of the station power supply.

Eisner walked among the huts, studying each. There were no windows, for it was continuous twilight within the dome and the light within the huts themselves was controlled to conform to the norms of day and night illumination. A few personnel were busy outside the huts, carrying routine maintenance and upkeep duties. A bright red snowcat rumbled in through the vehicle entrance storm lock, its metal tracks slinging snow and its top surface covered with several inches of it.

All in all, thought Eisner, it was not too bad a place. His watch reminded him of his meeting with Bormann.

'Well, we are here,' stated Bormann as he seated himself behind his desk.

'Are your quarters comfortable?' asked Eisner.

Bormann ignored the question. 'I have some things to cover with you. First of all, I want our people to be running this station by the end of the month and the Argentines out.'

'Including the power plant crew?'

'Yes. We have our own nuclear-trained personnel, do we not?'

'We do, but they need a complete familiarization.'

'The end of the month. I recognize that our presence here must be kept quiet; however, I wish the security force to remain in uniform to remind us of our purpose. There will be ample time to change in the event of impending visits from outsiders.'

'I would not recommend such dress outside the dome.'

'I agree. As for scientific personnel, they are minimum in number since this is primarily a colony of settlers. We cannot prevent the arrival of scientific visitors, but Mignone assured me that there will be few and we can prepare for them also. Once the Argentine turnover crew leaves, I intend to exercise control over all visitors.'

'The station will still be Argentine territory. There are the treaty provisions of open stations.'

'If forced, we will abide by those provisions, but we must resist them as a matter of routine. That will be your responsibility. I want the skiway kept too rough for use except for the times we are expecting resupply. I want no one dropping in on us unexpectedly.'

'Helicopters do not need a skiway,' cautioned Bormann.

'The closest foreign base is the West German camp on the ice shelf.'

'Don't forget the Americans at their Siple Base.'

'They and the Filchner people are too far for routine helicopter travel. We can maintain our isolation if we are vigilant. It is important, now that we have a complete community together with little risk of outside interference, that we establish ourselves as the first citizens of the New Germany. We must develop a model lifestyle. That is our primary purpose and this is our first opportunity to do so.'

Bormann left his mouth open as if he were going to say more, but after a few moments closed it and lowered his head in thought. Eisner waited several minutes before inquiring, 'Is that all, Mein Fuehrer?'

'No. I understand Scnell is joining us from Belgrano. I want him as my personal physician. Doctor Rarick can join the dispensary staff.'

'Doctor Scnell is involved in our special project. He will have duties that require much of his time. We have a February deadline on the delivery of the weapon.'

'Did everything arrive?'

'Yes. The laboratory is filled with our researchers at this very moment. We will have it ready. That is not the problem.'

'You speak as if there is another problem.'

'A minor one, Fuehrer. It is not worthy of your concern.'

Bormann grunted. 'You may go. I should rest. I will tour the complex tomorrow.'

Eisner stood, saluted with his heels and outstretched arm, and left Bormann's office.

'Welcome, Doktor,' greeted Eisner as Erich Scnell disembarked from the Argentine Air Force C-130. Within minutes the two men were in Eisner's office.

'You make our community complete,' said Eisner.

197

'I have been looking forward to this, to being with Germans again.'

'You wrote of some unpleasantness that hastened your departure from Belgrano.'

'An unfortunate incident, but a rather sensitive one. Involved in our weapons project, I was doing some basic research for the main team at Lake Argentino, here now, of course. One of the Argentine doctors stumbled upon some of my papers. I had to take steps, immediately of course. He had an unfortunate accident, but there was some friction. I was not too popular, I am afraid.'

'We will be comfortable here,' said Eisner, changing the subject.

'I think we will. We have only so many days remaining, you and I. It appears everything we need for our comfort is here – and our project. We came so very close before, Eisner. We have a second chance now.'

Eisner nodded. 'Yes – and everything is on schedule.'

The sky outside the dome was a brilliant blue, the intense white fire of the sun low on the northern horizon. Its angled rays struck the clean blue of the dome and bounced skyward in erratic bursts of shimmering reflection. Eisner had walked a half kilometer away from the station just to view the effect. The wind had died, and the blue and white flag of Argentina hung motionless around its staff atop the dome.

Eisner had to admit a certain harsh beauty about the scene. During the last two weeks, he had reconciled himself to this place. The colony was established. His people were rapidly taking over all of the station functions from the Argentines. Soon, only Germans would be occupying this lonely place. In just four months, the world would know of the return of the Third Reich.

And from the top of that gleaming staff crowning the blue dome would fly a different flag.

198

15

It was the third week in November before Brady returned, the six multinational inspection team members in tow.

Marc had finally sprung himself loose from his desk for a diesel fuel haul to Pole Station and was himself ten miles out of McMurdo on his return leg when he heard the admiral's plane call Williams Tower for landing clearance. Marc nosed over the Hercules and tried to close the gap between his and Brady's planes. If he could, they could all ride up to the Hill – the abbreviated name for McMurdo Station – on the same chopper.

'What's that vibration?' he asked Dare as the control column telegraphed a slight movement.

'Nose ski,' responded the plane captain. 'Mister Zinwicki nicked a fifty-five-gallon drum the other day while taxiing in.'

'I didn't hear about it.'

'No need to, sir. Some cargo yard idiot left the drum lying in the ice parking lot and it was half covered with snow. Visibility was lousy and he just scraped it. Loosened one of the edges of the Teflon coating on the bottom of the ski. Isn't noticeable until we indicate 260 knots or so.'

'I was riding right seat, Captain,' amplified Frosty, 'and neither one of us saw it.'

'Better get it fixed,' directed Marc.

'We keep gluing it back on and it keeps coming loose. We're scheduled for a Chi Chi check in another twenty-two hours. We'll get it repaired then.'

Brady's plane was on final approach. Marc was still five

miles out. A minute later, he rolled into his downwind leg and cut his base leg short. Too late. Brady's chopper was taking off in a swirling cloud of snow.

'This gonna be a carrier approach, Skipper?' inquired Dare as Marc continued his steep turn through the base leg and onto final with just enough straightaway left to drop full flaps and start a gradual flare.

'Might be. Should catch number three wire,' replied Marc.

'You transport types always have fantasies of flying fighters off the bird farms, like us carrier types,' needled Frosty. She liked to kid Marc about his multi-engine career as opposed to her brief but productive carrier duty.

'I'm qualified,' offered Marc in his defense, raising the nose just a tad more to let the Hercules settle onto the snow with barely a ripple. After all, like all naval aviators, he had qualified aboard ship before they would give him those wings of gold. 'Besides, this is a carrier bird.' A modified C-130 had, indeed, been taken aboard and flown from a carrier back in the sixties. An evaluation, the test had proved quite interesting. No tail hook involved, just a full-flaps, nose-high, slow-speed approach and a plop down on the angled deck. Reverse pitch and hit the brakes. All landings on centerline. Takeoffs were also innovative: full power, full flaps, release the brakes, and rotate. The carrier speed and wind over the deck allowed the bulky Herc to fly off, somewhat in the fashion of Doolittle's B-25s off the old *Hornet* early in World War II. Amazingly, the tests revealed that a C-130 could be operated from a carrier but not effectively; it took up too much deck space and a downed bird would have to have been pushed over the side to allow the carrier's complement of fighters and attack aircraft to operate.

'You missed number three,' taunted Frosty, evaluating in her mind where the third wire would have been.

'And number four . . . and number five . . . and . . .'
added Dare, getting into the spirit of things.

'Mind your gauges, petty officer Dare,' admonished
Marc good-naturedly.

By the time they slowed to a stop by the fuel bladders,
the helicopter was returning from the Hill. Marc crawled
from his seat and was aboard the Huey for its next run to
the Hill.

Disembarking, he walked the short distance to the
squadron hut. Entering his office, he was hailed by his
chief yeoman.

'The admiral's steward called, Captain. Dinner at 1900
at flag quarters.'

'Oh? Wonder who the guests will be?'

'I guess you'll be one of them, sir,' said the chief as he
placed another pile of papers atop the stack already
overflowing Marc's in basket.

'Technically. The admiral likes to use me as a buffer
when the conversation strays. Usually good chow,
though.'

'Steaks at the mess tonight, cooked the way you like
'em,' added the chief.

'Steaks are not just cooked in the admiral's mess, Chief,
they are "prepared."'

'Blessed are those who are wheels – for they shall go
around in circles.' The chief spoke the words over his
shoulder as he left Marc's office.

Marc took a disgusted look at the stack of papers and
followed him out.

At dinner, the steaks were perfect, as individually
ordered, and complemented with Ramon's special
McMurdo Fries – thick potato slices fried in oil laced with
beer – a fresh salad, and a bottle of New Zealand red
wine.

Brady's guests included Ben Molder, the senior

USARP scientist at McMurdo; Berel Kosciusco; Anatolii Kakushkin, the newly arrived Soviet exchange scientist; and Marc.

'I apologize for not being able to make the flight over to Vostok to pick you up, Doctor Kakushkin,' remarked Brady, motioning for Ramon to refill the wine glasses.

'No need for apology, Admiral. Your chief of staff was gracious substitute. I understand how duties sometimes alter plans. Was very good flight back to here. Lady pilot very competent.'

'Lieutenant Kohn. Yes, this is her third year with us. She has quite a background.'

'Very pretty, also. Tell me, Mister Kosciusco, is this your first time to Ice?'

'Yes,' replied the Israeli.

'Berel is a professor of behavioral science at the University of Colorado,' interjected Brady, using Kosciusco's cover identity as an explanation.

'You have fine Polish name, Professor.'

'It is a historical one.'

Brady wished the Israeli would offer more than simple replies. He could understand the slight discomfort Kosciusco might be feeling in the presence of the Russian, but this was a time for hospitality and civility.

'What are your projects for the season, Doctor?' asked Marc, directing his question to Kakushkin. Right on cue, Marc, thought Brady, let's keep the evening moving.

'I have some solar experiments, mostly the testing of small power generators.'

'Electric power, I presume.'

'No, actually mechanical energy, transformed from energy of sun's rays. On very small scale. Can also be converted for electrical energy if desired. Perhaps you would like to come to laboratory and I show you.'

'I'd like that,' responded Marc.

202

'Ramon!' Brady bellowed to the Filipino, who had retired to the small galley.

'Yes, sir?' immediately responded the messman, sticking his head through the partially opened door.

'What's the movie tonight?'

'I have a John Wayne movie, Admiral. *Stagecoach*.'

'I've got it on tape. Hell, take the rest of the night off. We'll chat for a while.' Turning back to his guests, Brady continued, 'Seen that one twice already this past month. Love the Duke.' Brady chuckled to himself and took a deep swallow of his bourbon and water before going on, 'Doctor Kakushkin, Berel, the winter-over crew a year back got hut fever halfway through their isolation. Cut all of the bedroom scenes out of the winter-over films and spliced them into a two-hour extravaganza of Hollywood sex, the scenes unrelated of course, but devastatingly funny when you viewed them one after the other. The movie exchange got so damn mad, they won't give us anything but old Westerns this year. Of course, with the closed-circuit TV in the camp now, we have plenty of video stuff, some of it pretty raunchy.'

'I like cowboys,' volunteered Kakushkin, 'American shoot-'em-ups! Virtue always triumphs. Man in white hat rescues maiden and lives happily ever after with horse! Not very Russian, I think.'

'You don't have Soviet cowboys, Doctor?' asked Marc.

'Nyet! We have Cossacks and the Steppes; glorious revolutionary battles.' Leaning forward, he added, 'Sometimes as outlandish as your cowboy stories! Only Cossack does not live happily ever after with horse.' He winked impishly. 'In my country, we prefer womens!'

During the laughter, Brady placed a fresh decanter of coffee on the table, along with bottles of brandy and scotch.

'That was an excellent meal, Admiral,' spoke up Kosciusco.

'Thank you. Coffee? Brandy? Scotch?'

While Brady poured the whiskeys, his guests rearranged their chairs in a more conversational grouping.

Kakushkin alone accepted the offer of a cigar. He bit off the tip and leaned forward to accept a light from Brady. He drew in a satisfying puff and glanced over his glasses at the admiral. 'I have asked that my name be put on inspection party list. I did not mean to be presumptuous, but it is such opportunity since our designee at Vostok not able to participate. Is that all right?'

'Of course,' replied Brady. 'We are trying to firm up the schedule now. Showa and the Aussies over at Davis Station have replied. We are waiting on the Argentines.'

'I understand their new base, Argentino Station, is complete and is being staffed now. Will we get opportunity for visit there?'

'I don't know. We've requested it, but this is the first year's operation and they may desire a bit more time to make it presentable. We will be going to Belgrano I. Will you be taking the flight, Marc?' asked Brady.

'I intend to. I've never been to Belgrano or Showa.'

'Belgrano is not suitable for large airplane is my understanding. How will we reach it? asked Kakushkin.

'With skis we should be able to get in all right,' explained Marc. 'The timing is good this month to complete the inspection. December and January have many field support requirements and the helicopters will be heavily scheduled for scientific support.'

'This must be a fascinating operation for you flyers,' commented Kosciusco, 'and very demanding.'

'Right on both counts,' agreed Marc.

Brady pointed to a wall map of the continent. The long finger of the Antarctic Peninsula pointed almost to the tip of South America, but the scale was misleading as there was more than 500 miles of open water between the two continents. With the peninsula at the top of the map, the Filchner Ice Shelf was just to its right, and on the easternmost edge of the permanent sea ice was a red circle designating the Argentines' Belgrano I Station. 'The weather over on the peninsula is some of the worst, and it can get damn lousy over the ice shelf, but there are no mountains around Belgrano, if we discount the continental rise thirty miles to the east. We could get aced out, but with any kind of ceiling and visibility we can let down to seaward and get in.'

'What about Argentino Station? Is in much better position for skiplane access, no?' asked Kakushkin, knocking an inch-long ash from his cigar.

Brady rose and walked over to the map. Using a pencil as a pointer, he continued, 'No, not really. Here is Argentino, over on the east side of Joerg Plateau, just off the base of Mount Edward. Heavily crevassed around that area, although they do have plans for a skiway. Not a place you would want to wander very far from on the surface.'

'Why did they put it there, then?' asked Kosciusco.

'There have been some interesting mineral finds in the nearby Wilkins Mountains, here. Even preliminary indications of possible uranium deposits. In keeping with the Argentines' colonization program, which establishes stations near important areas of their territorial claims, it was a very desirable spot.'

'But, is so remote. Resupply most difficult, particularly when you consider needs of women and children,' observed Kakushkin.

'True. We used to have a station near there, old Eights Station, here just about 150 miles west. Abandoned now, although the Kiwis plan to use it for a couple of weeks this season. Actually, our current Siple Station is in the same general area. We'll be stopping there for a phase of the inspection also.' As he talked, Brady indicated Siple, roughly 200 miles closer to McMurdo than the old Eights Station. 'Eights used to be a bear of a place to get into. A four-and-a-half-hour flight from McMurdo and you never knew what the damn weather was going to be. So, we can expect the same circumstances if we go to Argentino.'

Ben Molder had been characteristically quiet through the evening. A large man, with thick black hair that had a tendency to kink, and small brown eyes that required the assistance of thick glasses, he was a man of few words, but when he did speak it was always with authority and expertise. 'That makes Argentino Station an ideal test bed for their advanced-concept base. If they can live there, they can live anywhere on the continent. And they have done a remarkably fine job. The interior buildings are all prefabricated modules, complete with wiring, plumbing, and heating facilities. They just sort of plug together and are all connected to the central reactor unit, which is several times more capable than but actually smaller physically than the old Martin plant we had on the side of Observation Hill back in the sixties. They will chemically grow a great deal of their food, have plenty of water by melting the snow, and have available education and entertainment facilities by the extensive use of closed-circuit TV and computer terminals. Solar energy is an iffy thing, since the cloud cover at the base of the peninsula is considerable year-round, but the nuke plant solves that problem. And the exterior dome eliminates many of the weather hazards – blizzard winds and visibilities, for example. When it is bad, they simply stay inside, all self-contained. Of course, they will still require extensive resupply, but that can be fitted in during periods of good weather.'

'Remarkable,' observed the Israeli.

'And expensive,' added Marc. 'But, they are quite serious about colonization and have sacrificed scientific budget money for living requirements. As I read the last report of their proposals, they will populate Argentino Station with ordinary family types with sufficient skills to sustain a small settlement: teachers, tradesmen, medical people, cooks, and so on.'

Kakushkin raised his head and checked the time on the wall clock. 'Admiral, gentlemen, it has been most pleasant evening but I must excuse myself. I have meeting with your USARP solar study group. Please, excuse me, Admiral. I go now.'

'Of course, Doctor. Thank you for coming. We are looking forward to your work with us.'

The three men at the table rose in unison as the Russian reached for his parka and black leather-trimmed fur hat.

'I should excuse myself, also, Admiral,' volunteered Kosciusco, but remained in his position as Brady raised a hand in mild protest. 'Please, Berel, if you can, stay for a nightcap. You too, Marc.'

Kakushkin thanked everyone a final time as he stepped into the storm lock.

'Please, sit down,' invited Brady. 'I couldn't address this subject with the Russian here, but this might be a good time to discuss this Erich Scnell thing, Kosciusco.' By switching to the Israeli's last name, Brady was indicating that the conversation had now switched from the casual exchange over dinner to official talk time. 'Just what do you plan?'

'I must confirm that the man is present at Belgrano.'

'And if he is?'

'Then, we must think of some way to convince the Argentines to extradite him.'

'You recognize the American position on all this?'

'As your State Department representative briefed me in Washington, yes, at their Office of Oceans and Polar Affairs.'

'I was not privy to that briefing. Perhaps you would care to inform me of what was said.'

'Your government agreed to reserve a place for me as a member of the US team, under the cover you are familiar with.'

'Nothing else?'

'No.'

'Suppose he is there and the Argentines refuse extradition?'

'Then, I must find a way to kill him – forgive me for speaking so frankly.'

'Not on my goddamned watch! We have a different set of rules down here, Kosciusco. They have resulted in an unprecedented atmosphere of cooperation and coordination. There's no way I will jeopardize that, certainly not by condoning murder.'

'You do not understand, Admiral. I wish to confirm the man's presence this time. That is all. After I return to Israel, my government will request the extradition. Then, and only then, if the Argentines refuse, I must find a way to kill him. He is a war criminal, an SS doctor who mutilated and executed thousands of innocents. He must be brought to justice, and if that justice is death at my hands, then it will be.'

'I'll see you don't get a chance to rejoin us for that, believe me. Not that I'm not in sympathy with your cause. Hell, I'd like to shut the bastard's air off myself. But the war is long over.'

'Not our war,' said Kosciusco quietly. 'In any event, I suspect the Chileans will be cooperative.'

'Oh, shit. That, they will,' admitted Brady, recalling to

mind the long-standing feud between the two antarctic-active nations. Mentally, he could see several results stemming from the identification of Scnell, one being a miniwar right on the antarctic snows. 'Is our State Department aware of all this, what you say you must do if necessary?'

'I have spoken to them with the same words I have used with you.'

'How about the National Science Foundation? This is their ball game down here.'

'I only talked to them as a behavioral science professor. I assume your State Department has briefed all concerned parties.'

'Jesus, they better have. NSF takes a very dim view of any hanky-panky on the Ice. That's another reason I must ask for your discretion and why I asked Ben to sit in on this, also.'

Marc had completely forgotten the senior USARP was present! As Kakushkin had left, Molder had eased himself into the easy chair in front of the picture window and had not entered into the discussion.

Now, he did. 'We are aware of Berel's identity and his mission. I am the only one here in the scientific community who knows, of course. And we support it. A man of science, like the herr doktor, who abuses his skills in such an evil way, can expect no understanding from any true scientist. I hope Berel cuts his heart out, right on the spot.' Seeing the stunned expression on Brady's face, he modified his remark, 'Exaggeration for the sake of emphasis, Admiral.'

'Well, we will see you get your chance for identification, provided – and I say this most strongly – you do not in any way embarrass the United States on this inspection visit. If the Argentines want to keep the man hidden, they can do that. We have no right to probe their station any deeper than their hospitality permits.'

'I am prepred to live with that. Just get me there, Admiral. I will know if Scnell is at the station.'

Marc could see that Brady was not pleased with the possibility of Kosciusco overstepping his authority. The Israeli also sensed the admiral's concern, but that was secondary to the importance of his mission. 'Perhaps I should excuse myself now, unless you wish further information, Admiral.'

'No, just so we understand one another, and I believe we do.'

'I am sure of it. Goodnight, sir, and Commander Bradford. Ben.'

The four exchanged handshakes and Brady saw the Israeli to the door.

'I don't trust that man,' said Brady after the outer storm door slammed shut. 'Let's have a drink. We need to talk.'

Marc and Molder both accepted the scotches over ice, but Marc added a finger of water to his glass. 'I think all we have to do is keep an eye on him while we're there. That should not be difficult.'

Brady's grin was devilishly wide. 'Okay, my squadron commander, you've got the job. I don't want him left alone one second while we're there. I'll be busy taking care of protocol items, you know that.'

'I'll handle it, Admiral.'

'Those people are fanatics about retribution, you know.'

'Understandably so.'

'No, not in Antarctica. It's a new game down here. Man's last chance to live with himself. But, I grant the point. If Argentina is using the Ice to harbor a Nazi war criminal, the Jews have the right to take a crack at him. I just don't want them using our knife, that's all.'

'I'll be able to keep an eye on him, also,' added Molder.

'Good. Now, anybody for the Duke?'

'Hell, why not?' answered Marc, relaxed in the glow of the premium scotch. Molder shifted the position of the easy chair, and Marc sat down on the sofa, saving the best side for Brady.

The admiral slipped the tape into the VCR on top of the television and the opening credits of *Stagecoach* appeared.

'Hot damn,' said Brady. 'I surely do miss the Duke.'

'Wake up, Skipper! Tilley's on his way.' The words carried the soft southern accent of the exec. Marc sat up sleepily and reached over to the nightstand beside his bunk. Even in the darkness, he could see that it was only 0515. His cubicle was windowless so he could sleep regardless of the twenty-four-hour daylight outside the building. He switched on his lamp.

He had stayed much too long at the admiral's quarters. After *Stagecoach*, he and Ben Molder had joined Brady in several nightcaps and they had sat there until after two in the morning, swapping sea stories. He had been asleep less than three hours.

'You told me to let you know the moment Tilley was airborne,' added the exec, suspecting that it might have been more prudent to let his commanding officer sleep another hour or so. Tilley wouldn't hit the Ice for another three hours.

'Thanks. What's his ETA?'

'It's 0820.'

The trip to Belgrano I was scheduled for a 1000 departure. That was good. He wanted to be present when Tilley arrived. The flight in the DHC-7 was an epic one, in a sense. It had been more than twenty years since VXE-6 had flown anything down to the Ice other than the

211

C-130s. And the much lighter, smaller, four-engined DeHaviland turboprop had never been designed for long overwater flights, so there was some satisfaction in taking the aircraft beyond its normal capabilities.

'It's about time the old stud got here,' commented Marc, rolling upright and yawning as he dropped his legs over the side of the bunk. Today was November 20, but the first requirements for Tilley's Ranger were not until bearly December, so he had made his deadline. Eight weeks was no record, however, for a flight from Point Mugu to McMurdo, on either end of the scale. Back in the early days, the ancient C-47s had taken months, due to wind requirements and frequent mechanical difficulties.

After breakfast, Marc stopped by his office, signed out a couple of pieces of paperwork as a formality, and caught a helo shuttle to the airstrip. As he stood in the maintenance shack, waiting for some word from the control tower that Tilley was reporting in, he sipped coffee and made small talk with Boneyard Davis. Boneyard was actually one of Tilley's crew – the cargo and passenger handler – but there had been no room for him on the Ranger for the marginal flight down. With the added fuel requirements, there barely had been room for Tilley, his copilot, and his plane captain. And there certainly had been no cargo or passengers.

'I'm real anxious for Mister Tilley to get here with our airplane,' observed Boneyard. The black loadmaster striker was a favorite with his shipmates in VXE-6. A conscientious worker and a proud sky sailor, Boneyard could make the strings on an electric guitar not only sing but rock with the wildest and soar with the most classical musicians in the squadron. Whenever there was a lull, there was lean, lanky Boneyard and his instrument, treating his fellow men to sounds they never knew could come from a single instrument. A self-taught virtuoso, he was one of those rare individuals who had a perfect ear for music but could read not a note.

'Well, your wait is about over. We should be hearing him soon. How's your mother?'

Marc recalled the previous season when Boneyard had received news of his mother's cancer. Already a providing son, he started sending almost all of his pay for her medical bills. The crew had taken up a collection to help, but Marc knew that the money Boneyard could provide – a few hundred a month – and even the startling $6,300 raised by the squadron would be but a pittance compared to Boneyard's mother's medical bills. She couldn't qualify as a dependent since there were other children who should have been able to assist her. But Marc knew Boneyard was her principal supporter.

'She's just fine, Captain. The medicine hurts her, though.'

Radiation and chemotherapy did that.

'Well, you keep me informed. If she gets bad, I want you off the Ice and back home.'

'I will, sir. Thank you.'

The tower operator's voice came over the squawk box, 'VXE-6 Maintenance, tell your captain that the DeHaviland is twenty miles out.'

'Great!' exclaimed Marc, slapping Boneyard on the back. 'Let's go see your airplane.'

Together with the Quack, who had just walked in, Marc and Boneyard hurried out onto the ice parking apron and joined the growing group of squadron personnel. Control tower personnel had apparently called several offices and work spaces to announce Tilley's impending arrival.

'There he is!' shouted one of the men, pointing skyward beyond the west end of the airfield complex.

The tiny black blob was descending rapidly and as all watched, it grew wings and a high T-tail.

'And here he comes,' enthusiastically added Boneyard, fidgeting with sheer excitement. That was *his* airplane and *his* pilot.

'We're going to get dusted,' observed Marc.

The DeHaviland was now in an all-out dive, dropping toward the ice like a giant hawk swooping down for a hare.

'Uh-oh,' said Boneyard with some concern, 'he's got number four shut down.'

Sure enough, the right outboard propeller was rigid.

'Go, Mister Tilley, go!' rang out an anonymous voice over the excited chatter of the crowd. Everyone recognized that the swiftly diving Ranger was going to make a flyby, feathered number four notwithstanding.

Tilley leveled his arc less than fifty feet over the surface and came roaring right at the gathering of spectators.

Damn you, Tilley, thought Marc, you screw up this pass and bend that airplane and we'll all have fun before the accident board explaining why you ignored a bad engine for a flashy arrival.

Tilley was not about to screw up anything. He passed so closely overhead, everyone could see the cigar stuck in the middle of his arrival grin. Rolling sharply right, he pulled the screaming DeHaviland up into a contrail-creating climb, reversing his direction neatly and leveling his wings at the end of a perfect three-engined chandelle maneuver. Then he was back into the bank, smoking around a brief base to roll his wings level, with only a fifty-yard final to the ice runway. From the ice parking lot, it appeared to Marc and his men that the DeHaviland simply sank out of sight into the snow, for the ice runway was actually a trench, formed by scraping the thick layer of snow from the sea ice. The scraped snow was discarded on both sides of the iceway in long burrs that rose more than twelve feet. The effect was a trench, but it was wide and long, with the surface ice chopped and mixed with chemicals to give some friction for braking.

By the time Tilley taxied up to the waiting group, he had cut the other outboard engine. Finally, he cut his two inboards as the Ranger slid to a halt, its nose just ten feet from Marc, Boneyard, and the Quack.

'All right, where's the goddamned medicinal brandy for us heroic aviators?' shouted Tilley out the open pilot's window, his gapped teeth clamped firmly around the moist remnant of a cigar.

His copilot and plane captain followed him off the plane and all three were immediately enveloped by the happy throng of squadron mates. The Quack fished down deep into his parka pockets and came up with both hands full of pony bottles of brandy, saving a couple for himself and Marc. To the clamoring men he apologized, 'Sorry, no firewater for the Indians!' but hastily relented as the crowd loudly protested. He pointed toward a cardboard box held high by his chief hospital corpsman. 'They're animals, Chief! Save me!'

The chief passed out the tiny bottles.

'Welcome, Bud! We thought you had taken a wrong turn somewhere,' said Marc. 'What's with number four?'

'Well, the damn thing's been running as quiet as a Honolulu whore's moan – they all have. But a couple hours back, the fire warning light came on. Woke us all up, I'm telling you! No signs of a fire, though, and all the gauges read okay, so I feathered the sonuvabitch as a precaution. Probably the fire warning circuit. Hell, only you Herc drivers need four fans to drag your asses down here. I coulda glided the last hundred miles.'

'You go to Eights Station first week in December with a load of Kiwis.'

215

'No problem. We'll be ready. You all can just relax,' yelled Tilley above the din. 'Ole Bud Tilley is back on the Ice and the season is saved! I'm buyin'! A round for my friends, Quack!'

The chief passed out the few remaining bottles and ran for his life. The happy crowd began to disperse.

'How do you like the bird?' asked Marc, walking around the Ranger.

'Listen, I think this old girl is gonna open some eyes. She is all airplane, Canadian arctic in heritage and sturdy as a musk ox. I went out so heavy from Mugu that I left dents in the concrete, but she stuck her nose into the air and muscled her way up to cruising altitude as if she were filled with helium. Fuel-consumption figures right on the button. Are the skis here?'

'Yes.'

'We'll have them on by this afternoon and I'll give the old girl a snow checkout. The internal fuel tanks are rubber, bladders actually. We'll drain and purge them and then they'll collapse and we can get them out the cargo door.'

'Well, let your crew catch their breath. You can test fly tomorrow. You've had a long haul.'

'Shit. We've been partying for eight weeks, waiting for the weather and that damned generator at Hickam. We're ready to go to work. Boneyard, you black bastard, your vacation is over!'

Boneyard had been standing aside and Tilley grabbed him by the shoulders and kissed him square on the nose.

'Mister Tilley, it's good to see you, and we're going to show these Herc crews what flying and cargoing is all about!'

'Right on!' exclaimed Tilley as they exchanged high fives. Boneyard took a step backward.

'Mister Tilley claims he's a brother, Captain; his great grandfather married a slave.'

216

'No, Boneyard, I said my great grandfather *laid* a slave. My black blood is 100 percent illegit! And right now, I've got this strong cravin' for fried chicken and watermelon – what's over at the mess hut?'

Laughing, Boneyard excused himself and climbed on board the DHC-7. There were things he had to do, now that *his* pilot and *his* airplane were on the Ice.

'How's his mother?' inquired Tilley quietly.

'Apparently holding her own. I have a Red Cross contact who will let us know when it's about to happen.'

'She's a lucky woman to have a son like Boneyard. It's gonna break him up.'

'We'll get him back there in time.'

Tilley sagged. His audience was gone. 'Christ, I'm tired.'

'Why don't you go get yourself a rack? Maintenance has a crew ready to install the skis and take out the tanks. I'm flying the inspection party over to Siple and Belgrano I in an hour or so. We'll talk when I get back. I want a good evaluation of that airplane.'

'You're gonna love her. She's a good airplane.'

'Well, it's your project, including the paperwork.'

'That's what I've got a copilot for!'

Marc watched Tilley walk off toward the flight crews' sleeping huts. It was good to have the whole squadron finally on the Ice.

16

Siple Station welcomed the inspection party with a special lunch of steaks and hot apple pie. The inspection itself was carried out with the usual mix of scientific interest and professional examination, but everyone realized it was more of a formality than anything else. There were never any discrepancies, as all nations routinely obeyed the word and spirit of the Antarctic Treaty, so such occasions became opportunities to exchange ideas and see a few stations that the members of the inspection party were not familiar with.

By early afternoon, 129 was cruising at 26,000 feet in the cold, clear air over the Filchner Ice Shelf enroute to the Argentines' Belgrano I Station. Brady and Kakushkin were seated on the lower bunk seat and Berel Kosciusco was standing behind Marc, his eyes glued to the white panorama of sea ice passing below. Far off to their left, he could see the rugged mountains of the Antarctic Peninsula, most of them shrouded in multilayers of vicious-looking gray stratus. Marc had removed his head-set and the two men were exchanging comments about the passing scene.

'This is fabulous, Commander Bradford. I had no idea this continent could be so spectacularly beautiful.'

'That area over on the peninsula could change your mind. It's an awful place to get into, with countless inlets, bays, tiny harbors, islets, terrible terrain. Those clouds you see are dumping tons of snow, and inside some of those clouds is solid rock. We pick the best days for flights over there, believe me. How did you find Siple Station?'

'Very interesting and very isolated. It's a long way from McMurdo.'

'It's one of our main stations. Very strategically located for a number of scientific disciplines.'

Kosciusko leaned farther over to the cockpit windows to his left. 'Where is Argentino Station from here?'

'Just off our port wing, about 200 miles.'

'Hmmm.'

'We probably won't get to see it this season.'

'I envy you such duty. It is different from what a professional naval officer would normally expect.'

'Yes. But it is the best – and the worst – flying in the world. I feel very fortunate.'

'Can we expect this weather all the way to Belgrano?'

'Yes, we've picked a good day.'

Kosciusco studied the passing scene in silence for the next hour. One-two-nine droned effortlessly on toward Belgrano. Over Berkner Island, 15,000 square miles of unseen rock buried under the snow cover of the ice shelf, Marc reduced his power and started a cruise descent toward Belgrano I. From their present altitude, the island was indiscernible despite the snow-covered highest peak rising more than 3,000 feet.

'We're there?' questioned Kosciusco, stretching toward the windshield.

'About a hundred miles out. We should see it soon.'

Kosciusco peered ahead and out to the left. The edge of the sea ice provided a definitive reference point for his search for Belgrano. The deep blue Weddell Sea stretched beyond the left wing as far as his eyes could see. When they paralleled the edge of the ice shelf, Belgrano I would sit just inside the break between ice and ocean.

'There it is,' reported Marc. They were passing through 12,000 feet and dead ahead a cluster of black dots marked the camp's location. As they closed, the dots became buildings and huts, topped with all sorts of erect and dish antennae. To the south of the station, a long stretch of scraped snow waited for the descending Hercules.

'You'd better strap in,' instructed Marc.

Kosciusco turned and left the flight deck for his landing station back in the cargo compartment.

'I see a couple of aircraft off to the side of the skiway. Look like C-47s. And there's a Twin Otter,' reported Zinwicki.

'Looks smooth,' commented Marc, letting his eyes sweep the length of the skiway.

'We'll know in a moment.'

'There's the welcoming committee.'

A group of perhaps thirty people standing beside the parked aircraft waved excitedly as Marc took 129 down the skiway, barely fifty feet above the snow. 'Couldn't resist,' he said, pulling up and into a left turn for the downwind leg. 'I could see some wind streaks. I don't believe they've scraped it lately.'

'I noticed them, too. In fact, this side looked as though it had some rough spots. I'd stay left of center if you can.'

'Roger.'

Marc touched down with full flaps.

'Holy shit!' shouted Zinwicki as the Hercules shook and bounced across the rough surface. The navigator's coffee cup flew across the flight deck, slinging the dregs of cold coffee into the air.

Marc pressed back the power levers into their full reverse position. Finally the instrument panel stopped its Saint Vitus' dance and the Hercules vibrated to a stop. Cautiously, Marc taxied over to the waiting Argentines.

'Well, let's get out of this thing. I don't even want to look at the nose gear strut,' said Marc. Rough snow could pound the relatively fragile strut to pieces. But the nose didn't seem to be sitting low and the aircraft had taxied as normal. Disembarking, Marc left the postflight inspection to Dare and followed the inspection team and their hosts into the main hut.

In keeping with the norms of antactic hospitality, the Argentines had a buffet of snacks and hot drinks, the tables tended by women and young girls of the station. They were among the first permanent colonists of Antarctica and their cheeks glowed with excitement as they welcomed their guests and encouraged everyone to partake of the treats. Several heavily iced cakes had been prepared. Marc accepted a napkin full of cookies and a steaming mug of coffee before joining Brady and the others in a small anteroom.

'Welcome, gentlemen.' The station leader was just starting his informal speech, speaking in English, which was a common language to the members of the international group. 'We have been looking forward to this visit. You will find Belgrano I Station open to you, including the family living quarters. We have you berthed in hut number 27, which I feel you will find quite comfortable. For those in the inspection party, we have scheduled visits to our outlying facilities for this afternoon. Dinner at 1900 hours and we have a small celebration in your honor this evening. In the morning, we will be pleased to escort you through the buildings of the main camp and have set aside the ten o'clock hour for your critique. Please, I know you wish to depart after lunch, but you are welcome as long as you would care to stay with us. In your honor we have scheduled a special American classic film to be shown this evening, the production of *Stagecoach*, with your great John Wayne as the star.'

Marc watched Brady's face. There was not the slightest change in his smiling expression of interest. Standing, the admiral shook the station leader's offered hand. 'Thank you, Doctor Ginaldi, we appreciate this opportunity to enjoy your hospitality and exchange views and comments with your people. General Belgrano Station enjoys an enviable reputation as a forerunner in permanent settlements on the Ice and we shall try not to interfere with your normal routine.'

'Thank you, Admiral. Now, if you wish, we can break up into small teams and my people will escort you wherever you like.'

Marc and Zinwicki joined the team inspecting the airstrip. There was a lone primitive shack, perched on the edge of the parking area, which held the two C-47s and the Twin Otter. A large fuel bladder – Marc estimated a 15,000-gallon capacity – lay half buried beside the parking area. The single skiway was marked with fifty-five-gallon oil drums, similar in placement to those at McMurdo, and there was a TACAN facility. Apparently, the Argentines had no precision approach system.

By 2000, dinner had been consumed, after-dinner drinks had been enjoyed, and all were seated in the tiny theater hut for *Stagecoach*.

'I love the Duke, but would just as soon have waited a few weeks before another showing,' muttered the admiral over his shoulders as Marc took the seat behind him.

'American shoot-'em-ups,' replied Marc, parroting Kakushkin's succinct description of the Western genre. Berel Kosciusco took the seat to Marc's right.

'A very complete camp,' remarked the Israeli.

'See anybody you know?' asked Marc cryptically.

'Not yet. But our Russian friend and I have managed to get ourselves scheduled with the medical team. Tomorrow morning, we meet with the station medical officer and his staff.'

'That should prove interesting.' Marc was acutely aware that Brady had charged him with the responsibility of keeping an eye on Kosciusco. 'Who are the other team members?'

'Ben Molder and your Naval Support Force staff physician.'

Good, thought Marc. Ben could babysit the Israeli.

'Good morning, gentlemen. I am Doctor Steinhoff.'

Berel Kosciusco and Anatolii Kakushkin, each ignorant of the other's purpose in the visit, sat erect in their chairs, their ears tuned to the German accent and their eyes searching the face of their medical host. Obviously, the doctor was the right nationality but it was not Scnell.

'My assistant and I are at your disposal. Please feel free to familiarize yourself with our facility, which you can see is quite complete. We provide medical support for this community of men, women, and children, and I am happy to say our standard of health is equal to that on the mainland of Argentina.'

Kakushkin fingered the small plastic pouch in his pants pocket. Could Scnell have altered his facial appearance? Even if he had, the man before them was not the right physical size or age. He was young, perhaps still in his forties.

The tour of the medical facility took only forty-five minutes, after which the inspection team accepted Doctor Steinhoff's invitation for coffee and tea in his small office. His assistant had provided folding chairs and they sat around Steinhoff's desk in a compact cluster.

'Well, may I answer any of your questions?' solicited Steinhoff.

As they talked, the assistant poured the hot liquids and passed them around the group. Steinhoff sat his on his desk. There was no way Kakushkin could use the pill at the moment.

Brady's staff physician spoke up, 'Doctor Steinhoff,

you have an excellent facility for minor surgery, but what about major problems, for example, serious accidents or critical surgery – things of that type?'

'Everyone is given a thorough physical before coming here, of course, so we hope to eliminate potential problems. We cannot predict accidents, obviously. And serious illnesses do sometimes surface.' As he replied, Steinhoff rose and walked around to the front of his desk, taking his coffee. He sat on the edge of the desktop between Kosciusco and Kakushkin. 'There is the rare condition that requires surgical attention beyond our means. In that case, we have air evacuation facilities – you saw the aircraft – or we can radio the mainland for necessary personnel or a pickup.'

'Do you have a large staff here?' asked Kakushkin.

'Just me and one other physician,' answered Steinhoff. 'Doctor Raphael Ligussi. A gynecologist – for the ladies of the settlement. He was the dark-haired gentleman sitting at the other table at dinner last evening.'

Kakushkin recalled the man. He recalled every man at the dinner. Scnell had not been one of them. 'I had the impression there were three medical doctors here,' persisted Kakushkin, preempting Kosciusco, who had the same question on his lips.

Steinhoff appeared to hesitate before answering. The Russian was asking a lot of questions. 'There was another physician. He has been transferred to our new Argentino Station.'

Bingo! Kosciusco clenched his hands in his lap. That *had* to be Scnell, but the devil had slipped away, perhaps knowing full well one of the visiting team was Jewish, maybe even knowing Berel's true purpose. The bastard was clever. And the inspection team was not scheduled to visit Argentino. Suddenly, Berel was very tired and disgusted. It would take another year at least.

Kakushkin inwardly shrugged. So, there was no war criminal at Belgrano I. Perhaps he could ask for an early replacement at McMurdo. He fingered the pill and thought about his surroundings. A good KGB agent should never let an opportunity pass to sow a little discord. Certainly, Argentina would be embarrassed if one of the inspection team were to die at their station. Who more logical than the Polish Jew? Steinhoff had walked around in front of his desk and had sat his cup next to those of the Israeli and the Russian, the three containers forming a small cluster.

Kosciusco was busy writing something in a small notebook and Kakushkin, eyeing a four-drawer file cabinet against the back wall, saw a possible opportunity.

'Perhaps you have some statistics that would be of value to us,' suggested the Russian.

Steinhoff nodded. 'Let me give you a copy of last year's summary.'

Kakushkin tensed. Steinhoff was leaving the desk and walking to the file cabinet! Instinctively, the others in the room followed the doctor with their eyes. Kakushkin leaned forward, appearing to watch the activity as he reached for his cup. Allowing his fingers to extend beyond it, he dropped the pill into Kosciusco's coffee.

'Here we are.' Steinhoff returned to the front of the group holding a manila folder. 'I will have copies made for you.'

'Would you like a copy for your files, Toliya?'

Kakushkin turned to answer the voice behind him, flattered that someone would use Toliya rather than the more formal Anatolii. It was Ben Molder who had asked. 'Yes, I think that would be valuable, Ben.' Turning back around, he immediately saw that Kosciusco's cup was missing.

Steinhoff was still speaking. 'I have also prepared a

225

small listing of our equipment and . . . Mister Kosciusco, are you all right?'

Kosciusco was staring straight ahead, his eyes stretched open until they seemed to be ready to pop out. Rigid neck muscles thrust his head out and up and he gasped through a wide-open mouth.

'Heart attack!' shouted Kakushkin.

The staff physician jumped to his feet just as Kosciusco's body lurched forward and into the desk, his chin slamming down on the edge before his head slid down the front of the piece of furniture. Quickly, Steinhoff rushed forward and turned the Israeli onto his back. The staff physician started a CPR pounding of Kosciusco's chest while Steinhoff pried open his mouth and reached for his tongue to clear the air passage.

'Get him into the examining room! Quickly!' ordered Steinhoff.

On the table, Kosciusco turned deep blue and then all color began to fade from his rigid body.

Steinhoff's assistant had rolled a crash cart over to the table and thrust a filled hypodermic syringe into the doctor's hand. Steinhoff let it remain there. 'It is too late. He is gone.'

'We may be able to bring him back,' said the staff physician, continuing his CPR pounding.

'No, Doctor. He is an old man and you saw the severity and suddenness of the onslaught. A massive occlusion, I would say. If we are able to bring him back, it will be only a matter of minutes perhaps. Why put him through that? It is strange. It must be his heart, yet I have never seen such an intense eruption of rigidity of the whole body. He indicated no chest pain.'

Kakushkin had walked over to the doorway and stood with Molder and the two other members of the medical inspection team.

'God, he looked like he was in such agonizing pain,' remarked Molder.

'An autopsy will be required,' said the staff physician, 'but it will have to be in Christchurch. I will go alert the admiral.'

'Doctor, is such thing necessary?' asked Kakushkin. 'The old man just met his time.'

'We must assume one will be required before the New Zealand authorities will process the body through Christchurch. Unless we can certify the cause of death, the body will be quarantined until after the autopsy.'

'I see.'

'Well,' said Brady as 129 lifted from the rough skiway at Belgrano, 'this has been one hell of a day. Too bad. I liked the man.' He was speaking to the staff physician, who sat next to him on the flight-deck seat bunk.

'Admiral, that was no heart attack. Maybe a seizure of some kind that brought on heart collapse.'

'We've got a mess on our hands. An undercover Israeli agent dies on a mission like this. Could there be any connection?'

'We've maintained tight security on this. You only mentioned it to me before we left McMurdo.'

'That was because I was itchy that he was going to try something and I figured the more people keeping an eye on him, the better.'

'Admiral, it could very well be from natural causes. I didn't mean to infer anything.'

Brady nodded. 'God, suppose Steinhoff was really Scnell. If that bastard Nazi killed him, we've got a real donnybrook on our hands. But why would he? He had no way of knowing that Kosciusco was anyone other than who we listed him as – a member of our team. Surely, he

227

wouldn't be so reckless as to do anything just because the man was Jewish.'

'Let's wait for the autopsy.'

A long week passed before the autopsy report arrived from Christchurch. Brady was in his quarters when Marc relayed the message from communications.

'Natural causes, Admiral.'

Brady took the message and read the words. 'That's a load off my mind.'

Later that day, Kakushkin learned of the message and its comments. That night, he sat at the bar with mixed feelings. The pill had worked too well and left no trace of any foreign substance in the body. There would be no mystery or suspicion to cause any political disturbance. He almost regretted using Kosciusco for his attempt. The old man had been pleasant enough and had seemed to be so enthusiastic about going on the inspection.

17

'Well, Scnell, what do you think?' Kurt Eisner peered through the plastic viewplate of his safety suit and waited for Erich Scnell to reply.

'Everything is in order. Our people did a magnificent job of transporting the laboratory. If anything, this is a better facility than we had back at Lake Argentino. And certainly more secure. Let us go into the office and talk. I think we may be able to revise our completion date.'

The two men walked through the inner door of the double lock and closed it behind them. Instantly, a fierce shower burst forth from the ceiling, walls, and floors, the water steaming. Three minutes later a bell rang and the water stopped. Batteries of orange heat lamps lit the space as if they were standing in the sun. A minute later, the showers resumed their washdown, only instead of hot water there was a bright green liquid. Should there have been any leaks in their protective suits, they would have coughed from the penetration of the strong ammonia smell. Just as abruptly as it had started, the green-liquid shower ceased and the bell rang for a second time. The orange lights remained on.

Scnell watched a large dial on one wall. The six-inch black needle began a slow climb from the orange zone toward the green. As it steadied at the safe position, Eisner opened the outer door and the men stepped into an anteroom. Two attendants stood by as Scnell and Eisner pulled off their heavy fabric helmets and dropped their coveralls to the floor. They walked through a five-inch-deep footbath and dried their feet. The attendants watched carefully as an automatic retrieval device wrapped the plastic floor covering from where the men had dropped their discarded garments. The bag was sealed and the attendants placed it in an incinerator built into the wall. Scnell and Eisner passed through another door on the far wall, walked twenty feet down the narrow corridor, and passed into Scnell's office. The doctor poured them two large glasses of orange juice.

'You mentioned a possible speedup of the completion date,' observed Eisner.

'Yes. Of course, the weapon itself is, for all practical purposes, perfected. All that is required is its maufacture in sufficient quantity. Also, there is some design work to be done on the transportation containers. They must look like they hold ordinary articles of some kind. I have not decided just what ruse we will use. But it must be 100 percent accident proof.'

Eisner raised his eyebrows, 'I would hope so.'

'The main effort ahead of us is the vaccine. It must be equally effective and preferably in oral form. There is no way the Arabs could pass among their people, giving them injections, without detection. Even the logistics of such a method would be beyond their capability. Thus, a simple method of distribution must be provided. A solid pellet that could be easily swallowed would be best, I think.'

'How long would it be effective?'

'Long enough. The weapon cannot be passed from one recipient to another, even by body waste contamination. But anyone not taking the vaccine will positively die within a day, perhaps two. We will give the vaccine a safety factor, hopefully.'

'Hopefully?'

Scnell laughed. 'We are in a most dangerous area here. One slip, one inadvertent mistake in transporting or handling the weapon and the wrong people will start dying. When we deal with such a thing, there is always the possibility of an unknown factor creeping into our process.'

'We cannot afford any unknowns. We must have absolute control over a misuse of the weapon.'

Scnell sipped his orange juice. 'There is only one way to make sure.'

'What is that?'

'We must try it on someone who has been vaccinated.'

'Then, it is just a matter of selecting someone.'

'Someone we can do without, need I remind you? Just in case.'

Eisner laughed. 'Too bad this is not the old days. We had many volunteers then.'

'Ja!'

'All right. We will select someone when the time comes. Meanwhile, I wish to have a daily report on the progress of the project. I wish to know when you have decided upon the amount we will give the Arabs, how we will get it from this place to their hands – by that I mean what kind of container we will use – and finally, I want to know the instant the vaccine is ready.'

'Of course. I must rely upon you to ensure that the Argentine station keepers who are here are afforded no opportunity to become curious about these spaces.'

'That should not be a problem,' replied Eisner. 'This complex is a self-contained unit, the front dormitory being the only space of which they are aware. You and your people can come and go as you please, and I encourage that, commensurate with your time frame, of course. It would not be good for the others to feel you were too isolated from the normal camp life.'

'I see no problem there. My staff is fully capable. I completed all of my necessary basic research while I was at Belgrano. The actual manufacture does not require my constant presence. We will rotate.'

Eisner stood. 'Then I will go and brief Bormann.'

'He will be pleased, I am sure.'

'Pleased? The old bastard will jump for joy!'

18

There are days when all seems to be at peace with the world, although admittedly they come along not too frequently. But December 10 was such a day, despite the lingering regret over Kosciusco's death at Belgrano I. Marc had a long letter from Dorothy and a new snapshot of Jim. The inland resupply flights were on schedule and all six Hercules were in an up status. The science programs were going extremely well, and a happy scientist meant a relaxed senior USARP representative and a relaxed commander of VXE-6. Marc was so relaxed he had invited himself along on a quick helicopter trip over to Cape Crozier to pick up one of the two-man USARP teams studying the Emperor penguins.

The day was unbelievably beautiful. Antarctica was a land of contrasts. The most harsh of lands but the most comfortable when one was prepared. The most vicious with weather but the most calm when clear. The most lonely when compared to the other homes of man but the most crowded when two people stood together on the Ice. The most colorless – a vivid study in black and white – and yet a place of incredible color contrast when the blue sky dominated and the orange sun shone brightly. Such was Antarctica when Marc arrived at the helicopter pad next to the squadron spaces at McMurdo. He climbed into the left seat beside the pilot, Lt 'Chopper' John Fitch. Chopper John should have been a member of the Royal Navy of Great Britain, for his handlebar mustache set off an angular face that seemed to have been created only for the purpose of displaying a most magnificent nose, the kind of macho proboscis had by grandfathers, not young helicopter pilots. He was six feet four in his stocking feet, an inch taller in his white arctic bunny boots, and he sat a helicopter cockpit as John Wayne had sat a cow pony. Chopper John's size overpowered the bucket seat and his crash-helmeted head touched the glass over his position. He was one of that special breed of naval aviator who was born to fly, the kind of consummate pilot you suspected was conceived in the darkened lounge of a 747, was raised in the shadow of an airport fence, and had soloed his first airplane at age sixteen. The last presumption was quite true for Chopper John. He was the kind of professional who didn't climb aboard an aircraft, he strapped it to his rear. The UH-1N Huey lost its individual identity when Chopper John fastened his seat belt and shoulder harness. The bird became an extension of its pilot's hands and feet, as sensitive to the situation and environment as his own flesh and as responsive as his own muscles. A three-year veteran of antarctic flying, he knew every square yard of ice, every canyon and mountain, every crevasse and glacier within 200 miles of Ross Island as well as he knew every bolt, nut, lever, wire, line, circuit, system, and specification of the Bell bird that was his ultimate love. He could make the Huey dance, sing, and think, sometimes all at once.

The twin turbojets roared to life and Chopper John engaged the main rotor. 'It's all yours, Skipper.'

That was another reason Marc liked to fly with the dean of the VXE-6 chopper jocks – he got to handle the controls. Not a qualified helicopter pilot, he nevertheless accepted every opportunity to try his hand at the world of the cyclic and the collective.

'It's just like chewing gum and whistling at the same time,' Chopper John had told him. 'An impossibility at first, but once you get the hang of it, you can even blow bubbles, too.'

Marc nodded, twisted the throttle grips on the collective arm, and neutralized the cyclic. The Huey lifted cleanly off the pad and swung around to face the distant airstrip as Marc transitioned from his takeoff hover to forward flight. He kept the skids only a few feet above the snow surface, the more to enjoy the effect of their forward speed as they raced across the ice-blanketed McMurdo Sound. Well clear of the tip of Hut Point Peninsula, he leaned into a wide, sweeping left turn and paralleled the eastern edge of the long finger of volcanic ash. Twenty minutes later he was abeam Mount Erebus, having climbed to 1,000 feet to enjoy the view of the smoking volcano and beyond it the dormant Mount Bird. The magnificence of Erebus always carried with it a slight sadness, for on the far side, near its base, was the site of the 1979 crash of Air New Zealand's Flight 901. On November 28 of that year, the crew of the sightseeing DC-10, unaware of a fatal error in their inertial navigation system, had driven the jumbo smack into the base of Erebus, releasing all 257 souls on board to their ultimate destinations. Better than anyone else, the aviators of VXE-6 understood the pull of the White Continent that could so easily lure you to an instant death if you did not remain always wary, always alert and have a system of double-checking position if the weather simply became too hazardous to continue. To press on with inadequate charts and lack of personal experience in the sky over Antarctica was to invite tragedy. Nothing illustrated that lesson more than the snows on the north slope of Erebus, which forever would cover the remains of the DC-10.

Marc turned inland and crossed over Terror Glacier, the wide river of superfrozen snow that flowed southward from Mount Terror, the third volcanic mountain on Ross

Island. Almost a mirror image of Erebus, Mount Terror rose 10,702 feet into the frigid sky – 1,544 feet short of the elevation of the crater rim of Erebus but equally as spectacular. Ahead, on the extreme eastern tip of Ross Island, lay the rookeries of the Emperor penguin, not only the largest of the antarctic flightless birds but also the heartiest, breeding and hatching its young in the dead of the fierce antarctic winter. Surrounded on the south side by dangerous ice pressure ridges and on the north by open water now that the summer was present, Cape Crozier presented a challenge to the helicopter driver who needed to touch down on the volcanic island. Winds were often high and gusty, sometimes in excess of a hundred knots. Then there would be no approach, much less a landing attempt. The USARP biologists who worked in the area were often stranded for days, occasionally weeks, while the weather roared and kept them in tents that somehow resisted the forces around them. Today, the weather was almost ideal, but there could still be hidden eddies of invisible atmosphere that would test the sklls of the most qualified helicopter aviators. Marc relinquished the controls and Chopper John swooped down over a long-deserted rock igloo, then turned into the wind to approach the two huddled figures who stood with bundled possessions, waving energetically. Their pickup was three days overdue and Marc suspected they were much wiser penguin students than when they had been delivered to the rocky and remote home of the Emperor a week back.

The wind was erratic and as Chopper John neared the pickup point, the Huey bounced and yawed, then tried to tilt and pitch in the rough air. Deftly, he matched every force with countercontrol input of his own and gradually they neared the two standing men. The scientists, in their ignorance of helicopter capabilities, had selected too steep a portion of the slope. They should have moved farther down the side of the hill where the terrain leveled somewhat. Marc was tempted to signal them to do just that, but he didn't want to preempt Chopper John's plan. After several aborted tries, Chopper John sat one skid of the Huey on the steep rocky slope and held the other clear in a level hover while his crewman hopped out and assisted the two scientists in boarding. The operation took less than a minute and Chopper John lifted the helicopter swiftly into the air, turning and transitioning as he did so.

'Want her back, Skipper?' asked the expert, nodding his head towards Marc's controls.

'I coulda done that,' announced Marc with false bravado as he once again guided the Huey across the slope below Mount Terror.

'Ha!' laughed Chopper John. 'And I can loop a loaded Hercules! Okay, next time over, you get to do the honor.'

'No way,' countered Marc, recognizing that what appeared to be a simple pickup was made that way by Chopper John, who had balanced the Huey and held it steady with a finesse that was not quite within Marc's capability.

They climbed halfway up the southern slope of Mount Erebus on the way back to McMurdo, then brushed the tip of Hut Point Peninsula before entering a graceful hover and settling back onto the helicopter pad with only the hint of a skid.

'Thanks, John, that was fun,' said Marc as he disembarked.

'Any time, Skipper, any time. Nice flight.'

The rotors wound down along with the shrill whine of the engines as Marc ran down the slope away from the pad and entered the back door into his office. As usual, the first sight that greeted him was the overflowing in basket. Begrudgingly, he grabbed the bottom papers and started reading.

He was almost through the stack when a soft knock interrupted his concentration.

'Come in, Sheila.'

Lieutenant Kohn acknowledged the invitation with a nod, entered Marc's office, and lowered herself into the straight-backed chair positioned across from him.

'Coffee?'

'No, thank you, Captain.'

Marc studied the young woman as he drained the last swallow from his cup. Their working relationship in a squadron that was frequently in the public eye had caused them to consult frequently with each other on a professional basis, and he had shared a number of flights with her, including the long series down across the Pacific from Mugu. He was very satisfied with her, both as his PR officer and as a pilot. Still, he had never tried to penetrate that invisible cloak of cool professionalism she seemed to wear twenty-four hours a day. Humorously, he had told himself that such a penetration, however slight, would constitute an offense. Consequently, he didn't feel that he really knew her intimately, yet they had shared some close times and he considered her a friend as well as a subordinate officer and aviator. He was comfortable with their relationship.

'How's the airplane?' he asked casually.

'A few minor gripes. We're scheduled for a Pole run this afternoon.'

'How many hours have you flown this month?'

'Oh, gosh . . . sixty-some-odd so far.'

'Well, I wish I were more available, but the paperwork keeps piling up. So, tell me, you look like you may have a problem.'

'Tilley.'

'Oh?'

'Captain, I am an officer in the United States Navy. It

238

is demeaning to have to put up with Commander Tilley's constant sexual harassment.'

Deep down in Marc's gut a little scratchy knot formed and sat heavily. All he needed was a sexual harassment charge to ruin what had started out as a very fine day. 'Tilley? Hey, I know he's aggressive when it comes to women, but I don't think he means anything out of line around you. It's all part of our camaraderie.'

'Patting a junior officer on the ass is not camaraderie.'

'Hey, professional football jocks do it all the time.'

'Women don't play professional football. If they did, it would be out of line there, too.'

Marc could see that his lone female officer was very serious with her comment and felt guilty that he had intially taken her opening remark so lightly. Maybe there was a real problem. But, the woman before him had a reputation for standoffishness. As he had so often observed, no one approached Frosty Kohn, not in a sexual way, not even in a romantic way, without a very chilly rebuff, and she had always handled the situations very well all by herself. Perhaps it was the pressure of being on the Ice, having the responsibility of leading a crew, being in what was for all practical purposes an all-male environment that was metamorphosing her natural irritability into a sense of harassment. Or it could be the incident with that reporter at the start of the season that was making her supersensitive.

'I'll talk to him if you like,' he offered.

'I don't know. It's just that I want to be one of the boys, so to speak. And then, just when I'm feeling comfortable, someone like Tilley comes along.'

'You'll never be just one of the boys, Sheila, and I don't mean that facetiously. You're an attractive young lady and you have to accept normal male-female interactions.' *That sounded dumb.*

'It's undignified. If I were in hot pants in a singles' bar – God forbid – then I'd expect it and cope with it. Here, I'm in the air 200 hours a month, and the few hours I get off I need to relax. I don't need a pat on the ass or on the head or anywhere.'

For the first time since she had entered, Marc recognized the early signs of fatigue. It was almost mid-December. They had flown together perhaps a half-dozen times since their October arrival. Other than that, he had seen her only another few times. She was either in the air or sleeping or they had just missed each other in the mess area or bar. He had taken her for granted. That was his mistake. She probably had logged more than 400 hours of demanding flight time in the past seventy days.

'I agree. When Tilley gets back from Siple, I'll talk to him. Are there any others that . . . act that way or show disrespect?'

'No, sir.'

'Sheila, I want you to take two days off. I'm in a lull here and can fly. I'll take your Pole run this afternoon.'

'Captain, you misunderstand. I'm not complaining about being overworked, I'm complaining about Tilley being oversexed.'

'Are you sure you're not overly irritated about this? Do you have it in the right perspective?'

'I think so. And I don't want to be grounded because I sounded off about Tilley.'

'You're not going to be. I understand your feeling and I am in sympathy with it. I do feel that Tilley doesn't mean the disrespect you attach to his actions, but I agree that they are uncalled for. Now, you go ahead with your Pole flight. When you come back, it's two days off. Period.'

'I don't really need that.'

'I need to fly. Let's put it that way.'

Sheila smiled. 'Maybe I am a little pooped. I just don't want it to show.'

'Sheila, let me say something between us as friends, man-and-woman friends. You are a fine officer and you know what I think of your ability as an aviator. Hell, if I had a dozen of your type, I could put the rest of the squadron out to permanent happy hour. But you're trying too hard to be something you simply can't be – a man. Now, hear me out. You want to be equal to a man with respect to flying and being a naval officer. You are. I could even turn that sentence around and say that some of my men want to be the equal of you as an aviator and officer. And they can be that. But none of them can be a woman. And there is no reason for you to want to be a man, nor them to be women. No matter what each of us is, we are ourselves first. And that is good and normal and expected by God and the chief of naval operations. I want you to be completely honest with me. Don't you ever look at any of your shipmates and wonder how a social evening would be with one of them – a date?'

'Of course. I date. You talked to Barry Gordon on the station ship when we came to the Ice.'

'He's a Kiwi, Sheila. He presents no competition to you. When is the last time you dated one of your fellow officers in the squadron?'

'I don't like to mix a business relationship with pleasure.'

'Hell, Sheila, this isn't a business. This is the US Navy. I have a drink with my officers, including you. We play racquetball together and watch football and do men things when we're away from home.'

'That's not dating.'

'Because same sexes don't date, Sheila. Opposite sexes date. And a normal male-female relationship between business associates – or naval aviators – is perfectly normal. Look, I'm no psychiatrist. Maybe this difficulty with Tilley is exactly what you make it to be, a simple out-of-line pass. Or maybe there's more to it, more in your frame of mind. If there is, as your commanding officer I need to know about it. Anything that can affect your flying ability and judgement is my concern, especially emotional stress. Maybe we need to bring in Doctor Holley on this. He's trained to recognize stress symptoms in flying personnel.'

'No.'

'It's nothing to be concerned about. The Quack is a good flight surgeon. He may be able to help with this.'

'Captain, I just don't want to be patted on the ass in broad daylight in front of my peers. Can't you accept that?'

'How about not in front of your peers?' asked Marc, trying to keep his smile fatherly.

Sheila hesitated for a second before replying. 'Under the right circumstances, it might not be out of line.'

'Good! Then all you and Tilley disagree on are the circumstances.'

Sheila relaxed in her chair. 'I guess so.'

'I hopes so. You're too valuable to this squadron to have such problems. Look, Sheila, maybe I can put the cork in this bottle by mentioning that even I have looked at you as other than a fellow officer. When you hit the deck of that swimming pool at Hickam in that string bikini, you would have aroused a monk. Surely, you are aware of that aspect of human nature.'

'It wasn't intentional.'

'Sure it was. Not for me. I just happened to be there. But you were conscious of all the young officers around the pool. The eligibles. That's healthy and normal.'

'I'm embarrassed. I didn't mean to attract you.'

'Of course not, but aren't you flattered? You should

242

be. I've a beautiful wife and a fine son, yet, when I see an attractive woman, I react. I keep it in perspective, that's all. And Tilley's perspective is different from mine. Am I making any sense?'

'As my commanding officer, yes.'

'As a man?'

Sheila hesitated for just a moment. Then, 'With all due respect, Captain, I almost think you are as horny as the lot of them.'

The impasse was broken. Somehow, Marc had penetrated that cool exterior. Their shared laughter testified to that.

'I'm sorry, Captain. I guess I just needed to talk.'

'Have a good flight to Pole, Sheila.'

'I will, sir.'

As she rose to leave, Marc added, 'And when you get back, two days off.'

Smiling, Sheila nodded. 'Aye, aye, sir.'

19

December continued to be a good month. The men were so busy, Christmas came and left with a minimum of disturbance to their frame of mind, although Father O'Gorley arrived on December 23 and spent the holiday season spreading his special brand of good cheer around McMurdo and among his countrymen over at Scott Base. The countless boxes of candies, cookies, and other sweets from families and friends added close to a half ton of accumulated weight to the officers, men, and women of VXE-6, but it quickly began to disappear under the work schedule, which remained close to eighty hours per week. Frosty Kohn used her two days off to ride with Chopper John on several of his runs to the penguin rookeries and to catch up on her letter writing and reading. Returning to the crew, revitalized and with a fresher look on her relationship with Tilley, she resumed her heavy flight schedule duties. Bud Tilley, at Eights Station, remained equally busy supporting the small Kiwi group of geologists and topographers with daily flights of the DeHaviland DHC-7 Ranger. The aircraft was proving to be the workhorse he predicted and his plane captain, along with Boneyard Davis, had only a minimum of routine maintenance to perform to keep the plane airworthy.

New Year's Eve saw the customary impromptu hut parties with an unusually large attendance, since Mother Antarctica started the new year by ushering in a three-day blizzard that stopped air operations cold – literally and figuratively. The weather delay was costly and the squadron was faced with an even more intensive effort to make up the lost time.

The visitor load at McMurdo slackened except for the working types, who required no special consideration, and Marc found himself free of much of the PR and administrative load of running the squadron. January 4 found him back in the command seat of 129, approaching South Pole Station.

'Full flaps,' ordered Marc as they passed through 9,500 feet, the radar altimeter indicating their distance above the polar plateau at 375 feet. The two figures did not quite agree with the latest computation of the elevation of the South Pole airstrip, but 35 feet of radar altitude was lost in the deep snow due to the peculiarities of wave reflection, and there could be other variables such as their altimeter's pressure setting. In any event, Marc had the Hercules set up for an instrument landing with a 150-knot airspeed and a nose high attitude.

Zinwicki lowered the flaps and a moment later announced, 'Skiway in sight.'

South Pole Station loomed out of the gray-white ice fog a half mile ahead. Seventy-three tons of airplane settled toward the two-mile-long frozen skiway like a pregnant swan, graceful despite a belly full of cargo.

Touchdown came with an almost imperceptible nibbling of Marc's seat cushion, the subtle vibrations telegraphing the instant of contact as the main skis ticked against the small imperfections of the dragged-snow skiway. Easing off the power, Marc allowed the nose ski to gently lower onto the two-mile-thick layer of polar snow. Then, back into reverse pitch, the heavily laden turboprop decelerated rapidly, immersed in an ice cloud of its own making. It majestically slid along the skiway until it came to a stop, exactly opposite the turnoff to the off-loading area.

'Hey, Skipper, you're getting as good as Lieutenant Frosty,' announced Dare from his flight engineer's perch.

'Lieutenant Kohn,' corrected Marc, gently reminding the petty officer of normal protocol with respect to enlisted types referring to their officers.

'You've got to fly with us more, Captain. You're getting as horseshit as those staff officers,' retorted Dare, adding, 'with all due respect, sir.'

Marc shook his head in surrender. He knew Dare would never refer to their female pilot as Frosty in her presence and would be very diplomatic whenever he did use the term. In the unique way of their special enlisted-officer relationship, it was actually a term of the most utmost respect. The enlisted troops never let down their hair with the officers unless there was that mutual respect and special camaraderie that was a hallmark of the all-volunteer antarctic air unit. It was a good relationship, informal but never slack, sometimes intimate but always professional. Partially as a result of that relationship, the officers were continually requesting tour extensions and the squadron enjoyed the highest shipping-over rate in the navy.

'There's the D-8,' said Zinwicki, referring to the giant Caterpillar tractor, which would reach into the open cargo bay of the Hercules and extract the giant suppository of cargo that had been inserted into the rear of the aircraft back at McMurdo. Within thirty minutes, 129 had been off-loaded; the crew had grabbed sandwiches from the galley building deep within the metal dome covering the station; and the C-130, now lightened by some twenty-five tons, was climbing above the fog bank, heading northward – grid south – back toward the giant Beard-more Glacier.

A loud and very sharp explosion startled the flight-deck crew.

'Window!' explained Dare before Marc or Zinwicki could react. Relieved that it was nothing critical, Marc twisted in his seat to see Dare pointing to the small side window over and just short of the navigator's position on the right side of the flight deck. It was glazed with a myriad of tiny cracks. Apparently cold-soaked while they had been shut down at Pole Station, it had been reheated rapidly during the climbout. Coupled with the normal flexing of the frigid fuselage frame holding it in place, it had been overstressed and had collapsed. Fortunately, it was a double-pane window and the outer panel was intact, so pressurization integrity was maintained.

'Maybe the window heat circuit was faulty,' suggested Zinwicki, not bothering to look up from his well-thumbed copy of *Naval Aviation News* magazine.

'Can we replace it back at McMurdo?' inquired Marc.

'I'm sure supply has some replacement panels,' replied Dare.

'When's our next flight?' asked Zinwicki.

'We have an Eights Station run with Frosty . . . Lieutenant Kohn . . . at 1700. That gives us plenty of time,' answered Dare, bowing his head slightly toward Marc at the words 'Lieutenant Kohn.'

'You're learning, sailor,' commented Marc. 'We'll make a petty officer out of you yet.'

Frosty Kohn moved her head close to the replaced window and ran her fingers around the edges to check the sealant and fasteners. 'Did you check the heating circuit?' she asked.

'Yes, ma'am. It checked okay,' replied Dare.

'That's the second one we've lost. Let's be more careful in how we heat them. Maybe keep the flight deck warmer when we're on deck.'

'Yes, ma'am, will do.'

'Then, let's do it.' Frosty strapped herself in the command pilot's seat.

Flight time to Eights Station was just under five hours and the flawless skies back at McMurdo were replaced by an angry mixture of ragged cloud layers and mischievous snow showers, a relative rarity within the supremely dry atmosphere over the continent. A solid overcast lay beneath 129 by the time the instrument panel clock indicated their estimated arrival time. Frosty used the temporary low frequency homer to position 120 directly over Eights Station and turned outbound for the descent. She would drop to 5,000 feet and then reverse her course back towards Eights, always remaining above known terrain elevations. The 3,600-foot Mount Rex, just a couple of miles north of Eights, was a reliable radar checkpoint and she guided the Hercules down through the broken layers of dirty stratus until her pressure altitude read 5,000 feet. That meant a distance of approximately 2,000 feet stretched from the underbelly of the C-130 to the unseen snow below; the figure would vary as she closed back towards Eights Station. She would go no lower until a favorable break in the clouds would allow a safe visual descent. The hole came ten minutes later and she spiraled down until she was below the base of the lowest layer of clouds. Her radar altimeter read 580 feet.

'It's pretty shitty down here,' observed Zinwicki.

'Eights should be ahead about eighteen to twenty miles,' reported Sergeant Wineman, his body leaning over his navigator's table and his eyes pressed into the rubber shield of his radar scope. 'I think I have it ten degrees starboard, fifteen miles.'

'If this garbage gets any worse, we'll make a one-eighty to the right and climb out,' decided Frosty, taking into consideration Mount Rex, whose peak was now almost 1,000 feet higher than the aircraft. They were over open snow, and the lack of exposed rock eliminated the possibility of any definition to judge visually their position over the surface.

'Ten miles, dead ahead,' ordered Wineman.

'Landing check,' ordered Frosty. Within the next minute, the giant skis were in position and the black blotches of the prefabricated buildings at Eights Station were in view. Frosty dropped down to 100 feet and eased the nose of the Hercules just enough to the right to line up a few yards away from the camp.

'Full flaps.'

'Flaps going full,' reported Zinwicki. A snow shower was moving right across in front of them. The top third of the camp structures, the only parts protruding above the snow, began to fade, obscured by the falling snow.

'We need the camp for depth perception,' announced Frosty. 'Come on, snow, hold off just a little longer.'

'I've lost them,' announced Zinwicki.

'Me, too. I'll stay on the gauges. Call contact if they reappear . . . we got it wired, folks.'

Zinwicki watched the radar altimeter drop from fifty to forty to thirty-five to . . . they were on. The C-130 settled onto the snow and Frosty held the yoke back as it plowed to a stop. Before they could even retract the flaps, the snow shower was passing and Eights Station came back into view thirty yards off their port side.

'You could have at least put it by the main hut, Lieutenant,' teased Dare, the words reflecting his awe at the precision with which Frosty had carried out the approach and landing.

After the short taxi, they parked the C-130 beside Tilley's DHC-7 Ranger, cut the power, and stepped off the airplane.

'We just about gave you up,' announced the Kiwi party leader. A ruddy-faced Scotsman, he stood bundled in a

249

heavy wool knit turtleneck sweater and had his teeth clamped around a curved pipe with a natural burl knot bowl. The pipe and he were puffing smoke in unison. 'Come'n inside, and we'll warm ya up a bit.' He led them down the dug trench to the storm lock of the first structure and they entered. Eights was a series of several prefabricated units, all flown in by C-130s and connected together after being put in place. The camp, more than twenty-five years old, had long been abandoned until the Kiwis dug it out and made it livable. They would be using it for a short time for topographic studies of the surrounding Ellsworth Land, primarily by a series of carefully planned snow soundings. Frosty, Zinwicki, Dare, Wineman, and the loadmaster gratefully accepted the hot tea and coffee.

'Where're Tilley and his crew?' asked Frosty.

'They're asleep, curled up in their bags like wee children. First time in more than thirty hours. I say, that man loves to fly and we couldn't ask for better support. He's something else, that Bud Tilley is, eh?'

'That he is,' replied Frosty dryly, pulling one of the straight chairs away from the wall. As she did so, it momentarily caught on a floor seam, which caused her to slop coffee onto her woolen shirt. 'Ah, doodle,' she exclaimed, embarrassed.

As they sipped the hot beverages, the wop-wop of an approaching helicopter penetrated the snow-covered walls. Within moments of its landing just outside, a snow-encrusted teddy bear walked into the hut, his hard flight helmet still in place. He peeled it off and pulled himself from his overstuffed parka. Grinning, he held out his hand. 'Well, hello, Yanks, a bit o' rough stuff out there, eh? I saw you touchin' down. Thought for a moment you were going to drive right inside the storm locker . . . name's Murray . . . Bill Murray.' He wore the epaulets of a squadron leader in the Royal New Zealand Air Force.

'Lieutenant Sheila Kohn,' said Frosty, returning his warm handclasp, 'and this is Lieutenant Zinwicki, Petty Officer Dare, Sergeant Wineman, and Sergeant Tanaka.' The group shook hands in the order of their introduction. 'Are you going back with us?' asked Frosty.

'No, we've a few more soundings to make. The outer team – they're about thirty kilometers from here – will be going back with you. I just checked on the inner team. They're in fine shape. Been carting them all over the northwest segment of our area. Just came back to refuel and I'll be going right out to fetch the others. I hope you don't mind the wait. We didn't expect you for another hour or so.'

'No problem,' replied Frosty. 'We've got a loose schedule for the rest of the night.'

Squadron Leader Murray blew on his hands and wrapped them around a mug of coffee. He walked over and plopped himself onto a worn plastic loveseat. 'We've had stinkin' weather this week. How's it over at McMurdo?'

'Been pretty good,' replied Zinwicki. 'We were surprised to hit the snow showers.'

'I know. They're a rarity over here. Too bloody dry, like everywhere else on this godforsaken continent. My old, tired Huey doesn't like the damn stuff any more than I do. She's pretty short on de-icing capability, you know.' He chuckled at the obvious. 'I bet you don't sweat the slush in your bird, eh?'

Frosty smiled. 'No, we can handle whatever comes along. The visibility gives us the same problems as everybody else, though.'

'I could see that! You drove her onto the deck out there and I was sure you must have been blind. Can't do that with a chopper, you know.'

'I thought you could just hover in zero airspeed and bring her on down,' commented Zinwicki.

'At the risk of your backside. Zero airspeed is with respect to the wind, not over the snow. You could be hovering sideways in a thirty-knot gale for all your airspeed'll tell you. That's one hell of a skid with respect to the surface. Touch her down in that and you'll roll up into a ball about the size of a pumpkin.'

Zinwicki was embarrassed at his oversight of a basic aerodynamic principle, the relationship of an aircraft with resepct to relative wind, which was independent of its path over the earth.

Squadron Leader Murray checked his watch and emptied his cup. 'We should be all tanked up by now. I'll be on my way.' As he pulled on his parka, he glanced over at Frosty Kohn. 'Lieutenant, would you like to ride along? We're only going to pick up two men and their personal gear. Have plenty of room. I can show you a bit of the antarctic bush. You probably miss the good stuff, cruising along there at high angels.'

'Why not?' answered Frosty. Her rides with Choppy John had given her an appreciation for the whirlybird side of operations. 'But I'm not too sure about this weather. I get enough thrills driving the Herc around.'

'Oh, it'll be all right. This bloody stuff comes and goes. We've been fighting it every day, almost. I'll be careful. Promise.' Murray crossed his heart and bowed.

'I should leave this shirt here to dry,' commented Frosty, starting to unbutton it. Quickly, she added, 'Don't worry, gentlemen, I have several layers on.'

'Darn,' exclaimed Zinwicki, snapping his fingers and cocking his head.

'Here, take my parka,' offered the camp leader.

'Thank you.' Frosty followed Squadron Leader Murray out the storm lock. The Kiwi Huey, an old B model, was only a few yards from the hut and the crew chief had restarted the engine. Instinctively ducking, Frosty accepted Murray's assistance in taking the right-hand seat. Within moments, he had strapped himself in, engaged the rotors, and lifted off. The immediate area around the camp was clear with only the low broken ceiling to remind her of the conditions when they had landed. Murray nosed over the whining Huey and they rapidly accelerated toward true east.

'They're ahead about ten minutes. Should be ready for us.'

Frosty nodded, starting to comment about the reduced visibility, which seemed to be right between them and their destination, but decided it might not be appropriate. She was Murray's guest. Still, as they swept across the snow, keeping their skids only a few feet above the surface, the situation didn't seem like it would clear. Murray altered his heading to the right.

'Looks a little closed in. We'll swing over here and pick up the rocks of the Lowell Thomas Mountains to keep us honest. I guess he was quite a celebrity, eh?'

'I suppose so. A bit before my time.' Frosty felt comforted by the appearance of the black rock outcroppings, surprised that the visibility to the southeast was so much better than to the east. The weather around them was mixed – very intense and solidly white in many areas while breaking up and providing good visibility in others. This was the environment she normally missed, except for takeoffs and landings, in the high-flying Hercules. At 30,000 feet, there was little impression of speed; at 30 feet, the impression was overwhelming.

'We'll go around and come in behind them. It looks like this stuff's moving west,' said Murray, picking his way among the patches of falling snow. Frosty watched the overall scene. It seemed to her that additional moisture was condensing and freezing all around them, but Murray unerringly guided the Huey through the areas of the most promising visibility. Nevertheless, Frosty could see that the farther southeast they flew, the farther they would have to work their way back to the northwest, and the terrain back that way was wearing a white veil. She knew that flying into that, either in a Hercules or a Huey, would be extremely hazardous. There also seemed to be a haze forming all around them, filling in the remaining clear areas and giving the few landmarks still visible a pale translucent coating. She felt as if she were looking at Antarctica through a camera lens that needed focusing.

For the next half hour, Murray worked farther southeast until they were within several miles of the base of the mountain cluster that ran out toward the Antarctic Peninsula. There was at least one 5,000-foot peak amid the snow-mantled rock.

They passed through a snow area, excpecting to come out the other side in a matter of seconds. Instead, the outside world disappeared. Murray reduced power and pulled back on the cyclic, allowing the helicopter to slow, nose high. With a great deal of peering and squinting out his side of the cabin, and hurried looks down to where the surface was supposed to be, he managed to reverse his direction and broke back out into the relatively clear area he had just left. Circling, he searched all around him.

'The bloody stuff's closing all around us. I don't like this at all.'

'Maybe we should head back,' volunteered Frosty.

'Wherever "back" is. I knew about where we were fifteen minutes ago. Right now, with all the twists and turns we've been making, I'm not so sure. One thing we can't do is work farther southeast. There are some good steep snow-covered slopes over there.'

Frosty felt her stomach muscles tighten, reflecting her brain's message that all was not well. 'Maybe we should just land and wait it out.'

'Not a bad idea. But take a good look at the surface – what you can see, of course.'

Frosty wiped the Plexiglas with her glove to get a clearer view. Gossamer wisps of snow were snaking across the surface, thousands of them, side by side, racing across the ripples and cracks of an area crisscrossed with fine crevasses. She didn't need to hear Murray's explanation that to touch down in this particular area could find them alighting on a fragile snow bridge across an unseen chasm. If that happened, the snow could collapse and the helicopter would be swallowed in the depthless mouth of the greatest white whale of all time.

'Let's see if we can find a more solid spot,' declared Murray, dropping to just above the surface and air taxiing across the crevasses. They seemed to be over an area where the weight of the snow piled up against the sides of nearby mountains was pressing down and out, forcing the surface under them into an endless series of pressure ridges. Some deterioration far down under the surface allowed sections of the snow to collapse, forming deep crevasses, which in turn were covered by more snow, either under pressure of the flow or from the precipitate's constant shifting and falling. Some of the crevasses could be seen by the telltale surface cracks; others were completely hidden. Either configuration could be lethal to the unwary who walked over them – or tried to set down a helicopter.

Another thirty minutes crept by. Frosty made some mental calculations. They could be as far as 100 miles from Eights Station by now, probably in a general south-easterly direction. Although they were unseen in the heavy weather, the coastal mountains had to be just a few

255

miles to the south and just beyond them the flat ice of the Filchner Ice Shelf.

'Maybe we should climb and head out over Filchner,' suggested Frosty.

Murray nodded and tried his radio. He was due for his hourly position report. 'Hello, Aights, this is Murray, position, over.' He tried again, and again. No answer. 'Isn't that the bleedin' way things always happen? In bunches. Going over the top to the ice shelf isn't a bad idea, providing this stuff doesn't go on out over the ice. Unfortunately, with this wet snow, I suspect we'd pick up a load of clear ice on the way up. Can't handle that. Also, if we set down out there with no communications, no one will ever find us. We better stay at least somewhere near our planned area.'

Frosty was not reassured by the slight quiver in his voice. She knew it wasn't panic or confusion. He was handling the situation about as well as it could be handled, and his control of the Huey was positive and considered. It was more probably anger, anger at himself for letting them get into such a predicament. He knew full well that he should have aborted the pickup try at the first encounter with the rapidly deteriorating weather.

'Well, I'll tell you what we're going to do. We'll ease a few miles north – this pressure area ends out there somewhere – and we'll set her down and wait it out.'

Not a bad decision, thought Frosty. I just hope it's not a tad late. We should have tried that when we could still see. She checked the tightness of her seat belt and harness. Murray continud to try to raise Eights on his radio. Apparently, the station had dropped off the face of the earth.

Fifteen minutes later, Murray set up a hover, heading the helicopter into his best estimate of the wind's direction. There was absolutely no visibility; they were suspended in a white void – a netherworld of the unreal.

Very slowly, Murray allowed the Huey to settle, both he and Frosty straining to catch even a momentary glimpse of the surface below. The radar altimeter read forty feet. They were close. The miniature snowstorm created by the downwash of the main rotor on the surface was all about them, but still there was no feeling of anything except space. Frosty knew that the electronic signals from the altimeter would penetrate the snow for a number of feet before encountering sufficient solid resistance to bounce back. In the Hercules they always used the thirty-five-foot figure as zero. Right now, the indicator in front of her registered thirty-five feet.

Despite the tension of the past hour and her resignation to the fact that they were in deep trouble, Frosty was still startled at the suddenness with which the situation had now become critical. She braced herself and tried to breathe slowly.

The initial impact was surprisingly soft and her apprehension was replaced by a momentary feeling of relief. It was premature. Either they had touched down on a steep slope or they were in a violent skid. The helicopter plunged over on its right side, Murray frantically trying to disengage the rotors before they hit the snow. There was no chance. The blades dug in and torqued the fuselage violently into the deep snow, left side up. A crushing force on Frosty's chest forced out an involuntary yell as she was battered around in the cockpit. Her back wrenched as her torso twisted violently in the grip of her shoulder straps. Then a thousand hammers pounded her head and all sensation ceased.

Marc was just preparing to call it a day when his duty officer walked into his sleeping cubicle.

'Skipper, we got trouble,' he said softly. Marc knew the

meaning of the set of the young lieutenant's eyes. Immediately, he grabbed his parka and pushed away from his writing table. 'What is it?' he asked, his body growing cold with the premonition of impending disaster.

'Frosty's missing – over at Eights.'

'Christ! What happened?'

'First of all, Skipper, 129 and her crew aren't involved. They landed over there early this evening to bring back a part of the Kiwi field party. She hopped a ride on the chopper going out to pick them up and they're three hours overdue. There's been no radio contact and the weather's lousy. Eights is on the horn over at the flight-following shack.'

It took less than three minutes for the two men to reach the room in the operations building set aside for monitoring the progress of logistic flights. Marc grabbed the microphone. 'Eights, this is Commander Bradford, what's the latest?'

A Kiwi voice replied, 'This is Duncan, the station leader, Commander. We've a bit of a tight situation here. Our logistic support helicopter is three hours overdue from a routine pickup. We have no radio contact and suspect he is down somewhere. Your Lieutenant Kohn is with him.'

'What was their last position?'

'We got none after they took off. Ordinarily, they would have made a position report an hour out.'

Marc cursed under his breath. 'What's your weather over there?'

'Blowing snow and stratus overhead. Visibility zero. We have alerted Lieutenant Commander Tilley and his crew and they're standing by.'

'Let me speak to Tilley, please.'

Tilley's gruff voice reported in, 'Tilley here, Skipper.

We're ready to go, but it's garbage outside and we won't see a thing even if we can get off.'

'Okay, Bud, use your own judgement and start a search as soon as you can. We'll divert a C-130 over – 131 is enroute back from Pole. I'll bring another Herc over ASAP, and an extra plane commander. That'll give us three 130s and your DeHaviland.'

'Why not throw a chopper in the ass end of that Herc you bring? There are shit-bad crevasses all over this area. They could be down in a bad place.'

'Will do. Stay on the horn. I'm putting the duty officer back on.' Marc relinquished the mike to the duty air controlman and pulled the duty officer aside. 'Call the admiral and tell him what's going on. I'll alert the strip to get . . . let's see, 132 has search-and-rescue duty . . . to get 132 alerted. Get hold of Chopper John and tell him to crank up the ready bird for a trip down to the strip.'

Marc stood aside while the duty officer carried out his instructions. Double-checking his decisions, he called the airstrip ready shack and instructed them to alert the SAR Hercules. Seeing that everything was being done that could be, he started to leave but met Brady at the storm lock.

'Anything further?' asked the admiral, peeling off his parka. 'I alerted the chief of staff. He's putting a clamp-down on the press who are here. I don't want any premature releases.'

'No, Admiral. I just talked to Tilley. The weather has him grounded. I'm diverting 131 on the way back from Pole Station. I'll take 132, with a Huey on board and an extra pilot. That'll give us three Hercs, Tilley's DHC-7, and a chopper for the search.'

'Good. They may have just made a precautionary landing.'

'God, I hope so.'

'How about Siple? Are they alerted?' asked Brady.

'No, I'll have the duty officer give them a call. They don't have any aircraft, but they can start a surface search by snowcat. Also, we should notify the Argentines over at Argentino. They may be of some help.'

'I'll take care of it. You go on down to the strip. Give me a call as soon as you reach Eights Station.'

'Will do, Admiral.'

'And Marc,' added Brady, touching him softly on the shoulder, 'don't worry about Frosty. She's tough stuff.'

'So's the Ice, Admiral.'

Marc could see Tilley's Ranger taking off as the Hercules dropped out of the cloud layers and touched down abeam Eights Station. Station leader Duncan was waiting.

'Still no word, but Tilley's out. I would recommend waiting until we get his weather report before launching anything else.'

Marc knew he should not be irritated at what was merely the Kiwi's attempt to be of assistance, but deciding whether to launch or not was his decision, not Duncan's. 'We have to off-load a chopper first, anyhow.'

Inside the camp complex, they stood by the radio and waited for some word from Tilley. They didn't have to wait long.

'Eights, this is nine-four-echo. We can't see a frigging thing out here. The only clear spot is at the camp. We have multilayered stratus and snow showers. Poor visibility underneath. We're going to proceed to your outer field party position and work back from there. Over.'

Marc answered, 'Roger, Bud, this is the captain. We've got Chopper John and a Huey with us. He'll be ready to go in about forty-five minutes. Any suggestions?'

'I'd have him stay underneath and retrace the Kiwi bird's track. I have to tell you, though, Skipper, there are places out here where the snow is damned heavy and blowing like the winds of hell. If they've pranged the bird, they'll be covered over before long.'

'Let's pray that's not the case. They could have just set down to wait it out.'

'I bet Frosty's pissed. I wouldn't want to be that chopper driver.'

Marc chuckled nervously. 'Me neither. She'll make him wish he'd never left his mother's knee. Who is it, anyhow?'

'Squadron Leader Murray. He's good. They must have had something unexpected happen.'

'Okay, Bud. Keep us informed. I'll let you know when the chopper's airborne.'

'Roger.'

Frosty felt she was encased in ice. She had no idea how long she had been out, but the first sensation she had been conscious of after the blow to her head was the strong smell of jet fuel. The smallest spark would cause a raging fire. Horrified, she had forced herself awake and now found she was immobilized by the torn metal of the forward fuselage. She couldn't see any blood or feel any broken bones, but there was a disturbing numbness in her left leg. She lay on her right side, as did the battered fuselage. Murray? Where was Murray? There was nothing but snow packed under and around her. 'Oh, God!' she uttered and tore into the snow with her hands. Scooping and probing, she dug deeper until her fingers caught on frozen cloth. Frantically, she plunged her hands deep and threw heavy clumps of snow away from his buried form. One hand struck the flesh of his face. She yanked off her glove and pressed her palm against his cheek. It was as cold as the snow and rock hard. 'Oh, Jesus, let him still be alive,' she prayed, knowing full well that he was not. It took the better part of an hour to uncover his head and shoulders. With her twisted back screaming silently in protest, she laid her bare face against his and reached inside his shirt to massage his chest. There could be no life. Neither the warmth of her body nor the tears that dripped from her cheeks would soften the hard flesh of the frozen squadron leader. Perhaps that was best. As she raised herself and scooped away additional snow, she could see a twisted piece of the cockpit door frame sticking into his right side, right through his rib cage. He had not suffered long. There was only a foot-wide stain of frozen blood.

She stiffened. A new noise was emerging above the whine of the wind – a low throaty chorus of hums. It was the unmistakable sound of turboprop engines! Not a C-130 – too high-pitched for that. It was Tilley's DeHaviland! Bud Tilley was overhead! 'Tilley!' she screamed. 'Down here! Down here! Down . . .' She mustn't panic. They were looking for her. They would find her. But, in time? Already, the twisted Huey was wearing a blanket of snow. It had to stop falling. 'Don't do this to me, God,' she whispered. Reaching up, she brushed back her hair. It was thickly matted on top with blood. She was cut somewhere.

Her body shook several times and suddenly overhead there was nothing but blue sky! A brilliant blue sky, full of soaring white gulls! 'No, no!' she yelled, forcing her stomach muscles to contract. I'm hallucinating, she thought. Shock! I've got to fight shock! She started to sing at the top of her voice, for some strange reason selecting the 'Battle Hymn of the Republic.' The exertion hurt too much. She let her body slump against her seat straps.

I've got to stay awake, I can't sleep . . . I must not sleep . . . Oh, God, Tilley, come and get me . . . Don't leave me down here, you bastard! . . . Come and get me, Bud, please . . . you can pat me on the ass, any time . . . just come and get me . . .

20

Even Antarctica seemed to be in mourning. The midday sky, which even when cloudless was normally a crisp blue with an eye-assaulting sun, was at the moment subdued, its color softened by a thin gray shroud of upper-atmosphere ice crystals. Several luminescent rings enclosed the sun, symbolic halos of the mood shared by the 73 officers and 475 men and women of VXE-6 who stood silently on the sea ice opposite the airfield camp.

The search for Frosty Kohn had been carried on for ten days, a maximum effort by the aircraft and surface vehicles of the US scientific and support forces. The New Zealanders at Eights had scoured the surface area around the camp and the Argentines at Argentino Station had provided their LC-47 and an Otter to augment the air search forces. But there were still vital operations to be continued and everyone knew that further efforts were futile. The weather had cleared and every square inch of snow surface within the range of the missing helicopter had been examined several times over. Everyone eventually recognized that the Kiwi Huey, with Squadron Leader Bill Murray and Lieutenant Sheila Kohn, had to be buried somewhere out there under the snows of the Joerg Plateau. The squadron had even dragged the area with an air-towed magnetometer, hoping to pick up a disturbance in the earth's magnetic field, which would have perhaps signaled the presence of buried metal debris. But there was no disturbance, just as there was no visual clue as to the fate of the helicopter.

Marc and Rear Admiral Brady arrived at the airstrip

formation by way of Chopper John and his helicopter shuttle. They stepped out and took a position facing the formation. Father O'Gorley and members of the admiral's staff were off to one side and behind the squadron personnel were small groups of station support people.

'Have the squadron stand at ease,' ordered Marc.

The exec, at attention in front of the amassed men and women, spoke softly, 'They have indicated they would prefer to remain at attention, Captain.'

Marc nodded. Frosty would like that, he thought as he turned and surrendered the microphone to Brady.

'Today, with the utmost reluctance, I have directed that the formal search for Lieutenant Kohn, and her New Zealand Air Force pilot, Squadron Leader Murray, be ended. I have informed the Bureau of Naval Personnel that Lieutenant Kohn is missing and have sent her next of kin condolences from all of us here standing on this ice. We all know what has happened, despite the lack of any positive confirmation that it has. It is the way of Antarctica, and we who come down here, year after year, know that we pay a price for our intrusion. At times like this, we wonder if that price is worth it. I believe Lieutenant Kohn would say it is. I am very proud to have served with her – and you.' Brady stepped back. Marc placed himself before the microphone.

'This is a rare day. For the first time in my memory, we stand here on the Ice as a squadron, momentarily forgoing our other obligations, to pay tribute to one of our own. We won't stop looking for Frosty Kohn; we love her too much. But we will resume our duties as she would want us to. The greatest tribute we can pay to our fallen shipmate is a continuation of our efforts here on the Ice. Frosty set the pace. We'll be hard-pressed to match it. But we will.

'I suspect she sees us assembled in her honor, and she

264

may be a little bit embarrassed. We're not, Frosty. We're very proud of the frozen tears on our cheeks and the cold lumps in our throats. You are the best of us and we will miss you.'

While Father O'Gorley gave the benediction, Marc searched the faces of his crew. The irreverent, boisterous, devil-may-care, hard-working men and women of VXE-6 were rigid at attention, eyes straight ahead. Six paces out in front of them, at the center of the formation, stood the exec, and at the conclusion of the priest's final blessing, he executed an about-face and gave a loud command.

'Antarctic Development Squadron Six, hand salute!'

Navy personnel in ranks normally did not salute. Their officers saluted for them. But this day, 548 individual hands raised in unison. As Marc, the admiral, and his staff joined the tribute, a low roar sounded behind them. It grew louder and louder, the ear-shattering crescendo of the four turboprop engines of an approaching Hercules. Marc looked questioningly at the exec, who responded by mouthing the explanation through smiling lips, 'Zinwicki.'

The C-130 passed over the formation at 100 feet, the awesome vibrations of its passing accentuating the emotion of the moment. Directly overhead, the engine closest to the command pilot's seat – Frosty's seat – was shut down and the propeller streamed itself in the wind and became silent. The Hercules, with its unique three-engined interpretation of the missing man formation, pulled sharply skyward to climb toward the sun. It was 129, with Frosty's crew, in a final salute.

Operations continued unabated. Tilley and his crew returned to Eights Station for the final week. The C-130s quickly resumed their back-to-back schedule of logistic and trail support flights, their double crews augmented by newly designated Aircraft Commander Zin Zinwicki. The squadron Hueys, paced by Chopper John, continued their daily shuttles between McMurdo and the airstrip as well as providing field support for those parties around Ross Island.

The summer heat, with occasional temperatures as high as thirty-four degrees Farenheit in the McMurdo camp, turned the snow-covered volcanic ash into slushy mud, and the sea ice over McMurdo Sound began to thin and crack. The ice runway developed dangerous cracks and was declared unsafe for service. Even the ice parking area and the airfield camp began to crack open, and with superhuman effort the men and women of VXE-6, aided by camp support personnel, broke down the strip huts, loaded everything into the rear of the Hercules aircraft, and using them as ground-based taxis, ferried the entire complex farther out onto more solid ice. There, the camp was reassembled and operations resumed. The sorrow of losing Frosty Kohn didn't disappear; it just was overwhelmed by the daily demands on the personnel and aircraft of the naval air unit.

Marc had struggled for several hours in the privacy of his berthing space, trying to find words of comfort to write to Frosty's parents. He finally finished a two-page note and posted it to the States, wondering how anything that anyone could say would alleviate the deep grief felt by Mr and Mrs Kohn, who had watched their exceptional child grow into a young woman and achieve so much in her short life. Within a few days after that depressing chore, he began to come back to the realization that the loss of a friend, of a fellow naval aviator and valued professional associate, was not a first for him.

Nor would it be a last.

It was difficult for Marc to keep his mind on the proper subject as he gave the new airfield camp a cursory inspection. Things were still a bit jumbled, but the huts for the flight crews and the galley were as before. The men would be as comfortable as they ever had been within the crude environs of the airfield living area.

Exchanging a few notes that he had made with Doctor Holley and the squadron leading chief, he bid them a quick goodbye and trotted over to catch the Hill shuttle. Chopper John delivered him as usual to the pad above his office. With no interest in his in basket, Marc walked past the squadron spaces and continued on toward the personnel building. Passing the admiral's shack, he heard a sharp rap on the picture window. Brady was motioning for him to come inside.

'Glad I caught you,' said Brady. 'Got something I want you to do.'

Marc accepted the offer to sit and selected one end of the sofa.

'I want you to go back to Christchurch for a day or so.'

'I don't particularly want to leave my people right now.'

'I understand that. But it's necessary. A high mucky-muck from Langley is in and has requested a meeting with us.'

'Langley? CIA?'

'Yes. Something to do with those reports of Argentine neo-Nazis, I suspect. I received some correspondence the last time I was back there. Nothing earthshaking.'

'Why doesn't he come down here?'

'Those folks have their own ways of doing things.'

'Wouldn't one of your staff be more appropriate? My people are still in sort of a state of shock over Frosty. I wouldn't want them to think I was checking out for a day's R and R in Chi Chi. Not now.'

'I would like to go myself, but you know we still have Senator Evans on the Ice and if I don't babysit him and listen to his god-awful stories of how he spent three weeks

267

in the Arctic, his feelings will be hurt. Besides, soon I'll be going back to Christchurch for good and so will my staff. You'll be finishing up down here and if there is anything unusual that might come up, I want you to be aware of it, first hand.'

'I think you're just trying to get me off the Ice for a day, Admiral. Really, I don't need that.'

'God damn it, don't second-guess me. I do want you off the Ice. Ever since Frosty bought it, you've been driving yourself as if this were a combat zone. Every time I try to get you up here for a quiet dinner and a few drinks, you're charging off to the Pole or Siple or playing helicopter pilot. You've got plenty of flight time, Marc. Let your people do their thing. They're good at it. And this meeting with whoever is a perfect excuse for me to send you to Chi Chi. You might as well get used to this nonflying operational crap. VXE-6 is your last fun tour.'

'That's why I don't want to leave.'

'Well, I know that. But I do want you to go. Meet with this fellow and come back and brief me.'

'He's at headquarters?'

'No. These people like to play games. You'll be met by our contact at Harewood. He'll take you to the place where you'll talk.'

'Contact? We have a CIA contact in Christchuch?'

'Sure, it's . . . You don't know, do you?'

'No.'

'Well, good. I like surprises. You just go back on tonight's turnaround flight. By God, I'd sure like to see the expression on your face when you're picked up.'

'You're enjoying this, aren't you, Admiral?' asked Marc, appreciating the humor of the situation but hopelessly confused as to his contact's identity.

'You bet I am. We've had so little to laugh about lately. This'll get your mind off your problems. Hell, it might even be fun, sitting down with the spooks and letting them play their silly-ass games.'

'In that event, I'd better go throw some things in a bag.'

'Bring me back a couple of bottles of bourbon. The good senator from Georgia is drinking my bar dry. Two bottles should last the rest of my stay.'

'I can handle that.'

21

Marc stepped off the Hercules and ambled into the customs room. They had made near-record time, six hours and fifty-three minutes from McMurdo to Christchurch. The senior customs official recognized him and waved him on through. 'Thank you,' said Marc, returning the man's handshake. Bob Christian was standing just beyond the door.

'Welcome back, Captain,' he said. 'I'm sorry about Lieutenant Kohn.'

'Yes, it hit us all pretty hard.' For a brief moment, the thought occurred to Marc that Christian was the CIA contact, but the thought quickly vanished. Active duty naval personnel weren't normally on CIA rolls. He couldn't imagine that Christian would have the necessary ambition to tackle a double task, anyhow.

'I'm expecting someone to meet me,' declared Marc.

'You'll be picked up at the Christchurch Airport Travelodge at 1400.'

'No White Heron this trip?'

'They're full.'

'Who's picking me up?'

'I don't know. I figured you would know that. I was just told to relay the time and place.'

'By whom?'

'The admiral's aide.'

Marc climbed in the left side of the station wagon.

'We've transferred your clothes to the Travelodge. How long will you be here?' asked Christian, pulling away from the curb.

'Just overnight, I think. I'll be going back tomorrow night. Do you know anything about why I'm back here?'

'Only that the aide said you would be arriving and the information about your pickup. What's going on?'

'Nothing to concern yourself with. I'm meeting someone at the request of Admiral Brady. I think it's just an excuse to get me off the Ice. He thinks I'm under too much stress. I couldn't convince him otherwise.'

'He's stubborn.'

'Well, I'll make the best of it. I already feel like I'm in a different world.' As soon as they had exited the terminal amid the noise and activity of the airport, the Ice became the netherworld once more, a place far removed. Christian walked him to his motel room, then left. Marc suspected the man was still smarting after the rebuke he had given him on the way to the Ice. Oh well, he didn't have time to concern himself with Christian's exaggerated feeling of persecution.

The real-world hot shower was great and Marc dressed in casual slacks and sport shirt, laying out a sport coat as an afterthought. Christchurch was shirtsleeve warm, but the occasion probably called for a coat.

He grabbed a sandwich and a beer in the Travelodge coffee shop, enjoying the return to silverware, china, and cloth serviettes. The Kiwi holiday season was winding down, but the motel was still almost full and it was relaxing to sit in the lobby and watch the comings and goings of the clientele. Fifteen minutes before his pickup time, he raised himself out of the overstuffed chair to go back to his room and retrieve his sport coat. As he was slipping it on, he heard a knock on the door.

'Well, a good afternoon to me favorite Yank.' It was Father O'Gorley. Marc immediately began to figure how he could diplomatically cut short the priest's visit. He suspected his pickup would want to remain anonymous.

271

'Father. How did you know I was here? Come in.' The old Irishman entered but Marc was glad to see him decline his offer of a chair. 'What are you up to on this fine Kiwi afternoon?'

'God's holy work, m'boy, God's holy work. C'mon, we've a bit o' a drive ahead o' us.'

'I'm waiting for someone, Father.'

O'Gorley looked puzzled. 'Ye'r waitin' fer me, lad.'

Father O'Gorley? thought Marc.

'The admiral sent word ya'd be making this one.'

'I'm stunned,' said Marc.

'The admiral didn't tell ya who ya'd be meetin'?'

Marc understood the reason for the twinkle in Brady's eye back at McMurdo. 'That old seadog. He's back there, now, rolling on the deck at this little joke of his. I had no idea.'

'That is typical of the man. He loves a practical joke 'n this is as close as he kin come to one.'

Marc followed O'Gorley out to the car and slid inside beside the priest.

'How's everything on the Ice?' asked O'Gorley.

'On schedule. Everyone's pretty much on a downer, though. We miss Frosty.'

'She was a luvley young lady. Such a shame. But, ya just sit back 'n relax. We're off t' Lake Tekapo.'

'The cabin?'

'No, a little more elaborate retreat. There's someone waitin' fer ya.'

'It's not a good-looking woman, is it?'

'Stifle such evil thoughts.'

'Nothing will surprise me after this.'

They drove around the west side of Christchurch by way of a back road to avoid the midafternoon traffic and were soon cruising across the southern section of the

Canterbury plains, O'Gorley's Toyota purring quietly under his demanding foot.

'You've had a tune-up, Father. The car actually sounds good.'

'Yes, I finally got a wee bit of extra funds to treat the ole girl to a do. She sounds grateful, doesn't she?'

The clear, calm summer air and the tuned Toyota's effortless ride along the smooth two-lane highway would normally have lulled Marc into a sleepy stupor, but his curiosity kept him wide awake. They crossed the Rakaia River, some thirty kilometers south of the city, before either spoke further.

Marc had to ask, 'How did you get involved in all this? Surely, you're not CIA?'

'Gracious, no. I'm somethin' of an associate, ya might say, fer twenty-odd years, actually. Not really an agent, mind ya, just a friendly contact with sympathetic leanin's toward the States.'

'Why?'

'Well, I've a soft spot in me heart fer Yanks. We older Kiwis remember the Battle of the Coral Sea. Ya read about that one, eh? Before your time, o' course. If you Yanks hadn't won, we'd be speakin' Japanese down here. This is a quiet country now, a good place t'live. Very little excitin' enough to generate any international intelligence work, so I'm not in any danger of compromisin' me New Zealand loyalties. I couldn't do that, o' course.'

'Do we pay you?'

'Is the Pope Polish? Ha! Of course ya do! I'm patriotic, mind ya, but I also have a wee bit o' a drinkin' problem, or haven't ya noticed? And yer folks keep me in good whiskey 'n I don't have t' use me poor parish's collection money. Not only that, yer generosity keeps a few tiny Maori bellies full. So, everybody benefits from me good nature.'

'Twenty years,' murmured Marc. 'And no one ever let me in on it.'

'I guess ya didn't have a need t' know. Isn't that the criteria?'

Marc sighed. 'That's the criteria.'

The plains were flecked with green, moist from the summer rains. Off to the far west, the Southern Alps rose in snow-capped splendor. The passing countryside was uncluttered except for an occasional feed or grain sign, which was always low key and usually signaled the outskirts of one of the few towns along their route. As they continued south, sheep became more numerous and Marc watched them grazing the rolling hills, fat and puffy despite their recent shearing. Frisky sheepdogs bounded nervously around the edges of the flocks, their spirited yelps chasing the strays and working them skillfully back to the other animals. The Kiwi shepherd on horseback had little to do other than whistle instructions to his dogs.

'Who's waiting for us?'

'Waitin' fer you, not me. I'm just the arranger o' such things. He's travelin' under the name of Raymond Moody, or at least that's how he presented himself to me. For CIA, he's pretty well dressed.'

'American?'

'As apple pie.'

'Has he been here before?'

'I've never seen 'im.'

'Why didn't we meet in Christchurch?'

'Well, sometimes I do make arrangements in town. I was told this gentleman wanted as little exposure as possible. Maybe he has a face people might recognize. He's a stranger t' me, but then, what do I know, a simple parish priest out tryin' t' do good in the world?'

'You're practically a spy! What would Rome think?'

'The Holy Father has plenty funds fer his vices – he doesn't need to moonlight. I believe that's the term.'

They had been driving for just under two hours. O'Gorley turned to the right off the main highway and began to thread his way into the low foothills. In a short while they were climbing across Burke's Pass, and from their vantage point several thousand feet above the plains, Marc could turn around and see the broad expanse of rich Canterbury farm and grazing land extending back toward Christchurch. He sat spellbound in the grip of South Island's spectacular scenery and could only marvel at the unspoiled flood of primeval nature all around them. Ahead, the steep slopes of intertwining mountain ranges were draped in summer snow. From the towering, sharp-peaked mountains, permanent snowfields cascaded along the sides and fed the great glaciers flowing down the opposite side toward the Tasman Sea. Craggy rivers of tumbled ice chunks wound their way from the heights of distant Mount Cook and emptied into several long, narrow lakes. As the gutsy Toyota twisted and turned along the serpentine mountain road, Marc could catch glimpses of the contrasting greens and blues of the plains and the distant Pacific, and beyond the latter, the darkening horizon of approaching night.

What a contrast was the nature of his mission – a clandestine meeting with a covert agent to discuss sinister things – to the peaceful innocence of the land about him.

'It was nighttime when we drove up here last September. You missed all the beauty,' commented O'Gorley.

'It's magnificent.'

'God's handiwork, m'boy.'

Up ahead, Marc recognized the Lake Tekapo turnoff, and as O'Gorley swung off the highway onto the lakeside road, they passed the weathered arrow-shaped sign that read Lake Tekapo. The Kiwis, so accustomed to the intense beauty of their land, hesitated to erect anything artificial that would mar that beauty, but if a signpost were necessary, they kept it brief. The traveler needed not elaborate directions, only confirmation that somewhere around that nondescript wooden sign lay the lake he sought. If he had to search a bit more for it, so much the longer to enjoy the scenery around him. And if he didn't want the subtle game of finding it, he didn't deserve to enjoy it.

Several kilometers down the road, they pulled off onto a steep auto path leading to a gaily colored Alpine-style cabin, more of a chalet than the few others dotting the rim of the lake. The high-eaved structure rested precariously on the lakeside slope, supported by a half-dozen wooden stanchions, each of which was formed from a single tree trunk. A flat parking area had been bulldozed on the upslope side of the chalet, just opposite the main entrance, and although it was still covered with patches of rotted snow, O'Gorley was able to brake the Toyota to a stop by the main entrance. He was obviously very familiar with the approach and parking place.

As they stopped, the door opened and a tanned, fiftyish gentleman greeted them with a raised hand. Wearing tailored suit trousers, a white shirt open at the neck, and an unbuttoned beige wool cardigan, he placed his leather-slippered feet on the door sill but refrained from stepping out into the cool afternoon air.

'Father, good afternoon,' he said, his voice measured, yet genial.

'This is Commander Marc Bradford, Mr Moody. He's the commander of the antarctic air squadron and representative of Admiral Brady.'

Moody smiled but retained a slight look of disappointment. Marc suspected that he was unaccustomed to dealing with subordinates. 'Nice to see you, Commander,' said Moody, widening his smile and making a genuine attempt to be hospitable. He stepped back, holding the door open as Marc and the priest entered. O'Gorley stopped at an entrance closet and extracted a pair of hiking shoes.

'You two have a nice chat. I'll be taking a short walk through the bush of me favorite trail by the lake. Will an hour be about right, Mister Moody?'

'Certainly, Father, we'll look forward to your joining us for a drink, then.'

'Aye, that I'll be doin' with ill-concealed pleasure.' Walking stick in hand, O'Gorley headed back down the entrance path toward the lake shore.

Marc followed Moody into the handsomely paneled living area, a good thirty feet wide and about twenty feet deep, with a wall of glass at the far side broken only by a stone fireplace in its center. It rose the height of the room. Beyond the windows, the cold waters of Lake Tekapo shimmered in the late afternoon sun. Marc and the man sat down, each on one of the two overstuffed loveseats arranged in an L before the fireplace. In front of the sofas was a six-inch-thick slab of gnarled kauri tree trunk, stained and polished to a glossy sheen. It was supported by a single log leg which, in turn, rested on a large white sheepskin rug. Several bottles of whiskey sat on the table next to a wooden ice bucket and four glasses.

'I am Raphael Minochetti,' announced the man, 'special assistant to the director of the Central Intelligence Agency, I was present when the director wrote the note to Rear Admiral Brady, which you carried from Honolulu to Christchurch.'

Marc studied the man. Sitting, he was not as impressive as he had been when posed in the doorway. 'Forgive me, sir,' said Marc, 'I'm a little new to the intelligence game. May I see some identification?'

Minochetti seemed taken aback, but recovered instantly and allowed a tolerant smile to smooth the awkward moment of silence during which he extracted a leather card case from his shirt pocket. It featured a recent photograph and appeared to be authentic CIA identification.

'Thank you.'

'I expected Admiral Brady.'

'He sends his regrets, sir. We have a senator on the Ice. Evans from Georgia. The admiral would have to make some explanations if he ran off and left the senator to one of his staff.'

Minochetti nodded. That he could understand. 'I'm sure you and I can accomplish as much. I was very sorry to hear about the loss of one of your pilots. I understand it was a helicopter crash.'

'Yes.'

'Tell me, how is the situation?'

'I'm not quite certain what situation you are referring to.'

'Kakushkin. How is he taking his failure to stir the pot at Belgrano I?'

Marc felt as if he had entered in the middle of a spy movie.

'I feel awkward. The admiral didn't give me any briefing on this meeting. What about Kakushkin?'

'You know, of course, that Kakushkin is KGB?'

'No.'

'He was a substitute exchange scientist, was he not, for Chenenko? A last-minute substitute?' prompted Minochetti.

'I understood he was, but I was not aware of any explanation.'

'Kakushkin wintered at Vostok. He was to have been relieved and sent back to Moscow until the Soviets found out about Scnell. He was given the assignment to verify the presence of the herr doktor at Belgrano I. He was given the option of eliminating Scnell, although his main purpose was to verify what he could about Argentino Station. We monitored a satellite link with Moscow just before the season started. It was scrambled and took a while to unscramble. That's why we could give you no advance warning. It could have been a nasty incident.'

'We understood Kosciusco was the Nazi-hunter.'

'Oh, he was. In fact, we really had no suspicions about Kakushkin until we broke the Vostok communication. He's small-time KGB, not the best operator in their service, by far. Likes to strike out on his own. They don't like that. We suspect he was involved in the incident at Belgrano, the death of Kosciusco. The Israeli had ingested a poison.'

Marc felt the tiny hairs of an awful suspicion erecting on the back of his neck. 'You are aware of the details of the Belgrano incident?'

'Of course. Molder reported it to us immediately.'

'Molder.'

'Ben Molder.'

'He's CIA?'

'Brady really didn't tell you anything, did he?'

Marc shook his head. He really would have liked to have been in on the beginning of the movie.

'Well, if the admiral wants me to discuss this with you, he should have prepared you.'

Marc was still trying to sort out the plot. KGB and CIA on the Ice? He had thought he was privy to the entire operation.

'You said Kosciusco was poisoned. The autopsy said he died of natural causes.'

'There was a reason for that. We needed to get the body out of New Zealand quietly.'

The CIA was in on the autopsy? Marc thought incredulously. 'Who killed him?'

'Like I say. We suspect Kakushkin, or maybe Steinhoff, providing he knew that Kosciusco was an Israeli Nazi-hunter. We're not sure. In any event, we found evidence of the poison in Kosciusco's cup.'

'How did you do that?'

'Molder pocketed the cup and brought it back to McMurdo to analyze it.'

Marc was beginning to think that the bride, Antarctica, would not be going to her eventual wedding with the outside world wearing pure white.

'Commander, let me fill in a few blank spots for you. We have known for some time about Scnell, ever since we intercepted the information from a Mossad contact. We were quite agreeable to cooperating with the Israelis in arranging the cover for Kosciusco, understanding that he only wanted to make positive identification and would not take any action without our approval – in this case, from Brady, who was to monitor the operation. About the time you folks arrived at Belgrano, we came up with the Kakushkin input. Things were a little edgy for a while. State did not relish a member of an American-sponsored international inspection party murdering an Argentine citizen, in an Argentine camp. But, correct me on this, there are no more planned flights to Belgrano?'

'No. The season is almost over.'

'There must not be. That's the first message you must convey to Brady. There are a lot of sensitive political ramifications to all this.'

'I would imagine.'

'There is *more* – more than you imagine, Commander. In addition to Scnell, who really is a minor factor in the overall picture, we have reason to believe that there is an entire neo-Nazi community on the continent.'

280

Marc adjusted his coat. It was getting cooler inside the chalet. He knew about the suspicions of Argentino Station. Brady had shared that with him when they had read the original CIA draft back in Christchurch, but he would play dumb for the moment.

'You are familiar with the new state-of-the-art Argentino Station?' continued Minochetti.

'Only that it is on the Joerg Plateau and was activated for the first time this year,' replied Marc.

'Argentino Station is some idiot's idea of a New Germany. The permanent colonists are all of German extraction and we have irrevocable proof that there is some kind of governmental organization, based on the structure of Hitler's Third Reich, being nurtured there.'

'That's heavy stuff. Does Brady know this?'

'We mentioned our initial suspicions in the letter you carried from Honolulu. He has no idea of the real extent. That's why this meeting.'

'It's an Argentine station.'

'It's an Argentine-*sponsored* station, but once it's fully operational and in place, it's anybody's station.'

'The Nazi party is not a viable nation.'

'Nor is Greenpeace, but those loonies are in your neighborhood for the same purpose – colonization – but, thankfully, with a higher motive than the preservation of the Third Reich. As long as the Antarctic Treaty is in effect, Antartica is open to anyone.'

'Surely, we and practically all of the treaty nations won't stand for Nazis on the Ice.'

'Who's going to throw them off? Who has the jurisdiction?'

Marc fully realized that no one had, not under the unique structure of the treaty, which guaranteed the continent of Antarctica to be an open area, accessible to all.

'There must be some sanctions we can take against the Argentines.'

'Not according to State Department legal beagles. It's a fait accompli, my friend. We can't force Greenpeace to leave and they are American nationals. How in hell do we exercise control over non-Americans?'

'This is crazy.'

'You're goddamned right it is. But at this moment, it's the real world. We have even bounced this situation off our contacts in the UN. You know what those bastards say? We have no more say-so over Antarctica than Lower Slobovia.'

'Who on God's earth has any sympathy with a handful of dying Nazis?'

'Who? I'll tell you goddamn who. Every Arab nation on the globe, for starters. The Nazis started to eradicate the Jews. The Arabs want to finish the job. They're blood brothers when it comes to the Israelis.'

'A single Nazi colony in Antarctica can be such a force? I find that pretty far out.'

'In the international political arena, particularly in the UN, where it's one man one vote, an ally is an ally. If the German colony claims sovereignty, they're in. Look at Africa. Every spear thrower with a wife and six kids claims to be an independent nation! And their vote in the General Assembly is as big as ours. Look at Micronesia, where every little island suddenly goes sovereign and bingo! we've got a handful of tiny little nations, each with a vote in the international arena. The Germans aren't going to set any precedent.'

Marc knew that Minochetti had a point in principle, but he was still having difficulty in agreeing with the particulars of the CIA official's alarming argument. 'Suppose I agree with your analysis . . .'

282

'This is not my analysis,' interrupted Minochetti, 'it's the State Department's.'

'All right, suppose I agree with the State Department's analysis. Where does that leave Naval Support Force, Antarctica? Certainly, there is nothing we can do about it.'

'Absolutely correct. But you damned well better be aware of what is going on, and that it's a lot bigger than an aging Nazi doctor. That is the main thrust of my briefing for Admiral Brady. Any day, he could have a very sensitive international situation on his hands. Now, the season is almost over. Chances are you people will be able to complete a normal operation and leave the Ice. Nothing will happen over the winter. That gives the politicians and diplomats an opportunity to wrestle with this thing. In short, you don't have to concern yourselves with a solution, you just have to make sure that you don't allow any type of situation to develop, which could be the case if there was another flight to Belgrano I or a flight to Argentino Station.'

'There are none on this season's schedule.'

'Then we should be home free until this is all verified and checked out and the high mucky-mucks back in DC can decide what to do about it. We just don't want to be a party to the Israelis or the Soviets deciding to take matters into their hands. Admiral Brady has an independent responsibility on the Ice, thus we wanted to brief him on the picture so he would not inadvertently be drawn into a compromising situation.'

'The admiral, Mr Minochetti, has more than thirty years of military-politico experience. I doubt if he could be drawn into any potentially embarrassing international situation.'

'I admire your loyalty and I suspect you are quite right.

283

But we have to be sure. Now, let me tell you about the real ass kicker.'

There's more? thought Marc.

'I mentioned the Arabs. Well, there's one in particular, a Palestinian by the name of Ibrahim al-Abbadi, who's a known terrorist; he may have had a part in the bombing of the TWA flight in 1985. He's part of a radical cell of Palestinians who operate independently. That's the worst type. Absolutely answer to no one. And he has access to large sums of cash. We placed him at Lake Argentino – that was the Nazi's Argentine hideout – on three separate occasions. To keep a long story short, we think there's something going on between him and the Germans.'

'Such as?'

'The damned Germans are technological geniuses. We figure he is bargaining for some sort of weapon.'

'Nuclear?'

'No, no danger of that, even if they have the know-how. But how about biological or chemical? They have the expertise. Scnell, himself, was a pioneer in certain biological experiments. He's disappeared from Belgrano I. His comrades are at Argentino Station. Two plus two, Commander.'

'They have some facilities at Argentino to do such a thing?'

'A number of their people were in on the construction. Why couldn't they have prepared spaces and included their laboratory equipment and materials in the move from Lake Argentino? We found evidence they had a very comprehensive chemical laboratory at their lakeside villa. It's too goddamned frighteningly clear, Commander. And this puts a new spotlight on the whole sordid picture.'

'If we have the evidence, why not just go in and lower the boom on the whole bunch?'

'Because, at this point it's only a theory. And something of this proportion requires presidential approval, and the president, so far, poo-poos the whole business. We need some hard evidence.'

'We can't get you any. Not unless we go to Argentino.'

'Right, and you won't be going this year. So, we wait out the winter. No one will visit Argentino in the winter.'

'The Palestinian could make contact before the winter if one of the Germans gets back to Argentina, or even to Chile.'

'Absolutely. So, we have our people alerted for that. If there is a meet, we plan to be there. That would be the hard evidence.'

'Then, you have the situation covered.'

Minochetti chuckled. 'Yes, *if* we don't screw up and miss the meet. Like the US Navy, we're damned good but not infallible.' He reached over to the kauri-top table and poured a splash of bourbon over a single ice cube. It was barely a full swallow. 'Against doctor's orders, but I need just a touch,' he commented. 'The liver doth protest.' Smacking his lips, he continued, 'Don't get old, Commander. All sorts of things happen to you.'

'You don't impress me as old, Mr Minochetti.'

'I'm not, but my liver is, aged by overindulgence. A common failing, I suppose.'

'I'm sorry.'

'No need to be. Now then, do you feel fully aware of the situation?'

'I believe I can brief the admiral.'

'Good. And for the time being, there's no need for anyone other than you and the admiral to know that Kakushkin is KGB. At this point, he really has no mission. Molder already knows, of course.'

'Does Kakushkin know about Molder?'

Minochetti lifted his arms, palms up, and shrugged.

'I'm curious,' remarked Marc, 'why didn't you just come on down to the Ice under some cover as a working visitor and talk to Brady directly?'

'Well, first of all, I want low visibility. I was a field agent for more than twenty years. My face is too well known in some circles. Anyone going to Antarctica is subject to media attention in Christchurch, as you know. And I *thought* I was going to meet with Brady here.' Minochetti smiled, 'Besides, I don't like the cold and I understand you folks have an abundance of it down there.'

'McMurdo's not bad this time of year.'

Minochetti had been eyeing the bourbon as they talked. 'I hate going out of DC. I lose my self-control.' He reached for the bottle. 'Join me?'

'I'm not sure I want to contribute to your demise. Should you really?'

'No.' Minochetti poured two shots, his over a single cube, Marc's over a cluster. 'To your health, Commander.'

'And yours.'

O'Gorley entered as they touched glasses. 'Am I too early?' he asked.

'No, come and join us, Father,' answered Minochetti, reaching for the scotch. 'Ice?'

'. . .'n a finger of water,' replied O'Gorley, easing himself down beside Marc.

'To amplify our last point,' began Minochetti, adjusting his position so that he could lean back and study the outdoors through the wall window, 'you obviously can tell I've been down here before . . .'

You knew the Father preferred scotch, reasoned Marc.

'We keep this place as a sort of retreat. There's not much business down here for us. That's why I jumped at the chance to do this brief myself. Father O'Gorley here is an old friend. And he comes cheap.'

O'Gorley seemed embarrassed at the revelation that he had known Minochetti all along. 'Maybe I should be askin' for better compensation,' he suggested.

'And there is complete security here,' Minochetti continued without addressing O'Gorley's hint. 'This is such a sparsely settled country. My God, the Kiwis got a good thing going, only three million people and half of them in four cities. I haven't seen a soul since I arrived two days ago.'

O'Gorley freshened his drink. Outside the windows, the trees were beginning to weave under a fresh breeze from across the lake. Gray clouds replaced the blue sky, their bottoms irregular and dropping wisps of condensation. The inside temperature had dropped noticeably, the fireplace being cold at the moment. 'I have a suggestion, Marc,' said O'Gorley. 'I have t' get Mr Minochetti back to Harewood fer his departure this evenin'. Why don't ya just spend the night here? There's food 'n plenty o' firewood. You can meditate on yer past sins 'n be a better man by mornin'. I'll come 'n share a late breakfast with ya 'n ya can make yer evein' flight back t' the Ice.'

Marc considered the proposition. Why not? He had no obligations in Christchurch. A rare evening alone would be therapeutic. His mind had been filled and his body working around the clock since Frosty's loss. Now Minochetti had introduced another factor to be squeezed in among the myriad of mental considerations he juggled as commanding officer of VXE-6. He would probably feel guilty. He could return to Christchurch and meet with Christian to discuss the detachment's requirements and problems. Guilt be damned. 'Sounds good,' he decided.

'Foin! Then, are ya ready t' go, Mr Minochetti? Me housekeeper kin fix a good supper fer us while yer waitin' t' go t' the airport, or would ya rather dine out some-where? I know a little spot on the Brighton coast that would be inconspicuous.'

'I'll buy,' offered Minochetti.

'That ya will,' confirmed O'Gorley. 'We'll leave ya t' yer own devices, Marc. Everything ya need is here.'

A light drizzle was falling as the two men passed through the door and climbed into the Toyota. Minochetti waved as O'Gorley wheeled the automobile around and headed down the entrance road.

Marc watched the car disappear down the wooded slope. So, O'Gorley and Minochetti were old friends. Just how much into the CIA game was the good Father? Marc considered the bizarre developments. A Kiwi Roman Catholic priest and the senior USARP on the Ice – CIA agents. Their Soviet exchange scientist a KGB. An attempted international assassination on the White Con-tinent. And the ultimate disgrace, a Nazi colony in Antarctica.

There goes the neighborhood, for sure!

Over Mount Cook, a stream of cold air from across the southern Tasman Sea was vying for control of the local atmosphere with the warmer summer air mass sitting across South Island. The setting sun had added some stability to the warm air mass, but rapid cooling from the mountain snows and the influx of the cold air was creating a mixture of down- and updrafts. The warm air rose and began to divest itself of its moisture. With darkness, further cooling separated more high moisture from the clouds and a mild summer storm formed over Lake Tekapo. For several hours, the winds of the uncertain air gusted and the precipitate peppered the disturbed waters of the lake and wet its shores.

Marc built a fire and sat before it, watching the rain run

down the windows. The refrigerator had surrendered a
filet of firm Kiwi beef and a fresh head of plains lettuce.
Whoever was responsible for the comfort of Minochetti
had provided an overflow of provisions. His own dinner
had been classically American – steak and salad – but no
potato. Instead, he had heated a small serving of cauli-
flower, which seemed to be a staple of Kiwi dining.

In addition to the whiskeys on the kauri table, there
was a small, well-stocked bar. He had selected Kahlua.
Sipping the liqueur, he watched the flames of the fire and
enjoyed the warmth and security of the chalet. Having
absolutely nothing to do was hypnotic and for the first
time in many months he was completely relaxed.

Outside, the wind drove streaks of water across the
frosted windowpanes and stroked the tall trees around the
cabin. The erratic rustle of the leafy branches against
the shake roof announced the passing of the brief disturbance. A few desperate streaks of silver lightning triggered
the release of high-country thunder and tried to stir the
dark clouds into a full-fledged storm. But the cold stream
was passing too quickly and breaks began to appear in the
dark clouds, revealing patches of sparkling sky diamonds.

Directly overhead, the last remnant of a pre-earth
galactic explosion began its final miles of an eons-long
journey through space. It sliced across the blue-black
skies over Lake Tekapo, the clawing forces of earth's
atmospheric gases rasping across its uneven surfaces in an
ever-increasing fury of abrasive heat. The kilometer-wide
space rock glowed red, then orange. Finally, it began to
consume itself in the white-hot heat of friction, screaming
silently as it succumbed to the same force that drew down
the rain and snow. The plummeting meteorite curved
fatally downward toward South Island, its passage marked
by a slim silver stream of stardust.

In an instant, the pocket of trapped gases at its core burst forth in a violent release of extraterrestrial energy.

Startled, his thoughts returning to the events of the past few weeks, Marc watched the white flash light the valley floor. The symbolism of the heavenly phenomenon triggered a mental toast. He raised his cordial glass. Farewell, Frosty, you left this lousy planet just in time.

22

Kurt Eisner sat across the desk from Doctor Scnell. 'How is our patient?' he asked.

'As good as new, Colonel. She has had several days' rest and there were no injuries to be concerned about. She is also a very healthy and strong young woman. Don't you think we should notify the authorities?'

Eisner rested his chin on his folded hands. 'You have kept her isolated, as I instructed?'

'Yes, but she is ready to return to McMurdo. She is fine.'

Eisner studied Scnell's eyes, recalling the circumstances of the woman's arrival at the station.

'Fools! Why did you bring her in *here?*' Scnell had been irate.

The litter bearers had recoiled under the force of his words, and Martin Bormann, whom he had been examining, had mirrored his look of anger. Grabbing his tunic, he had hurried out of the dispensary door.

'She is unconscious, Doctor.'

'She *appears* unconscious. She may very well hear or even see if she opens her eyes. You were to take her to the emergency room only. Idiots. Put her on the examining table.' Turning to the pilot accompanying the men, he asked, 'What are her injuries?'

'She was unconscious when we found her. She was pinned in the helicopter but doesn't seem to have any severe injuries. We freed her and kept her warm, which was about all we could do. She has some minor cuts and bruises on her head.'

'Who is she?'

'We haven't searched her clothing. We mainly wanted to keep her warm and get her here as quickly as possible.'

'Is there anyone else?'

'A New Zealand officer, I assume the pilot. He was dead. We still have him in the aircraft, in a body bag.'

'Leave him there for the moment.' Scnell started examining the woman and searching through her clothing for identification. 'Nothing. Did you notify the Americans?'

'We tried, but we could raise no one. We have been having radio difficulties.'

'What is this?' Scnell removed a small silver bracelet from the woman's left wrist. Turning it over, he read the inscription, 'To Sheila, in remembrance. Barry.'

Kurt Eisner walked in and stood by the examining table. 'A woman. I heard the radio call saying our aircraft had picked up a survivor. I just assumed . . . she's very pretty. Who is she?'

'Sheila someone. Probably a scientist working with the Americans or the New Zealanders. Have you notified McMurdo?'

'No. I just assumed the aircraft did.'

'They were unable to.' Scnell studied the woman. 'She is not seriously injured at all.' A nurse was inserting an IV needle in the back of the woman's left hand. Scnell passed a small vial under the woman's nose. She winced and opened her eyes.

'Hello,' said Scnell in English. 'You are all right.'

'Where am I?'

'Argentino Station. This is an Argentine research station. What is your name?'

The woman seemed confused. 'Sheila . . . Sheila Kohn . . . I was in a helicopter . . . where is the pilot?'

'I'm sorry. He did not survive. Don't try to talk anymore. Just rest. We will take good care of you.'

'Please, notify McMurdo, I . . .'

'Yes, yes. Hush, you must rest. We will take care of everything.' Scnell patted her right arm and smiled in his best bedside manner. Taking a syringe from the nurse, he held it while the nurse cut open the sleeves of Frosty's sweater and cotton undergarment. As he completed the injection, Frosty murmured and closed her eyes.

'American,' proclaimed Eisner. 'She speaks English with an American accent.'

Eisner spoke very carefully across the desk to Scnell. 'I do not intend to return her to McMurdo.'

'What?'

'They have already assumed her lost. The wreckage of the helicopter is buried under several feet of new snow, and there will be much more over the winter. It will never be found. Don't you see, Herr Doktor, we have our volunteer for the weapons test.'

'I am not sure that is a good idea. The word of her recovery is known throughout this camp.'

'No, the word of her initial survival is, that's all. We have kept her isolated and sedated. As far as anyone need know, she died of injuries.'

'Wait. You are forgetting. The purpose of the test is to try out the vaccine. We know the weapon will work. Thus, if the vaccine works, she lives,' countered Scnell.

'For a while, until you can be sure it is a permanent deterrent to the weapon. Then we dispose of her.'

Scnell shrugged. 'Perhaps it is better than using one of our own people, is it not? The vaccine is ready.'

'It is, and animal tests have indicated it is perfected. Then, we proceed. Why not now?'

Scnell nodded. 'Why not?' Leaning over, he spoke into

293

his intercom, 'Nurse, bring the woman out of sedation. We wish to talk to her.'

'Yes, Doctor.'

Scnell rose. 'I will go to the laboratory and return immediately. We can give her the vaccine here. I would rather use the laboratory for the employment of the weapon.'

'When should we give it to her?'

'A full twenty-four hours before we use the weapon. That is the program lead time we have developed. Actually, when the Arabs use the vaccine, they will need at least seventy-two hours to ensure everyone gets it before they use the weapon. But, twenty-four hours is sufficient for our purposes. The vaccine has a full month of protection.'

'Why not a vaccine with permanent protection?'

The corners of Scnell's lips curled upward, but his expression was not a smile. It was more a look of supreme satisfaction, an evil twist of the lips that preceded a whispered single sentence, 'We may have further use for the weapon, even against those we give it to.'

'We will talk with the woman when you return.'

The impact of Scnell's last statement stayed with Eisner the entire ten minutes before the doctor returned. Ingenious. One vaccine for others, a temporary one. Save the permanent vaccine for the Third Reich. Good.

'Shall we go in?' Scnell reentered and led the way into Frosty's room. She was sitting up in her bed.

'How do you feel?' solicited Scnell.

'How long have I been out?'

'Oh, just a day or so. The people from McMurdo will be arriving in another day to take you back.'

'I want to talk to them.'

'Of course. Here, take this. It will help.'

Frosty accepted the pill and the paper cup of water.

'What is it?'

'Primarily vitamins. You will follow it today with some substantial meals. You are a steak eater, I presume. We will have you back to normal overnight.'

Frosty followed the pill with a large gulp of the water. 'I hate pills.'

'Now, in a while, we will let you get out of bed and walk around,' announced Snell, trying to sound fatherly.

'I hate to keep insisting, but I must talk to my commanding officer.'

Scnell looked at Eisner, who also suddenly wore a puzzled expression. 'Your commanding officer?'

'Yes. Commander Marc Bradford. He is the commander of my squadron, VXE-6.'

Neither Scnell nor Eisner spoke for a long moment. Finally, Eisner asked, 'You are military?'

'Lieutenant Sheila Kohn, United States Navy, Antarctic Development Squadron Six. Didn't you see my insignia and name plate?'

'You wore no insignia.'

The coffee stain, remembered Sheila. I took off my shirt back at Eights. 'I'm sorry, I forgot. I didn't have on my uniform shirt.'

'And no identification, except for the bracelet you wore on your wrist.'

Frosty felt her bare arm. 'Where is it?'

'Right here, in your bed table.'

Doodle! she thought. Even my ID is back with my shirt. Dog tags, too. Serves me right for not wearing them, even if they do scratch.

'Will you excuse us for a moment?' asked Eisner, taking Scnell by the arm.

'My call to McMurdo?' insisted Frosty.

'We will set it up immediately. Please, we will see you in a moment.'

Outside the room, Eisner rolled his eyes. 'This places a different connotation on the situation. The woman is a naval officer, in the American Navy!'

Scnell looked carefully at Eisner. 'We have already started.'

Eisner held up a hand. 'Only with the vaccine. If anyone ever finds out we used an American citizen – a member of the military, mind you – the complexion of our existence can rapidly change, open continent or not.'

Scnell walked a step away, then turned back around. 'No one knows. No one will ever find out. It is that simple. As for being an American citizen, perhaps I should refresh your memory. She is also a Jewess.'

23

'Wanna do the honors, Skipper?'

Marc had been leaning over the command pilot's seat of the Hercules for the past hour. Mother Antarctica was doing it to them again.

The more than eight-and-a-half-hour flight from Christchurch had admittedly been launched with a bad weather forecast for McMurdo, but not *this* bad! It probably would have been better to have delayed twenty-four hours, but Marc was anxious to report to Brady on his meeting with Minochetti. His impatience now had them facing a situation that featured a real old-fashioned winging of a ground blizzard with sixty-knot winds from due south and a direct crosswind for the ski runway. That was just too much for a C-130 to handle safely. The availability of the crosswind skiway was academic at the moment. It would take hours to realign the GCA unit – and the Hercules was already breathing jet fuel fumes. Without the precision assistance of the GCA unit, there was no way the aircraft could be lined up with the crosswind skiway with sufficient confidence that it would touch down on the 200-foot-wide strip of smoothed snow. That was a must, for to each side were debris and the clutter of the Williams Field cargo yard.

The weather overhead was beautiful. In fact, the weather down to 150 feet above the surface was CAVU – ceiling and visibility unlimited. But below that, a raging wall of blowing snow was obliterating everything: the ice shelf, airfield, snow roads, buildings, huts, debris – everything. To attempt a landing on the crosswind skiway would be to accept a surveillance radar approach by the GCA controller – and that would provide only an approximate lineup with the skiway. They would enter a white world at 150 feet, settle unseeing onto either the skiway, camp, cargo yard, or random debris of the airfield dump. Those were not very good odds, despite the fact that the Hercules would be going only about fifteen knots at touchdown!

The exec was strapped in the seat, balancing a cup of coffee on his lap, waiting for Marc's reply to his question. It was a courtesy; 130 was his airplane, but Marc was the squadron commander and the senior aircraft commander on board.

'No thanks, Don. You got us into this mess. You can get us out of it,' replied Marc good-naturedly. He appreciated the offer, but had every confidence in his second-in-command. The exec had just notified the tower that he was going out on the ice shelf and set the airplane down in the emergency landing area. It wouldn't be as smooth as the skiway, and there would be no ground radar assistance other than advisory, but it would be into the wind and they would be touching down at almost helicopter speed. To insist on a precision GCA to the main skiway would be to wipe out the main skis and landing gear – at best. The approach and letdown to the emergency area would be in accordance with the criteria on their homespun TACAN path to the alternate area: fly outbound on the primary skiway heading for six miles, descend to 600 feet, then execute a right 90-degree turn into the wind and ride it in.

As the exec made the right ninety, Marc sat back on the lower seat bunk and strapped in. They passed 150 feet on their descent and the world went white. Despite his confidence, Marc felt the familiar tightening of his stomach muscles. No matter how qualified the other pilot,

298

you always felt better if *you* were doing the driving! He monitored the airspeeds and rate of descent as the copilot called them out as a double-check to the exec. At eighty-one knots, twenty-five feet per minute down, full flaps, engines at substantial power to hold the Hercules in its nose high attitude but keep it out of a stall, and with the radar altimeter reading thirty feet, Marc felt the skis settle onto the unseen surface. Head-on into the blizzard, the Hercules had hardly any forward motion, and with the exec's prompt retardation of the power lever, they were stopped.

Marc unstrapped and peered out the exec's side of the flight deck. They might as well still be in the air. Nothing could be seen outside except the blowing snow scraping past the window.

'Nice job, Don,' complimented Marc.

'I didn't even need reverse pitch! That wind must be seventy knots out there.' The exec was still flying the ailerons, trying to keep the wings level in the violent winds. The copilot called Williams Tower and reported they were safely on deck.

'Roger, 130, we can't send anything out in this stuff.'

'We'll wait it out,' responded the copilot.

Three hours later, the winds died, the cloudless blue sky appeared, and the exec made a five-minute return flight to the airfield. All fuel gauges read empty as they taxied in.

All of the helicopters were down at various field camps, having been grounded by the sudden storm, and Marc rode a snowcat back to McMurdo Station, jumping out at Brady's hut. Senator Evans was just leaving, the admiral escorting him outside.

'Well, I understand you're just back from some ice shelf liberty,' shouted Brady.

Marc laughed. 'I'm going to miss all this. Are you free?'

Senator Evans raised his hand in greeting at he passed.

'Yes, of course. Come on in,' invited Brady.

The hot coffee was inevitable and Marc sipped it while Brady excused Ramon from the hut. It took only a few minutes to brief him on the discussions with Minochetti.

'I'll be damned. So, my preliminary report was basically correct, although it mentioned nothing of this scope. Just that it was suspected that some of the occupants of Argentino Station were ex-Nazis.'

'It appears that they're ex-ex-Nazis.'

'Ha! That's a good one. Those people over there must be mad.'

'Minochetti seemed to feel they were quite serious.'

'I'm certain they are, but they are just plain stupid to feel they can pull it off.'

'I got the impression there is a distinct possibility they may.'

'Well, there's nothing we can do. It's up to the politicians, now. I wouldn't even want to be in on the arguments. God, can you imagine the turmoil this is going to cause when it gets out? What did Minochetti say about classification of the information?'

'He really didn't say, but I gathered it is still held pretty close within the intelligence community and certain State Department and White House personnel. There apparently is no real confirmation, yet, of the Germans' intent. We just know that they are, in fact, on the Ice.'

'I don't like it,' started Brady, nodding. 'I've been suspicious of Kakushkin. He asks the wrong questions for a pure scientist. Let's not let him know his cover is blown. I think our main aim is winding up the season and getting the hell off the Ice before anything further happens. Incidentally, the Soviets are calling him home. We've been asked to provide him space to Christchurch. I want him on the last plane out.'

'That'll be with me,' commented Marc.

'The captain is always last to leave the sinking ship,' teased Brady, 'and our valiant ship, Antarctica, has some serious damage to her hull!'

'Do you want me to brief Ben?'

As if on cue, there came a knock on the inner storm lock door, and at Brady's invitation the visitor entered. It was Ben Molder.

'You bastard,' kidded Marc. 'You're a damned spook.'

Molder smiled. 'You've been talking to Minochetti. No wonder they took him out of the field. Must be getting senile. How is he?'

'Seemed to be okay to me, except for his liver.'

'He hasn't had one for five years. His body just doesn't know it yet.'

'Let's sit down, Ben,' suggested Brady. 'Marc has a fairy tale for you.'

'Boneyard! Get your black ass in gear! Storm's over, we're going home!'

'Right with you, Mister Tilley!' Boneyard Davis secured the last cargo strap in the rear of the fuselage and took his seat with the six Kiwi passengers. Strapping himself in, he gave Tilley a thumbs-up signal that everything and everyone were secured. The Ranger roared away from the once more closed Eights Station and raced across the bumpy snow. Boneyard watched the contents within the passenger-cargo compartment shake and rattle as their takeoff run continued. They were never on the surface long, the superb power of the aircraft's turboprops pulling it free with a grace uncharacteristic of its ungainly appearance.

This time was little different. After a bone-jarring series of encounters with the frozen snow ridges around Eights, the Ranger bounded into the air. With a final sad glance back at Eights, Tilley guided the Ranger up and away from the tragic scene of Frosty's loss.

'I think that surface's getting rougher all the time. Remind me to mention it back at McMurdo,' exclaimed Tilley.

'I'll say. I thought we were going to tear off the gear on that one,' replied his copilot. 'At least we won't be coming back here in this bird.'

'I dunno. She's done pretty well. The squadron may want to try a couple next season.'

'If we can get the bucks.'

'Well, I'll vote for the old girl,' stated Tilley confidently, reaching forward and patting the glare shield over the instrument panel.

Back in the passenger compartment, Boneyard settled down for the boring ride. There would be a brief stop at Siple Station to pick up mail and a passenger or two and then a five-and-a-half-hour ride to McMurdo. Then Boneyard could start thinking about more pleasurable things, such as the ride back to the States. The good Lord was sparing his mother until he could see her one more time, and he knew how that tired, wrinkled old face would spring to life and those drooping eyes sparkle with pure joy at seeing her 'baby' once more. Boneyard chuckled. He was twenty-four years old, but to Mama Tish he was her baby. She would admonish him, as always, when he gave her the roll of bills for her medical expenses. It would be more than a thousand dollars this time.

He and Tilley's plane captain would have only one major chore left – to seal up the Ranger against the winter snows and anchor it securely to the ice for its long wait until next season. Then, a redeployment ride aboard a Hercules back to Christchurch and a flight home on one of those plush chartered DC-8s, where he could relax for the first time since last year.

They topped off the fuel tanks at Siple and picked up only one passenger, a USARP climatologist who had been studying the deterioration of the ozone layer over Antarctica.

Five hours later, they were less than a hundred miles from Williams Field. Boneyard noticed it first, a faint sweet smell, then a stronger odor that tingled his nose. *Jet fuel!* Quickly, he unstrapped and walked the length of the cabin, cimbing over the legs of the sleeping passengers, none of whom seemed to be disturbed by the alarming odor. Just as he traced the strongest scent to the forward right side, near the wing root, Tilley leaned back and yelled, 'Boneyard! I smell fuel! Make a check!' Before Tilley finished speaking, Boneyard was joined by the plane captain. The chubby aircraft mechanic immediately screwed up his face and cursed. 'Shit! Something's let loose. That's too strong.' He joined Boneyard by the wing root and started pulling away insulation. There was a small access panel leading into the wing interior. Peering down his flashlight beam, the mech searched inside the wing structure.

'See anything?' asked Boneyard anxiously.

'No, it looks dry, but I can't see too far. The leak's in there somewhere.'

'You find anything?' came Tilley's voice from the cockpit. The plane captain hurried forward.

'Starboard wing, Skipper. It smells like we're pumping JP-4 like crazy.'

'We'll have to shut off the fuel supply and secure those engines.' Even as he talked, Tilley shut down the two right-side engines to eliminate the fuel pump action. If the leak were between the pumps and the engine burners, perhaps in the injection lines, it would stop. Ignoring the intercom, he directed, 'Secure all electrical power.' Together, he and the copilot shut down all sources of

303

electrical energy. They would be unable to talk to or hear anyone and would not be able to use flaps for landing, but those were minor inconveniences compared to the alternative. One spark and they would light the sky like another sun. Besides, the tower would see him coming, and Antarctica had anything but crowded skies.

The leak had to be major. The odor was strong.

Nosing over, Tilley started a rapid descent toward the Ross Ice Shelf, 19,000 feet below. 'Dump the cabin pressure. We need to air this thing out.' There was an ear-popping pressure change as the copilot hit the dump switch and the atmosphere within the cabin went from its 3,000-foot pressurized level to the reduced pressure of their 18,300-foot altitude. The air was thin, but they were diving at 6,000 feet per minute. The temporary scarcity of oxygen would not be a concern. Nevertheless, Tilley and his copilot pulled their oxygen masks over their faces. As they passed 11,000 feet, they placed the masks aside.

'I bet all that shaking over the past weeks has loosened something,' ventured the copilot.

'I wouldn't be surprised. Open your window vent, too. We need to maintain a positive flow. Whew! That's bad, but I think we've cleared some of it out.'

The passengers were wide awake, frightened by the rapid decompression and sudden dive, and sat silent, unsure of just what was going to happen. Boneyard climbed around to each of them and explained the situation, his smiling face offering reassurance. Thankfully, the airflow had eliminated most of the fuel odor.

But Boneyard, as well as the other members of the crew, knew that did not mean the fumes were gone from inside the wing.

'Well, we haven't blown up yet,' observed Tilley, trying to picture in his mind where the leak could be. It was obviously within the right wing, but he had instructed the

304

plane captain to replace the inspection panel to keep the fumes from the cabin. Maybe that was not so smart. 'Take off that panel again,' he ordered. 'Maybe the flow of air in the cabin will drain more fumes from the wing.'

Williams Field was in sight, probably twenty-five miles ahead. Eight minutes at most. 'We'll go straight in. As soon as we're on deck, I'll cut numbers one and two. I want everyone out ASAP. Tell Boneyard to brief the passengers. No moving around until we come to a complete halt. Then, anyone that isn't fast enough is going to have my boot prints across his ass.'

The plane captain again removed the panel and stuck in his flashlight. 'I think I can get my head and shoulder inside and maybe get a better view,' he suggested.

'Even so, you won't be able to do anything about it,' declared Boneyard.

The mech reached far inside with his right arm, his hand clamped around the flashlight. Managing to work his head through the opening, he stretched and searched further. The odor was overpowering. The leak had to be continuing. Suddenly, the beam of the light glanced upward, reflected by bare metal. No, not bare metal, a liquid! Fuel! There was a pool of the stuff shimmering on the bottom wing skin between several of the ribs just inboard of the closest engine. No wonder the fumes were so strong. That was raw fuel, maybe several gallons. He swung his flashlight around in the void of the wing. Groaning in disgust, he saw the source of the trouble. At the junction of the fuel line from the tank selector valve and the pickup line from the engine, the coupling nut was backed off. No safety wire. The two ends of the lines were just resting against each other. There was no way he could reach the faulty junction. How could it have happened? No one ever worked on the airplane except him and Boneyard, and he always checked Boneyard's work.

No one else could have . . . wait. They had refueled at Argentino Station while out searching for Lieutenant Kohn. The whole crew had been invited inside the line shack for coffee and hot soup while the Argentines had refueled the Ranger. They would have had no reason to have been in the wing void. But, suddenly he remembered one of the ground crew's comments about the wing void being a great place to hide booze when going through customs. How would he have known about the wing void since none of the Argentines had ever seen a DHC-7 before? And when he opened the fabric cover to the wing access, just now, there had been a loose snap.

The fumes were much too strong for him. He was suddenly very dizzy and disoriented; he had to get back into breathable air. Struggling against the pull of his flight suit, which was snagged by the sharp edge of the opening, he yanked his elbow back sharply and it hit a fuselage frame. The shock dislodged the flashlight and it struck the metal of a wing rib.

The spark instantaneously ignited the fumes which erupted into a ball of orange flame that turned his head and shoulder instantly into ash, and the pressure of the explosion separated the right wing from the fuselage of the DeHaviland.

In the cockpit, Tilley cursed, instinctively knowing he was only seconds away from death. Trying to accomplish the impossible, he was still working the control yoke and rudder pedals as the rotating fuselage, spinning up and over itself under the offsided lift of the left wing, smashed into the ice. His copilot had ridden the last seconds in rigid terror as had all of those in the passenger cabin except one. Boneyard Davis, thrown violently against the rear bulkhead by the explosion, forced out a final 'Mama' an instant before the fuselage crumpled around him.

* * *

'Oh, dear Jesus, look at that!' cried the lone operator of the control tower as he hit the crash alarm. He had followed Tilley's approach through his field glasses ever since he had first picked up the rapidly descending DHC-7, trying repeatedly to raise the aircraft on several frequencies. Spotting the two feathered propellers, he had alerted the crash crew, who were already in their vehicles when the orange explosion lit the daylight sky. Horrified, the tower operator watched the fuselage and left wing spin onto the ice, triggering a second violent explosion and a towering fire that belched black smoke skyward.

'We're on our way!' came the crash crew's reply over his radio. He watched the two huge tracked trucks speed over the ice, bouncing and bounding across the drifts and ridges. The DeHaviland was a good two miles short of the skiway. They would never reach it in time. Recovering some of his composure, he lifted the direct phone line to McMurdo Operations.

'Chief, we're going to bust right through this ice,' complained the young seaman driver of the lead vehicle. All around them were pressure ridges and watery spots of rotting ice.

'You keep this son of a bitch headed right for that column of smoke, *wide open,* or I'm going to bust right through your ass! There are men burning to death out there and if we go through the ice, your mommy will get a big box of medals from the Navy Department that she can set on the mantle and say, "My Joey got those for doing just what his chief told him to do"!'

If there was one thing worse than plunging through the ice into the frigid waters of McMurdo Sound, it was the wrath of the chief. Seaman Joey pressed so hard on the accelerator that his leg shook. Behind him, leaving a second trail of black diesel exhaust, the companion truck weaved and bobbed in the tracks of the first.

The smoke from the crash was boiling skyward, reaching several hundred feet before leaning over to spread along the wind line. Abruptly, it was joined by a white burble of steam and the black smoke began to thin rapidly.

'Oh, shit!' said the chief. 'They've burned through the ice. Take your time. Shit, oh dear.'

The two vehicles reached the scene and started spraying the scattered debris with the dry chemicals from their firefighting tanks. There were no pieces larger than a pie plate. Farther on, the severed right wing had fluttered to earth and lay smoking. The second truck flailed its way over to it and covered it with the fire-extinguishing agent.

The chief dropped out of the truck and cautiously walked as close as he dared to the ragged hole in the ice. The dark blue water of McMurdo Sound rose and fell within the open area, softly lapping against the sides. 'I don't know how deep it is here, but they're on the bottom, that's for goddamned sure.' A few air bubbles and wisps of steam were rising from the water. Placing his hands together, the chief dropped to his knees and crossed himself. His young driver dropped out of the truck cab and stood beside him. He wasn't cold, but he couldn't stop shaking.

Marc met Brady on the run as he passed the admiral's quarters on his way to the helo pad. Chopper John was a dozen paces in front of him.

'What happened?' asked Brady, pulling on his parka as they ran side by side.

'Tilley! The Ranger exploded on final.'

They reached the Huey and jumped in as Chopper John threw the switches and the turbojet whined into life.

He had the helicopter in the air before they had time to strap in.

'What the hell will happen next?' yelled Brady over the engine noise.

Marc could only sit, collapsed in the seat, holding the ends of his shoulder harness in his hands. They were passing over the airstrip camp before he could gather his thoughts sufficiently to attach the metal clips to the buckle of his seat belt.

'There are the crash vehicles. My God, where's the airplane?' asked Brady.

Chopper John took them down over the gaping hole. Two figures were off to one side, one kneeling, the other standing with his hand on the kneeling man's shoulder. There was no need for words aboard the chopper. It was obvious what had happened. They completed a circle of the scene and touched down next to the crash vehicles.

'They burned right through,' announced the chief as they approached.

'How deep is the water here?' asked Brady.

'Too deep for scubas, Admiral,' replied the chief.

Back toward the airfield, Marc could see a salvage party coming toward them. 'We'll have to gather up all of the debris, and the wing. Maybe there will be a clue for the accident board.' His voice sounded hollow to himself, as if he were speaking from deep inside his head. 'Do we know how many were on board?'

The chief shook his head.

Marc didn't want to leave. In his grief he kept thinking that there was something he could do, or should be doing. The suddenness of it all had temporarily interrupted his normally logical chain of thought. 'We don't have any divers on the Ice,' he announced in a low monotone, not even knowing why he bothered. What could divers do? Recover the bodies? Salvage the wreckage so the accident board could weigh the evidence and come up with a pompous decision as to why Tilley and his companions had either drowned, been blown to bits, or burned alive? Airplanes didn't just simply blow up in midair. If they did, it was because of weapons malfunction, or fire, or the ignition of explosive fumes. The DeHaviland carried no weapons. There had been no fire sighted by the tower operator. That left explosive fumes. A fuel leak. That's why the engines were shut down, thought Marc. Tilley had a fuel leak somewhere out in the right wing. That also would explain the lack of radio communications and the straight-in approach. There had been little wind, but it had been in the opposite direction from that required for a straight-in approach. Tilley had wanted the aircraft on the deck as soon as possible. He just hadn't gotten it there soon enough. Why convene a board? Tilley smelled fumes, suspected a fuel leak, tried to isolate it, but a spark set off the fumes. Why not just write it up, one sentence, and go back to work until the next crew died? Exhaling deeply to clear his head, Marc returned to the real world. An accident board would be convened. All of the standard procedures would be followed. And no other crews were going to die. Not this cruise. A merciful God just wouldn't let that happen.

It would be a month before qualified divers and equipment could be brought to the Ice. The deep water of McMurdo Sound in the area of the crash was churned constantly by swift and erratic currents. Depending upon the integrity of the wreckage, it could be scattered over several square miles before salvage attempts could be mounted. There was another vital factor. Summer was almost over. A deep dive, out on the exposed ice shelf during the month of March, would be overly hazardous.

The pitiful debris that was recoverable was examined

and the remnant of the right wing showed evidence of a violent explosion. The two engines were smashed beyond any kind of analytical examination. The accident board convened, studied the matter, and reported out the same day: Explosion from unknown cause, catastrophic damage to aircraft, all hands lost. The admiral endorsed the findings, recommending that salvage operations not be conducted due to the deep cold water with known dangerous currents as well as the unpredictable March weather. For the time being, at least, Tilley and his companions would join Frosty Kohn in remaining on the White Continent.

'Hell, there are worse places to spend eternity,' said Brady, offering Marc a glass of sherry in his quarters. It had been four days since the accident and the paperwork had been completed. All except the letters. Marc had four of them to write.

'What's happening?' asked Marc, gazing out over the ice shelf.

'The law of averages,' replied Brady quietly. 'We've gone almost eight years without a fatality. You can't fight this place forever and keep winning.'

'I disagree, Admiral. We run a sophisticated operation. Our people are not just professionals, they're handpicked from the best.'

'I suppose that means they can ignore the antarctic weather, or hold the pieces of an airplane together after months of pounding it to death in rough open fieldwork?'

'Granted – Murray and Frosty should have turned back. And maybe Tilley should have landed the moment he smelled fumes. But those are two separate incidents. I just find it hard to think that any law governs such things.'

'Well, the law of averages is a peculiar law. It acts in retrospect. You don't consider it until after something happens.' Brady set down his wine glass and grabbed a bottle of scotch. 'Why don't we just get blotto?'

They each drank two double shots in silence, watching the sun hovering over Minna Bluff, just a touch above the horizon. Brady poured them each another.

'You'll like the Naval War College, Marc. It'll be a sabbatical after this.'

It was the first confirmation Marc had heard of his impending orders. The exec would relieve him as commanding officer in June. That was predestined in the ordinary course of things. War college would be nice. Dorothy would like that. The genteel life of favored military officers, the academic atmosphere, the receptions and parties in Newport and days off to explore New England.

'Funny, isn't it?' remarked Brady. 'You go through something like 'Nam where you lose shipmates and wallow in the filth of an unnatural war, then you get a duty like this, away from the real world, actually. All peace and tranquility. And then, things happen and it doesn't seem any better down here than anywhere else. What could we have done, Marc, to have prevented the loss of that lovely young woman and Bud Tilley and his crew? Are we at fault?'

'Not according to the navy, Admiral, but I think we'll always wonder if there was something we could have done. I don't know. It's hit me so hard, and you, too, obviously. I appreciate that, Admiral. You're a good flag officer.' The room had a slight list to it, and Marc found some of his words dropping off his tongue before they could be fully formed. And a junior did not normally compliment his senior in such a fashion. Brady was pouring him another drink.

'You know, Marc, you're a good family man. That's awunnerful thing,' Brady's words were running closer together also. 'I wish Sarah and I had a kid, but we were always going to wait until the next year, the next duty. 'Course, I may have a little brown-skinned bastard scampering up a palm tree in the South Pacific. I had some hell-raising tours as a junior officer before I went to 'Nam. Christ,' continued Brady, shaking his head in disbelief, 'he – or she – wouldn't still be climbing for coconuts, the child would be grown by now. Twenty-five years.' He paused and sipped his drink. 'That was a lifetime for some of my buddies who bought it over North Vietnam. Now, I could have a kid just that age. Makes you think.'

'I never consider "ifs", Admiral. I've always made my decisions and never looked back.'

'Uh huh . . .'

'I wonder if I'll rework this tour in my mind. I don't think War College will erase these memories. I've had the best, and now the worst. That type of thing is supposed to season an officer, I understand. But I bet I see Frosty's gold wings over that feminine chest and smell Tilley's cigar for a long time . . . a long time.'

Marc waited for some response to his statement. Instead, a low vibrating sound caused him to turn away from the picture window. Brady was asleep, his head on one arm of the plastic sofa, his empty glass sitting on his chest, and one foot crossed over the other. Marc set down his glass, quietly left the hut, and headed for his own room.

24

Frosty stared at the glass.

'Drink,' directed Scnell.

'I'm not thirsty. And why have you brought me here?'
She stared angrily at the doctor, who wore a white
coverall and stared back at her through a plastic viewplate
in his headdress.

'Your blood gases show a marked discrepancy in electrolytes. Our research has produced a chemical medication to alleviate such a problem.'

Frosty had tasted fear before, in flight training, in that
first night carrier delivery, in Antarctica at the controls of
her C-130, in the chopper with Squadron Leader Murray
as they spun into the snow. This was a different fear.
They had refused to let her call McMurdo. They would
not answer any of her questions about treatment. No
visitors, but surely the people in the camp would have
wanted her to know their concern. Did they think she was
an idiot? Something was going on, and like a chapter of a
Stephen King story, the chilling bastards had a mysterious
evil air about them. And that German accent. At first,
she had thought nothing of it. Argentina was a mixture of
European societies. But she kept thinking back to the
movies she had watched about Nazi Germany and the
fictional flicks that always had a mad German scientist.
Had her predicament anything to do with such a bizarre
plot?

'Doctor, I have had enough. I won't drink your damn
medication and I demand to be taken immediately to your

communications shack, where I can talk to my commanding officer at McMurdo. I don't know what is going on, but if this is truly medicine, as you say it is, I still pass. My electrolytes can wait until I get back to McMurdo. I feel fine. My electrolytes feel fine. You are on the verge of committing an international criminal act, namely the kidnapping and unlawful detention of an American citizen. If I am not immediately released, with full freedom of this camp, so that I may contact my authorities, I shall prefer charges against you, your associate, Eisner what's-his-name, and every Argentine son of a bitch in this station who is putting me through all of this.'

'You will drink your medication.' Scnell lifted her hand with the cup.

'You drink it!' exclaimed Frosty, her voice firm and threatening. Incensed, she threw the contents of the cup at him.

Scnell frantically leaped back. 'Jew bitch!' he screamed and ran through the door. Frosty tried to follow, but it was locked and through the viewing window she could see the doctor standing in the midst of a powerful spray of steam, which hit from all directions.

That sure as hell was not medication, you bastard, thought Frosty. What is going on? She pounded on the door with her fists, tears of anger and frustration rolling down her cheeks.

Ten minutes later, three men entered, clothed in protective suits. She couldn't tell if the doctor was one of them. But one held her tightly in his grasp, another squeezed her nostrils together and yanked her head back, and the third poured a paper cup of 'medicine' down her gagging throat. Then they stripped her; dragged her into the shower; and held her through the cycle of the orange lights, then the green liquid that made her gag further on anmonia fumes and close her eyes from the intense irritation. Finally, they pulled her through the footbath, even though she had wrestled herself into a sitting position, and dried her off. Scnell handed her a robe.

'Cover yourself,' he snarled. 'I would not want my assistants to think you desirable.'

'Sex rears its ugly head,' muttered Frosty, wrapping the soft robe tightly around her and looping the ties together. She resisted the almost irresistible urge to attack the doctor. She could get in some good licks before anyone could help the old bastard. But that would not contribute to any solution to her problem. 'What did you pour down my throat?'

'Sit,' ordered the doctor.

What the hell, thought Frosty. She sat.

'You might as well know. It will make the waiting more interesting. You have just made an invaluable contribution to medical science – the development of a vaccine that will resist a rather common, but otherwise thoroughly deadly, biological weapon.'

'That's what you poured down my throat?'

'Exactly. And you swallowed the vaccine yesterday, so you see, you have nothing to be concerned with.'

'No ovens?'

'Ha! Such bravado! It must be the American influence. Jews have no such courage. They whimper and die like the inferior beings they are. I know.'

Frosty felt her insides grow cold and quiver. But Scnell would never know she was too scared and angry to think as clearly as she would have liked. She tensed every muscle in her body to hold back her fists.

'You will live, Jew, because of German skill and technology. The vaccine will work. But I will do you a favor, because you are spirited. When our time together is over, I will see that you have a painless and peaceful departure.'

316

'I am not a Jew, bastard, although I wish to God I were one now. My mother was a Catholic – Mary McBride – my father a Kohn, surely, but not a practicing man of any faith. He never saw the inside of any temple, and my mother stopped going to Mass after I was in my teens. I suppose I am what some people would call a generic American, if anything, so get your jollies if you want from all this, but not because you are killing another Jew. You're killing an American naval officer, and my country will take a very dim view of that.'

'They will not know.'

'Oh, yes, they will. If I have any faith at all, it is that they will know.'

Scnell rose as Eisner entered.

'I understnd our volunteer was not too cooperative.'

'The evaluation is underway.'

Eisner handed Frosty a message form. 'I thought you might like to see this.' She read the words to herself. It was an interception of Brady's notification to the Bureau of Naval Personnel that he was calling off the search and she was presumed lost. She handed it back to him. Eisner folded it and stuck it in his shirt pocket. 'Lieutenant Kohn, you have the choice of cooperating with us and enjoying a relatively comfortable stay, assisting us in this research, or you can continue to be a problem, in which case we will restrain you and you will get only minimal care.'

Frosty pictured Eisner with her spittle dripping down his face but opted for Plan A. She would settle down. Maybe there was some remote chance she could figure a way out. She was certainly no worse off than some of her more distinguished predecessors who had spent their vacations in the Hanoi Hilton. 'I am an American naval officer and I demand to be treated with consideration of the Geneva Conventions.'

317

'A – how do you say it? – a sea lawyer, I see,' responded Eisner. 'I am prepared to treat you as a fellow military officer, with certain constraints, of course. You will have private quarters, reading material, even video if you like. You will have proper nourishment, and as you can see, excellent medical attention. If you wish, I can have one of my young officers provide you with suitable . . . entertainment. In return, you will conduct yourself as we direct. Agreed?'

'For starters, agreed, but you can skip the social hour.'

'Then tonight, as a preamble to such a relationship, I shall invite you to dine with our fuehrer and several of his staff.'

Fuehrer?

'I protest! She must be kept in quarantine,' objected Scnell.

'You have assured me the weapon cannot be transmitted from one human to another.'

'It cannot. But I object most strongly to any exposure to our people.'

'Object to Bormann. It is he who asked me to see if I could arrange this. There will be only those of us who understand such things. You will join us also, of course.'

'I will, but I still protest.'

Eisner returned to the door and opened it. Two male nurses entered. 'Take her to her room.'

Frosty slapped the first hand that reached for her. 'I will go.'

The door closed.

'See, Scnell, it is a matter of diplomacy. The woman knows she will eventually die, but she is a military officer in the truest sense. It radiates from everything she says and does. I will give her that courtesy, as long as she is cooperative. An interesting person, is she not? A woman, a Jew, a pilot, an officer, a new American. We should try to understand her before she . . . leaves.'

25

Marc watched 130 lift into the antarctic sky. On board were Brady, the last of his staff, and the few remaining USARPs who ordinarily would have been returned to Christchurch a week ago. But the loss of operational time during the search for Frosty, and the day's standdown for the memorial services for Tilley and the occupants of the Ranger, plus a hellish preceding week of snowstorms and ice fog, had placed the squadron behind in its critical logistic requirements for end of the season. The last few days had been hectic, indeed, with a late retrieval of the people out at Cape Crozier. Chopper John had managed, on his fifth try, to finally work around the weather and recover the last two of the penguin study group, a married biologist couple who were down to their last three days' rations. One wag had commented that after that last week in their fragile tent, waiting out the winds and snowstorms, the couple probably had set some sort of record for sexual activity.

Siple Station was topped off with heating oil for their long winter amid an increase in falling snow, which made the last trips touch and go with respect to getting in and out of their skiway. Each flight encountered whiteout conditions. Pole Station had been evacuated three weeks back, except for the few scientists and support personnel spending the winter at the bottom of the world, but on the return flight to McMurdo, 131 had suffered an extremely hard landing and wound up with a hairline crack in the right main landing gear strut. It had been flown early back to Christchurch with the gear chained in the down position, depriving the squadron of its use for the critical airlift off the continent.

Finally, with their requirements filled, the helicopter crews had secured their Hueys for the winter, leaving only Chopper John and his reliable whirlybird to wind up the odds and ends of the season and provide the Hill-Strip shuttle.

Calendarwise, summer was still the season, not being officially over until late March, but the antarctic environment did not necessarily recognize that fact, and temperatures were already dropping at Siple and in most of the fieldwork areas. The weather at South Pole Station had become more unpredictable and the temperature was dipping into the minus seventies for short periods of time. The sea-lane broken through the ice over McMurdo Sound earlier in the season began to refreeze with the out passage of the last supply ship and the departure of the Coast Guard icebreaker. Traditionally, by February 28, the summer 'visitors' and VXE-6 would be off the Ice.

But today, March 1, Marc sat with Zinwicki in the dining hall at McMurdo, pushing the remnants of his evening meal around on his plate while he and his copilot discussed the final details to be taken care of before the departure of 129, the last plane on the Ice. Across from them sat Ben Molder, who would be wintering over, and Anatolii Kakushkin, who would be flying with them back to Christchurch.

'I think we've covered everything,' said Marc. 'Zin, we don't want to forget the last-minute mail.'

'I've already made arrangements to have a postal clerk put it on the shuttle with us in the morning.'

'Good.'

Ben Molder stopped stirring his coffee, a habit he indulged in despite the fact he didn't use sugar or cream. 'Marc, we know this has been a terrible season for you.

But, as usual with VXE-6, you folks did it again and we appreciate it. I'm sure that there's no better logistic support anywhere than what you give to us. I guess we won't be seeing you, individually, next season.'

'I hope not,' Marc replied with an exaggerated smile. 'Don will have the squadron and I'm sure he will do his customary outstanding job.'

A galley phone rang in the background.

'I, too, would like to express my appreciation for support of my projects here at McMurdo,' added Kakushkin. 'It is nice to work with you, with all Americans, who treat me with hospitality and consideration. My government will be told of American airmen who flew me around as own people.'

'Thank you, Doctor. We appreciate that.'

One of the messmen was hurrying toward their table.

'Well, Anatolii,' commented Molder, 'you have been a real asset to our own solar study program, we . . .'

The messman was standing by Marc, obviously impatient to deliver his message.

'Excuse me,' interrupted Marc. 'Yes?'

'Commander Bradford, they want you over at flight-following right away.'

Marc made a quick mental review of the day's flight schedule. There should be nothing in the air. Only the shuttle helicopter was still active on the Ice, and Chopper John was at the adjacent table, dunking cookies in his tea.

'I'll be right there.'

The messman hurried away and said something on the telephone before hanging it up.

'My last night and I still can't finish dinner. Excuse me, folks, shall we get together in the lounge later?'

'We'll see you there,' said Molder, waving Marc on with his hand.

321

Marc was met as he entered flight-following by a very agitated duty petty officer. 'Sir! We've got Siple Station on the primary flight-following frequency. They need to talk to you!'

Puzzled, Marc picked up the mike. 'Siple, this is McMurdo. Bradford here. Over.'

The immediate reply was broken up by some sort of atmospheric disturbance, but still readable. 'Commander, this is Frank Heller, the station leader. We have just picked up a very broken and garbled message that I think you should listen to. Rather than try and repeat it, I have it on tape and will play it. Can you copy it? I think it may need some interpretation.'

The duty air controlman threw a recording switch and nodded.

'Yes, Siple, we're recording. Go ahead with your tape.'

At first there were ten to fifteen seconds of static, then a high-pitched voice, but the words were unintelligible. The static continued and two words suddenly came through loud and clear, '. . . after me . . .' It sounded very much like a female voice. More static and then an interrupted series of words, '. . . this . . . cone . . . station . . . please answer . . . after me . . . read?. . .'

'Sounds like a woman,' commented Marc. 'Do we have any females wintering over at South Pole?'

'Sir, we've talked to Pole. They aren't sending or receiving any of this, and our communication with them is good.'

The static faded again and the voice continued, '. . . cone . . . cone . . . eights stay . . . please come . . . teens after me . . . do you . . .'

'What was that word? Cone? She keeps repeating "cone." Does that mean anything to anyone?' Marc looked around. Molder had joined him along with Zinwicki. The younger officer's face was dead white.

'No, Captain, not "cone" – Kohn!' emphasized Zinwicki.

'Hush!' admonished Marc. The voice was on again.

'. . . lieutenant . . . get me . . . I am at . . . shun . . . teens . . . to get me . . . do you read?'

'Dear God,' exclaimed Marc, leaning forward and straining to hear more of the transmission. 'It can't be!'

The static stopped and Heller came up on the circuit. 'Did you receive that, Commander?'

'Yes, yes, stand by, please.' Marc stood transfixed, his whole body tense with a mixture of joy and disbelief. 'That's Frosty Kohn!' He turned and slapped Zinwicki's shoulders. 'That's Frosty! How on God's earth?. . .'

'Have them play it again,' urged Zinwicki.

'Siple, play the tape again, please.'

The static and the faint, frightened voice were heard again over the flight-following loudspeaker.

'It has to be!' agreed an equally startled Molder. 'Don't you recognize that voice? And the words: lieutenant; Kohn; and eights; and shun. What's "shun"?'

'That's Frosty Kohn and she's at Eights Sta*shun!*' said Zinwicki.

Marc could hardly speak. It was just too much to even hope for. But he had heard the voice. He had heard the words. 'Siple, can you talk to her?'

'You just heard all we've been able to get. We picked it up on international air distress, VHF, 121.5 megahertz.'

'How long ago did you receive the transmission?'

'Approximately fifteen minutes ago.'

'Keep trying and notify us the moment you get anything else, the very moment, do you understand? We will be standing by this frequency. Over.'

'Yes, McMurdo, we will do that. This is Siple Station. Out.'

'I can't believe this. We need to talk. Let's go into the

ops office,' suggested Marc, turning to the air controlman as the three headed for the adjacent office. 'Leave the speaker up and call us the moment anything comes on.'

They hurriedly sat around the duty officer's desk.

'I can feel my heart beating,' said Zinwicki.

'It's a miracle! Do we all agree that it *is* Frosty?' asked Marc.

'Impossible as it is, it has to be,' stated Molder.

'I agree,' said Zinwicki, 'and she's at Eights Station.'

'How did she get there? No matter for the moment,' said Marc, ignoring his own question. 'But what is she telling us?'

'Come and get me,' said Zinwicki.

'Yes, but there was more. Who or what are the "teens"? She said the teens were coming to get her – Oh, my God!'

'What?' asked Zinwicki, leaving his mouth open.

'The Argen*teens*,' answered Marc, nodding his head in confirmation.

'From Argentino,' added Molder.

'Of course, only they are not Argentines. They are the Germans,' said Marc very slowly.

Molder leaned forward. 'Are you thinking what I'm thinking?'

'You're damned right I am. It has to be. That's the only possible explanation,' murmured Marc.

'What is? What are you talking about?' asked Zinwicki. He was sitting on the edge of his chair and while he fully agreed that the voice belonged to Frosty Kohn, he had no idea what Marc and Molder had come up with by way of explanation.

'Zin,' began Marc, ignoring Zinwicki's urgent question. 'You get down to the strip and alert the crew. Full fuel, sixteen JATO. We'll be down as soon as we can. I want 129 ready to go to Eights as soon as we get there. And the Quack; I want the Quack to go with us. Move!'

Zinwicki knew they were going after Frosty and that's all he had to know for the moment. He was practically out the door before Marc finished the sentence.

'Ben, I think Frosty's in deep trouble and I know what's happened.'

'The Argentines found her and Murray.'

'No, the Germans found her and Murray, or else they stumbled into Argentino trying to evade the weather. For some reason the station didn't report that to us. The fact that Argentino is a Nazi colony must have been compromised by her and Murray before they could contact us. Those bastards have been holding her prisoner!'

'How'd she get to Eights?'

'God, I don't know, but she's there. Maybe Murray, too. And I think she was trying to tell whomever she could contact that they – the Germans – are coming after her!'

'I agree.'

Marc stood and walked several paces, obviously trying to come up with a course of action. 'Do we have any small arms? You know, rifles or pistols that the biologists use to collect specimens?'

'We have a small USARP armory in the chalet. Maybe a half dozen rifles. Yes, six, I believe.'

'Ammo?'

'Some.' Molder looked in Marc's eyes. 'I have a revolver.'

'I figured as much. We'll need everything we've got, Ben.'

'What are you going to do?'

'First of all, I'm going to run out there and tell that air controlman that he is not to breathe a word of this to anyone. If he does, I'll get him permanent duty at South Pole. I don't know the political ramifications, but we better play it close to our chest until I can get some word to the admiral. You run over to the chalet, get every weapon you've got, and meet me in Brady's hut. It's empty and we can plan there. Also, bring anything else you can come up with that we might need. I have two marines down on the strip, Sergeant Wineman and Sergeant Tanaka, my loadmaster. Plus my plane captain. Dare's a sailor, but he's a hunter. We'll add whomever we have to, to use all of the weapons. That's all I can think of at the moment . . . wait!. . . does Siple have any transportation?'

'They have a snowcat and several snowmobiles, but they are 150 miles from Eights. Besides, they are only five scientists. It would take them twelve hours to get over to Eights, even if the weather is good.'

'It'll take us the better part of six, but that's still much faster. We can't take enough fuel to ensure a round trip, though.'

'Refuel at Siple after we get Frosty,' suggested Molder.

'I hope to God we have left some fuel there. I'll have them informed to be ready. Let's do it.' Marc headed back toward the flight-following room while Molder left for the chalet.

Ten minutes later, they met in Brady's hut.

'Three old M-1s, one with a telescopic sight; three military carbines, all thirty calibers; plenty of ammunition,' reported Molder. 'I also picked up three walkie-talkies, then ran into Chopper John coming back from taking Zinwicki to the strip. The weapons and radios are on his chopper and he's standing by – hopelessly confused.'

'I can imagine. With your revolver, that's seven weapons.'

'You think the Germans are armed?'

'I don't know what to think, but after that briefing by

326

Minochetti, I would say we can expect anything. At least, we'd be foolish not to assume it.'

Marc walked over to the picture window to gather his thoughts, but stepped back quickly.

'What is it?' asked Molder.

'Kakushkin. It looks like he's coming here.'

The sound of the outer storm door opening confirmed the arrival of the Russian, who walked in uninvited. He reached inside his parka, pulled out an automatic, and offered it to Marc – handgrip first – smiling mischievously. 'I believe you have need for this. However, is Soviet weapon and would be more effective in Soviet hands.'

'How did you find out about this?' asked Marc.

Kakushkin shrugged. 'It is my profession. I think now is time for me to repay what you have done for me, and besides, I have love for your female officer. She is very professional also. I go with you and Ben?'

'Eight weapons is better than seven,' offered Molder in support of the Soviet's request.

'Why not? But are you aware of what we may encounter?'

'Of course. Soviet intelligence is particularly effective when dealing with former – or future – Nazis. You know who I am. What better credentials can I offer?'

Marc was beyond further surprise. Everyone in McMurdo had played the game, but everyone seemed to know who everyone else was. There was no time for further discussion.

'Let's go, we can plan on the plane. Besides, if further word gets out about this,' said Marc, glancing at Kakushkin, 'everybody in the station will want to go.'

Marc sat up front with Chopper John as they flew down to the strip.

'Skipper, what in the hell is going on?' asked Chopper John.

Marc briefed him on the radio message. 'But keep it quiet, John, until we get back.'

Chopper John was so excited about Frosty's appearance that he was practically jumping under his seat straps, 'Frosty's alive! I can't believe it! But I'm a terrible blabbermouth, Skipper, and the way I read this, you're one gun short.'

'One man short, John. I'll pick up somebody on the strip.'

'No, sir. You got your eighth gun right here.'

'Who'll handle the shuttle while we're gone?'

'No one needs to. They can use surface transportation. If I have to, I'll prang this bird when we get to the strip. Then, even I won't be needed back here.'

'All right, then it's me, you, Zinwicki, Dare, Molder, our two marines, and Kakushkin.'

'That's a right sharp little firefight team, Skipper.'

One-two-niner was turned up and standing by when Marc and the others arrived at the strip. Chopper John shut down the Huey and left his crewman to secure it to the ice tie-down stakes. Within four minutes Marc had the Hercules airborne and pointed towards Eights Station as they climbed.

'Damn! I forgot to try to reach Christchurch and brief the admiral,' he said, punching on the autopilot.

'We can crank up the single sideband and try them,' suggested Wineman.

'No, it's probably just as well. The admiral can't help us and he might disagree with our approach. Besides, that circuit is clear language and anybody could pick it up. I don't think we're ready to announce this to the world yet.'

'It's already all over McMurdo,' interjected Zinwicki.

'I told that air controlman to keep it quiet!'

'I took the liberty of contacting the Officer-in-Charge of the winter-over party. I gave him a brief rundown and told him nothing was to leave the Ice. He's put a hold on all radio contact,' said Molder. 'I didn't mean to overstep my authority, but I knew you had so many things on your mind.'

'Good. Thanks, Ben. I should have thought of that. My heart is just starting to slow down, now.' Leaving his seat, Marc stood on the flight deck with Molder, Chopper John, Kakushkin, and his two marines. The Quack had crawled into the upper bunk to give the others room. 'When we get to Eights, I want Frosty on the airplane as fast as possible and we'll get the hell out of there.'

'What if the Germans have already arrived?' asked Wineman.

'That's *our* station, even if it is abandoned.'

'You think that'll make any difference to those people? After as far as this thing has gone?' asked Molder.

'No,' replied Marc. 'This can be a real can of worms. It depends on how many there are. But we're not leaving without Frosty.'

Kakushkin leaned toward the others to be better heard over the flight-deck noise level. 'We must hope they send someone in authority and not just search party. We can argue political side with someone familiar with that aspect. If just armed search party, maybe they do not listen to reason.'

Marc peered outside at the cloud deck underneath. 'You know, we're getting there close to low light. With this cloud cover, it could be fairly dark underneath. How much twilight do we have over here, Ben?'

'Well, this time of the year the sun does drop below the horizon for a short time, maybe an hour or so.'

'What time?'

Molder checked his watch. 'We're probably six hours from sunset. I'm not exactly sure.'

'It'll be light for our landing, then.'

'Yes, but if these clouds hold, it won't be good daylight.'

Marc nodded. 'We've been into Eights a number of times. I don't anticipate any difficulty.'

'Sir,' spoke up Sergeant Tanaka, 'if I may make a suggestion?'

'Of course.'

'If the Germans are already there, I think we should put our cards on the table right away. Sergeant Wineman and I can accompany you off the aircraft, with our weapons. The others can make a show of force around the aircraft and even try to fool them into believing we have more personnel inside. We just march right up and say we've come for Lieutenant Kohn.'

'It could work,' suggested Molder.

'Do Germans play poker?' asked Chopper John.

'I hope not,' replied Marc.

'Okay, Sarge, take us down.' Marc had retaken the command pilot's seat and their radar indicated they were over Eights Station. The top of the overcast was at 9,300 feet and it seemed to extend from horizon to horizon. Wineman double-checked his identity of Mount Rex and the location of the camp radar reflectors. They would use their standard radar approach, departing to the north toward the Bellingshausen Sea coastline.

They started their procedure turn at 7,000 feet, in the clouds. Inbound, they would not descend below 5,000 feet unless they were visual.

'Looks good, Captain,' reported Wineman, his face glued to his radar scope. 'We're coming out of the turn with Eights dead ahead, twenty-three miles.'

330

'Five thousand, five hundred feet,' reported Zinwicki. 'We're coming out of it.'

Marc let the Hercules drop another thousand feet. They were well below the base of the cloud layer and visibility was good despite heavy snow showers. The radar altimeter indicated 2,300 feet.

'I've never seen snow like this down here,' remarked Dare, leaning forward between the two pilots' seats.

'Look at that outside air,' commented Zinwicki. 'It's a heat wave, only minus twelve and we're still 2,000 feet up.'

'Yes, and the surface around Eights is 1,500 feet or more. This could be a wet snow compared to what is normal around here,' commented Marc.

'There it is!' announced Zinwicki. 'Ten o'clock!' The tops of the Eights Station huts sat ahead, just to the left – two dark blocks in the white snow.

'Twelve miles,' reported Wineman.

'Good vis,' observed Zinwicki.

'Thank God for small favors,' murmured Marc.

'Skipper,' said Zinwicki cautiously, 'there's an airplane down there.'

'Where?'

'Just to the left of the station.'

Marc strained to see. Molder, Chopper John, and Kakushkin all were forward, eyes dead ahead.

'It looks like an Otter,' observed Molder.

'It is,' confirmed Zinwicki, 'with Argentine markings. Germans?'

Marc dropped to within 500 feet of the surface.

'See anybody?' asked Molder.

'There! Running from the hut – it's Frosty!'

The hatless figure was jumping and waving her arms, long raven hair streaming in the wind.

Marc descended to just above the snow and roared by,

dipping his wings as everyone on the flight deck waved and cheered. Frosty Kohn dropped to her knees and placed her hands over her face.

'The Otter has a collapsed right gear and a crumpled wing,' announced Chopper John as they pulled up. Marc had not even bothered to look at it. 'That surface may be rough under the new snow cover, Skipper,' he added.

'That, I noticed. We'll stick with the normal landing area. It should be as smooth there as anywhere.'

On final, Marc studied the snow below. It was criss-crossed with interlaced sastrugi, some of the ridges looking a yard across. It was impossible to tell how high they were. Even six to eight inches would be a serious hazard.

'Problem,' announced Dare. 'We got a chip light on number one.'

Marc glanced back over his shoulder at the orange glow over Dare's head. The light meant metal particles in the oil, and metal particles could mean an imminent engine failure. 'That's our high time engine, isn't it?'

'Yes, sir. Oil pressure's fluctuating.'

'We'd better shut it down,' decided Marc.

'We don't have to,' answered Dare quickly, 'there it goes!'

The oil pressure needle was plummeting toward zero.

'Shut down number one,' ordered Marc.

Zinwicki leaned forward and placed the farthest left of the four engine condition levers into the full feathered position. Instantly, all fluids were cut off from the engine and the propeller blades twisted to their feathered position.

Marc continued his approach. With full flaps, nose high, and three engines turning, he sat the Hercules down as slowly as he dared.

'Hold on,' cautioned Zinwicki.

The initial contact was smooth, but as the Hercules slowed and settled into the snow, the ride became brutal.

'Jesus!' exclaimed Zinwicki, reaching forward to help Marc hold the yoke in its full back position.

The C-130 entered a series of rapid shudders as the main skis rode head-on into the hardened snow ridges under the fresh snow.

'They must be pure ice!' yelled Marc, holding the shaking yoke full back, trying to keep the nose ski off the surface as long as possible. They slowed rapidly, but just as the airspeed passed forty knots, the flight deck jerked violently, there was a loud crack, and the nose gear plowed unsteadily into the snow as the aircraft came to a stop.

'Shit!' announced Zinwicki.

'Secure the engines,' ordered Marc. 'We've popped a nose strut for sure. To hell with it. Let's go see Frosty!'

He was first out of the lowered crew entrance door and met the running figure twenty yards from the plane.

'Frosty!' he cried as she jumped on him and they fell into the snow, laughing and hugging. Zinwicki piled on top of them and they rolled over and over in sheer jubilation. Molder and Chopper John were next and pulled Frosty to her feet. She kissed each of them and hugged them both at once.

'Wineman! Tanaka! Do you guys look good!' shouted Frosty, turning her attention to the two marines. They returned her enthusiastic hugs. 'Gosh, I'm crying like a baby!' she exclaimed. Spotting Kakushkin, she reached out to him and he grabbed her around the waist.

'Is good to see you, Lieutenant!'

'Thanks, Doctor Kakushkin, it's good to see you! Dare!'

The plane captain was just running up. He had been unable to resist his paternal urge to take a look at their nose ski. 'Lieutenant Kohn!' he shouted above the laughter and happy chatter. As Frosty kissed him hard on both cheeks, his face flushed.

'And the Quack! This is too much!' screamed Frosty, releasing Dare and embracing the flight surgeon. His tears were matching hers and for a moment they stood, pressed together. Everyone crowded around and the compact group made their way over to the nose of 129.

'What have you done to my airplane?' cried Frosty in happy despair.

'Got a busted strut,' said Dare to Marc.

Marc got down on his knees in the snow and examined the wheel well. Getting up, he was still grinning like a schoolboy. 'Who cares? Come on, let's get inside, out of the air.'

Frosty pulled him toward the huts. 'I've got the oil burner going.'

Inside, they settled themselves around the stove and the Quack handed out mugs. A large pan of boiled coffee was on top of the stove.

'Hey,' announced Zinwicki, 'you look like you've set up housekeeping.'

'Everything we need is right here, except for a radio.'

'All right. First things first. Where have you been? Where's Murray?' asked Marc.

Frosty sobered. 'Dead. We got caught in the weather and he tried to set the chopper down. We couldn't see, of course, and we must have hit in a skid. When I came to, he was buried under the snow with a piece of the helicopter through his side.'

'We launched everything we had, looking for you,' said Marc, refilling his mug.

'I know you did. I heard Tilley overhead once, but the clouds were down to the deck. God, I'll even be glad to see him, the lecherous old bastard!'

Marc covered the awkward silence with a further ques-
iton, 'And then what?'

'Well, I must have been out for a while. When I came
to, I was freezing in the back of an Argentine C-47,
strapped in a litter. They fed me hot soup and took me to
Argentino.'

'They never told us!'

Frosty's voice steadied and slowed. Her look of elation
vanished. 'Captain, there's a real problem over there.
Argentino is a Nazi colony. Real Nazis.'

Marc nodded. 'Yes, we've been getting reports. We
don't know what they're up to.'

'We do now,' announced Frosty. 'We need to get forces
over there, right away.'

'Slow down. Tell me,' said Marc.

Frosty spoke of her arrival in the dispensary, her days
sedated, her first meeting with Scnell and Eisner, the
vaccine, and finally, the forced drink of the mysterious
substance. 'It has to be some kind of biological weapon,
maybe a virus or strain of anthrax or something like that
– they spoke German but that word kept cropping up.
They're obviously planning some sort of biological warfare operation.'

'That's the hard evidence!' exclaimed Marc, recalling
to mind Minochetti's remark that before the president
would consider action, he needed to have more than just
reports. 'We've got them. But you? You may be in
terrible danger.'

Frosty, her eyes wide and head forward in emphasis,
continued, 'I feel great! But, they're real sickos! When
they carried me into their dispensary, someone had
screwed up his signals, I guess. They thought I was out,
but I was really half conscious. The first person I saw
inside was a real old guy in a storm trooper outfit. He
tried to jump into a back room, but we just barged right

in on him and a doctor who had his head practically sticking in one of the old guy's ears. I guess it was a Nazi sick call or something. Anyway, everybody immediately caught holy hell from the doctor and another old guy who came in. Talk about some kind of mad. Everything was in German, and they just let me lie there while they ranted and raved.' Marc estimated Frosty's rate of speech at a new Guinness record.

'Were you hurt badly in the crash?' asked the Quack.

'Oh, I was pretty well chilled through and really almost out of it, but I knew what was going on. My head was banged and my left leg was throbbing like the devil. But nothing serious. After things calmed down, the doctor took care of me and they kept me in a private room for a while, six days, I think. Then they got serious about things.'

'Didn't you tell them who you were?' asked Zinwicki.

'Hell, yes, I screamed US Navy, the Geneva Conventions, international kidnapping, and everything I could think of. But I knew they had me by the short hairs.'

Marc smiled at the Quack. Frosty was not known to use such frank expressions.

'I'd better take a look at you,' offered the Quack.

'I'm great. Really great, at least now. The vaccine works!'

'When we get back to McMurdo, then.'

'With a female corpsman present, Quack!' Frosty leaned over and hugged the doctor as he threw up his hands in mock dismay.

'I tried, I tried,' he said in a singsong voice.

Frosty's eyes sparkled with concentration as she returned to her narrative. 'They put me in the women's quarters eventually. A sort of military officer's agreement between the colonel, Eisner, and me. I would have some restricted freedom and in turn promised to be a good girl.

336

Captain, they've got a whole breeding operation set up there, with computerized records of who slept with whom, when, and how many times they made it that night! I mean, those people are sick!'

Sensing the unasked question, she went on. 'Nobody touched me. Hell, if you want to be an instant persona non grata, drop in on a bunch of Nazis with a last name like Kohn. You would have thought I was an AIDS carrier. They knew I was an American naval officer as well, and they did treat me with a form of reserved military courtesy. But I was an enigma and they obviously weren't going to let me go.'

To spare Frosty the necessity of relating everything in detail, Marc told her of the briefing by Minochetti and the admiral's and his general knowledge about the neo-Nazi setup. It was news to the others, as well, except to Molder and Kakushkin. 'I don't think there is need for more security,' explained Marc to his people. 'This thing will be out in the open as soon as we get off the Ice.'

'Okay,' said Zinwicki, 'how did you get out of there? The Otter?'

'Yes. The old guy was their leader. They even called him their fuehrer. He said his name was Martin Bormann.'

'Incredible,' interrupted Marc.

'You know the name?' asked Frosty.

'He was Hitler's number two man. Everyone thought he had died in Berlin in 1945.'

'Well, that's who he said he was. Everyone kowtowed to him as if he were some sort of god. Anyhow, two days ago he died and they cremated him and had a big ceremony. They were so worked up, they sort of let their guard down. One of the breeders befriended me. She's six months gone and doesn't want to have her baby in that god-awful place, much less raise it there. She is

337

completely disillusioned. Several times we had talked about how I could get away and I told her all I needed was to know when the Otter was warm, and I could do the rest. She was able to monitor the flight schedule; she worked with one of the pilots during the day on records or something. Last evening, as they were burning torches and singing all sorts of martial songs and God knows what all, she took me aside and said that the Otter would be returning from a local field party support mission and would be kept ready as a search and rescue airplane. The whole camp boozed it up – maybe they were celebrating or drowning their sorrows at losing their fuehrer. In the early morning, I had her start a small fire in the women's quarters for a diversion and in the confusion hauled my rear out of there. What she didn't tell me, or probably didn't know, was that they had not refueled the bird. I got into the air and managed to climb on top this stuff and headed for the general direction of Siple before I really paid any attention to the fuel gauge. Not that it would have made any difference – I would have taken off on empty. But I could see I'd never make Siple, so I veered toward the coast, looked for a hole, and found Eights. I didn't expect it to be so rough. I must have bounced twenty feet into the air before I came down – right wing first. Ker-prang! You saw the result.'

'We didn't do a hell of a lot better,' commented Marc.

'I checked out the station and fired up the stove. Plenty of food. Couldn't get the generator started – there's an old Honda portable unit in a back room – so I went back out to the airplane and tried the radio until the battery died. That's about it.'

'What is that?' asked Kakushkin abruptly, holding up his hand for silence. All heard it immediately, the up-Doppler effect of an approaching aircraft. Racing outside, the group peered skyward.

'C-47,' announced Marc, his ears recognizing the slightly out-of-synchronization beat of a pair of reciprocating aircraft engines. 'Sounds like he's in the soup.' The engine noise was faint but definitely passing overhead, probably at around 6,000 feet.

'He's trying to work his way down,' said Frosty.

'Theeeey're heeere,' muttered Zinwicki, imitating the popular saying of an old science fiction movie.

'All right, everyone inside,' ordered Marc. 'We've some things to do.'

Back around the stove, Marc laid out his plan. 'Zin, you and Dare get out to the airplane. Turn it up and get on the horn to McMurdo. Try to get them directly, but go through Siple if you have to. They are to launch the exec from Christchurch ASAP. Have him bring air bags and a new nose strut and whatever else Dare tells you we need. The exec is to refuel at McMurdo and get here pronto! Have them tell him to come up on squadron tactical and we'll find a suitable landing area for him.'

'Why don't we go for the whole enchilada?' suggested Molder. 'The Germans aren't party to the treaty. Have Don bring a squad of Kiwi soldiers. We may have to fight our way out of this.'

'If we do, it'll be before the exec can get here. But, that's a good idea, Zin, so pass it on.'

'Come on, Tom, let's get out there,' said Zinwicki, pulling on his parka.

Marc stood. 'I want everyone to look around in the huts and see what you can come up with, anything we can use to defend ourselves against these people if it becomes necessary. Make an inventory. Tax your ingenuity. We've got eight weapons. That's all. Frosty, you stay put.'

'I'm back in battery, Captain.'

'I know. I just want you to take it easy for the moment.

Help the Quack. Doc, check and see if you can set up a secure place to treat wounded.'

'Do you think it will come to that?' asked the Quack anxiously.

'I don't know. But, that's why I brought you along.'

'I thought it was just to check Frosty.'

'That, too, of course. But we had to be prepared and my skin is certainly not bulletproof. Wineman – you and Tanaka check outside and see if there is anything we can do to better our position.'

'Right, Skipper.' Wineman turned to the big Japanese-Hawaiian. 'Let's go play like we're marines.'

'All in all, I'd rather be surfing,' said Tanaka, carefully laying his M-1 on the galley table.

26

Marc studied the inventory sheets. With only eight weapons, they needed some form of tactical advantage. Surprise could be one – he doubted that the Germans would expect an armed party of defenders. But there was the big unknown: How many would be in the Nazi search party – a squad? Platoon? No, they wouldn't send that many, not in a C-47. He looked up as the sound of the aircraft approached again.

Wineman, on watch outside, stuck his head through the storm lock inner door. 'They're underneath and making another pass!'

'Everyone stay in here,' ordered Marc. 'I'll check.' He joined Wineman outside. The clouds had lowered and the visibility had dropped dramatically. Heavy snow was still falling and in addition there was a hazy pall. Marc took a quick glance at the weather panel on the outside of the hut. 'Temperature and dew point are only two degrees apart. We could have ice fog. There's no wind.'

Wineman pointed to the east. The C-47 was at about 500 feet and closing.

'Let's stay out of sight. Keep them guessing,' suggested Marc. He and the marine squatted in the entrance trench, pressed up against the snow sides. The Argentine Skytrain passed overhead and disappeared into the haze. 'Well, they know someone's here with Frosty,' observed Marc, nodding toward the crippled Hercules.

'If they intend to come down, they damn well better do it now. This stuff is closing in fast,' remarked Wineman.

'Yes,' agreed Marc, 'and I think we've got a sunset.

Look over there.' Wineman followed Marc's upraised arm pointing at the area of maximum light. It was now barely twilight, with an absence of the brighter area that the sun above the horizon would have pushed through the clouds. 'They may have to call it off. It's pretty dark down here, now.'

Both men stood on the snow surface and listened. The engine noise faded but steadied at a low level. The airplane was keeping its distance a few miles to the east. 'I bet the son of a bitch is looking for a place to set down. He saw the pranged Otter and 129 nose low, with number one feathered. He knows it's too rough right here. We better get inside.'

'What's he doing?' asked Molder as Marc and Wineman rejoined the group.

'I think he's coming down. Let's see that inventory.'

Frosty handed him two tablet pages. Marc studied them while Wineman made a suggestion. 'Captain, we've got two things on our side, darkness – or almost darkness – and surprise. I suggest Tanaka and I go outside and dig three snow holes about fifty yards out, 120 degrees apart around the camp. That way, no matter from which direction they approach, we'll have a crossfire field.'

Marc nodded, 'Excellent. Get busy and let me know when they're ready. I think the rest of us can take a station on the roof. It still sticks up about four feet and we can add a snow wall to give us protection. That'll give us a slight height advantage plus cover. John, you and Doctor Kakushkin get hot on the snow wall. Make it thick. It'll have to stop small arms fire.'

Chopper John and the Soviet hurried out.

'Now, Ben, we've got dynamite, detonators, wire, and an exciter box left over from the geologists' projects. And white star flares . . .' Marc ran his fingers down the inventory sheets. '. . . and flashbulbs?'

342

'They're old. Left over from before the electronic flash. But they're still good, I suspect.'

'Do we have any aluminum foil?'

'There's Reynold's Wrap in the galley,' volunteered Frosty.

'Great! How long a light will the star flares give us?'

Molder pursed his lips, then replied, 'They're search and rescue gear. I'd say three minutes or so.'

'All right, here's the plan, and interrupt me at any time. Wineman, Tanaka, and Dare are digging the three snow holes. Between each pair we'll string a series of land mines – dynamite clusters wired to a central control point on the roof. The three perimeter positions will be the points of a defensive triangle around the camp. We'll also lay mines in front of the two entrances, even though a lot of snow blocks the back way.

'The roof of this complex is designed to carry a winter snow load, so it should hold us, no problem. I wish it stuck up higher, but we can't do anything about that. Incidentally, Frosty, I want the stove as hot as you can get it. The roof will radiate some warmth for us. Now, Quack, you and Frosty make me three clusters of flash-bulbs – shoot for a hundred in each cluster. Push the bases through Reynold's Wrap for a common ground and tape wire to the bottom contacts for the hot lead. Use a cardboard box or something to hold them steady. We'll place them just inside our defense perimeter, between the snow holes.'

As he briefed, Marc sketched his plan on a piece of computer paper. 'The roof will be our command post – that will give us some elevation. And when we're on our bellies, the snow wall will give good protection, particularly if we have time to melt some snow and cover it with ice.'

'I don't think we have that kind of time, Marc,' interrupted Molder.

'You're probably right. We'll make do with the snow. The control panel for the dynamite mines and the flash-bulb clusters will be up there with us. Doctor Holley and Lieutenant Kohn will man the medical room . . .'

'Captain, I'd be more valuable up on the roof. I've qualified as expert marksman every year,' broke in Frosty.

'We don't have a weapon for you. But stay near the roof hatch. We can pass wounded down, and if one of us does get pinged you can come up and take his weapon. Okay?'

Frosty nodded, satisfied.

'We need a floodlight,' mused Marc.

'How about the two on the corners of the huts?' suggested Molder.

'Okay, last priority. Take them off and put them on as high a stand or pole as you can. If we have time, we'll orient them toward the Germans. First, get busy on the dynamite mines.'

'Right.'

Marc studied his plan. Time was the critical factor. How much of it did they have to get ready? Wineman stuck his head in and gave him part of the answer. 'Captain, I think they've landed – to the east.'

'How far out?'

'It's hard to tell, but I'd say at least three or four miles.'

'They can't cover that on foot in less than an hour, not on this snow surface.'

'The ice fog is here, too, Captain. They'll have to feel their way. They may want to wait for better visibility, or more light.'

'They're going to be cold out there with no shelter.'

'They can wait in the plane,' suggested the marine.

344

'Not unless they turn it up and use the heater. Otherwise, it will cold-soak and they'll be better off outside. Can we hear them if they run their engines?'

'I doubt it if they stay at idle or low power. I could barely hear them when they landed.'

'Or flew away. Are you sure they touched down?' asked Marc.

'Yes, sir, I think so.'

Zinwicki and Dare arrived and pushed past Wineman, who closed the door as he returned to his task of digging the snow holes.

'As soon as you warm yourself, Tom, give Wineman a hand with the snow holes,' requested Marc. Dare immediately turned and started outside. 'I can warm myself later, Skipper.'

'We talked to McMurdo,' announced Zinwicki, peeling off his parka and rubbing his hands together over the stove. 'They talked to Christchurch. The exec will launch within the hour.'

'That still puts him fifteen hours away. We're on our own.'

'What can I do?' asked Zinwicki.

'Give Ben a hand with the dynamite and start stringing the wire.'

'Wire?' questioned Zinwicki.

Marc had forgotten that Zinwicki and Dare had been in the airplane during the briefing. 'Ben will fill you in.'

Marc checked the M-1s and the carbines. All were in good shape, clean and well oiled. Silently, he gave thanks for the provision in the Antarctic Treaty that allowed a few weapons on the ice for the collection of seal speciments for biological study. Trying to think of anything he might have overlooked, he loaded all the clips, inserted one in each weapon, and arranged the rest in individual piles. The M-1s were semiautomatic, as were the carbines.

345

The Germans, if they were armed, and he felt sure they would be, would probably have more modern equipment, certainly automatic rifles. If only there weren't too many of them. Suddenly, he remembered Wineman's information that the Argentine C-47 was landing to the east. That could eliminate the need for one snow hole. He hurried outside. Wineman had already anticipated the direction of the Germans' approach and he and Tanaka, along with Dare, were finishing up the two easternmost snow holes.

The positions were flush with the surface and Wineman was covering them with white canvas while Tanaka covered the canvas with a thin layer of snow. A small flap was left free for entry.

Colonel Kurt Eisner stood in the open cargo door of the C-47. How the pilot had ever gotten them down through the clouds onto the surface was a mystery to him. Even now, as his troops prepared to disembark, he could see only a few yards from the plane. The thickest ice fog was still to the west, but the low, thick cloud cover and the fact that the sun had dipped below the horizon turned the normal twilight into near dark. He felt a presence by his elbow and glanced back to see Erich Scnell standing behind him.

'This is madness. I have no business being on this mission. This is a young man's task,' said the doktor angrily.

'I hold you responsible for the woman's escape,' said Eisner with equal anger. 'There is no way we can let her get back to McMurdo. Or any of them, now. Just keep hoping they have not already relayed the information about us back on the radio. You let her go, so you come with me to get her back. I keep in shape. You should not drink so much.'

'I'm almost seventy years old. A march though this snow will kill me, for sure.'

'You won't march, you'll be pulled along like the rest of us. Besides, I need you to ensure the vaccine is still working. No one must touch her if she is ill, regardless of your claims that the disease cannot be transmitted. And we have to ensure we cover ourselves against any of the Americans finding out what takes place here. Stand aside.'

The two men cleared the doorway as the troops disembarked and the crew pushed a small green snow tractor to the exit. The troops lifted it in unison and set it in the snow. With only a seat for the driver, the wide-tracked diesel was standard Finnish Army equipment, a tow vehicle for skied troops.

Scnell slipped on his backpack. Inside were syringes to incapacitate any Americans at Eights. Initially, it had been merely a precaution, since their interception of Frosty's radio plea for help indicated she was there alone. Then, if the Americans had heard and did arrive after the troops secured the station, Scnell would administer the powerful sedatives and they would leave the Americans – including the female lieutenant – to die of exposure in the snow. Any subsequent rescue party would find only bodies, with nothing to implicate the Germans or the Argentines. In retrospect, now that they had spotted the Hercules nosed into the snow, the precaution was most fortunate. There *would* be other Americans at the station – the crew of the disabled aircraft.

Two troopers were passing out long, thin cross-country skis and others were aligning them on the snow behind the tractor. Stepping into the simple bindings, each trooper bent down and picked up his section of the tow rope. The squad leader, wearing the insignia of a Wehrmacht lieutenant, reported, 'We are ready, Colonel.'

347

Eisner took the seat of the tractor and two troopers assisted Scnell in mounting his skis and grabbing the rope. He would be next to the last in line. At least, thought Scnell, it was not as cold as he had feared, and there was no wind, thus no chill factor. But as soon as the tractor moved ahead, even though it went forward at only five kilometers per hour, there was an artificial breeze. Scnell pulled up his parka collar and lowered his balaclava so that only his eyes were exposed. Over them he pulled down clear goggles. Surprisingly, he was reasonably comfortable and little effort was required to hold onto the rope once their forward motion was steady. Perhaps he and Eisner would survive this insane situation, after all.

In the antarctic silence, the engine noise was disturbingly loud, prompting Eisner to decide they would use the tractor only up to the last kilometer. Since it was technically the middle of the night, there was a chance they could approach Eights Station undetected, provided they could find it. The pilot had oriented them and they had a magnetic compass, which under most circumstances would be useless in Antarctica's areas of extreme magnetic variation. But they were going only five or six kilometers and the variation would not change appreciably over that short distance. True, the heading they had been directed to take was not accurate, compasswise, but it need not be. They had only to keep it constant and they would go in a straight line. If they did not sight the camp at the end of six kilometers, they would return to the aircraft and wait for better light.

Scnell leaned comfortably against the pull of the towline, as did the entire squad. On foot, their progress would have been exhausting, indeed. He was pleased to find himself breathing normally.

The Scandinavian arctic pants and parkas, worn by the troopers as well as by Scnell, covered several layers of woolen clothing, and next to their skin were loosely woven cotton undergarments. The combination was much more suitable than the heavier and bulkier clothing favored by the Argentines back at Argentino. Most of them were already gone, anyhow, but Scnell was grateful that Eisner had insisted on Scandinavian rather than South American cold-weather gear. Like Scnell, each trooper wore clear snow goggles. Eisner, in front driving the tractor, also had field glasses hanging from his neck, and as they progressed he would periodically raise them and try to penetrate the fog ahead. Along with the troopers, he wore a small field pack, inside of which were bars of high-protein meat and raisins, and candy bars fortified with vitamins. Scnell had directed that at half-hour intervals they were to eat one of the meat bars. Despite the relative ease of their travel, the frigid air would quickly sap their energy, whether they felt the loss or not. The troopers also carried lightweight, collapsible, automatic rifles, slung loosely over their right shoulders. They carried no survival gear. There was ample in the aircraft should they have to return. Otherwise, the American camp would provide emergency provisions and shelter should they need it.

As he drove the clanking tractor over the wide sastrugi, Eisner began to resign himself to the task at hand. It was not nearly as demanding as he had imagined and it gave him a great boost to be leading young German soldiers on an actual war mission. Just as he had forty-five years earlier, he was advancing through winter snow to assault Americans.

The Quack went about his chores, arranging the contents of his medical bag and assorted bandages to prepare for any eventuality. He was living a nightmare and was completely aghast at what was happening. It was almost beyond his comprehension. Nevertheless, he was a doctor of medicine first, a naval officer second, and a political analyst way down the line. As bizarre as it all seemed, he could see his duty clearly.

Marc began his tactical briefing. 'What we have here is a good old-fashioned American ambush, although I pray to God we don't have to execute it. We're set up for an approach from the east, from where we think the C-47 touched down. They could circle around, but it would add some exhausting travel and I suspect that once they step from the airplane and this cold hits them, they'll stick to a straight-line approach. They know a C-130 crew is here, but they have no idea we're armed, and the snow holes and our position on the roof ensure one hell of a crossfire field if we're engaged. Of course, two of our weapons are handguns, not too accurate at long ranges, but I think Molder and Doctor Kakushkin are well versed in their use.' His grin was slightly devilish as he thought, certainly a CIA agent and a KGB officer would feel at home with handguns. 'Wineman, Tanaka, and possibly Dare will be in the snow holes.' He laid out his map.

'The perimeter positions are designated Alpha, Bravo, and Charlie; Wineman, you're Alpha; Tanaka, Bravo; and Dare, Charlie, if need be, but start out on the roof with us. The mine locations are numbered one through twenty, arranged in a circle around the huts. The flashbulb clusters are Tom, Dick, and Harry, with Dick in what we think will be the direct line of approach. The other two will be insurance. Zinwicki, you will fire the flashbulbs under my command. The Germans will have to pass between two of the snow holes unless – God help us – they inadvertently head directly toward one. Wineman and Tanaka will have walkie-talkies. We're going to have to let them get pretty close before we execute.

'I'll start a count from one to five. On three, everyone

close your eyes, *tightly!* On four, we'll fire off the flash-bulb cluster closest to their approach path. On five, we'll fire the first white star flare and open our eyes.

'What will happen is this – I hope. They will have been marching in greatly reduced light for at last an hour, perhaps longer. They'll be coming in with pupils dilated. When we fire those flashbulbs, their pupils are going to snap tight like assholes on an ice block.

'On five, when we fire the white star flare, there they'll be, gentlemen – and lady – standing blind and bare-assed on the level snow. It'll take at least thirty seconds for some of their sight to return. Before that, I'll give them the word that they're in Indian territory and it is too late to circle the wagons.'

'What if they keep coming?' asked the Quack.

'If we do this right, we will achieve a heart-stopping surprise. If they are foolish and start a firefight, we have the tactical advantage, although I don't know yet about the numerical odds. We open fire on my command, put up another white star to keep them exposed on the open snow, and hit the floodlights, which will be aimed their way. Zap! Their pupils will retract a second time. That's why we've positioned the lights on the end of the farthest corner of the huts: they'll draw fire. We'll keep the star flares in the air as long as necessary. Wineman – you and Tanaka must not look at those flares; the troops will be your only concern.

'Now, these guys may be good, perhaps veterans of Argentine military service, maybe even of the Falklands fracas. When they fall, hit 'em again, in case they're playing possum. If we're lucky, they won't even be able to see our muzzle flashes. We'll have a slight height advantage on the roof. It'll be about a hundred-foot range or so and we'll be right on top of them, from three sides. Assuming they approach in column, Wineman and

Tanaka will take the rear ranks; we'll start off at their front.

'Depending upon how fanatical these bastards are, they want Frosty, bad. And us, too, now. Any questions?'

Sergeant Wineman asked the first. 'My dad fought the Nazis and he always used to say they were bad bastards. If they have kept a core group together this long, I think they're pretty goddamned dedicated, excuse me, ma'am, and I don't have any qualms about opening up on them as soon as they're in range. Why give them a chance to counter us?'

'I think they will see the hopelessness of their position right away. They'll be tired, cold, surprised, and confused.'

'And if they're pros,' countered Wineman, 'they'll hit the snow and start covering their asses with concentrated fire toward you folks on the roof.'

'Provided they can see. I really think we're going to damn near shut their eyes. It's pretty dark out there. The sudden light will blind them.'

'Quite possibly. But I'd still rather hit 'em first and worry about it later.'

'Everyone. Open fire only at my order, or immediately upon their opening fire. We want to avoid bloodshed if we can. Surely, they are not suicidal.'

'They are quite serious about their purpose in life. I can attest to that,' observed Frosty dryly.

Marc noded. 'If they attack, pull out all the stops.'

Wineman persisted. 'Captain, in combat it's one hell of a lot better to act rather than react.'

'I agree. And that is exactly what we're doing. After it's over, if you can justify an "I told you so," I'll kiss you full on your lips and pat your ass at the same time,' offered Marc.

Wineman grinned. That type of final decision he could

live with. 'How about the other way around, Skipper?' he asked.

The laughter was good for them all.

Eisner studied the visibility. He really couldn't see much more than twenty or thirty yards due to the continuing snow and darkness. It was not the darkness of night but more of an early morning gloom, a heavy gray fog that was almost solid. He could see no light area, which would have betrayed the position of the sun just below the horizon. The low clouds and fog had to be very thick to maintain such a uniform color – or lack of color. The tractor pulled strongly and Eisner could feel the whispering rhythm of the ease with which his troops rode behind him. He strained his eyes, opening them wide, in a concerted attempt to peer through the freezing moisture.

Marc felt he could wait no longer. 'Wineman, you and Tanaka man the snow holes. If they're coming tonight, they may be getting close.'

The two marines grabbed their M-1s, stepped outside, and made their way the 150 feet to their snow holes.

'Give 'em hell, haole,' whispered Tanaka as they parted.

'*Semper fi,*' returned Wineman. It had been relatively easy to dig down the five feet, and they had lined each hole with slabs of Styrofoam ripped from the solar laboratory room at Eights. The inch-thick layer of plastic provided a welcome insulation from the cold snow. Molder had also brought along a supply of butane hand warmers and had given one to each marine. Once inside his cramped hole, Wineman pulled the canvas flap tight and lit his warmer. For a moment he was concerned about fumes, but noting the cracks around the canvas covering and the low intensity of the fire inside the warmer, he decided the fumes were of no consequence. The hole became surprisingly warm. He had noted that the outside temperature was only minus forty-five degrees when they left the complex for the snow holes. Not too bad. He wore his heaviest antarctic gear, and the hand warmer provided enough warmth to keep down the chill. He had been colder.

Back at the huts, Zinwicki, Dare, Chopper John, Molder, and Kakushkin had manned the roof, prepared to stay until the light and the visibility increased. Then, if there was no sign of the Germans, they would revert to two-man, two-hour watches.

Zinwicki made a radio check with the two marines. Communication was good. Next, he checked the control panels for the identification of the dynamite mines and the flashbulb clusters. The flare gun was beside him, along with the small box of white star flares.

Marc passed paper cups of coffee through the roof hatch to those already in position. 'Call me the instant you see anything. I'm going over some last-minute details with the Quack and Frosty.'

'Will do,' replied Zinwicki quietly.

Marc sipped from his own cup, sitting across the medical table from the Quack. Frosty stood to one side, leaning against one of the mattresses that she and the Quack had used to line the walls and give them some protection from random fire. 'God, this whole thing stinks,' uttered Marc.

'I'm with you, Captain,' agreed the Quack. 'I don't see how this can actually be happening. What can the Germans be thinking?'

'They are thinking, Doctor,' replied Frosty, 'that they have royally screwed up by letting me get away and their whole damned scheme of self-preservation is on the line. They've nothing to lose by eliminating us, and they know that if they can, there's a good chance no one will ever know they did it.'

'I have no doubts that is their intent,' began Marc, 'but I also am confident that once they see we're ready for them, and can reason that we've told someone in the outside world what is happening, they will reconsider. I intend to identify ourselves as soon as those flashbulbs go off and inform them that they are surrounded . . .'

'By two marines,' interjected Frosty with a broad grin.

'. . . and we will open fire if they do not immediately lay down their arms and return to their aircraft. Then, when we get back to the States, we let the politicos sort all of this out.'

'What I really don't understand,' commented Frosty, 'is how the Argentines are letting this take place. They know their responsibilities under the treaty and that this will seriously jeopardize their position on the Ice.'

'I don't think they know anything at all about the intent of the Germans, certainly not the biological warfare research,' said Marc. 'You said only a few maintenance personnel were still at Argentino. They would have no idea what is going on.'

'They're still responsible,' insisted Frosty.

'It's academic at the moment,' commented the Quack.

'Time to go,' said Marc, tossing his paper cup into the trash. He must not let Frosty and the Quack know of his own doubts. He was no more confident of what course the action would take than they. The whole thing was unreal. Within a few minutes, he and his people could very well be locked in a firefight with a group of radical fascists whom the outside world had figured were destroyed forty-three years ago.

He took a final look around the medical area. Between the mattresses and the walls were metal doors that the Quack and Frosty had removed and leaned in position to provide additional protection. The result was a secure bunker, reasonably protected from outside fire. The old Honda generator had finally been started and there were lights, but Frosty had placed several oil lanterns in reserve, just in case. The inside lights would not be seen by the approaching Germans, as the huts had no windows and all cracks had been tightly sealed when the complex had been assembled.

Holley appeared calm despite the deep furrows in his brow, but as Marc gave him a reassuring smile and started to leave, the Quack nervously called after him, 'Captain . . . this is crazy . . . has everyone lost their sense of morality? I'm scared.'

Marc paused. 'They're dealing the cards, Doctor.' He placed his hand on the Quack's shoulder. 'As for being scared, Harold, I am, too.' His frank admission seemed to bolster the Quack, who managed a weak smile.

'We're all scared,' added Frosty. 'We wouldn't be normal if we weren't.' Her sympathetic look broadened into a wide smile. 'I'll take care of you, Quack.'

Holley stiffened. 'I think I'll take my chances on the roof with you, Captain.' His confidence and ability to spar with Frosty had returned.

Marc pulled himself up through the roof hatch.

27

As Marc crawled up onto the roof, the degree of darkness pleased him. The flashbulbs, star flares, and floodlights would have a great deal of effect. Zinwicki was in the center of the small group, beside the mine and flashbulb cluster control. To his left was Ben Molder, and beyond, the senior USARP, Tom Dare. To Zinwicki's right was Chopper John, lying casually on his back, arms raised and hands clasped behind his head, eyes closed. The relaxed helicopter pilot was not one to waste energy, not yet. On the far side of Chopper John was Anatolii Kakushkin, looking every bit the Russian bear with the fur collar of his heavy leather coat turned up around his neck. His matching black leather and fur cap was placed firmly on his head, the enormous flaps pulled tightly over his ears. Like Molder and Dare, he was sitting with his back against the two-foot-wide snow wall that lined the roof. Marc examined the snow block barrier. Between the two rows of foot-thick snow blocks was a series of two-inch-thick planks, ripped from the floor of the generator room. Good. He squeezed in between Zinwicki and Chopper John. As he squatted, he could feel some warmth radiating from the roof, but it was obvious that they would have a limited time outside before having to go back through the roof hatch to warm themselves below. Still, the slight warmth would make their wait more comfortable, and he had a gut feeling that it would not be too much longer. He felt for his marines out there in the frigid pall of fog-laden air, crouched in their snow holes. It must be colder than the proverbial witch's tit.

He had ordered all outside lights turned off except for the single red bulb that marked the main entrance. He wanted the camp to have a normal look.

There was absolutely no breeze. They could be thankful for that. The fog would hold solidly, at least for a while. Marc would just as soon see the snow stop, however. He wondered about the Germans. Would they be out there now, just beyond the edge of his visibility, approaching the way a serpent slithered toward a hare, or would they be waiting out the darkness with their aircraft?

Suddenly Marc heard what sounded like a momentary flutter of metallic vibration, slightly muffled but definitely repetitious, reminiscent of the clatter of steel tracks as they passed over the drive wheels of a tracked vehicle. Or had it been merely a transient surge of the generator as someone inside turned off or on some piece of electrical equipment? He strained hard, but the noise did not repeat itself.

Wineman shifted his weight in an awkward effort to prevent his leg muscles from stiffening. He should have made his hole a few inches deeper. But he could manage, and he felt good about the combat sense his commander had displayed in setting up the defense of the camp. One didn't expect that kind of expertise from a navy fly-boy, no matter how sharp an aviator he was. Grunt combat was a different game, yet Bradford had planned his tactics like – well, like a marine. Wineman would still have opted for blasting the Germans at first sight. Zinwicki's quiet voice from the walkie-talkie alerted him.

'Okay, Alpha and Bravo, crack your covers and keep a sharp lookout. They could be close.' Wineman clicked his mike button twice in response and heard Tanaka's double click of acknowledgement. He positioned himself so that his eye level was just above the rim of his hole, allowing

358

the canvas cover to drape his raised head. Visibility was lousy, as if a thin layer of night itself was stretched across the snow surface. He could barely make out the dim profile of the top of the hut complex, jutting above the snow. The single red bulb at the entrance cast an eerie deep rose glow against the thick ice fog, as if to portray a surrealistic painting of some frigid hell from Dante's *Inferno*. As he turned to scan eastward, he thought of the Germans, quite possibly approaching his hole this very minute. The last of the Jew-hunters from Europe. Or were they? The Soviets seemed to have taken over the role of the Nazis, but they were a bit more subtle about it. Still, the scientist, Kakushkin, seemed like a regular guy.

The thought made Wineman think about his own heritage. He had never been a practicing Jew, never known a rabbi, never been inside a temple. He did remember his mother's prayers and her stories about Moses and the old prophets – fairy tales from the shadows of his beginnings. He had only a vague recollection of her face, but he did remember that it always looked tired, and that when he was five years old she had taken him to the place of other children and left him. He had never known his father, and suspected, once he had grown, that she had not, either. He had been placed in a series of foster homes, but times were hard and no one developed a deep attachment to the scrawny kid with the dark skin and even darker eyes. Finally, at the age of sixteen, he stole his small stack of official papers, walked out the front door, and took to the streets. A year later he joined the Marine Corps. He had been a twenty-seven-year-old staff sergeant when his barracks blew up around him in Beirut and he lay for ten hours amid the rubble and pieces of his friends. Wanting no further ground-pounding assignments, he had switched to marine air and had quickly become a highly qualified aerial navigator, the lingering bitter taste of the carnage in Lebanon prompting him to volunteer for the noncombat tour with VXE-6.

Now, ironically, he was nose deep in an antarctic snow hole, waiting to do combat with a team of maverick Germans. He shifted uneasily, wondering how it was going to be, shooting other human beings. As a marine, he recognized his preordained destiny, he supposed, but up to this moment, with the exception of the Beirut experience, he had seen no actual combat. For all of his confused thoughts, however, uppermost was his pride as a marine, and those bastards stalking toward him and his shipmates were a freakish carryover from another, most evil time. With that in mind, there grew within him an almost eager anticipation, a rising desire to kill. It was a very new and strange feeling for him. Perhaps, it was because, in Lebanon, he had seen a sample of senseless killing, and the Germans had been masters of the art. Or maybe it was simply because he had become attached to the serenity of the Ice and the White Continent's promise of a more dignified human experience. Those creatures out there in the fog were not only going to defile that promise, they were going to vomit their evil philosophy all over the continent if given the chance. Wineman didn't like that.

Marc had been lying with the others on the roof for fifteen minutes, and despite the smattering of warmth from below, his back and legs were getting cold-soaked. He found himself squirming restlessly. Like the others, he kept his rifle beneath him, wanting it warm to his touch if he had to use it. He would have to remove the bulky leather outer mitten to fire, but he would still have on the woolen inner liner with the separate trigger finger. The cold would seep right through it without the cowskin outer shell.

Chopper John had changed from his relaxed back position to a crouch, his arms wrapped around his raised knees. 'I don't know about you, Skipper, but I'm freezing my ass off!'

'Think of Wineman and Tanaka in the snow holes,' commented Marc. 'This fog has killed off any residual warmth from the sun.'

'At least the Germans are getting the worst of it. I sure as hell wouldn't relish a stroll on a night like this.'

Marc chuckled. 'We're getting old, John.'

'Bullshit! When you get right down to it, this is where it's at in our profession – combat – although I always fancied myself doing my bit in a gunship, not flaked out on a rooftop in Antarctica with an assorted bunch of ersatz warriors. My God, here I lie with a goddamned hunting rifle in my lap, waiting for my first ground-bound firefight.'

'I know what you mean,' responded Marc. 'If I'm going into combat, it should be as a department head or XO of some nuclear bird farm, not on the ice-covered tin roof of a remote field camp in the middle of Antarctica.' Shifting positions, he continued, 'But, what the hell. This puts things in the proper perspective. We live in a dream world of peaceful coexistence down here. Let's face it, that's what's really unreal. In the final analysis, we're warriors, just like those misguided bastards out there who think they've a monopoly on solving the world's ills.'

Chopper John nodded. 'You know, Skipper, we've got a pair of mighty hellacious marines out there. They didn't bat an eye when you gave them the dirty job. And I must say, you put this thing together like you knew what you were doing!'

'That's a laugh,' remarked Marc.

'I know.' Despite his jest, Chopper John felt strangely confident. His commander was a sharp naval officer. Of course, he was probably wondering how in the hell he ever wound up in this position, leading a ground defense team consisting of two fellow aviators, an American scientist, a Soviet KGB agent, an airdale sailor, a pair of sky marines, a female lieutenant, and a flight surgeon. Chopper John had always thought about writing, and now he had one bodacious idea for a story.

Wineman froze in his position. Something had moved out there, at the limit of his visibility. He fixed his stare at where the movement had occurred. There it was again! An almost imperceptible bobbling of tiny irregularities in the darkness. Rapidly, they multiplied. He grabbed his radio. 'Command, this is Alpha . . . I've got 'em! They're coming right down the pike!'

Eisner plowed along at the head of his double column. They had left the tractor several hundred yards back. Without skis, his was a difficult walk. But, ahead, he could see a faint red glow. It had to be a camp light. A moment later, the dark low silhouette of a rectangular building began to take shape off to one side of the light.

He held up his arm and the column halted. Raising his binoculars, he fine-tuned his focus. Slowly, he scanned every inch of the camp. There was no movement. Certainly, they had heard him and his men fly over in the C-47, and the woman was smart enough to reason that he would come after her. Were they lying in wait? Or had they been so naïve as to feel that the weather and induced darkness would give them a temporary respite from the inevitable. He wondered what messages they had sent back to their main camp on the radios of the crippled Hercules. Really, it was of no matter. His troops could easily establish control over the personnel in the camp. Scnell could use his syringes, then they would turn off the heat at the camp and be gone. When the American rescue party arrived, they would find only frozen corpses. Besides, if worst came to worst, he knew the second C-47 was following with more troopers.

The cold was getting to him. He could almost taste the delicious warmth inside the huts barely a hundred meters ahead. Swinging his right arm over his head and forward in an arc, he resumed his slow but steady pace. The troopers unslung their weapons by force of habit and carried them casually at their sides, in the way of professionals who expected no resistance but enjoyed the comfort of having their weapons at the ready.

Eisner was breathing hard and suspected that Scnell was breathing even harder. One of the troopers had been assigned to assist the less fit doctor, however, and they had only a few score more meters. Within a few minutes, they would be inside, warming their leaden legs and rubbing numb hands together, refreshing themselves with hot drink and savoring the natural high of conquering forces. The fog and lack of decent light would continue to provide some cover through those last meters ahead, should the occupants of the camp plan to conduct some kind of foolish resistance.

Wineman silently watched the bobbing blobs metamorphose into the plodding shapes of ski troopers on the march. They were going to pass within thirty yards of his position. From this point on, he would avoid looking back at the camp. If his walkie-talkie failed to pick up the count, he didn't want the flashbulb bursts to catch his eyes. He fingered his parka pocket full of M-1 clips.

The Nazis were approaching two abreast in a column seven rows deep. The one in front must be their officer.

For some reason, he was the only one not on cross-country skis. Breaking trail by foot? thought Wineman. Shit! A real leader would have his two biggest and dumbest privates doing that! They apparently were very confident that their aproach was undetected; Wineman could read that by the way they hung their heads and concentrated only on their feet or the back of the trooper ahead. He dropped down in his hole and raised his radio to his lips. 'Command, Alpha. I count fifteen, one apparently exhausted and being helped.'

The reply came back as two clicks.

Eisner cursed the fresh snow. He had been at the head of the column since they had abandoned the tractor. Each step, now, was labored. He could feel the cold wetness of the tiny beads of perspiration that had popped out on the inside of his thighs, across his chest, and around his waist. He must stop and catch his breath one more time before they made their entrance. Holding up his arm, he turned and called softly, 'Lieutenant.'

'Yes, Colonel?'

'From this point on, the operation is in your hands. I will drop back and assist Doctor Scnell. I suggest we close quietly and listen for any activity inside, then rush them.'

'That is my plan. I will leave two men outside with you as a precaution.'

Eisner nodded and stood aside as the column passed. Scnell was proceeding unassisted and Eisner walked beside him. 'It will be over momentarily,' said Eisner.

'Thank God for that. I will never do this again.'

'They stopped for a moment,' murmured Chopper John, peering through a slit cut in the snow wall. 'I wonder what they're thinking.'

'Probably that they should have stayed the hell back in Argentino,' observed Zinwicki.

'Or, they've seen something, maybe the perimeter positions.' Marc sounded concerned.

'I doubt it,' said Chopper John. 'They're coming on too relaxed. Probably within a hundred feet of Wineman. Thank goodness it's still dark. We better get ready, Skipper.'

Marc raised his walkie-talkie. 'Alpha . . . you still got 'em?'

'In my sights, Captain.'

'Did you hear that?' asked Eisner, alarmed.

'What?' wheezed Scnell.

'I don't know. Maybe my ears are playing tricks. It sounded like a short burst of radio static. Very faint, muffled.'

They could hear the little Honda generator clacking away. Perhaps he had just heard a variation in its sound. In any event, he was much too cold to give it further thought. They needed to get inside.

Marc watched the figures approach the mine line. He started his count, 'Stand by . . . one . . . two . . . three . . .' He closed his eyes as he continued, '. . . four!' Zinwicki already had his hand on the firing switch labeled DICK, and on four he closed it.

The German lieutenant was staring straight ahead when the brilliance erupted directly in front of him, the whole world instantaneously and incredibly white. His pupils contracted so sharply, he could feel them move! Instinctively, he dropped, shouting, 'Down! Down! Down!'

His troops had already anticipated his command and as they threw themselves forward, each flipped off the safety catch of his weapon and slammed into the snow with it held firmly in firing position. Their reasoning power numbed by the terrible cold and energy expenditure of their march, they reacted instinctively: make as small a target as possible and cover your ass with a curtain of protective fire. But where should they aim? Like their lieutenant, they were blinded! If they were confused about other things, it was nevertheless clear that the occupants of the camp were putting up some form of defense. The obvious shook them to a man. They were being ambushed! They squirmed belly deep into the snows of Antarctica.

Marc never had a chance to offer the Nazis an opportunity to lay down their arms. Standing, he had cupped his hands around his open mouth, but the words never came out. Instead, his heart tried to jump through his chest wall as an awesome staccato of shots rang out to his right. 'No!' he yelled as Kakushkin continued emptying his automatic at the prone Germans, a look of rage contorting his face and curses screaming from his mouth. Immediately, a return volley of automatic fire erupted from the figures in the snow. Marc had no way of knowing that the deadly noise also masked the German lieutenant's desperate pleas to his men to hold their fire. Even as Marc lunged at Kakushkin, he knew it was too late. Like Pavlov's dog, the Germans reacted instinctively, spewing forth a steady stream of lead saliva in their conditioned response to the situation, and the horror of armed combat was spreading its sickening stench across the white desert of the last peaceful continent on earth. The last virgin was being violated.

His companions on the roof were returning the Nazi fire – they had no choice now. As Marc pounded his fist into Kakushkin's face, he realized he was not even hurting the man. There was a spreading bloodstain on the KGB colonel's chest.

'. . . five!' Zinwicki had picked up the count and Marc heard the swish of the rising star flare. Almost immediately, it reached its zenith and burst. The flat snow around the camp was bathed in light and the dark forms of the prone Nazis punctuated the white surface, a double row of ink spots shaken from some giant pen.

Wineman saw the Nazis drop and sink into the snow, almost disappearing, but their backpacks protruded above the surface and gave him an aiming point. He lowered his sight just below the surface at the closest figure and squeezed off his first clip.

The German lieutenant had sickened at the instinctive reaction of his men. They were too exposed. He kept his eyes tightly closed, hoping that the darkness under his lids would cause his pupils to relax. He could hear and feel the bark and whine of attacking fire around him, and his head and body were being covered with chunks of snow thrown up by incoming rounds. He didn't know what to do, but he did know he couldn't stay where he lay. Yelling in fury, he jumped to his feet.

Without a pause, he started running ahead in a zigzag pattern, firing his machine pistol toward where the dark building should be. He had his eyes open but could see nothing except that all-enveloping whiteness that was much brighter overhead. Just as he was beginning to make out the vague form ahead, a clump of steel chunks ripped into his chest. He pitched forward, dead before he hit the snow. Two of his following troops stumbled crazily over his inert form in their sightless rush to reach the hut. One fell only a few yards beyond the lieutenant's body, while the other miraculously kept going, screaming obscenities and firing blindly in all directions. Then, he disappeared in a fiery blast that erupted under his heavy, snow-clogged boots.

Marc watched several of the Nazis charging ahead toward the complex. Deliberately, he waited until they reached the line of dynamite mines strung beneath the snow before twisting the T-handle of the exciter. The few Germans who got through the flesh-tearing blast were felled almost immediately by the rain of fire from the roof. It was a turkey shoot.

Wineman reached for a fresh clip and rammed it home. When he looked back up, a dark form was racing toward his snow hole, jinking left and right and firing from his hip, spraying death from an automatic weapon. Wineman emptied his M-1 at the onrushing figure, his last round at point-blank range. As he fired the final round, he felt a searing hot and very sharp pain as the right side of his face was blown away. Simultaneously, a great weight slammed into his chest and propelled him backwards hard against the Styrofoam lining of his hole.

The wounded German dropped hanging over the rim, head and one arm only inches from Wineman's mangled face.

The marine could feel the sticky warmth of his own blood oozing from his uper body. His face rapidly became numb and the pain was gone. He still retained the blurred sight of his left eye and he slumped, horrified, as the red life drained from him.

The Nazi's balaclava had been ripped from his face and he was working his jaw while bloody bubbles dipped from his lips. Slowly, he was raising his arm and pushing his upper body forward. Wineman could see his other arm snaking ahead, his weapon still held in his clenched hand.

Wineman was not sure he could move but did feel the touch of his arctic pants as he slid his right hand down and gripped the handle of his survival knife. While they had been waiting in the hut complex, he had honed its edge to razor sharpness. He withdrew it, but could not raise his arm. Sucking in a giant breath, he yelled to tighten his stomach muscles and forced the blade upward. It took every ounce of his strength and every molecule of his last lung full of air, but his dying effort drove the blade fiercely into the Nazi's throat.

Marc and the others kept firing until all of the Germans lay motionless in the snow. The entire firefight had happened in the space of one star flare. Zinwicki fired a second to be sure. While it burned, Marc called his forward marines.

'Alpha . . . Bravo . . . report.'

There was a delay, then Tanaka replied, 'They're all down. I'm okay here.' Alpha was silent.

'Check on Wineman,' directed Marc and he watched Tanaka sprint across the snow to Alpha hole. He stooped down and then his call came. 'Wineman's bought it. Everything is secure out here.'

Incredibly, they had suffered only two casualties. The loss of Kakushkin was no big disturbance, but Wineman's death would be heavily felt.

'Come on in,' ordered Marc.

'I'll check for wounded,' replied Tanaka.

'Roger. Be careful. I'll send Dare and Chopper John out to give you a hand.'

Leaning over, Marc turned on the floodlights. In the excitement of the firefight, he had forgotten about them.

The Quack and Frosty met Marc, Dare, and Chopper

369

John at the bottom of the roof hatch and they placed the Russian on the table in the makeshift dispensary. The Quack worked over him, compressing his chest to slow the loss of blood. Without any substantial medical supplies, that was about all he could do. After a few minutes, he pulled a blanket over Kakushkin's body and turned toward Molder, who was patiently standing by, holding his left upper arm. Frosty had helped him strip off his parka and shirt. The Quack cleaned away the semidried blood from the gouge in the USARP's bicep muscle. It was a flesh wound and the Quack quickly dressed it and provided a makeshift sling.

Dare and Tanaka came in, carrying one of the Germans. 'The only one left,' announced Tanaka.

'Put him over here,' directed the Quack as Marc and Zinwicki lifted Kakushkin from the table and placed him on the floor. The Quack checked the trooper's pulse and pupils, then placed a blood-pressure cuff around the German's arm. Before he could pump it, however, he pulled it off. 'There's nothing I can do except give him something for the pain.'

Tanaka walked up, holding a steaming mug of coffee. 'We sure did a job on those troops. They never had a chance. Somehow, I feel sorry for them, poor misguided bastards. Captain, there are two old toads out there. Look to be in their sixties. How they made that march is beyond me.'

Marc tilted his head, curious as to why such old men would be with the assault troops.

'I bet I know who one of the SOBs is,' said Frosty, pulling on her parka. Marc joined her in exiting the hut. They made their way among the bodies until they reached the farthest two. Both were crumpled face down in the snow, only about ten feet apart. Frosty rolled over the first. 'That's the number one honcho.'

370

Together, they rolled over the other body. 'Scnell,' announced Marc.

'That's the doctor who treated me,' added Frosty.

'War criminal,' amplified Marc. 'He's the one Kosciusco was after.'

'He's a good Nazi now.'

'Aren't they all?' asked Marc, standing and looking around. A lightening area off toward the hut complex indicated that the sun had returned above the horizon. The fog was still thick, but there was more light penetration and it would soon fade.

As Marc and Frosty reentered the hut, the others were sitting around the galley table with their coffee, silent and obviously exhausted.

The navy ritual, thought Marc, giving thanks.

The long exposure outside and the intense emotion of the firefight had drained them all. The shock of the slaughter was still reflected in eyes that did not want to blink. The fact that the Germans had brought it all on themselves was of little comfort to those in the room who had never killed before.

'If only that son of a bitch Kakushkin had not opened fire. We had them,' observed Marc dryly.

'Things surely happened fast,' said Zinwicki, shaking his head.

'What do you think will happen now?' asked Dare.

'Well, we have some things to do,' replied Marc. 'As soon as we collect our thoughts and settle down, you and Tanaka go outside and drag the bodies up by the hut. Cover them with a thin snow cover. I don't know how long they'll be there, but I don't intend to take them out with us. The Argentines can have them next season. There's going to be hell to pay there.'

'What about the C-47?' asked Frosty.

'I suspect he'll wait until the weather lifts and hightail

wheel well, examining the chains reinforcing the nose gear. 'Looks good to me,' he declared.

'We'll know soon,' remarked Dare.

They waded through the deep snow over to the main gear. 'I've never seen anything like this,' exclaimed Marc. The main skis, easily eighteen inches thick, were sunk below the snow surface. Bending over, he picked up a handful of snow. 'Heavy. Not quite wet, but certainly not as dry as we're used to. The first part of our takeoff is going to be a snowplow run. Well, let's do it.' As he climbed up the lowered entrance door, he thought of last November's early landing and takeoff at Byrd Station under somewhat similar conditions. He had come close to not getting off that time, with four engines and on a prepared skiway! On the other side of the coin, Byrd was at 5,000 feet.

Zinwicki and Tanaka were just finishing hanging the JATO cylinders. Each hung horizontally – four on each it back to Argentino. There must have been some sort of prearranged signal that would have been sent once the Germans took the camp. In the absence of that, I'd leave! I suspect he will, too. There's a good chance he heard the firing.'

Dare and Tanaka rose to leave.

'Just a moment,' said Marc, also standing. He looked at each of the faces around him as he spoke. 'You all did fine. Once the firefight started, it was out of our hands and for a weird collection of airdales and scientists, we did all right. None of us can take pride in what happened here today, but in doing what we did, we may have averted a much greater evil. This will finish the Nazi community at Argentino. I am very proud of all of you, and for what it's worth, I share your deep disgust that it had to be. Now, before we do anything else, let's bring in Sergeant Wineman.'

Three hours later, the Germans had been buried under the snow on the north side of the Eights complex, except for Scnell and Eisner. Along with Sergeant Wineman and

after side of the fat fuselage, just in front of the paratrooper doors – on quick-release brackets, with the electrical firing wire plugged into a receptacle built into the side of the Hercules. After a double-check, the two men secured the doors and Zinwicki proceeded forward to the flight deck. At Marc's invitation, he took the copilot's seat.

Marc was anxious to get into the air. Every moment they sat there, more snow was falling, and any minute he expected to see a second German C-47. The ceiling had lifted and the visibility was better, but there was still little wind. What direction they took off seemed immaterial. He advanced the power levers, and the whine of three good engines deepened as the huge four-bladed props took bigger bites of the cold air and the Hercules strained against the grasp of the deep snow. It took full power to break loose and then, with the rudder ineffective due to the slow forward speed, the two engines on the right side pushed the nose of the C-130 slowly to the left.

'I don't believe this,' said Zinwicki. With full power they were indicating thirty knots and accelerating very gradually. At forty knots Marc had rudder control and could straighten out their path across the snow.

'Gimme half flaps,' he ordered.

'Half down,' responded Zinwicki.

The airspeed built to fifty-five knots and stayed there, the needle resting on the two fives as if it were glued. They needed sixty knots before firing the JATO if they wanted a reasonable chance for the additional 8,000 pounds of thrust to boost them into the air.

'Full flaps,' ordered Marc.

'You got 'em.'

The airspeed slowed five knots.

Marc rocked the yoke, the C-130 rocked, and the airspeed fell to forty-five knots.

'Pick 'em up.'

Zinwicki placed the flap lever in its up position and the huge flaps retracted into the undersides of the wings.

Forty knots.

Marc pulled back the power. The Hercules plowed to a stop.

Grinning sheepishly, Marc looked over at his concerned copilot. 'Okay, let's try it again. Give me half flaps when I have full power on all three.'

Advancing the two middle engine power levers forward, Marc held back pressure on the yoke and watched the airspeed climb. At thirty-five knots he felt rudder control and started in with number three engine. As it reached full power, Zinwicki gave him half flaps. The airspeed climbed to fifty knots.

'JATO!' called Marc.

Zinwicki hit the firing switch and the eight bottles of solid rocket propellant exploded into life. Eight thousand pounds of additional thrust pushed the airspeed to sixty knots, then sixty-five.

'Full flaps!'

Marc pulled back hard on the yoke as Zinwicki hit the flap switch – and the fifteen-second JATO thrust expired. The airspeed dropped back to sixty knots and stagnated.

'No way,' came Dare's disgusted voice over the intercom.

Marc retarded the throttles. 'Well, when all else fails, go by the book,' he remarked, and continued a slow taxi straight ahead.

'And that is?. . .' asked Zinwicki.

'Hang the rest of the JATO. We'll taxi for two to three miles, turn around, and wait. We will have compressed us a three-track takeoff path and the friction of our skis will have melted a top film of snow. In this temperature, the film will refreeze in about fifteen minutes. If we're lucky, it'll be hard and slick. Then we pour on the coal, fight like mad to keep this bird in those same tracks, and pray.'

Zinwicki grinned. 'Why didn't we do that in the first place, Skipper?'

Marc continued taxiing. 'Good question. Remind me to have you transferred to some remote base in Kansas where you can develop your sense of tact around commanding officers.' Back on the lower seat bunk, Frosty and the Quack joined in the laughter.

A suddenly appearing form dead ahead silenced any further mirth.

'Look at that!' yelled Zinwicki, pointing to the diving C-47, which had just dropped out of the overcast. It barely nosed up before hitting the snow surface. 'He almost bought it!'

The aircraft passed barely a hundred feet overhead.

'The brazen bastards!' yelled Marc to those on the flight deck. The C-47 was wearing Luftwaffe colors, with swastika insignias on the wing and fuselage.

Swinging the Hercules around, Marc lined up in his tracks. The C-47 was in a steep bank, probably three miles ahead, obviously fighting to stay under the overcast and to keep the C-130 in sight.

'I bet they could use new skivvies after that dive. I don't see how he recovered in time,' said Zinwicki.

'They want us bad,' added Marc.

'Let's get out of here!' hollered the Quack.

'We wait,' replied Marc. 'We have to let our tracks freeze.'

'Here he comes again,' remarked Frosty, who was now standing behind Zinwicki's seat.

The German aircraft passed over them once more, off to the right side, where they could see the pilots clearly.

'I'm glad that the old bird isn't armed,' said Dare.

The C-47 faded into the gloom.

'How much longer?' questioned Zinwicki.

'At least ten minutes. We can't hurry it,' replied Marc.

Frosty leaned forward. 'A watched pot never boils.'

'Thank God we brought an extra load of JATO.'

'We may not need it, Skipper,' comforted Dare. 'If those guys start shooting at us, there's enough collective pucker aboard this airplane to lift us right into the ozone layer.'

'They're landing!' announced Frosty, pointing ahead. True enough, the C-47 had reemerged and was touching down on the snow off to the left of their takeoff path. Slowly, it turned and started toward them.

'Patience, patience,' murmured Marc. 'Frosty, strap in.'

Frosty resumed her seat beside the Quack.

The silence on the flight deck was almost complete. Only the mild whine of the three engines and the breathing of the plane's occupants disturbed it. One minute passed, then two.

'We can't wait any longer. They're stopping and I suspect they'll have plenty of weapons. Give me full flaps.'

As Zinwicki started them down, Marc advanced the two inside engine power levers smartly forward. The Hercules hesitated for a very long second, then surged forward in an awkward waddle as Marc fought to keep the skis within the narrow tracks. Gradually, the aircraft settled into a loping but steady acceleration.

'Hey! That's better!' shouted Dare.

At forty knots, Marc came in with number three.

'Ride 'em, cowboy!' Sergeant Tanaka, on the phones back in the cargo compartment, broke his customary silence. One thing about this crew, thought Marc, they even enjoy disaster!

The wing flaps hung almost straight down, and as 129

picked up speed, they forced the onrushing air onto the snow surface. The growing air cushion began to press against the underside of the wing, and with each nose oscillation, the cushion literally lifted the C-130 a tiny bit higher on the compressed landing gear oleos. With less weight on the skis, surface friction decreased and the Hercules slid faster and faster.

The C-47 was stopped and soldiers were dropping from the open cargo door.

'We've got a bubble!' Marc could feel the effect of the bunched air under the wing. It felt good. 'Fire JATO!'

'Hang in there, Skipper!' Dare was practically exuberant.

'Sixty knots!' shouted Zinwicki, ignoring the intercom in his jubilation.

The soldiers were kneeling in the snow. unslinging their weapons. They still were too far away for effective fire, but the Hercules was eating up the distance at more than a hundred feet per second.

Marc horsed back on the yoke and the nose of the aircraft rose confidently to its takeoff attitude. At seventy-four knots he wrenched the galloping beast clear of the surface and booted the left rudder to skid the aircraft around toward the kneeling soldiers. Letting the charging C-130 rapidly build up speed, he kept it within feet of the surface. Zinwicki sat transfixed. His commanding officer seemed intent on smashing the huge skis right into the assembly, half of whom were firing and half of whom were breaking away for dear life! Instinctively, Zinwicki ducked behind the instrument panel as they swept through the German force. A pronounced thump signaled that someone had caught a massive ski with his body. Marc pulled up into the overcast.

'Flaps up – slow,' he said quietly.

'I think we hit one,' said Zinwicki.

'I hope so,' replied Marc. He felt a pair of soft arms around his neck.

'Forgive me, Captain, but I have to do this.'

He felt Frosty's lips pressed against his cheek.

'Me, too,' replied the Quack, maneuvering into position.

'Just buy me a beer!' spouted Marc laughingly as he jerked his head away. 'To use a cliche, let's go home.'

Early on the morning of March 4, Marc pulled 129 free of Williams skiway for the last time. As he swung the big machine around in a wide, low arc to pass close aboard the tip of Ross Island and its McMurdo Station, he rocked his wings in a salute to the somber waving figures of the men left behind to winter over. They stood, scattered among the almost deserted streets of the continent's largest station.

One-two-nine climbed past Mount Erebus, the majestic white cone of the ancient volcano breathing forth a long wisp of steam. The sea ice was beginning to reform and the path cleared by the icebreakers only a few weeks before was already clogged with brash.

The Royal Society Range slipped by their left side, then the deserted Hallett Station. Too high to see the Adélie penguins roaming Hallett's rocky shore, Marc satisfied himself with the thought that the little flightless birds were surely there, waddling across the ice as they had for centuries. He felt shame for his part in violating their peaceful home.

They leveled at 32,000 feet and he engaged the autopilot.

Back in the cargo compartment, his passengers and crew returned to the routine of making themselves comfortable for the eight-hour flight to Christchurch. Soon, most of them were asleep.

The four in the rubber body bags slept the most soundly of all.

Marc relaxed in his seat with the ever-present cup of coffee. Like the White Continent, the events of the past few days were falling farther behind with each revolution of the purring four-bladed propellers of the Hercules.

Even as they cruised through the clear antarctic air, he knew that Admiral Brady was standing before a covey of international media representatives in Christchurch, breaking the news of the Nazis' last stand to the world. And far to the east of 129's present position, a United Nations expeditionary force, made up of troops from the countries who had signed the Antarctic Treaty, was advancing on Argentino Station. And in the back of his aircraft was all of the proof they needed for whatever action they had to take.

Only his concern for Frosty marred his feeling of relief. Was she contaminated with some lethal Nazi bug? The Quack had assured him that if she were, there should be symptoms by now. And there was the technical reputation that the Nazis had always enjoyed. They were generally good at what they did, so why *not* a successful vaccine? For once, mankind could be thankful for their misguided expertise.

Marc leaned back in his seat. There were still questions, but all in all, he had a feeling that the crisis was past. Frosty was sitting with her feet up on the footrests, munching a thick Spam sandwich and nodding her head in time to music she had tuned in from the McMurdo Station.

Way to go, Frosty, thought Marc with a smile.

Epilogue

Sometimes, in the late summer, the limitless skies around the north shore of North Island of New Zealand are alive with the full-throated rumblings of tall cumulonimbus clouds. The billowing gray ocean thunderstorms do not tower to the heights, or develop to the intensities, of the summer giants over the land, and their thunder has a more muffled, faraway sound. Their electrical discharges are more playful than threatening and the darting silver streaks happily chase each other from cloud to cloud.

The stately stands of condensed water seem to be trying to imitate the fierce, warlike charades of the now peaceful Maoris. Like their wide-eyed, tongue-thrusting human counterparts, the clouds growl mostly for show, for they dance in isolated fury and can easily be bypassed.

In such a sky, 129 climbed northward, threading the deep, white cloud canyons and reaching for the incredibly blue sky that stretched ahead for more than 6,000 miles to the West Coast of the United States. Marc declined Frosty's offer to engage the autopilot, preferring the personal satisfaction of manually guiding the Hercules on its long ascent. These were the times that made his profession a spiritual experience unique to only those who rode the breath of God. Every tremor, every vibration, every response to the invisible sea of air that the airplane experienced was telegraphed through the structure of the complex machine to the hands that lightly gripped the control yoke and the feet that rested on the large rectangular rudder pedals. This was the time when the eighty tons of aluminum and steel, fuel and hydraulic oil, and cargo and passengers became a mere extension of the flesh-and-blood creature who was its master. Man and machine symbolically merged into an android of the air, interreacting within itself in a symphony of aerodynamic cause and response. Whatever Marc willed, the airplane did. Whatever the airplane did, Marc knew.

The ocean fell farther below, a blue-green expanse of water that was the primeval source of all life on planet Earth. Despite the affluence of columns of rising warm air, the passage of 129 through and around them was smooth. Only an occasional bounce reminded the crew that the same gentle currents now lifting them toward the heavens could on another day become the most deadly of winds, an unseen force that could dismantle their flying machine as thoughtlessly as a child would pull apart a toy.

Flight was a demonstration of man in harmony with nature – as long as man respected the rules and appreciated the hospitality of the gods of the air.

Marc watched the coast fall behind them, finally disappearing completely within the broken wall of Kiwi clouds. Ahead, all the way to Honolulu, lay blue water, the vast Polynesian portion of the Pacific, tranquil and romantic.

Frosty rested unconcerned in the right seat, having won her battle of words with the Quack over her physical ability to resume flying status. Marc had to smile, recalling her brief but spirited argument when the Quack had the audacity to suggest that maybe the physical and mental ordeal of being a prisoner at Argentino and a participant in the Eights incident was sufficient cause for her temporary removal from flight status. In no uncertain words, Frosty had informed the conscientious doctor that in no way would she be flying back to the States as a *passenger,* citing her thorough physical examination at the hands of New Zealand doctors, which revealed no trace of any biological disorder. The Quack had wisely backed down.

M. E. Morris is a retired naval aviator and his years of antarctic flying and international affairs background form a solid base for this fascinating story. He is a member of The Antarctican Society and the U.S. Polar Society and is author of the novel *Alpha Bug*. He lives in Colorado Springs, USA.

By the same author

Alpha Bug